Praise

"Whip smart, hilarious a͟   ͟ ͟ͅ
it in one sitting!"

Emma Grey, author of *The Last Love Note*

"A side-splittingly witty rollercoaster ride through every woman's Hollywood daydreams. Kat Alley is who I want to be when I (don't) grow up!"

Nina D. Campbell, author of *Daughters of Eve*

DEAD FAMOUS

RUBY FOX

Copyright © 2023 Ruby Fox

All rights reserved.

No part of this book may be reproduced in any form or by any electronic or mechanical means, including information storage and retrieval systems, without written permission from the author, except for the use of brief quotations in a book review.

Cover Design: Elizabeth Mackay

Interior Design: Brad Fennell

ISBN: 978-0-6455648-6-0 (print)

ISBN: 978-0-6455648-5-3 (eBook)

For Lola, who is most definitely a showgirl.

Chapter One

There was a good reason why I was standing in Mitch's office wearing my pyjamas. Unfortunately, they weren't even nice pyjamas. Not that the situation would have been made better if I'd been wearing Peter Alexander—you know, the fancy ones that presumably have magic sleep-inducing properties, otherwise why would you pay so much for sleepwear? No, mine were baggy-arsed, threadbare, and covered in crazy monkeys and ripe bananas. Speaking of ripe, I'd been wearing them for approximately eight days.

I had really messed up. And I don't mean something small. I mean epic. We're not talking getting drunk at the office Christmas party and kissing your boss. We're not even talking about walking out of TK Maxx without paying for a pair of sunglasses—not that I would ever do that. Except for that one time when I did, but it was honestly a complete accident.

My head was on the chopping block because I was single-handedly responsible for the near death of a national icon. The entire country was baying for my blood and I'm not being over-dramatic. It was categorically the biggest fuck up of my entire life and I felt like the worst person in the entire world. Even Charles Manson would have shaken his head at me.

Pyjamas aside, a couple of concessions to basic decency had been made before leaving the house. My shoes were at least on the right feet, I'd thrown a stylish satin trench over my monkey pants and I'd attempted to brush the Cheezel crumbs out of my hair—it might have been dried Weetbix, I'm not quite sure to be honest with you.

Looking back, I could have tried to pass the look off as *effortlessly shabby chic* but to be fair I looked like I'd escaped from a commune somewhere and was still high. The dodgy outfit made dodging the paparazzi a little bit harder, but somehow I'd managed. After all, I knew how their brains worked. On any other day, you could've called me their fearless leader.

I wasn't fit to be out in public really. I'd been hiding underneath my bedcovers for more than a week and—without my usual access to Channel Five's make-up department and the office fashion cupboard—I was a mess.

But Mitch's phone message had been unmistakable.

"Kat. My office. Today." Clunk.

Mitch was the editor-in-chief of MeridianCorp's entire stable of magazines, both print and digital. She was also my boss, which meant I didn't have a choice. Personally, I would have preferred a dark room and a truckload of Tim Tams to Mitch's office and the imminent threat of unemployment but ignoring the summons would have been a fatal mistake, and I didn't fancy dying that day or any other.

STAR NOW, Australia's highest circulation gossip magazine and my home away from home, took up the entire top floor of a big pink building on Sydney's North Shore. The sprawling office was a maze of cubicles; the occupants' crowded pin boards and screensavers a clear indication of who was hot or not—something that changed by the week, the day or even by the hour. Over the years the walls had witnessed Kylie and Jason, Brangelina, too many Kardashians to mention, the handing of the boy-band 'traitor' baton from Robbie to Harry and, more recently, everything Hadid and Delevingne.

The hush enveloping the space as I'd shuffled towards Mitch's closed office door that morning was eerily reminiscent of that awkward scene in *Jerry Maguire*—the one where Tom Cruise has a conniption and adopts the office fish and Renee Zellweger.

A single kind person behind me—I think it might have been Dawn, our eager-to-please intern, with a penchant for socks-n-Birkenstocks and a teeny-tiny crush on me—squawked a self-conscious *good luck*. She was shushed with an audible elbow jab, right before I'd stepped through Mitch's door. It had swung shut behind me with a hostile, metallic clunk. I now stood in front of her gigantic wooden desk like a wayward primary school kid, called up to the principal's office for sticking chewing gum on the rungs of the monkey bars.

When I say in front of her gigantic desk, I mean in front of the yawning space in front of her gigantic desk. The room itself took up the entire corner of the building. All floor to ceiling glass and neutral paint, with the gargantuan desk the only real furniture, the room screamed success. Meanwhile, the sun bouncing off Sydney Harbour screamed through the banks of glistening windows to pierce my red and swollen eyeballs. I blinked painfully as my eyes adjusted to the glare and wondered momentarily whether eyeballs could actually explode.

Mitch sat at her desk, glowering at me from behind bony fingers, which were steepled sharply together like she wanted to stab me with them. With my stinky pyjamas and food-filled hair, I must have looked like a mucky blot on the shining ecru plush pile. Her carefully made-up eyes travelled slowly down to my fidgeting feet and back up again. She twitched one artfully-tweezed eyebrow.

"Wow, Kat, you look like shit." She waved a hand at me. "Is this some kind of disguise to try to outwit the paps or have you finally lost your marbles?"

At the mention of the paparazzi, I hiccupped. And then hiccupped again. Over the past week, the stress had reacti-vated my teenaged nervous tic—chronic hiccups that broke out like a cuckoo clock on helium as soon as my heart rate went up.

"There was a photographer—*hic*—hiding underneath my car this morning. I nearly—*hic*—ran him over, for Christ's sake." I took a gulp of air and held my breath as Mitch pursed her lips.

"I'm glad you didn't. We don't need another law suit, cour-tesy of the great Katherine Alley." Her deceptively soothing voice was loaded with disapproval. "It's not much fun when the shoe is on the other foot, is it?" I shook my head, still holding my breath in my best impression of a miserable puffer fish. "Cardinal rule of gossip, darling," she continued. "Never become the story. Kelly is going to be fine, by the way, thanks for asking. They'll release her from hospital tomorrow morn-ing. Her agent called me."

I exhaled with a rush and paused, waiting for a hiccup and hoping the breath holding had worked because the next step was standing on my head to drink water and I had a feeling that wouldn't go down well. No hiccups were forthcoming so I risked squeaking a question.

"Are you going to fire me?"

Mitch was silent as she drummed her fingers on her desk. I waited, staring at the floor and cringing on the inside, until the silence became awkward. I peeked at her from beneath lowered and somewhat crusty eyelashes. She was studying me. Calculating. Maybe she wanted me to beg. "Mitch, please. You can't fire me."

"Actually, Kat—I can," she snapped, before pausing and folding her spindly arms. "But, luckily for you, I'm not going to."

I was stunned.

"What?" After the public backlash from my three-pronged and ultimately unfounded exposé of pop-star, Kelly Craig, I was certain getting fired would be a fait accompli. Mitch motioned for me to sit and I did, my legs shaking with relief. Mitch eyed me like a hawk eyes a mouse before swooping in for the kill.

"The fact is you make me too much money and you've got too many contacts for me to lose you." *Wow, so heartfelt*. "But... Kelly Craig is Australia's darling. Everybody loves her. The fucking Prime Minister loves her. Christ, even that horrible radio jock who hates everyone thinks she's Madonna incarnate and by that I don't mean like a virgin. The fact is, Kelly's in hospital because of you. Personally, I couldn't give a shit. Circulation went through the roof last week—suicides are always massive sellers." She shrugged. "Even if they don't take."

Ugh. I grimaced. I might have fucked up but at least I had the common decency to know how heinous that statement was. The horrid truth of the matter though, was she was right. Whenever anything like this happened—and it seemed to be happening more and more often—the public couldn't get enough.

Celebrity death was big business; memorial covers, special editions, pages and pages of *the life and times of*, complete with insider stories from every person who ever loved them or simply did their dry-cleaning that one time. Not to mention the scores of secret offspring who would suddenly emerge from the woodwork.

And, if the death was self-inflicted? The morbid fascination ramped up a notch. Was it disbelief that a celebrity could have anything truly bad to worry about? Or was it the realisation that being rich and famous didn't preclude you from having a shitty life? Either way, people wanted to know what had gone wrong. Maybe it made them feel better about their own lives, who knew.

"Of course, the public want your head on a platter. Hypocrites." Mitch snorted and then echoed my thoughts, unnerving me slightly because Mitch is the last person you want inside your head. "Sure, there's plenty of noise being made about how horrible you are, but that doesn't stop them buying the magazine or watching the show or feeding into the whole bloody machine, does it?"

I still wasn't quite sure where her train of thought was going. I wiggled my head, a confused cross between a nod and a shake, to cover all bases. "Look, I have to show that I'm doing *something*, otherwise there'll be a fucking backlash and I need that like Donald Trump needs a spray tan." She sighed heavily. "But I'm not going to fire you. Okay?" A loaded pause. "So? What do you have to say for yourself? Any explanation at all?"

I stared at her, caught off guard, then scrambled for words.

"Mitch, I swear I had no idea that guy was her psychiatrist. Honestly, they seemed way too friendly. Like *get a room* friendly. How was I to know she was so close to the edge; that she'd do something so—" I hesitated, grappling for the right word "— stupid?"

"So, she's stupid now as well as being suicidal and a home wrecker?" *Nope, definitely not the right word.* "You're on fire, Kat."

"I didn't mean that." I backtracked rapidly. "*Extreme*. How was I to know she'd do something so extreme?"

"Here's a start. Maybe you should have verified your story

before you accused her of having an affair with a married man on your blog, in *my* magazine and on national television." She glared at me. "Mental health issues, depression, they're hot topics right now. We come out of this like heartless bastards. Channel Five is extremely embarrassed. So embarrassed in fact that they've dumped you from your *Rise and Shine, Oz* segment. They've replaced you with that agreeable little blonde girl that used to do *Funniest Home Videos.*"

"What? But *The Kat's Whispers* is mine," I squeaked, outraged. "I built that segment. How can they have *The Kat's Whispers* without a Kat?"

Mitch shrugged.

"Sorry, they own it. I suppose they'll change the name. Besides, you brought this on yourself, you need to take responsibility. Be thankful they're not suing us. Two law suits would be, let's just say *unmanageable.*"

I shrank.

"Two?"

"Mm-hmm. Kelly's people are in talks with legal as we speak. That one shouldn't be too bad. Like I said, circulation was way up and it counter-balances what we have to pay out. It's a trade-off, everybody does it, you know how this works. You've been here long enough. If we end up in the black it's worth running the story."

I hugged myself tight, hands tucked into my sleeves like a little kid, and nodded at her. It might be worth running the story to her but for the first time in a long while it left a really bad taste in my mouth. How the hell did I end up here? I must have looked wretched because Mitch's flinty countenance softened for once.

"Kat, I know you've been struggling since your Dad died, and I feel for you, I do. I had a lot of professional respect for your father." A wry smile crossed her lips. "Even if it wasn't exactly reciprocated. *He* was an exceptional journalist."

"Yeah thanks, Mitch," I muttered. "Can I have some tequila and lemon with that salt? It rubs into the wound better." Sarcasm never went down well with Mitch and she straightened, her face assuming its regular stone-like visage.

The mention of my Dad stung like a Portuguese man-o-war but I wasn't about to open up to her about that awful last conversation I'd had with him. The one that proved her words were on point. How could I tell her I was almost glad he wasn't around to witness my spectacular fall from grace, being that it would have simply consolidated what I knew he already thought of me? I couldn't tell her I had no doubt he'd be mortified, and more than a little pissed off that Mum had given me his two Walkley Awards in a fit of misguided sentimentality?

Like Oscars for Aussie journalists, Walkleys were only given to the best—not journalists like me. War crimes in Rwanda and shonky politicians—my Dad's *raison d'être*—outranked celebrity sex tapes every time. The pointy metal trophies had been sitting in a box in my apartment since his funeral, like shiny, stabby reminders of how tarnished my personal interpretation of the word 'journalist' had become.

It hadn't always been the case. When I first started out as a cadet on the *Bayside Sun*, I did everything by the book. Armed with a truckload of gleaming idealism, I knew my media law inside out. I was an ethical powerhouse. I would check and double check facts and sources; nothing was committed to paper that I didn't know was absolutely true. Plus, I had great instincts. The award for my hard-hitting piece exposing the widespread bribery of the jam judges at the Benbridge Fete was still a high-point in my career.

Dad had always said my thirst for incontrovertible proof started when I was six and lost my first tooth. Excited to meet the much-lauded tooth fairy, I'd forced myself to stay awake long past bedtime by licking my fingers and repeatedly poking them in my eyes every time sleep threatened.

Hearing the door open, I'd lain perfectly still under my Care Bears doona, feigning sleep and peering sneakily through the tiny gap between my scrunched eyelids and my eyelashes. Long story short, Mum was busted trying to sneak two dollars —that was pretty good in 1992—under my pillow and the jig was well and truly up.

In my six-year-old wisdom, if the tooth fairy wasn't real it stood to reason the Easter Bunny and Father Christmas were a load of crap too. I had to be pulled out of Sunday School because I kept asking the nuns to prove God was real. My Mum was extremely embarrassed, but Dad defended me by saying it showed I had an enquiring mind and strength of character. More recently he'd said it was a shame that character so easily went AWOL with the lure of a big pay check and my own fifteen minutes of fame. But to be fair, that wasn't entirely correct.

I had fallen into celebrity gossip quite by accident, after an investigative piece I'd been working on went horribly pear-shaped. I'd been convinced that a particular high-profile lawyer was taking bribes and had been staking him out for weeks. My gut told me it was going to make my career, be my first really big break as a journalist. Unfortunately, my gut was wrong— very wrong—and to make it worse the lawyer accused me of stalking. I'd missed a key bit of info, something that apparently *everybody* knew. Except me, clearly. The oversight made me a laughing stock at the paper.

I'd thought my dad would be supportive – people make mistakes, don't they? But I had overheard him in conversation with a colleague who was going on about the importance of procedure, of *not* running on instinct. He was a stuffy-looking bald man who wrote about real estate, and he'd said pointedly to my dad, "It would be much easier if women stuck to writing about things they know, don't you agree?".

My dad had made small murmurs of what sounded like agreement as the stuffy man continued, "Investigative journalism simply takes a particular level of intelligence." I stood there, silently, waiting for him to stand up for me.

My dad had cleared his throat.

"Well, I think you're right there, but—"

I'd turned tail before he'd finished the sentence, mortified. If my dad didn't think I had the brain power for the job, what the hell was I thinking?

Fortunately, a silver lining presented itself soon enough. The photos I'd taken of the lawyer had also snapped Tim Bailey—a very famous television host—kissing his long-rumoured mistress in the background. I wouldn't have picked it without the eagle eyes of my editorial coordinator—who was so immersed in pop culture she could have told you how many fillings Tom Hardy had—but, either way, *Hello* magazine paid me handsomely for the shots and asked me what else I had.

And the rest, as they say, is history. I discovered unexpectedly that I enjoyed writing about the entertainment industry; it was fun and the perks were fabulous. As a result, I never tried to write anything too serious again. I also never confronted my dad about the conversation I overheard, and things were never quite the same between us.

The more my career as an entertainment journalist took off, the more disappointed Dad seemed. He simply didn't understand why I wanted to write what he called *fluffy rubbish*. He was never one to pull any punches. As far as I was concerned, I was simply playing to my strengths. Looking back, I think maybe I was also scared. I'm sure my dad could have told me the difference, but it was too late now, wasn't it? His sudden heart-attack had seen to that.

I dragged myself out of memory lane as Mitch made her way around the desk. She perched on the edge and looked down at me.

"Kat, at the end of the day, these kinds of mistakes shouldn't happen and it's not the first time. Things have been shaky with you for a while. You've been so caught up with getting the scoops before anyone else—"

"But that's my job—" I protested. She silenced me with a raised hand.

"—finding bigger scandals, playing celebrity. You've been sloppy. Legal is getting twitchy and I can't ignore this one."

"What if I publish an apology on the blog?" I was desperate to make amends.

"Pop Vulture's gone." Mitch could always be counted on to be blunt. "I've taken it offline. I've also deactivated all of your social media accounts."

My eyes bugged in horror.

"All of them?"

"All of them."

"Even Instagram? Snapchat?"

Mitch gave a curt nod and I reeled. *Holy shit.* Even I'd forgotten what I looked like without a filter.

"No," I wailed, "Mitch, you can't do that."

"I can and I have."

"What about Twitter? I hit half a million followers last month, the same on Instagram. It's taken me years to build my platform." A thought struck me. "Oh my god, my TikTok."

"Also gone".

"NO! Mitch, you don't understand. I am an *influencer*. You can't just delete me. And... and..." I floundered in complete panic at the thought of being cut off from my social network.

"Oh, for god's sake Kat, grow up. You are not an influencer. You're a thirty-six-year-old *journalist*. You do not need to be making stupid voice-over videos like an attention-seeking twenty-two-year-old with too much lip filler and ridiculous eyelash extensions. Your followers are not your friends, I'm sure they'll cope. Christ, I rue the day I ever suggested 'cross-platform' to you."

"But, what are people going to read if *Pop Vulture*'s gone?"

Mitch's icy glare nearly froze my eyeballs in my head.

"I would imagine they'll read my magazine. You know, the one you write for?" She folded her arms. "You are not the celebrity here, Kat, despite what you might think. You'd be wise to start remembering that. Look, it's temporary. The best thing you can do right now is lay low and wait until this all blows over. The public have very short memories. As soon as the next scandal comes along, you'll be forgotten."

It came out before I could stop it.

"What if I don't want to be forgotten?"

"Pardon?"

I should have shut up then and there but for some reason my tongue kept flapping. Stupid tongue.

"I mean, if you think about it, I am sort of a celebrity. Even other famous people know who I am. Some of them are even scared of me. I mean, when I walk into a room people actually whisper that I'm there and if you ask anyone who the Pop Vulture is, I bet loads of people would—"

"Are you listening to yourself?"

I was. And I was disappointed. I sounded like one of those whiny, self-important ex-reality show kids who think they have something special and important to offer the world because they'd showered nude or performed impressive fellatio on a wine bottle on national television. All they had was bad grammar and a disturbing lack of self-respect. I puffed my chest out a little, defiant. At least I had good grammar.

"You're treading a fine line here, Kat. If you would rather be fired, I can certainly oblige, just keep talking the way you're talking. I'm offering you a chance because I like you, not because you deserve it. If I were you, I would shut up and take it and learn the lesson."

"Fine," I still couldn't help sulking a little. "So, what now? Are you demoting me to the mail room? The switchboard?"

Mitch waved her hand dismissively as she moved back to the other side of her desk. "Don't be so dramatic. I'm bumping you to staff writer for a while and sending you on assignment. You can get back to your roots." The last bit was said with a definite smirk. There was no point in arguing so I slumped in my chair and chewed my nails as she reached into her desk drawer.

"Let me guess, you're going to punish me by shipping me off to Gympie to write a 'where are they now?' about a soap-star turned llama farmer."

"While that would be amusing... not exactly." Mitch handed me a computer printout and a black and white photograph. The printout was an airline reservation, a return flight to Los Angeles. The photo was of a vaguely familiar face. I stared blankly at them both. "You'll be writing a story on Xander Hill."

Now I stared blankly at her.

"Huh?'

Mitch frowned, "Xander Hill, *the actor*." She spelled it out slowly as if I was extremely thick, then took a breath, about to repeat the name again.

"I know who Xander Hill is, Mitch." I let out a laugh of disbelief as I tossed the photo on to the desk. "I get paid to know this stuff." I rattled off the bit of trivia I knew. "Xander

Hill, small-time actor in Hollywood back in the late sixties, early seventies. Died before he really made it big, *allegedly* slept with a lot of women, high profile affair with a movie star. Mitch, he's been dead for a long time, he's not exactly big news."

She shook her head like you do when you can't believe you are wasting time talking to somebody really dumb. I flushed.

"The point is, he's been dead exactly fifty years this week. I want you to write a retrospective, how he got started, who he dated, who he shagged, the usual."

"But, why?"

Mitch finally snapped, exasperated.

"Oh, for god's sake Kat, stop arguing with me. He didn't just *die*, you know that. And you know they never figured out who killed him. It's *interesting*."

I was still puzzled.

"But isn't the anniversary of James Dean's death coming up? Wouldn't people be more interested in a big star rather than some obscure up-and-comer? Why aren't we covering that instead?"

"Because everyone's doing James Dean."

"Would you like to rephrase that?" I winked at her, attempting a grin, and was rewarded with a withering look. Clearly not the time for double entendre. My face straightened as she continued.

"There's nothing new about Dean. Everyone rehashes the same stuff. We're going with something different. Think of it like this, Hill is to Dean what Mansfield was to Monroe. Not as big a star but still a fascinating story."

"You're the boss. Are you sure people will be interested enough to buy the magazine though?"

"If they weren't interested there wouldn't be more than

one hundred Facebook groups dedicated to Xander Hill," she said triumphantly.

"That's not saying much, Mitch. There are hundreds of Facebook groups dedicated to "Which Sesame Street Character Are You?" and the difference between their, there and they're".

"Smart-arse."

My chuckle screeched to a halt and I cleared my throat.

"Sorry. Look, okay, I get why you want me to write it, but I still don't understand why I need to go all the way to LA? Can't I write it from here—you know, using the internet?"

She was losing patience with me.

"No. We have a scoop—an exclusive interview."

"So? Surely I can do that by Zoom."

"It has to be done in person. Not negotiable. My source is old school. Says he has some sexy new secrets about Xander Hill." She waved her hands like an overenthusiastic game show host, "*Never before revealed*," then dropped them as quickly. "So, you're going and that's that." Her eyes were ringing dollar signs like a lit-up pokie machine and I admit my curiosity was piqued.

"So, who is it?"

"I'll send you the details once you're there, I'm still finalising some things. It could take a few days but let me assure you, it is a coup. If he tells us what I have a hunch he's going to tell us, this could be really big. Kat, you're lucky I'm not booting your arse out the door, be thankful this is getting you out of Sydney. Two birds, one stone and all that."

I retrieved the photo and studied it intently. I couldn't help thinking it was weird that the smiling face in the picture simply didn't exist anymore. My dad came involuntarily to mind again and I squashed the thought. Today was hard enough. I snapped myself back to the present in time to hear Mitch wrapping up.

"—so, the basic whodunit theories, the *scandal*, but don't

get too serious. It's the sexy stuff our readers want. Focus on that."

That, I knew I could do.

"Well, I guess it's a done deal then. So, when do I leave?" I started to flip to the reservation sheet, mentally calculating how many pairs of shoes I should pack.

"In three hours. You'll need to head straight to the airport."

"What?" I stared at the flight time in disbelief then glanced down at my crusty pyjamas. But—"

Mitch shot me a pointed look.

"Maybe you should have made more of an effort with your appearance today. Hmm?" She patted my hand across the desk. "Don't worry kiddo, I took the liberty of packing you a bag from Sarah's cupboard over in *Style* and I raided Miranda's beauty trunk." She nudged a grey hold-all from beside her desk with her foot. "Your passport is kept here anyway, you know that, there's a proper camera in there—SLR—and I've booked you a room at the Chateau."

My eyes widened.

"Marmont?"

She rolled her eyes at me as if to say *what other Chateau is there?*

"I don't want you going home and I certainly don't want you around when they release Kelly from hospital tomorrow. Clearly the press is still camped out. It's best you're gone and I don't want anyone knowing where you're going." With that she plonked an archaic flip-phone on the desk along with a piece of paper. "Here's your new email address and phone number."

"Huh? My new what?" I nearly had to peel my eyebrows off the ceiling. This was all happening way too fast.

"This is all I want you to use. You won't have your laptop either, you can use an internet café to check emails and file your story. Research only. Got it? I want you to stay off social media.

Do not try reactivating your accounts. This phone has the main numbers you'll need in it and I'll send your temporary number to any important contacts for you. In the meantime, I'd like your iPhone please."

She held out her hand and I stared at it, incredulous.

"Are you serious?"

"Completely." She pushed a pen and notepad at me as I reluctantly put my iPhone on the desk. "It's not going to kill you to unplug. This is damage control, Kat. Your number is public property, you're easy to get hold of. You can't tell me you haven't been fielding unwanted calls 24/7 for the past week and a half. This way it all dies down. Nobody can photograph you, call you, talk to you and get some shitty comment out of context. You of all people know how it works. In the meantime, you get to keep your job and I get the story. Simple."

"Are you sure that phone even works? It looks like it belongs in a museum," I muttered, imagining answering the thing and copping an earful of dust.

Nausea washed over me as I jotted down a short list of names I wanted out of my contacts list. It was like a scene from a spy movie, *your mission, should you choose to accept it*, blah blah blah, except I wasn't a spy and 'choose' was not the word for it. *I'll take ultimatum for a hundred, Alex.* Although granted, ultimatums didn't usually involve swanky, iconic hotels.

"And the Chateau? What's with that? It doesn't exactly feel like I'm being punished here," I was more than a bit mystified.

Mitch made a little moue and hunched her shoulders. "If I want you in the thick of things, where better? Anyone who's anyone stays at the Chateau. Keep your eyes open." Was she deliberately trying to confuse me?

"But I thought I was supposed to lay low, steer clear of all that? Learn a lesson?"

The *you're an idiot* expression crossed Mitch's face yet again.

"We still have a magazine to fill. This is not some kind of intervention, Kat. I simply want you to check your facts. Focus on this story first but if you happen to see anyone of note behaving badly, you know the drill."

"But—"

"But nothing. Would you rather I get you a room at the motor inn, downtown?" Images of grotty dumpsters flashed in my mind and I quickly shook my head. "Good." Mitch stood and moved toward me, arms outstretched. She was definitely not a hugger so the overall impression, with her scrawny arms and emotionless face, was zombie-like and I flinched involuntarily. She stopped and patted me awkwardly on both shoulders instead. "Everything will be fine, Kat. Trust me. You're not well-known in LA. Enjoy being a nobody, get the job done and then we'll talk when you get back."

Being a nobody? *Ugh.*

Before I could argue any further, she hoisted the hold-all onto my shoulder, shoved my passport, flight reservation and the photo of Xander Hill into my hand and bustled me out of her gleaming office. "I'll email you everything else you need, Okay? Oh, and one final thing, Kat—" She shoved me unceremoniously into the lift and pressed the down button.

"What's that?" I raised my eyebrows in query, expecting well wishes for a safe trip, considering my fragile state.

"Please wash your hair. You smell like Cheezels."

The lift doors slid shut.

Chapter Two

8221 Sunset Boulevard. Some things in Hollywood never change and the infamous Chateau Marmont was one of them. Castle-like and secretive it hovered above the North side of Sunset Strip, all white washed gothic arches and turrets.

"Well, Ma'am," the Tom Cruise look-alike working the front desk drawled as he shot a white, toothy grin at the woman checking in before me, "I can't put you in Bungalow Three, but if it's a ghost you're after, Apartment Four often has an elderly gentleman visitor we believe is Helmut Newton. How 'bout we put you in there?"

I chuckled. Only in LA.

Maybe I could get some real help with this stupid article. I conjured a mental image of myself in a purple turban, fingers poised over one of those spirit board thingies, eyes rolling in my head and chanting *speak to me Xander Hill, speak to me.* I shook my head. It was a silly idea. I believed in ghosts about as much as I believed Kim Kardashian's arse was completely *au naturel*.

I had cankles after the sixteen-hour flight and the unwieldy bag was chomping brutally into my shoulder. I shifted from foot to foot, tapping a staccato rhythm with the toe of my shoe, waiting my turn. After what seemed an eternity, the woman was handed her room key. Plump and in her sixties, with her silvery hair teased into a dated beehive, she nevertheless looked like a kid in a candy store as she turned and held the key aloft like a prize.

"Oh, Katherine, isn't this exciting?" She squealed at ear-splitting volume. "Los Angeles. The Chateau Marmont. I can't believe I'm here. It must be terribly tedious for you but me, Marjorie Brent, in Hollywood? You don't know how long I've dreamed of this." She kissed her room key dramatically and threw her arms skyward. "Thank you, Channel Seven!'

I cringed and glanced around, hoping nobody thought she was a friend of mine. Marjorie was also from Sydney, Parramatta to be exact. She'd cleaned up on the ever-popular TV game show, *Quizmania*, enabling her to take the trip of a lifetime.

Encased head to toe in pink terry-towelling and with the demeanour of an over-zealous spaniel, she was also a widow and had assumed because we sat together on the flight, we were now best friends. Clearly not, because only people who didn't know me (or didn't like me) called me Katherine. She waited patiently, but not quietly, while I checked in, only taking a breath between words to sip on a fizzy cherry cola.

"I was hoping to stay in bungalow three; that's where John Belushi died, you know. Oh, of course you would know, silly me. So tragic, such a talented and funny man." She paused to emit a small burp. "You know, other guests have said they've seen his spirit; he kept them awake through the night telling joke after joke after joke. Isn't that thrilling?"

"Only if you believe in ghosts," I grumbled over my

shoulder as I handed my credit card to the clerk. He appeared to be flirting with me, his smile so wide I could see his wisdom teeth. I scowled and he hurriedly dropped his eyes to the computer terminal. Why were Americans always so bloody happy? Couldn't he tell my life had just imploded?

Awkward now, he presented my key and half-heartedly chirped, "Have a nice day." I blinked at him like a cranky owl then turned and plodded wearily through the decadent lobby, weaving between sofas with Marjorie still yapping at my heels.

The rugs under our feet were a touch worn—shabby-chic —and the vaulted ceilings echoed with whispers of a luscious, rich past. Everything from the velvet lampshades to the deep red carpet had a tarnished patina, a wicked glow that might have been my imagination, fuelled by countless stories of Hollywood scandal, romance, and flat-out debauchery.

Years earlier I'd interviewed Ben Affleck in this very lobby; sinking into one of the opulent striped sofas, awestruck by the surrounds but not the company. Most celebrities were unimpressive in person. I'd lost count of the times I'd turned up to interview the latest and hottest heart throb only to find a shorter, pimplier version in his place, with questionable personal hygiene and an even whiffier attitude. It left a person somewhat jaded.

To be fair, the interview with Affleck was about a year after the widely-panned *Gigli* was released. I was suffering from the mother of all hangovers. The combination of a slightly defensive Affleck, a few too many personal questions about his 'inevitable' split from J-Lo, and the fact that half-way through the interview I'd vomited all over his expensive sneakers, led to me being blacklisted by his publicist. Not my finest moment. I should have registered the start of my decline way back then.

Unfortunately, my wish for Affleck's star to fade so I'd

never again have to face him did not come true. In fact, the
opposite happened and—to top it all off—who'd have thought
'Bennifer' would rise from the ashes twenty years on? Wasn't it
taking the whole *everything old is new again* thing a little bit
literally? I mean, good for them; clearly true love finds a way. I
was just hoping it didn't signal a return to ultra-low-rise jeans,
because having to wax your bikini line just to wear Levi's?
Nobody needs to see that. Regardless, with all that in mind, I
simply prefer to feign confusion every time someone mentions
the Oscar-winning actor turned director. *Hmm? Ben? Ben who?
Sorry, what?* The thought of having to face him again at some
point didn't thrill me.

This legendary hotel however, still did. It was a shame I was
too jet-lagged and bad moody to appreciate it. I picked up
speed, hoping Marjorie would eventually fall behind.

"They all stayed here you know, all the Hollywood greats,"
Marjorie prattled, "Clark Gable, Marilyn Monroe, Greta
Garbo. In fact, James Dean and Natalie Wood first met here
during a script rehearsal of *Rebel without a Cause?* That was
back in the day when the studios cared for their stars. I believe
caviar was on the lunch menu that day ... was it caviar? Yes, it
was caviar because I remember reading that James Dean apparently kicked up a heck of a fuss about eating fish eggs. Did you
know that?"

Christ. The woman was a walking encyclopedia. Jet lag had
shot my patience levels to pieces but I was too tired to do
anything apart from listen to her waffle. I sighed instead,
clenching my jaw, and tried not to notice that fizz from the
cherry coke was decorating her little old lady moustache.

"No, Marjorie, actually I didn't know that."

"Really?" she squeaked, "I thought celebrity journalists
knew everything there is to know about celebrities? Isn't that
your specialty? You always seem to know things before

everyone else on that internet thingy you do, what's it called again?"

"It's called a blog, Marjorie."

She laughed loudly.

"That's right, such a funny name for it. Sounds a bit like a poo if you ask me," she covered her mouth and snorted as she glanced around, as if saying something terribly rude. "Although, it's not as funny as what you call yourself, is it?" She wrinkled her nose and continued on guilelessly. "The Pop Vulture's not very complimentary. Sounds quite mercenary, don't you think?"

"That was kind of the point," I muttered miserably under my breath.

I'd almost managed to get away without talking about my job at all. Marjorie had recognised me from somewhere as soon as she'd squeezed herself into the seat beside me on the plane, but she couldn't quite place the face. It must have been the red puffy eyes and greasy hair disguise I was wearing.

She'd stared quizzically at me for a few uncomfortable minutes then shrugged, fastened her seatbelt and proceeded to tell me all about her son, Barry, who'd moved to LA five years earlier and who didn't have a steady girlfriend, even though he was forty-two and, in her opinion, that was leaving it a bit late. Didn't I agree? But she supposed he did have a very important job with the LA Police Department which kept him far too busy for romance, you know—and on and on and on. I don't think she took a breath for the entire flight.

Quizmania had been her late husband, Geoffrey's, favourite television show. He'd been an armchair player and had hypothetically won thousands of dollars, week after week. He'd always wanted to give it a shot for real and shake host, Garry Marks', hand but somehow never got around to applying.

Then he'd died. A sudden stroke in the middle of a Tuesday afternoon episode.

Marjorie had grabbed my hand earnestly, pinning it to the armrest, and whispered tearily that going on the show was a tribute to her Geoffrey. And wouldn't you know it, it was like he was right there with her, choosing the boxes that held questions she knew the answers to. Even the jackpot question, about Charlie Chaplin's dog in *A Dog's Life*, had been right up her alley, being an old movie buff and all.

That's when it hit her. She'd startled me with a sudden *A-ha!* and, right now I was wishing I'd simply answered, 'Nope, not me ... you must have the wrong person. I'm a juggler...' when she'd pointed her finger at me with a triumphant grin.

"You're that gossip girl," she crowed. "Kat – er – something,"

Great.

"You got me. I'm that gossip girl."

I'd rubbed my forehead with an increasingly sweaty palm.

"Oh dear, that's certainly a bit of a mess you're in at the moment, isn't it?" she'd said in a shocked voice. "All over the papers back at the airport it was. I was reading about it while I was waiting to board. Awfully tragic news about that pretty little singer. Well, you must feel horr—"

"Horrible?" I'd snapped, immediately regretting my tone as she'd recoiled. "Yes, I do feel horrible. So horrible in fact that I'm leaving the country. Now, if you don't mind, I'd prefer not talk about it."

To her credit, she hadn't pursued the topic. She'd smiled and patted my hand and said, 'That's okay, dear, we can talk about something else'. Then she'd started the interrogation.

Is Kat short for Katherine? *Yes.* How old are you? *Thirty-six, although I'm sure at the moment I look fifty.* Do you live in Sydney? *Yes.* Don't you find it dirty and overcrowded? *No. Well yes, but I like it that way.* Do you prefer dogs or cats? *What an oddly random question but, uh, dogs, I guess.*

Robotically, I'd answered every one of her enthusiastic questions. It had taken my mind off things for a short while at least.

"Are you married? Do you have a boyfriend?"

Ha! You'd have to have spare time for that. Besides, I'd given up on men a long time ago thanks to the dawning realisation that I had a knack for choosing completely inappropriate partners and was pretty crap at the whole love thing.

Combine a string of my own disastrous relationships with the number of famous love rats I'd personally splashed across the tabloid pages and you can understand that I was a touch cynical when it came to affairs of the heart. Wasn't celibacy cool these days? I'm sure there was some kind of coloured wristband for it.

I hadn't been on a date in nearly two years, let alone have an actual boyfriend or husband. The closest I'd come to any kind of romantic activity in a long while was some ill-advised, drunken and never-to-be-repeated fumbling with an up-and-coming sports reporter, six months ago, in one of the Channel Five editing booths. Considering it didn't get past second base due to the fact one of his contact lenses fell out, it hardly counted.

"No, Marjorie, not married. No boyfriend to speak of."

"Oooh, are you a lesbian?" Marjorie had peered hopefully at me, as if my potential gay-ness was as fascinating as if I'd sprouted an extra head or given birth to a pterodactyl.

"No, unfortunately, I am not a lesbian." I'd said, almost at the end of my tether. "But my best friend, Chrissie, is bisexual if that helps."

Gorgeous Chrissie Maxwell - heavily tattooed and perpetually half-cut music journo/TV presenter, chronic practical joker, and the only friend I have who understands my occasional need to get drunk on Bundaberg Rum and dance with my eyes closed to Dave Dobbyn's *Slice of Heaven*.

If she'd been in my situation, she would have jammed her AirPods into her heavily pierced ears and stared Marjorie into quiet submission. Or asked her politely to 'please shut the fuck up'.

I'd actually tried to leave Marjorie in the airport taxi queue once we'd landed, even after I knew we were staying at the same hotel. I'd felt mean of course but my ears were about to bleed and I was cranky and desperate for a pillow, copious amounts of vodka and some generic cable television.

Blame the jet lag, blame the guilt I was carrying around like expensive luggage, whatever, but I'd made the mistake of glancing out of the side window before the taxi pulled away. There stood Marjorie, by herself with her garish, hot pink suitcase and matching tracksuit, looking rather lost. The sight of her triggered something in me. Probably insanity now that I think about it.

Don't do it.

A tiny, tattooed Chrissie had appeared on my shoulder, wearing a pair of red-sequined devil's horns and smoking a cigar.

Don't do it, Kat.

I couldn't help myself.

"Hold on, driver," I'd leant over and wound down the window. "Marjorie," I'd called, wanting to kick myself immediately. But it was too late. She'd stepped eagerly up to the kerb and leant into the window. "Hop in, we'll share the ride."

My imaginary Chrissie had shaken her head in disapproval and blown smug cigar smoke rings at me before proclaiming, *'Alley Kat, Alley Kat. Man, are you going to regret that in the morning.'*

So you see, there was nobody to blame but myself for the fact I was being followed through the hotel lobby by a needy housewife whose enthusiasm was directly proportionate to the size of her hair-do; or for the migraine introducing itself slowly to my cerebral cortex.

"So... Xander Hill. Wow. That'll be an interesting article to write, I'm sure." Marjorie was unrelenting, oblivious to my silence as we waited for the elevator for an interminable amount of time, "Katherine, did you know the last time he was seen alive he was arguing with Lola Tennant in this very lobby? She was his co-star, you know. Much older. Married too."

Of course, she would know the entire story. Maybe she should write my article and I could just get drunk. She lowered her voice to a theatrical whisper and nudged me. "They were having an affair. Terrible that is. There's no excuse for cheating you know."

My eyes were starting to glaze over but I managed to mutter my agreement as we finally stepped into the elevator.

"No, Marjorie, you're right. There's no excuse for cheating."

"Then BANG, just like that, Xander Hill was found shot dead in his car. They never solved it."

"Yes, Marjorie, I know," I mumbled, struggling now to hold my head up.

"Personally, I think it was the husband."

I was on autopilot by then. I felt numb.

"Really Marjorie? That's super."

The doors of the elevator opened onto a dimly lit corridor.

"Well, this is your floor," Marjorie said brightly.

I'm ashamed to say I didn't even answer. I stumbled out of the elevator, faintly registering the shouted reminder of her room number before the doors closed behind me and I was left in silence. Finally.

I searched for my door number, running my fingers along the silky, flocked wallpaper. I vaguely recalled reading somewhere that a young William Holden was told by Harry Cohn, the founder of Columbia Pictures, 'If you must get into trouble, do it at the Chateau Marmont.' Clearly, Xander Hill got more trouble than he bargained for.

I pushed the heavy door to my Junior Suite open with relief. The cherry-wood parquetry floor glowed in the sunlight that streamed through the gauzy white drapes, clean and bright. In the other room, a king bed beckoned and I tottered gratefully towards it, dropping my bag with a loud thunk. I was utterly exhausted. I collapsed onto the soft bedding, my body sinking deep into the luxurious white quilting.

Local time was 10am Monday morning but my body told me it was 3am Tuesday in Sydney and I hadn't slept yet. At my age, pulling an all-nighter without the aid of a bucket load of cocktails and some cheesy dance music was akin to being forced to watch all eight *Harry Potter* movies back-to-back with no sleep and your eyes sticky-taped open. It did bad, bad things to your sanity.

Being a weeknight, all of my friends back home would have been tucked up in bed. All except Chrissie who thought midweek nights out meant shorter queues at the bar for a start, and who was actually at that moment living it up at the World Music Awards in Monaco.

My feet throbbed painfully so I sat up to take my shoes off. I caught my image reflected in the large gilt framed mirror on the opposite wall. *Oh dear.* I might have changed out of my pyjamas and tried to freshen up at Heathrow, but I still looked like hell. I certainly fitted in at the Chateau Marmont and not in a good way.

I was reminiscent of one of those paparazzi photos people seem to love, of an inebriated star sitting in a gutter or falling out of a flashy car. My impossible-to-style-on-my-own haircut stuck up in matted tufts on one side and my mascara had decided to migrate to underneath my eyes, presumably to party on with the dark circles already lurking there.

I scowled at my reflection. I was entitled to look like crap. I kicked off my sneakers and socks and stomped barefoot over to a peach-coloured art deco cabinet. It cleverly concealed a tiny bar fridge behind its carved façade. *Aha! Mini bar, mini bar, oh how I love thee.*

I perused the selection for about two seconds before deciding on the lot. I gathered up as many of the miniature bottles as I could, hungrily adding two Snickers and three packets of Pringles to the mix. The bottles lined up on the bedside table like tiny alcoholic soldiers ready to march valiantly on my depression.

Scotch! *Yessir.* Gin! *Yessir.* Vodka! *Present.* Another vodka. *Excellent!* Vermouth! *Vermouth?* I eyed the tiny green bottle suspiciously. Yuck. There's no Bundaberg Rum (that was to be expected) only some kind of sweet Jamaican equivalent. And, of course, some tequila. Who could forget trusty old *Jose*?

I wondered momentarily if the concierge would be able to find some Bundy anywhere in downtown Hollywood. Probably not. Although they did say the concierge at Chateau Marmont could (air quotes) get you anything. No doubt that had been tested a million times, with a million substances, but I found it hard to believe he or she had ever been sent out in search of the Bundy Bear.

Emptying the first of the vodka minis in two swigs, I glared at my handbag. It lay on its side on the floor where I'd unceremoniously dumped it. The black and white picture of Xander Hill peeked out from between rumpled, leather folds.

Get to work! It shouted at me. *Get stuffed,* I shot back telepathically. I imagined Mitch echoing *I'm not paying you to get pissed. You've got work to do.* Poking my tongue out defiantly at the smiling photo, I cracked open the tiny tequila and crawled fully clothed into the bed. Xander Hill had been dead for fifty years, he could wait another day. It wasn't like he was going anywhere.

Chapter Three

From underneath my pillow—which for some reason was wedged firmly over my head—I could hear an insistent and annoying beeping. I didn't remember setting the alarm and reached out blindly from underneath the tangled bedclothes, groping around on the bedside table for the offending clock. I found nothing except the massacred remains of my tiny bottle army, little glass bodies clinking morbidly together under my hand.

I groaned at the sound, pressing my face into the bed. *Urgh.* The tinkling of glass sounded more like a window shattering and the back of my skull throbbed in response. Ever since Brad Peters' birthday party in Year Twelve, where I got completely plastered on Nikov vodka and orange in a cask and ended up sleeping in my own vomit on an inflatable swimming pool li-lo with my Guns 'n' Roses t-shirt over my head, I hadn't been very good at hangovers.

I usually tried to avoid them these days. Not by drinking less mind you, because how the hell could I maintain a friendship like Chrissie's with such a defeatist attitude. No, a piece of

Vegemite toast and some *Berocca* in a litre of water before collapsing into bed usually allowed me to wake vomit and headache free. This led both Chrissie and I to think whoever invented the fizzy orange magic should be awarded a Nobel Prize.

The shrill beeping had stopped for the time being and I inched myself onto my back, thinking my head would hurt less facing the other way. Nope. It hurt the same amount and the inching made my stomach heave in protest. Something sticky and warm oozed under the small of my back where my t-shirt had scrunched up in my sleep. I reached hesitantly down and retrieved half a *Snickers* bar from between my crumpled jeans and the chocolate covered sheet. Gross. That was going to look like something else entirely to housekeeping.

My throbbing head, which seemed to weigh approximately the same as a watermelon, peeled slowly away from the pillow and I blinked blearily at the harsh Californian sunlight. Suddenly – bip - be-beep, bip bip – bip - be-beep - bip bip. *Grrr*. What the hell was that and why wouldn't it go away? I peered around the room, trying to locate the source of the mysterious chirruping while my inner mogwai shrieked *bright light! bright light!* I made a note to myself—next time I chose death by mini-bar, to think ahead and close the freaking curtains.

I tried to move only my eyes, so my brain didn't slosh around too much in my skull. It didn't work. It only made my eyes hurt. Aha! The sound was coming from my bag and, as I attempted to focus, I could feel tiny intrepid fingers belonging to a vital piece of information clawing their way towards my foggy frontal lobe.

Recognition finally dawned. It was that stupid unfamiliar phone I'd been lumbered with, cheerily announcing the arrival of several text messages with a weird, old-fashioned beep. No wonder I didn't recognise it. It didn't have anything at all to do with the fact my brain was alcohol-impaired.

How on earth did those tiny bottles get me so drunk? I thumped cross legged on to the floor and found the culprits. Two tiny green bottles. Empty. Damned Vermouth. I kicked them accusingly under the bed as if they—and not the other fourteen bottles—were the sole reason for my hangover.

I wasn't sure how long I'd been asleep but it couldn't have been that long because it was still daylight. A thought occurred to me. Surely not. A quick check of the time confirmed that it was daylight *again*. I had in fact been comatose for more than twenty-four hours. Shit.

There were four text messages queued up, the latest from Chrissie. At least it confirmed Mitch had been true to her word about passing on the new number. The message was clearly sent after having a few, if Chrissie's wonky spelling was anything to go by. Never mind predictive text, someone should invent drunk-corrective text. I'm sure it would be wildly popular among trashed twenty-somethings, all too eager to text the ex after a few too many shots. I was used to deciphering her messages though. I knew that '*Miss you. No duo when you're not herd*' was nothing to do with the two of us and a bunch of cows and more to do with her having no fun without me.

It had been nearly a month since we'd caught up in person and the funny text reminded me how much I missed her. The other three messages were from Mitch. Two had apparently beeped through quite some time before.

'*Call me when U arrive & have chckd email.*' Uh oh. Then 12 hours later, '*Pls tell me ur plane didn't crash!*' How caring. As if I would have texted her back if I'd perished in a fiery mid-air mishap. The latest text was more business-like. '*Called hotel. Confrmed chck in. Assume U R 2 busy working hard 2 call. PS Don't touch the minibar*'.

Oops.

I tossed the phone on the bed and gave myself a mental shake, mainly because I was wise enough to know a physical shake would make me throw up. Then, I struggled up off the floor and hauled myself towards the bathroom.

Fifteen minutes later I felt halfway human again, my skin shining pinkly and my wet hair going somewhat towards soothing my pulsating scalp. The heat and steam of the shower (and several Advil) had soaked away a tiny bit of my jet lag and purged some of the remaining alcohol from my pores. The intentional quick spurt of icy cold water at the end had finished the waking up process, making me hop around the shower recess, gasping like a manic goldfish. It always did the trick.

The red light on the in-house telephone told me I had waiting messages there too. Surely I hadn't slept through that phone as well. Toothbrush in hand, I wedged the receiver between my ear and shoulder and scrubbed hard at teeth that were on the Fozzie Bear side of furry while I listened.

Mitch. Mitch. And Mitch again, by the third message sounding extremely pissed but still only checking in. Nothing new to report, just a directive to check my emails ASAP. The fourth message instantly made my brain hurt.

"Katherine, hello? Katherine, it's Marjorie, Marjorie Brent, you know, from the plane. Listen, I know you're very busy and all and far too important to worry about a silly request from little old me but I was wondering – uh, you see I belong to a bridge club and we have this newsletter that comes out and, well to cut a long story short, I do a bit of writing for it and thought that maybe I could pick your brains about writing, maybe. Or even interview you for it, you know, for practice. Not about any of this nasty rubbish that's going on, don't worry. Maybe you could talk about how exciting your job is. Um – well – think about it. Let me know. You can call me anytime. I'm in Apartment Four. That's Apartment Four. Okay. So, hopefully I'll hear from you soon. No hurr—"

Beeeeep.

Wow. She actually ran out of space on the voicemail. Sorry, lady. The thought of having my brain picked by anything at that moment brought on an involuntarily shudder. And the thought of willingly subjecting myself to a sit down with Marjorie, well, something pretty drastic would have to happen for me to even consider that. Plus, *hello*, bit busy being a real journalist and writing a real article and all that.

Speaking of which—as my discarded handbag and that stupid smiling photo of Xander Hill caught my eye—I was going to need caffeine.

Lots of caffeine.

Con-X, my favourite internet café and the purveyor of arguably the best coffee in Hollywood, was tucked away in a tiny strip mall near the corner of Vine and Fountain. Sunglasses firmly affixed to my face, I set off on foot. I hoped the long walk there would clear my head but in all seriousness all it did was make me sweat like a pig. A very hungover pig.

Within minutes, the back of my sundress—the first scrap of unfamiliar material I came to in the top of my bag—clung to my sticky skin. I could swear the faint whiff of vermouth was emanating from my damp armpits. It was not pleasant.

Despite my hangover, the multitasker in me was still functional. But only just. I decided to take a quick detour, double-checking my camera was in my bag and fully charged. Rather than walk directly down Sunset to Vine, I turned left at North La Brea and headed towards Hollywood Boulevard and the iconic Walk of Fame.

The famous trail of brass stars ran along both sides of

Hollywood and Vine, embedded in glossy pink and charcoal speckled terrazzo. Xander' Hill's star lay closer to Vine Street, near Bette Davis and Gary Cooper, but for now I was more interested in his concrete hand and foot prints in the forecourt of TCL Chinese Theatre.

I eventually reached Hollywood Boulevard and the familiar silver gazebo with its gleaming spire and Silver Screen goddesses at each corner. Wiggling my way through the throng surrounding it, I then headed across the busy road, continuing up the street and dodging tourists at every step like a matador.

Camera phones whirred and clicked around me every few seconds, the sightseers like manic paparazzi. I neatly dodged one posing family only to have my eye nearly taken out by the errant selfie stick of another. Kids pulled faces in front of street signs for posterity and took pictures of the gilded names at their feet. You could pick the influencers a mile off. They were the ones repeatedly jumping in the air for their Boomerangs and TikToks, clearly caring more about the right angle and facial expression than the history surrounding them. I recognised them because I'd done it a million times, although I'm absolutely certain I didn't look as silly as they did.

I stopped at the expansive forecourt of the theatre and gazed around. I'd been there many times but the grandiosity always impressed me. The forecourt sat slightly back from the street, the cement squares giving a chequered appearance to the ground in muted grey and pink and beige. Its imposing pagoda, with its coral red pillars, towered over the space. Guarding the theatre entrance were the spiky stone faces of the Chinese heaven dogs, fierce yet serene.

An excitable horde milled around, people kneeling here and there to compare their hands to those of a favoured star. Tanned beefcakes to Schwarzenegger's. Serious actor types to Pacino's. Gaggles of teenaged girls squealing and taking selfies, fondling the prints of whichever baby-faced heart-throb was currently flavour of the month.

As on any other given day, there were numerous young blondes reverently placing their hands and feet into the small prints left by Marilyn Monroe. Today there were two, one in red spandex and one dressed in the requisite white halter dress, her ample figure spilling from the top. She in particular was quite the attraction and I smiled as I wandered to the left, scanning the ground.

Xander's square was a deep grey. I knelt and fished around in my bag for my camera, then clicked off several shots. His name was scrawled in curly letters next to the date; 18th February, 1973, a month to the day before he died.

I put my camera down and leaned forward, placing my hands into the imprints. His hands had been large, with long fingers; strong hands I imagined. I wondered about his skin, if it was coarsened and rough—country boy hands. Or had Hollywood already smoothed the edges away by the time he'd knelt there.

I ran my hand back and forth over the rough surface of the square, touching the letters of his name. The sun-baked concrete warmed my fingers then seemed to heat up so rapidly it practically seared my skin. I jerked my hand back in shock and my arms erupted in goose bumps. The strangest sensation swept over me. Someone was watching. I knelt up, shielding my eyes from the sun, and swept the forecourt, unnerved.

Peering through the mob of people, I saw a tall man, standing alone by the entrance to the theatre. Shadows obscured his face and he was partly hidden by one of the pillars but he was clearly staring at me, head dipped. I stared back figuring that if he was aimlessly people watching, he'd be embarrassed by my attention and turn away. No such luck. He didn't move.

He made me more than a little uncomfortable, so I casually picked up my bag and sauntered to the other side of the fore-court. I felt his eyes burning into my back and when I surreptitiously glanced back at him, he had moved closer.

Crap.

Trying to appear nonchalant, I walked towards the street and headed right, picking up pace once I was out of sight in case he was a weirdo and decided to follow me. As I cut across the road and around the corner into Orange Drive, I took a chance and glanced behind me. Sure enough, about fifty feet back was the same guy, walking slowly with his head down.

I mentally catalogued his appearance—light hair, about six-two, dark jeans and a blue checked shirt. If only I could see his face. My pulse quickened and I walked more swiftly, dodging people standing stationary on the street and every few seconds turning to check if he still followed. When I thought he wasn't looking, I ducked into the nearest store.

The door of the tiny souvenir shop rattled noisily in my haste to hide. Slipping between shelves filled with Hollywood sign key rings and black and white clapper board fridge magnets, I waited to see if he walked past.

Minutes ticked by. I pretended to weigh up the pros and cons of a pair of Laurel and Hardy bobble-heads as opposed to a giant John Wayne coffee mug, for the benefit of the shop assistant, who was clearly keeping an eye on my strange behaviour. My stalker wasn't visible through the window so I inched towards the door, trying to peer sideways through the glass in case he was waiting outside. I saw nothing but cars, a Coca-Cola truck and a group of lost Japanese tourists.

I cautiously ventured outside and scanned the street both ways. No sign of him. I'd been holding my breath so I exhaled, slowly, letting my shoulders relax. Maybe I was imagining things. Jetlag and a killer hangover combined with too many

Advil was bound to do strange things to your mind. Why on earth would someone want to follow *me*? I mentally slapped myself for ridiculous paranoia and headed back towards Hollywood Boulevard at a clip. It was a ten-block hike down towards Vine and I needed that coffee. Stat.

Chapter Four

An icy blast hit my face as I stepped through the door of Con-X, nearly taking my breath away. I wish it had—the smell of Vermouth leeching from my skin was making me feel sick. I stopped short inside the door and let the air-con soothe me with its glacial fingers.

I'd forgotten since my last visit how bright the décor was. The citrusy walls—lime green, orange, yellow—were no doubt painted that way to keep the resident gamers awake for days at a time. As I squinted around, I pushed my sunglasses firmly against the bridge of my nose and gave thanks to the goddess of Prada for protecting my sensitive eyeballs.

At least it was quiet, apart from the mechanical hum unique to multiple banks of computers. In this strange silent vacuum, the gamers were literally in a world of their own, headphones and online personas firmly in place. Intermittently, violent expletives from wannabe elves punctuated the stillness (upon being killed by sword-wielding trolls, of course) . Aside from that, all I heard was the clacking of keyboards and the occasional creak of a swivel chair.

"Hey, look who's back." A deep, familiar voice boomed across the room and a couple of headphone-less nerds darted their heads up and grumbled in Elvish at the distraction.

"Leon, you're still here." I smiled at the towering Latino man behind the counter, "I was hoping you would be."

"Where else am I gonna go, eh?" He shrugged with a gap-toothed grin, stepped around the counter and grabbed me in a massive bear hug, squeezing me tight. "How's my favourite Aussie?" He pronounced the double *s* like the *s* in snake, a linguistic quirk I adored. I squeezed back hard, glad to see a friendly face.

"I've been better." The hug brought hot tears dangerously close to spilling. Oh god, I'd thought I was finished with the whole crying thing. Stupid jet lag and stupid bloody hangover. I hadn't had a hug from anyone in weeks. I was needy, pathetic and desperate for affection, even the platonic kind. Without letting go, Leon leaned back and studied my face, a concerned frown forcing his bushy eyebrows into a V.

"Coffee?"

I nodded, offering up a watery smile, "Coffee."

He patted my shoulder with his huge paw and pointed me towards a compact workstation next to an overstuffed blue couch. Then he set to work on a gigantic double-strength latte. He still remembered how I took my coffee. For some reason that made me want to cry even more. I'd practically lived in this place last time I was in L.A. My laptop had crashed and Con-X was the only place within walking distance with the two things I needed most, fast internet access and great coffee.

I'd initially fancied that its owner, with his bulging, tattooed arms and menacing stare, would be more at home on Venice Beach. Surprisingly, beneath Leon's intimidating exterior beat the heart of a true geek. The stare was simple short-sightedness and an unwillingness to wear glasses.

By the time I figured out how to log into my new email address, a large steaming mug was placed in front of me. Leon leaned against the white Formica desk top, hands in his pockets.

"So, what's going on, chica?"

I sat back and blew out a shaky breath.

"Don't get me started, Leon." I paused, not sure I wanted to talk about it at all. I stalled. "Hey, are you still chasing fake UFOs?"

Leon's thick, sausagey finger wagged at me.

"You *know* they're out there, don't you be makin' jokes."

"Who's making jokes? Not me." I laughed, relieved to have changed the subject.

"You won't be laughing when they arrive, mija." Leon gazed at me earnestly. "Just because you don't believe in anything you can't prove."

I raised a wry eyebrow at him.

"Oh, you are behind the times." I'd never, ever believed in UFOs or aliens much to Leon's chagrin. He knew this all too well and I chuckled at his solemn expression. "I'll tell you what Leon, IF they arrive on earth, IF I am totally wrong, I'll be first in line for an anal probe, ok?"

"Yeah, yeah, yeah," he threw his hands up in mock disgust. "Nice diversion. Now spill."

Damn.

In between filling him in on the Kelly Craig incident and why I was there in LA, I talked about Dad and how much I missed him and how utterly lost I felt. I gulped great mouthfuls of coffee, tears collecting against the side of the cup as I sipped, giving my latte a salty tang. For a split second I pondered the damage to my health if I main-lined the stuff instead. The standard method of consumption didn't seem to be making a dent in the Moby Dick of a headache still swimming around at the base of my skull.

Leon nodded sympathetically and, every now and then, handed me a fresh tissue. I finally stopped for a breath and deflated, sagging in my seat. Spent. Leon waited to make sure I was finished then stared at me, impressed.

"That's a lotta shit."

"Yup." I let out a small hysterical giggle that was more hiccup than laugh and nodded. "It's a *whole* lotta shit Leon."

He waved his hand at the computer, "So, what are you doing in here? If your laptop has died again, I gotta tell you, you should buy better quality hardware."

I laughed and explained my editor-imposed tech ban then turned back to the computer screen. Three emails from Mitch. That was it. I was used to literally hundreds of emails a day. Usually, I had to organise them into multiple folders and use those coloured flag thingies to keep track. With my inbox so empty, my feeling of being cut off was complete. Leon tapped the computer monitor.

"Your editor does know that you can still access Twitter and Facebook and whatever else from an internet café, right?"

"Yeah, but I get the whole being off-radar thing. It makes sense. I suppose she figures I won't bother with the effort of creating new accounts simply to get a fix." I shrugged. "I'm doing okay. Only minor withdrawals. Although I'll admit I had one dodgy moment at the airport. I had to stop myself tackling the guy in front of me for his phone so I could see his Twitter feed. It was touch and go there for a moment."

I opened the first two emails. Mitch had bundled together everything I needed to get started, probably to keep me off the internet and out of harm's way. Both emails had a long list of attachments and I clicked print on all of them. Reams of paper spewed forth from the industrial size printer nearby. It was going to take hours to wade through it all. Leon's eyes widened too, at the growing paper pile.

"I'm guessing your editor ain't too worried about the trees, huh?"

"Background info for the stupid article I have to write," I explained.

"About the dead actor?"

"Xander Hill, that's right. It's ridiculous. I have an interview lined up with someone who knew him, apparently. But I have no idea who it is and to be honest, I still don't see why I couldn't have done this from home, over Zoom, in comfy pants and with chocolate." I scowled and slumped in my seat, arms folded.

"But then I wouldn't have seen you, chica. And I can give you chocolate."

"Very true, lovely." I held out my hand expectantly with an accompanying grin. Leon chuckled and put my latte in my hand instead.

"Hey, maybe you can figure out who killed the guy," he said. "Isn't that what journalists do? Dig stuff up. That'd get you back in the good books with your editor, right?"

I snorted at him mid gulp and coffee came out of both nostrils. I laughed, putting my sleeve to my nose, "I'm not exactly Angela Lansbury. You've got the wrong girl, Leon. I don't do investigative journalism."

He shrugged at me.

"Okay, then."

"Besides, apart from this interview, there's nobody else to talk to. It's a fifty-year-old murder case. It's stone cold. The only digging I'd be doing would be in a cemetery because everybody involved is dead." I scooted the chair away from him on its zippy wheels and grabbed the wad of printed sheets from the printer. Waving them at Leon, I made a face. "In the meantime, I had better get on with this."

"No problem, chica." He winked and stood, "I'm over here if you need anything, okay?"

"Just keep the coffee coming."

I took my latte and the pages and settled into the blue couch. The articles on Xander Hill's murder were shuffled to the back of the pile so I could go over them later, but my mind kept backtracking.

What if Leon was right? What if I could actually solve it? After all this time, was it possible? *No, Kat, that's stupid. Where the hell would you even start?* Maybe this mystery interview would give me something to go on. *But you don't even know who it's with.* It could save my career. *Stop arguing with yourself, you sound like a psycho.*

I squashed the errant thoughts, reminding myself that there was a reason I didn't do investigative journalism. I kept reading, underlining important bits with a marker. Pretty standard stuff; his bio said he arrived in Hollywood at twenty-six, fresh off the farm from Iowa. I riffled through more pages, scanning —Iowa's a big state, whereabouts in Iowa? I couldn't find anything more specific. Strange. The oddity was logged and filed and I read on.

He worked as a waiter at De Luca's on Vine until he was discovered, scored his first few roles and the rest was history, so to speak. It was the same interchangeable story I'd heard a million times about any number of actors. Small town boy/girl makes good, discovered doing something mundane; walking the dog, buying milk, delivering pizza. The kind of thing that doesn't happen in real life but makes a great bio story. Publicists love that shit.

Nowadays, child-performers network on social media from the age of six. They upload slickly produced audition clips on their YouTube channels, go viral on TikTok, or pop out of generic talent schools like shiny, triple threat clones. Math isn't taught to them in schools—instead they learn to juggle figures by calculating an agent's twenty percent. I have this theory that Johnny Young (of *Talent Time* fame) still has a secret factory somewhere in Wantirna, where he grows them by the hundreds, in pods.

Xander Hill's professional bio was pretty limited. I knew he hadn't made many films, but I didn't realise quite how few. A handful of bit parts, two minor supporting roles then—within a couple of years of arriving in Hollywood—a coveted career jump to the co-lead in *Chase the Wind*, his best-known film and the one made right before he was killed. It also starred Lola Tennant.

I leafed through pages and pages of gossipy clippings from *Variety* and *Hollywood Today*. Spotted dining with this starlet; meeting with that director; rumoured to be signing on for Project X. Why the hell was there so much hype when he'd done so little? Although, if you skipped forward fifty years, doing practically nothing guaranteed you a TV show, cosmetics and clothing line, and a book contract. Who was I to judge?

I ran my finger down the list of high-profile actresses he was linked with romantically; Ann-Margret, British actress Mona Wallace, Elizabeth Taylor, and of course, Lola Tennant. He liked older women, that much was clear. It was also clear his reputation as a womaniser overshadowed his prowess as an actor.

I lingered over a particular photo. Shagging your way to the top must have been an easy option when you looked like Xander Hill. He was a complete cliché; tall and broad-shouldered with slim hips. Short, wavy hair, the colour of wheat, huge brown eyes and the biggest set of dimples I'd ever seen on a man.

He was almost too perfect to be truly attractive, with a plasticity I found unnerving. Then again, the photo was a formal publicity shot. Slick in a tuxedo, his posture was awkward. They obviously weren't big on the natural look back then.

I recalled my Mum gushing over him one Sunday afternoon when I was about fourteen. The ABC would program old movies until five o'clock and I remembered that day specifically because it was the first time I'd seen *Chase the Wind*. Dad had rolled his eyes at me, trying to change the TV to a documentary about illegal whale harpooning he wanted me to see.

Normally I would have preferred the whales. But, whether it was teenage hormones kicking in or something else, I hadn't been able to take my eyes off the screen. Mum and I had ganged up on Dad—two against one—swooning our way through the entire film as he grumbled behind his newspaper.

I flicked back to the biographical information and skimmed through it again. Something nagged at my brain and it wasn't the remnants of my hangover. I scanned the next page, and the next, and the next. There was nothing but the bio, the short list of movie titles and his extensive harem.

No old yearbook excerpts, no school details and no proud Ma and Pa photos back on the farm. No photos of Xander chewing a corn stalk atop a tractor. Not one. I padded quickly to the computer and tapped Xander's name into Google, thinking Mitch had simply dismissed the info as not sexy enough.

I typed in various search strings; *Xander Hill + parents, Xander Hill + high school, Xander Hill + farm, Xander Hill + hometown*. Nothing. It was as if Xander Hill didn't exist before he arrived in Hollywood. I flopped back onto the couch and curled my feet under me, clutching the wad of paper and chewing the end of my pen. Xander Hill, where on earth did you come from?

"*MANAMANA! Do doo do-do-do...!*"

From underneath the computer table, my phone did its

best Muppets impression. A bunch of nerdy heads swiveled accusingly in my direction as I scrambled for the offending handset, skinning hands and knees on the carpet. What the hell kind of ringtone was that? I was going to kill Mitch.

"Hello? Kat Alley." I risked a loud whisper. One bespectacled nerd in particular glared at me in an intimidating manner, but he was wearing an impressive set of plastic Spock ears so I couldn't take him seriously.

"Meow!" Chrissie's standard greeting purred out of the phone. Her voice was instant balm to my soul and I plonked onto my backside with my shoulders against the couch and a wide smile on my face.

"Heeeey!" I lowered my voice. "How are things in Monaco?"

"Why are you whispering?" she whispered back.

"I'm in an internet café."

I heard a throaty chuckle, "Kat darling, I don't think internet cafés are like libraries. You can talk, you know."

"Yes, but I'm surrounded by an army of wired nerds that have been hooked into *World of Warcraft* for at least twenty-four hours," I explained, still in hushed tones, "if I break their concentration they might snap and beat me to death with their joysticks." There was a pause. I could sense the innuendo rolling around in Chrissie's brain.

"I'm going to leave that one well-alone," she said wryly. "So, Monaco's okay. The awards are pretty crap as usual but there's still much fun to be had, you know me. That new rock band, The Stray, are here, they're a crazy bunch, and I got smashed with Miss Terra last night, now *she* is a kook." She chattered on. "That chick never wears pants, it's kinda hot. Weird, but hot. So—you know, same old shit."

"Don't tell me you too are disillusioned with this glorious

industry of ours?" Maybe it wasn't only me. Chrissie bridled immediately.

"No fucking way. I love it. I mean, it's all a bit of a wank and most musicians are complete tools but Christ, the parties are *great*." I couldn't help chuckling, much to my friend's approval. "Now there's a sound I haven't heard in a while. How's things, babe?"

"Well, I am severely jet lagged, I'm up to my eyeballs in research for this stupid story and I have a hangover the size of the Simpson Desert from cleaning out the mini bar last night. Apart from that, I'm tops."

"Excellent," she exclaimed with satisfaction. "The mini bar bit obviously, not the other crap. I have taught you well."

"Tell that to my head."

"Lightweight."

"Lush!" Without fail, no matter how shit I felt, our faux-bitchy banter made me laugh.

"So, not having fun writing about the dead hottie then?"

I snorted into the phone.

"Mitch filled you in? That's a surprise. I thought she didn't want anyone to know. How'd you get past the gatekeeper?"

"I called her to double check the number she sent through for you. What can I say, she likes me."

"Mitch doesn't like anyone."

"Well, she likes me. Ever since I found her in the bathroom after last year's ARIAs, coked off her face. She asked me to go down on her—says to this day it's the best head she's ever had." Chrissie let out a throaty laugh. "I could probably ask her for her credit card number and she'd hand it over."

"Ew. What? You never told me th—" I was momentarily gob smacked. I held the phone out, staring at it and shaking my head as if Chrissie could see me being all disapproving. Not wanting the mental picture to take root, I rapidly changed the subject. It took me a second or two to refocus. "What was I saying? Apart from yuck? Oh, right—no, I'm not having fun writing about the dead hottie. I haven't even started yet because I wasted a day passed out drunk."

"Never a waste, love."

"Maybe not for you. Anyway—" I trotted out my grumpy Google and comfy pants line again. "But, seeing as I'm being forced to stay here in LA, it would be nice if I could bang the thing out in a couple of days then do some mooching on the magazine's tab. I can't see that happening though."

"Mooching would be good." Chrissie was always very supportive of slacking on company time. "Why can't you?"

I sighed.

"I'm waiting to hear about this interview I'm supposed to be doing. I'm in limbo until then. I figure I'll go over the research and start planning out the article. There's not much else I can do? Unless—" The insistent thought poked at me again. I decided to sound Chrissie out. "Hey, I've had this idea."

"Mmm-hmm?"

"Don't laugh, okay?"

"Why would I laugh?"

"Promise."

"Okay, I won't laugh."

"What if I can figure out who killed Xander Hill?"

A beat. A long beat.

"Are you kidding?"

"No."

"You're going to do a Miss Marple?"

"I said don't laugh."

"Who's laughing? Honey, I know things have gone a bit pear-shaped with the celebrity gig, but when was the last time you investigated anything more serious than the total number of groupies Robbie Williams shagged? You know, before he went and got all married and sensible and shit."

"Thanks a bunch." I managed to sound wounded but she was pretty spot on. I slumped back. I couldn't even be bothered verifying who was hooking up with who properly. What on earth made me think I could investigate a murder, let alone one that happened half a century ago. Who was I kidding? "I thought if I can find out something new, I might have a shot at being taken seriously again, that's all."

"You were never taken seriously babe." Chrissie laughed." No offence."

"Some taken," I snipped back. "What if I want to be taken seriously now?" There was another long pause.

"Kat, is this about your Dad?"

"Is what about my Dad?" I was all innocence. I hated when she saw straight through me.

"The sudden Columbo urge. You know, your dad was proud of you."

"Firstly, I'm nothing like Columbo. And secondly—he wasn't."

"What do you mean? Of course he was."

I tried to swallow the sudden lump in my throat. I hadn't told anyone this, even Chrissie.

"No. He really wasn't. The last time I spoke to my Dad, we argued. He said I was wasting my talent and I'd obviously missed the class where they taught journalists about ethics."

"Ouch." Her voice was soft.

"Think about it Chrissie, my dad uncovered major political corruption. What have I ever contributed to the world of journalism apart from the word 'Brangelina'?"

"Hey," she chuckled, "the world would be a very different place if we didn't have Brangelina. Don't underestimate the importance of that."

"You're not funny."

"Oh sugar, I'm sorry. This whole mess with Kelly Craig has made you stop and reassess, correct? So maybe your Dad was right from that point of view. You are a talented person, you just lost your way a bit, got caught up in all the industry bullshit. It's an easy thing to let happen. Trust me, I know."

I sighed again.

"It kills me to think he was disappointed in me. I feel like I've got to fix things. God, that sounds so lame." Then it all poured out, before I had a chance to think. "Chrissie, everything I've done in my career is worth nothing." My words croaked out of a tightening throat and I sniffed back more tears. *Don't start blubbering again, Kat.* "Nothing! None of it matters."

"I've spent literally years of my life on trivial rubbish. I mean, who gives a stuff about an obnoxious pop star's hair or whether some snotty actress with a head too big for her body bothered to crack a smile today? Huh? And tell me, where the hell did the Kardashians even come from? Can you explain that? No. Nobody can. It's insane. I don't even know who I am anymore. When did I become the person who makes stuff up about other people simply to get a headline, without giving a shit about the consequences?"

"And why do people buy it anyway? Why do we even care about movies and celebrities and music and TV and *stuff* when there's oh—I don't know—people starving in Africa. And AIDS babies and...and gangs... and refugees—" I trailed off miserably. I didn't know where the rant had come from, or where it was going. It didn't sound like me at all. And maybe that was the problem."

"People care about it so they don't have to think about all the crappy stuff," said Chrissie, her voice quiet. "So they don't have to feel guilty they're not doing more. It's escapism. Always has been. It's nothing new, babe."

"It's horrible. It's turned me into an arsehole, and I don't want to do it anymore."

"Listen to me. To be fair, you *have* to write this article or you're going to get fired. Even if you do manage to solve this thing, it's still a Hollywood murder—you're not exactly removing yourself from the machine, are you? So, unless you're going to resign from your job and fuck off to Calcutta to volunteer in an orphanage—which you know, is all very noble and such—" Chrissie cut herself off mid-sentence and huffed heavily down the phone. "Kat, art is important too. You can write about what you love, but maybe you need to come at things differently. But what would I know? I get paid to drink with rock-stars. So," she switched topics briskly, "do you have any leads? See, I watch NYPD Blue."

"NYPD Blue was axed years ago dummy." I smiled and made the effort to quash my existential crisis. "Not really. I guess I'll wait for this interview and take it from there. It's probably a dumb idea, forget I said anything."

"I say go for it."

"Really?

"Yeah, why not?" she said. "You know me, never one to stand in the way of crazy ideas."

"Thank you. It means a lot. I needed to bounce it off someone."

"Glad to be of service, chicky-babe. So, you'll be kind of like Magnum PI, right? Hey, you should get a sports car—and a fake moustache." Now Chrissie did laugh. "Do you need a side-kick? I'm available."

"Shut up, I'm serious and that's three different detectives you've compared me to in five minutes. Make up your mind."

"I know you're serious. Look at it this way, if all else fails and the whole thing goes tits up, Mitch can always fill the pages with pictures of the dead hottie. That is the best bit after all."

I gasped in mock indignation.

"Are you dissing my writing?"

"No honey, but face it, he was straight up fire. Even I would have given him a roll in the hay."

"He was okay, I suppose. These photos are probably airbrushed."

Chrissie snorted.

"Okay? Kat, trust me, if he was alive now I would have his pants off in—"

"Alright, I get it," I did *not* need to hear the rest of that sentence. I was still trying to recover from the lingering mental image of Chrissie with her head between my editor's thighs in a toilet cubicle. Any more sharing and I'd be wishing for a flip-top head so I could sanitise my brain. "Xander Hill was smoking hot. Hot, hottity, hot. I agree. Happy?" The noisy chatter in the call background increased. "It sounds pretty crazy there."

"Yeah, it is." She shouted over the growing din and I held the phone away, "I'd better go, Mara Calais is doing jelly shots with those cute boys from Stratosphere 5, it could get real ugly, real fast. Although, she's looking mighty grown up these days. She's certainly come a long way since those little Mickey Mouse ears. Maybe I'll go join the party." She laughed lasciviously. "Take my advice, go back to your hotel with those photos. It's about time you took care of yourself," she gave a dirty chuckle, "if you know what I mean."

"Funny. You're the queen of the double entendre." Unbidden, The Divinyls '*I Touch Myself*' played in my head and I hastily flicked the off button. That was not going to happen. Not thinking about a dead man anyway. Yuck.

"Miss you." Chrissie said.

"Miss you more. Have fun, and behave. Do not swipe anyone's underwear."

"You're always spoiling my fun. What if I—"

I cut her off.

"I said BEHAVE!" I laughed and hung up, smiling broadly and climbing to my feet. I shook out pins and needles as I checked for more emails. Two more publicity photos sat in my inbox. I brought them up on the screen.

In one, Xander posed with arms tightly wrapped around a pretty blonde showgirl. She pressed against his tuxedoed chest dressed only in a sequinned g-string and sparkly nipple pasties. Viva Las Slutty. She also had what appeared to be a stuffed-and-mounted Ossie Ostrich on her head. It clashed terribly with her pout. I doodled a moustache, glasses and a pair of squiggly horns on the screen with my marker pen, right across her head. Much better.

In the second photo, Xander and Lola Tennant stood shoulder to shoulder. The candid black and white photo was taken on the set of what must have been *Chase the Wind*; extras and crew milled around in the background and a large camera set up intruded onto the left-hand side of frame. Lola stared directly into the camera, hands clutched in front of her; inky tresses piled high on top of her head, her dark eyes wide and heavily made-up. Xander was staring at her with complete and utter adoration.

I studied the image, trying to figure out the strange body language. I clicked print, there was something about the photo and I wasn't quite sure what it was. But it was worth filing. A big hand plonked another cup of coffee in front of me. Leon studied the screen over my shoulder.

"Isn't that whatshername?" he licked his finger and rubbed at the black squiggles I'd made on the glass. I gave him a sheepish grin and mouthed *sorry* before answering him.

"That's Lola Tennant. The actor I'm writing about was supposedly having an affair with her."

Leon scratched his head.

"Isn't she the woman from that horse movie, with Carey Grant? And that mini-series in the early eighties, what was it?"

"*Orion Point,*" I glanced at him, surprised. "Good call, yeah that's her. She was in a lot of stuff, even won an Oscar. Started acting quite late, from memory, and didn't do much after the whole scandal broke and Xander Hill turned up dead. It wasn't exactly a career booster. Not in those days. These days however —" I trail off with a wry purse of my lips. "She went all Greta Garbo after that. When she did *Orion Point,* she hadn't worked for years and then never again after that. Sad really, she was good."

"Why don't you talk to her as well?"

"Well, first I'd need a Ouija board, then—"

"She's not dead, chica. If it's the woman I think it is, she lives up in the Hollywood Hills. My brother—Luis—he takes deliveries up there every other week - groceries, that kind of thing."

I frowned and turned back to the computer. A few swift key strokes and *voila*, one obituary paying tribute to Lola Tennant. Dated 1986. I waved my hand at the screen with a flourish.

"Ta-dah. Definitely dead."

But Leon was adamant. He said maybe she wanted people to think she was dead but he swore on baby Jesus it was the same woman. His brother had told him she'd gone bat-shit crazy; would rant and rave at him in a mix of English and Spanish, had a million cats and talked to people you couldn't see. The clincher was when he told me she'd once tried to pay Luis with a 'small statue of a gold man' and a can of cat food.

I couldn't believe it.

"But she'd be almost a hundred years old by now."

Leon didn't say anything more. He simply put hand on heart and held the other up as if taking an oath. I fell silent—stunned. Maybe the universe was saying *do it!* My stomach fluttered in anticipation. Then someone pulled anticipation's wings off. How would I get to her? Did I simply knock on her door? I was sure she'd welcome me with open arms and kibble. *Not.*

"Can your brother get me in to see her?"

Leon shook his head. "She doesn't let anyone in apart from Luis. Not for years. I wouldn't want to get him fired."

"No, of course not. Does she ever come out? Surely she has to leave the house sometimes."

"Not usually. I guess that's why she gets deliveries, so she never has to go out." Of course, it made sense. "Although, there has been a couple of times—maybe once or twice in the last few years—she's asked Luis to take her out, at night."

"Did he say what for?"

"Yeah, sure. He drove her to pick up flowers, then to one of the cemeteries downtown."

Bingo. It had to be her and no prizes for guessing whose grave she visited. *Whoa, slow down Kat.* I yanked at my own reins. Maybe it wasn't her. Maybe it was the wrong cemetery. I didn't know anything for sure but was powerfully excited all the same.

"Leon, could you call your brother for me? The anniversary of Xander Hill's death is in a couple of days. Find out if she's asked him to take her again and when? If it is her, I reckon it'll be soon." I was willing to bet the farm on it. It's what my Dad would have done.

Leon patted my shoulder with a wink.

"Anything for you, mija."

Chapter Five

Unsurprisingly, I dreamed about Xander Hill that night. Exhaustion overwhelmed me and I crashed like an out-of-control NASCAR as soon as my pyjamas were on—quickly and despite all efforts to slam on the brakes.

The dream wasn't one of those disjointed nocturnal adventures; you know the ones where you're you but you don't look like you and your Mum is there and she looks like Kylie Minogue (but somehow you still know it's your Mum), and together you're searching for a lost circus elephant at your old primary school and then you fly home. As dreams go, it was actually quite a normal one.

Xander sat next to me on a large puffy couch, scattered with lolly-bright cushions. We were clearly in a television studio because blinding white spotlights were set up all around us. A halo-esque glow radiated from behind his head and his smile was directed solely at me. He locked eyes with mine, staring intently and stroking my hand with feather-light fingers.

The conversation revolved around my ex-boyfriends. I was describing failed relationship after failed relationship to him in great detail. This is how I knew it was a dream. No guy would voluntarily sit and listen to a girl yammer on about her ex-boyfriends, right? Unless he was gay, trying to score brownie points, or trying to get laid. Or—case in point—was a dead guy in a dream.

I also knew it was a dream because in real life a movie-star like Xander Hill wouldn't look twice at me, let alone stare with such affection and longing. To be honest, he probably wouldn't even look at me the first time, unless he had astigmatism and was trying to figure out who I was.

Regardless of his level of hypothetical vision-impairment, dream-Xander's voice was as I imagined, deep and throaty with a subtle country twang. He was saying all the right things. About Grant, the bricklayer I dated at nineteen, 'You had nothing in common.' He stroked my hand more firmly, fingers trailing up my wrist, sending shivers up my arms.

Mmm-hmmm. That feels great and you are so right.

Angelo, the bilingual and quite possibly bisexual Italian student, took over my life from twenty-one to twenty-three. Xander brushed my hair back and his hand cupped around the nape of my neck as he whispered, 'He only wanted to stay in the country. Honey, you deserve better than that.'

Yes. True.

At twenty-five; Peter, the surfer. 'You were too smart for him.' Xander turned my hand over and stroked his thumb down the centre of my palm.

My thoughts exactly. I gasped, giddy.

Xander moved closer until I could feel his breath, warm on my neck. 'It's not you. You are enough,' he murmured, sending tingles up and down my spine. *Uh huh. Mmmm.* My lips strained towards his, my body arching, no longer registering the words. I leaned forward as he suddenly and inexplicably shifted away from me. 'Wait." He frowned. "Are you enough? Are you really?'

Huh? I tried to brush off the sudden flip. I was far too concerned with Xander's immediate proximity. *No, don't go.* I stretched forward towards him, desperate lips puckered like a horny giraffe. *Come back. Kiss me. KISS me.*

CRAAASSHH!

My head and shoulders introduced themselves violently to the parquetry floor as I tumbled face first out of the bed, arms and legs tangled in 1000-thread-count Egyptian cotton. Halfway between waking and sleep, I didn't know where I was or what the hell had happened. It took a few seconds for me to come around and, for a brief moment, I cared more about the fact I'd woken before my neck got nuzzled than I was about the egg forming on my forehead or the possibility I'd dislocated my shoulder.

"Gaaah!" A twisted loop of sheet wrapped tightly around my feet, binding my legs together. I thrashed them like a demented mermaid. Flopping back, breathless, I took a few moments and blinked in the darkness, waiting for my heart to stop pounding. There's nothing worse than being ripped unexpectedly from sleep. My body jittered. I was literally vibrating on the inside, and not in a good way.

I struggled to sit, then reached for the phone charging on the bedside table. 3am. Still a few hours of sleeping left. If I got back to sleep quickly enough, maybe we could pick up where we left off, dream-Xander and I. Although, dreams never worked that way. I knew I was more likely to dream about being spanked by Woody Allen than I was likely to slip back onto that cushy couch.

Considering the length of my self-imposed celibacy and the way my hormones were jangling, I was willing to take the risk. I could always go to therapy if I ended up in an S & M version of *Annie Hall*. I extricated my legs from the twisted sheet, padded into the bathroom and half-filled a glass with water. My breathing returned to normal while I took tiny sips, standing in the patch of moonlight that shone through the small window. Unbidden, dream-Xander's question echoed in my head. *Are you enough?*

Enough for what? I had no clue and it was too big a question for 3am. Plus, I was too horny to waste time on philosophical musings. I pushed the thought aside and closed my eyes. Instantly, Xander's warm breath caressed my neck.

Yup, back to bed.

Stepping into the dark bedroom, I felt immediate unease. An electric charge crackled in the air and the hairs on my arms stood up like follicular sentries. My skin prickled as a cool breeze slid around my legs, though I could have sworn I closed both windows and the French doors leading out to the balcony. Sensing movement behind me, I spun around in time to catch the curtain shifting, floating away from the glass-paneled doors.

Willing my spider-senses to stop tingling and thinking the doors must have simply popped ajar, I tiptoed to close them. They were firmly shut. I rattled the doors in an accusatory fashion to make sure.

Movement caught my eye again and, as I whirled sharply, my throat constricted in alarm. A shadowy figure loomed in the bathroom doorway, completely blocking any light from the moon. My heart thumped wildly against my ribs, my pulse thudding in my head.

"Who's there?" My voice ricocheted off the walls, far too loud. The motionless shadow seemed not to hear me. Despite the urge to run, my feet stayed stuck to the floor. I would have had to pass the bathroom door to get out and, even in panic, I wasn't stupid enough to run towards an intruder; no matter how many self-defence classes I'd taken at the Woolloomooloo PCYC last summer.

My mind, and my heartbeat, raced. I've always thought that to be such a cliché but right at that moment my chest felt like it was filled with galloping horses, all intent on winning the Melbourne Cup. The guy from the street. It was him, there couldn't be any other explanation. He'd followed me. But, how the hell had he gotten in?

I imagined the inevitable headlines; 'MORE SCANDAL AT THE CHATEAU MARMONT'; 'CELEBRITY JOURNALIST FOUND DEAD IN CELEBRITY PLAYGROUND'; or my favourite, 'MURDER AT THE MARMONT'.

Adrenalin pounded through me and my body shook as I hunted frantically for something heavy or sharp, or preferably both. I snatched up the only appropriate object visible in the dark—the plastic TV remote control—pretty useless as weapons go, but it would have to do.

"I said, who's there?" My voice trembled slightly. *Bugger*. I was aiming for authoritative. I held my breath as the shape shifted, almost imperceptibly.

Shit. Shit. Shiiiit!

A low male voice murmured out of the shadows as if talking to himself and not me.

"Lady, you wouldn't believe me even if you could hear me." His words were burdened with resignation, not menace. He sounded strangely familiar. What the hell? What was he talking about? My panic increased. This guy was completely cracked.

"I *can* hear you, freak." My voice went up an octave, "Now, who the hell are you and why the fuck are you in my room?"

Silence for several seconds.

"Firstly, ma'am, language. Secondly, you can hear me?"

Did he seriously reprimand me for swearing? What a nut

job. I inched towards the phone. "That's what I said, weirdo, and if you don't get out of my room right now, I am calling the police."

"You can hear me?" Excitement rang in his voice. Familiarity tickled my brain yet fell short of absolute clarity. The figure advanced and I retreated hastily, waving the remote in what I hoped was a threatening manner.

"Whoa, stay right there, buddy. Yes, for the third time, I can hear you. I can see you too, so I know exactly where to aim when I kick you in the—"

"Wait, you don't understand." He halted and had the cheek to laugh. "I'm not going to hurt you."

Arsehole!

"Yeah right," I growled, anger overtaking fear, "I suppose breaking into a woman's hotel room and scaring the shit out of her is a harmless pastime in LA. Crazy stalker fun?"

"Turn on the light."

"What?"

He lowered his voice, "Turn—on—the light." I scrambled to place the insistent and honeyed tones. "You'll understand if you turn on the light."

I paused. If I turned on the light, that would mean I could describe him more accurately to police. Then again, once I'd seen his face he would *have* to kill me. I wasn't stupid, I knew how it worked. I'd seen CSI.

"Okay, fine," I snapped, "but you move one inch and this extremely hard remote gets embedded in your head." All I heard was an amused chuckle. "And stop laughing, it's creepy." I side-stepped towards the wall and fumbled for the switch, keeping my eyes fixed on the murky shape that may or may not have been an axe murderer. My fingers finally found the switch and I froze. What if this guy was hideously disfigured, that being the reason he hated people and had turned to crime? What if he was covered in blood from an earlier killing spree?

I wasn't ready for that. I didn't want to turn on the light. Maybe dark was better. *Chicken.* What would Chrissie do? She would turn on the light and go on the offensive, that's what; she'd race across the room and kick him right in the bloody balls before he knew what hit him.

Right! That's the plan. Yes, I'll do it. I'm not scared. I am an Amazon. Okay that last bit sounded crap, but you know what I meant. I inhaled and clenched my teeth, scrunching my face. *Flick the switch Kat. You can do it.*

I flicked the switch. Light flooded the room, illuminating the intruder. I blinked rapidly, partially because I was momentarily blinded, but mostly because my brain wouldn't compute what was in front of me. I backed up against the foot of the bed in shock. The dark jeans, blue checked shirt and sandy blonde hair were instantly familiar from earlier that day. But, it was his face that jolted me the most. Standing in the bathroom doorway in all his gorgeous glory, was Xander Hill. The movie star. The *dead* movie star.

Then I did something ridiculous. Something I had never done before in my entire life. I fainted.

The artificial chill of the hotel room had me groping around for the blanket before I opened my eyes. I was freezing, despite wearing PJs and fluffy socks. In contrast, the hot slices of sunlight coming through the window turned the inside of my eyelids fiery red. *Urgh, morning.* I cursed the fact I'd forgotten to close the curtains again.

I yawned, eyes still squeezed shut against the glare. Suddenly, I flashed back to the sexy dream. I smiled despite myself. *Nice.* Stretching languidly, I threw my arms over my head and allowed my memory to slide back over the yummy bits like hot caramel.

It was no surprise that Xander had featured heavily in my nocturnal fantasy. All the info and images stuffed into my brain had to overflow somewhere and okay—I'll admit it—he was pretty delicious. Besides, no real-life sex for Kat meant the occasional blow-off-some-steamy dream. It was totally normal and healthy.

I had no idea my relationship baggage was a handbag, a whole set of suitcases, and a cargo trunk to boot though. I hadn't thought about any of those guys in forever. In fact, I hadn't had anything approaching a serious relationship in nearly eight years. I'd realised I had a habit of choosing completely the wrong guys then limping along for a while before it inevitably imploding. It was always the same and had become easier to just avoid relationships all together. I was busy enough that I didn't really notice—well not much anyway. I certainly didn't understand why it would all come leaking out now. I frowned, my eyes flickering open.

And, what was with the psychoanalysis at the end there? *Are you enough?* I blinked heavily as dream-Xander's question poked annoyingly at me again with its tiny pointy fingers. Nope —I flicked it away like a bug—still way too early to think about that stuff. What was left of my self-esteem wasn't even awake yet. I rubbed my eyes, trying to unglug sleep-sticky lashes, and my fingers accidentally brushed my forehead.

Ooww. What the—? *Oooooooowwwwwww!* The bump felt like a Volkswagen beetle was parked on my head. My fingers gingerly explored the damage and the not-so-dreamy part of last night whooshed back in full roaring technicolour.

Oh. My. God.

Sheet clutched to my chest, I lurched upright, my head spinning in the process. It was not possible. It couldn't be possible. My eyes darted anxiously around the bedroom. I was being ridiculous. If Xander Hill was there it would have meant he was a ghost and I didn't believe in ghosts. The only person who apparently believed in ghosts was that silly lady—Marjorie—in Apartment Four.

I wasn't exactly doing a stellar job of convincing myself; the egg on my head felt real and I remembered the feeling of shock vividly.

"Hello?" Yes, I was actually talking to an empty and silent room. *Of course it's silent,* I snorted to myself. *There's no such thing as ghosts.* Clearly it was one of those dreams where you think you've woken up but you haven't. The kind of dream that usually ends in disaster because you've either dreamt you've woken up and gone to the toilet but you're actually still in bed (note, accidental bedwetting as an adult is never pleasant or joke-worthy and should never be spoken of again), or you sleep-walk to the petrol station in your cookie monster underwear and a singlet (also never to be spoken of again).

I must have had one of those dreams and rolled over and whacked my noggin on the side table. A perfectly plausible explanation. No ghosts in this room, thank you very much. No ghosts at all.

My internal bravado didn't stop me peeking cautiously around the bathroom door, or from creeping towards the shower and yanking the curtain back like the token about-to-be-slaughtered babysitter in a B-grade slasher movie. Finally, satisfied my hotel room was spook-free and feeling a little foolish, I relaxed and laughed.

Chrissie was going to have a field day. I would tell her the story over a glass or five of Pinot, knowing she'd laugh so hard her wine would spurt out of her nose, guaranteeing more mirth.

Room service delivered a pot of steaming coffee and I

turned the TV on. The news was all doom and gloom as usual so I switched channels with a sigh, not in the mood for doom. The *Wake-Up USA* hosts' shiny, plastic faces filled the screen. I wrinkled my nose. Uber-perkiness wasn't much better.

Before I could hit the remote, they crossed to Lana Seeley. Lana was the U.S. version of me, with better teeth and hair and without the recent idiocy. I tried to press the off button, I did. I shouldn't have watched it but, like any addict, I caved. I knew it was bad for me and I didn't want to do it but my thumb jacked up the volume, completely independently of my brain.

A photo of current it-girl, Milli Tanner, flashed up on the screen and my hands shook so hard I had to put my coffee down. The biggest entertainment news that day— NEWS-FLASH—the diminutive actress had been seen several times holding a gigantic handbag in front of her stomach which of course *must* indicate the presence of a baby bump and her desperate wish to hide it from ageing rival, Jenna Ford, who apparently still wasn't over her toy-boy ex-husband, Eric Lorimer, who was now of course dating Milli Tanner, although the *official* line was still 'close friends and co-stars'.

Amateur. Didn't Lana know Milli was absolutely tiny? That handbag was enormous. She could have been holding it over her head and it still would have obscured her belly. Pfft. It meant nothing. I would lay money on the fact any hint of a bulge was simply a food baby. More carbs than foetus. I bet I could put a call in to Milli's—

Whoa. What was I thinking? I whacked the remote to my forehead and winced. Focus on the job at hand, Kat. I rubbed my face and glared at the television. Stupid Lana Seeley. How come she was allowed to speculate about stuff and she got to host the pre-Emmys? I did virtually the same thing and was more hated than Yoko Ono.

I was in the middle of gesturing rudely (and redundantly)

at Lana, who had moved on to waxing lyrical about Bradley Cooper's chest hair, when my phone squawked at me from across the room. Finally, the message I'd been waiting for.

INTERVIEW TODAY W/ QUENTIN MILLSON.
2231 BENEDICT CANYON DVE. BVLY HILLS. 1PM.
DON'T B LATE. M.

Quentin Millson. Holy crap.

Like most people, I knew Quentin Millson purely by fearsome reputation. A shrewd and bitchy old queen, he was the Edmund Hillary of my profession. The first of my kind. Back in the day, his columns made or broke whole careers. He had shocked and titillated Hollywood by ruthlessly trading in secrets; praising stars on one page, backstabbing on another.

Rumour had it he'd known a little secret about absolutely everybody. That's why he'd eventually wielded more power than some of the studio heads. He was more than a gossip columnist, he was the stuff of Hollywood legend. I had no doubt at the top of his game, Quentin Millson would have crumbled me *and* Perez Hilton up and sprinkled us on his cornflakes.

He'd transitioned from newspapers to magazines, of course to TV, and even had his own game show at one point. His turn as Oscars host in the seventies was so biting and sly, even Ricky Gervais would have cringed. He'd retired years ago—made his fortune then bowed gracefully out of the limelight as tabloids took over and celebrity gossip became a multi-million-dollar machine. He'd paved the way for journalists like me.

As far as the industry went, he'd long been obsolete. He'd be at least in his eighties. Most ordinary people would never have heard of him. Even I thought he was dead by now—the second time in as many days I'd mistakenly assumed someone had shuffled off this mortal coil. A sign of our times? As soon as someone was no longer in the public eye, no longer relevant, they might as well be dead? It was more than a bit horrifying.

I grabbed my coffee and the manila folder that held my printed research, rapidly scanning page after page. Just as I thought; every clipping from *Hollywood Today* had Millson's by-line, column after column featuring a few lines about Xander Hill. All complimentary, all talking him up.

What was the connection? Did Millson see talent or titillation? I squinted at the tiny headshot at the top of each column. With a rotund face and narrow eyes, Millson even looked snarky in print and a shiver of anticipation tripped up my spine. Half talking to myself and half to the piece of paper, I murmured, "What exactly have you got to say, Mr Millson? Hmm?"

"You do know talking to yourself is the first sign of madness?"

The voice was mere centimetres from my ear and my feet literally left the floor as I screamed in fright. My flailing arms sent hot coffee flying out of my mug and down my chest, the scalding liquid soaking straight through to my skin.

"Gaaaah!" This time I yelled in pain. My feet tried valiantly to spin me around but the floor was slick with spilt coffee. My socks should have provided some kind of woolly traction but I succeeded only in skating briefly on the spot before my arse hit the parquetry with a mighty wallop. I banged my elbow hard, sending painful tingles shooting up my arm. I've never understood why it's called your funny bone because I was not bloody laughing.

"You know, I could never stand that little toad."

I attempted to swivel on the floor, craning my neck backwards. The speaker continued, oblivious to my panicked contortions, "Quentin had these beady little eyes that—are you okay?"

Oh god, that voice. The person standing over me—who looked exactly like Xander Hill but couldn't possibly *be* Xander Hill because that would be insane—was staring down at me, bemused. I stared back, gobsmacked. I didn't care in the slightest that I was sitting in a pool of coffee. Xander-who-couldn't-really-be-Xander smiled at me. "Do you always make this much noise?"

My mouth hung open, village idiot-like.

"Huh?" I squeaked, my voice box not wanting to cooperate. He frowned and leaned down towards me.

"Okay. Let's start again. Hello there." Another devastating smile. "I'm Xander Hill."

He could not be serious. My mind was a riot. This was somebody's idea of a joke. Mitch? No. Chrissie? YES. Chrissie! It was exactly her style. A light pinged on in my brain. Of course... he was a lookalike. They would be so easy to find in this town, just check the closest diner. Good likeness, very well done. I was going to kill her.

I started to laugh. I couldn't believe she got me. Me, the skeptic. She actually had me believing the ghost of Xander Hill was paying me a visit. Fake Xander eyed me curiously and I winked at him.

"Nice one, buddy. Great acting. How much did they pay you for this little ruse?" I reached out towards him. "Now, seeing as you've done your job very well and scared the bejesus out of me—*and* made me spill my coffee—I don't suppose you'd mind helping me up?" He stared at my hand, bemused. I waggled my fingers at him and raised my eyebrows. "Assistance would be good."

"I can't."

"What do you mean you can't?"

"I would like to help you up of course, Ma'am, but it's not possible you see." An antique lamp stood on the teak side table near the wall. He strode over to it and swiped a hand at the ornate brass base as if to knock it clean off the table. I gasped, anticipating the breakage bill. It didn't budge. Not in the slightest. Xander's hand passed straight through the solid metal. I gawped at the lamp and then at him.

"How the hell did you do that?"

"I can't touch anything." He shrugged and I gawped even more while he swiped back and forth through the lamp several times, in case I was having trouble catching on. He dropped his hand to his side and smiled sadly, "You see?"

"I don't believe it," I whispered, "it's some kind of trick."

Xander shook his head. "Sorry to disappoint you. I'm sure it'd be easier to believe."

"Easier to believe than what?" I hiccupped. *Great.* "That a movie star who's been— *hic*—dead for fifty years is standing in my—*hic*—hotel room doing magic tricks?"

"Thank you for the compliment, Ma'am, but I was hardly what you would have called a star and I told you, it's not a trick. I can't touch anything. I can't pick anything up, I can't move a thing."

"Right. Because you're all—*hic*—ghosty and see-through and stuff." My head was swimming, my thoughts syrupy inside my brain.

"I believe the term is non-corporeal. Why are you hiccupping?"

"It's a—*hic*—stress reaction." I held my breath. Not the smartest idea considering I already felt dizzy and a little sick.

"Why are you stressed?" Xander wrinkled his forehead and I expelled air with a whoosh.

"Why am I stressed? Are you—*hic*—freaking kidding me?" *Dammit.* I stared at him, incredulous. My pulse throbbed rhythmically in my temples and I pressed my fingers to the sides of my head, squeezing my eyes tightly shut.

Did Hamlet feel like this when he met his dead dad? Hang on, wasn't Hamlet crazy? Or was that Macbeth? That was it; with all the crap I'd been through, I'd finally gone bonkers. Maybe I'd had too much caffeine and booze and chocolate and it had all combined in my body into some toxic, insanity-inducing cocktail. I hoped desperately that the room would be empty when I opened my eyes.

I lifted one eyelid slowly, peering out. No, he was still there. *Fuck*. I closed it again, hot tears pricking behind my lashes. It was all too much. Way too much. Dad, Kelly, the jet lag, the hangover, the shock of last night, even the purpling lump on my head. The sudden urge to vomit overcame me. I wailed like a petulant six-year old.

"Go awaaaaaay. You're not reeeeaal."

"I'm afraid I am," he chuckled ruefully, "even if you don't want me to be." I was so glad he found me amusing.

"But, I don't believe in ghosts!" I clapped both hands over my ears as he started to speak again, "La-la-la-la-la-la-la-la-la," I chanted, so I couldn't hear him. When I finally stopped and opened my eyes, Xander was still standing in the middle of the room staring at me, like I was a mental patient. I groaned.

"You're not going away, are you?"

"No. Sorry."

Crap. I drew in a deep breath and in that one moment of pause, of fresh oxygen, of clarity, it sank in that I was holding a conversation with an actual ghost. A bona fide, real as they come, walking, talking and absolutely drop dead (pardon the pun) gorgeous ghost.

Ho-ly shit!

Might I add, a ghost who was inside my head the night before if my toe-curlingly sexy dream was any indication. Ghosts must be able to do that, right? I allowed myself to look at him properly for the first time and a flush crept unbidden up my neck and warmth flooded my belly at the memory of his breath on my neck and his fingers trailing along my—

"Has it been that long?"

His voice interrupted my lapse into pornographic daydream. My face flushed red and hot as I spluttered with indignation.

"What? Um, no—uh, of course not—I, uh, you know, I'm very sexually—" I faltered. How rude. What kind of person, dead or not, asked a question like that? I glared at him, pursing prim lips. He wore a perplexed expression and it occurred to me that maybe he wasn't commenting on my recent dry spell at all. I straightened up, trying to assume a professional bearing which was pretty hard while sprawled on the floor covered in coffee. "I'm sorry, what?" I feigned ignorance.

Xander looked totally confused by that point. His next words shocked me into dumbfounded silence.

"You said 'a movie star who's been dead for fifty years'. Have I really been dead that long?"

Chapter Six

How did a ghost not know how long he's been dead? He was freaking me out. I consoled myself with the thought that at least he knew he was dead because, let's face it, that conversation would have been awkward.

"Do you really not know?" I asked. He shook his head. I clambered up from the hard floor and skirted gingerly around him. He put his hands up in mock surrender and wiggled his fingers to remind me he couldn't touch anything.

I still didn't trust him; how was I to know he didn't have some weird ghostly force-field thingy that would zap me if I moved too close, or that he wasn't planning to body-jack me and do weird things with me. Or to me.

On second thoughts, I wouldn't mind— I shook my head. Stay on topic, Kat. I sat on the edge of the bed, ignoring the brown stain my coffee-soaked PJs made on the linen. I couldn't believe I was having a rational conversation with a dead person. I rubbed ferociously at one of my eyebrows then managed to stop myself.

A whole eyebrow almost got rubbed off once. I did it

completely unconsciously. It usually happened when I was perplexed or overloaded with information, my mind a soup of jumbled thoughts. I'd had no choice but to draw it back on every day—a la Tammy Faye Baker—until it grew back. It was not a good look.

Think Kat, think. Of course, nobody would believe me about the ghost, I couldn't publish that. I'd get thrown straight into the nuthouse. But I had to think of the inside information. He could tell me everything. So what if he didn't know how long he'd been dead—maybe time moved differently when you're dead, how should I know?

I cracked my neck to one side with a loud snap making Xander cringe. A squeamish ghost, who'd have thought. Then I planted my hands on my knees and leaned forward authoritatively.

"Okay," I said. "Yes, if you really are Xander Hill, in two days' time you'll have been dead for exactly fifty years."

"Wow." His eyes widened and he shoved a hand in his pocket, studying the floor and frowning. His other hand pushed through his hair, resting palm down on the back of his bowed head for a second. I studied him.

If Xander hadn't done the hand thing with the lamp, I would never have guessed him to be—what did he call it—non-corporeal? I recalled the snippets of Latin I'd learned in high school. *Corpus* - body. Okay, the words made sense.

But weren't you supposed to be able to see through ghosts? Weren't they supposed to look a bit deader? Pale and ghouly? A ghost was not supposed to look like it had floated out of the pages of GQ Magazine. This guy was as robust as Matthew McConaughey on a good day. He must have won the after-life lottery, if there was such a thing.

The light caught the golden hairs on the back of his hand and the shadowy flecks of what looked like two days' worth of stubble on his face. Quite amazing. His eyes were downcast but I made out the flicker of dark lashes as he blinked. He seemed so real, so solid. Not alive though..

"You're staring."

I jumped.

"Sorry." I'd evidently intruded on his thoughts of being dead. Thoughts that should be private, I supposed. I tried to think of something to say that didn't sound totally lame. "It's just, I've never met a ghost before." *Yeah, not lame at all.* "This is a little weird for me.".

He nodded, eyes guarded, and offered a thin smile, his famous dimples appearing in miniature on both cheeks and then disappearing as quickly.

"Me, too. I have no idea why or *how* you can see me. I couldn't believe it when you heard me, spoke to me. I wanted to talk to you last night but I scared you and then you fainted and—you know I haven't had a conversation with anyone in a very long time." He paused, troubled, then shook his head in disbelief. "Fifty years apparently."

His reaction to the time lapse puzzled me.

"Surely if you've been hanging around—" I wasn't sure it was the technical term but it'd do "—all this time, you'd know how long you've been uh—" I trailed off awkwardly.

"Dead?" He finished the sentence for me, one eyebrow raised.

"Yes, dead." I didn't know why I felt embarrassed saying the 'd' word, he obviously knew he was dead, but it felt kind of like to talking to a person with alopecia about how terrible it is losing a bit of hair down the shower drain.

Xander crossed the room to stand by the window, his face angled away from me. The shafts of sunlight sheering through the curtains rested on him as if he was standing there, flesh and bone. His skin was tanned and smooth in the sunlight. But something was a little off and I realised with a start —he had no shadow.

"I guess that's something I should know, right?" He turned and looked at me. "I've forgotten a lot of things. I know I have. There are big gaps in my memory. It's funny, I can remember being five years old and playing in the yard, but I can't remember where I lived here in LA."

I listened with a sinking feeling. Just my luck, a ghost with amnesia. There went my inside story. Xander rubbed at his face, looking for the entire world like a tired kid. Was it even possible for ghosts to feel tired?

"I remember moments." He turned back to the window. "I get flashes of names, even lines from scripts. I know I made films of course, but the details are hazy. I remember people, sort of. I recall fragments of conversations I had. But sometimes I can recollect the words but not who said them; or that I knew somebody but I can't remember how or what they meant to me." He fell silent and gazed through the glass, eyebrows knitted.

"That must be difficult." It was a redundant thing to say but I was floundering and remembered a therapist once saying that the most important thing in difficult situations was acknowledgment ... or was it empathy? *Gah!*

"It is. It feels like I'm trying to grab onto something but I can't quite reach it. Like wreckage from a ship—splinters of broken wood that would make a whole memory if I could piece them together. On the other hand, I remember so many small things; parties I went to, tiny details, I remember not liking certain people—like Quentin." He grimaced at the name.

"Why? What did he do to you?"

"What makes you think he did something to me?" Xander rounded on me then caught himself, taking a slow breath through flared nostrils. "I don't remember the details, but I can assure you I detested Quentin Millson with a passion. I can feel it in my gut."

"Okay, Okay." Wow, he wasn't defensive at *all*.

"There are others that I feel—that I *know*—were important to me. I don't remember how or why but when I see them, I feel so strongly. It's strange."

"Like who?" I frowned as Xander glanced sharply at me.

"Well, I don't know who they are exactly. I said that, didn't I? People." His face screwed up with confusion.

"So, you just pop around and visit random people then?" I imagined him like an ethereal Jehovah's Witness, visiting home after home. *Ding Dong. Casper calling*. Clearly there was the distinct possibility my brain was suffering from hysteria. His almost inaudible answer sobered me.

"There's nothing else for me to do. It stops me going mad."

In that instant, I understood. He was stuck in a tragically futile loop. I shuddered, horrified at the thought.

"So, who do you visit? Is it the same people all the time?"

"Not always. Sometimes. I check up on old friends, or at least I think they were friends. People I never got to meet when I was alive but wanted to, people I don't even know. Anyone. Everyone. If I get close enough and really concentrate, or if somebody walks through me—not knowing I'm there—I get snatches of their thoughts, feel what they're feeling. It makes me feel less alone. Sometimes I see an interesting person on the street so I follow them for a while, watching while they go about their day." He looked at the floor, a wistful smile on his face. "That's how I found you."

"That's a little bit stalkerish don't you think? Why did you follow me?"

He shrugged.

"You seemed interested in me. I watched you touch my handprints and I sensed something different."

"Oh," I murmured. "So... you watch random people every day? All the time?"

He nodded, "Except when I'm not here."

Huh?

"Not here? Where are you if you're not here?"

"I honestly don't know," he said. I stared at him, befuddled. He was going to be no help at all. "I'm simply not here. It's like there's nothing, like sleeping without dreaming. One minute I'm here and then the next I'm not and when I come back all I know is that time has passed, I've missed things. Sometimes I think I'm gone for days, at other times weeks. I think I've even been gone for years. I honestly don't know. How would I know?" He shrugged again, his face a mix of bewilderment and sadness.

I waved a hand at him, struggling to get my head around it all.

"Let me get this straight. You can remember some conversations but not who they were with, you can remember some things about some people but there's far more that you can't remember. You know whether you liked or hated people but you have no idea why. And you pop off into nothingness all the time but you don't have a clue where you go or for how long."

"That about sums it up. It's all fragments, never a complete picture. I've learned not to think too hard on it. It frustrates me, pushes things even further out of reach."

Trust me to find a ghost that didn't remember anything. What was the point in that? Admittedly though, it triggered an immediate and delicious curiosity—something that inevitably grabs writers when they hit on a complex, fascinating story. It had been a really long time since I'd felt that particular thrill, that all-consuming drive to find proper answers, to know why.

I wished I had my notebook and pen in my hand so I could fire more questions at him, but the sad puppy dog eyes were putting me off my game. Was this how a doctor felt when they discovered a person with a brand-new incurable disease; torn between compassion for their patient and excitement at their new discovery?

Xander seemed so lost and, despite my better judgement, I felt myself softening. I snapped myself out of it with a big blink. Dead or not, the man was a renowned womaniser and I was not getting suckered in. He was not deserving of tender, smooshy feelings, only hard-nosed professional ones. I straightened up and cleared my throat. I needed to ask him an important question.

"Xander." It felt so weird saying his name out loud. "Can I ask you something?"

"Of course," he stepped towards me, palms out, "anything you want." He attempted a little smile. I wasn't quite sure how to put it gently but everything hinged on this.

"Do you know how you died?"

He stared at me with a completely blank expression. Not a good sign.

"I—uh—" He paused then abruptly turned away from me. I waited. He closed his eyes as if trying to recall some distant detail. The seconds stretched on and still he stayed silent. Reluctantly, I prodded further.

"Xander, the night you died—"

"No," he turned back to me, eyes full of anguish, and I was jolted by the depth of his turmoil. "I don't know. I can't remember any of it."

My eyes locked with his and they were frightened and black. I felt my insides twist and then he disappeared. Just like that. Gone. *Poof!* I think I would have felt better if there actually was a puff of smoke or something to mark the disappearing act but maybe I'd watched too many episodes of *Charmed*.

As it was, the instant absence of a focal point made my

vision go wonky and the floor tipped, the same feeling you get
when you spin around fast with your eyes closed, stop, open
your eyes and then attempt to walk in a straight line. Nausea hit
me hard and my hands shook uncontrollably.

He was definitely gone, that much was clear. I thought back
to only a few hours earlier, when I'd woken in the night. I'd
sensed him as soon as I'd walked into the room, known
somehow that he was there. Right now, I was just as certain he
wasn't.

I lay back, the cool softness of the linen soothing my skin,
and took a few deep breaths. What was I supposed to do now?
What if he came back? What if he didn't come back? I couldn't
decide which I wanted more.

The television chatter filtered back into my awareness as I
curled sideways on the bed, tucking my knees to my chest and
wrapping my arms around them. *Wake-Up USA* was almost
finished and the hosts were wrapping up with toothy platitudes
and tired jokes. As the credits rolled, one of them chirped,
'Have a great day America, it's good to be alive.'

I sighed and coiled myself deeper into the foetal position,
staring at the freckles on my knees. Xander didn't even know
how he died, let alone who killed him. Oh, God. How on earth
did you tell someone they were murdered? You didn't normally
have to tell people how they died because they were—you know
—dead. It made my brain hurt.

I couldn't imagine not being able to talk to a soul in fifty
years. That would have driven me crackers. I was surprised
Xander was so lucid, that he hadn't ended up a babbling mess
of insanity. What an incredibly lonely existence. The blank
spots had me flummoxed though. Was that simply what
happened to a ghost when they were stuck here for too long? I
didn't have a clue. Hell, an hour ago I didn't even believe in

ghosts. I huddled in the middle of the bed, immobile and deep in thought. Minutes later my cell phone shattered my reverie.

'MITCH' flashed up on the little blue screen.

"Hi, Mitch." I hoped my voice sounded relatively normal despite the wobble I felt. Maybe I should tell her. Was I mad? It occurred to me—in light of things—that I probably was.

"I hope you're on your way." Her voice was cool and slightly delayed down the long-distance line. No *hello*, no *how are you*, no *made friends with any attractive ghosts lately*? None of the normal pleasantries.

"Huh?" was all I managed and her voice instantly took on a razor-sharp edge.

"Quentin Millson. Please tell me you are on your way."

I jerked upright. Shit! What was the time? 12.15pm. Fucking hell. Even without the ever-present LA traffic, I'd be cutting it fine.

"Of course I am, Mitch," I lied. "I'm in a cab right now." I started frantically tugging at my soggy socks, phone jammed between my ear and left shoulder. I hopped on one leg towards the small bathroom.

"Good," said Mitch. "You can't afford to miss this interview. Without speaking to Quentin, you'll have nothing for this article except the same tired old stuff. We don't want the same old stuff, remember? This is the only reason you're there."

Panting slightly, I wriggled out of my pyjama pants. They clung to my legs, cold and damp. Yuck.

"Actually Mitch," I wobbled dangerously close to the door jam, with one foot still stuck in the leg hole, "I've had a bit of an idea."

A loaded pause on the other end of the phone.

"I'm not paying you to have ideas, Kat." There was another pause. "But okay, I'm listening."

"I'm wondering if I could dig a little more into how he died."

"You mean the murder case?"

"I can't write this piece and not talk about his murder. It'd be like writing about Elvis without mentioning deep-fried peanut butter sandwiches. But there's got to be more to it than the stuff people know."

Mitch chuckled.

"Our readers want to know about his sex life, not crime. They buy James Patterson novels for that. Focus on the sexy stuff. It's what we're about. We don't do investigative journalism."

I decided to go out on a limb.

"What if I've managed to find a couple of other interviews. People who also actually—uh—knew Xander."

"Really?" She sounded more than a little skeptical.

"Really. Think of the headlines, Mitch." My shirt muffled words as I tugged it over my head, staggering closer to the shower recess.

"Kat, what the hell are you doing in that cab?"

I thought fast.

"Oh, it is so hot here Mitch, you wouldn't believe it. I was taking my jumper off to make the most of the sun."

"Right. Well, you're not there to sun bake, Kat," she snipped. "You're there to work. Look, I don't know what else you think you could possibly find out. If the police didn't figure it out fifty years ago, you're not likely to. But fine, if you want to dig—dig. Just make sure that whoever you speak to, you get solid proof of their story. We don't want another mess like the last one."

"Of course, Mitch, you know me."

"That's what I'm worried about."

Of all the times to decide she wanted solid proof. Oh, the irony. How the hell was I going to do that? Call Ghostbusters? The last time I checked, Bill Murray was a bit busy. But it didn't matter, I technically had permission. It was decided. I was really going to do this. I rang off, promising an update as soon as I was finished with the interview and showered so quickly even the Wicked Witch of the West would have survived. Tightly wrapped in a white fluffy hotel towel, I bolted for my bag to find something suitable to wear.

I had no idea what else Mitch had packed for me apart from the jeans and t-shirt I'd flown in, the sundress from yesterday and my PJs. What on earth did you wear to interview one of the bitchiest, most judgmental people on the planet anyway? This was someone who lunched with Marilyn Monroe for Christ's sake. *The pressure.*

Bending down, I tossed garment after garment over my shoulder, unselfconsciously letting my damp towel drop to the floor. Blue T-shirt. Red T-shirt. No, too casual. Jeans? No. Sequined mini-dress? Huh? Did Mitch pack anything decent at all? Aha! Hang on.

I stood, torn between a filmy blue slip dress in one hand and a slightly crumpled tan suit in the other. Both were infinitely better than jeans and a T-shirt.

"I like the blue." Xander's voice piped out behind me and I jumped. Again. Thankfully I wasn't holding hot coffee, because this time I was stark naked.

"Will you please stop doing that?" I yelped as I whirled around. "Someone should put a bell on y—" I froze, registering my nudity. I stared at him, aghast and too shocked to even attempt covering my exposed and slightly wobbly flesh.

He was sitting casually in the arm chair near the television cabinet, leaning forward with his elbows on denim-covered knees, hands clasped loosely together. A tiny smirk tugged at the corner of his mouth but—to his credit—his eyes stayed firmly locked on mine instead of dropping to cop an eyeful.

"You appear to have dropped something," he said smoothly.

Heat flew up my neck and took up roost in my cheeks as I dropped the clothes and snatched up the towel. I had a feeling it was too short to cover every inch of my thighs but it was either that or continue to show him my boobs and that was a complete no-brainer.

"You're back." I pursed my lips at him.

"Uh-huh."

"And I suppose you don't know where you went?"

"No idea."

"Handy."

Xander shrugged and I felt a stab of irritation. I might have been over-reacting due to embarrassment but his nonchalance was annoying. What happened to sad-puppy Xander? I quite liked him. I waved my hand at him, holding the towel up with the other.

"Do you mind?"

"Oh, sure. Sorry." He had the decency to feign embarrassment as he placed both hands over his eyes like one of the three wise monkeys.

I hurriedly dressed in the suit; partly because it was more professional but—if I was honest—mainly because Xander said he liked the strappy dress better and I didn't give two figs what an extremely sexy but dead movie star thought I should wear.

"It's a little late for modesty don't you think," he said from behind his hands, "How do you know I didn't see everything last night?"

I gasped.

"Typical. You're invisible so the first thing you do is use the fact nobody can see you to spy on naked women. I—"

"Whoa," he chuckled through his fingers, "down girl. I was teasing, Katherine, relax. I promise, I am a gentleman." I glared at him and in that second registered two things. He knew my name and he was sitting in a chair. A solid chair.

"Hey!" I pointed at him accusingly. "Firstly, how the hell do you know who I am? And secondly, I thought you couldn't touch anything? Why aren't you falling straight through that chair, huh? Explanation, please!"

He still had his hands over his face.

"Are you decent yet?"

"Yes."

He took his hands down. This time he didn't stop his eyes travelling slowly up and down the length of my body. I tried not to think about the fact his eyes were a deep and gooey chocolate brown and that—just like in those ridiculous romance novels—they were twinkling at me as he smiled, which is really quite absurd, because stars twinkle, not eyes and—

"Very nice," he said and I narrowed my own eyes at him as if to say *I don't care what you think*. "Now which question did you want me to answer first, the name or the chair? Both of which can be easily explained." He was getting more infuriating by the second.

"Whichever," I growled, folding my arms.

"You're very demanding and aggressive for a woman you know," he smirked again, "It's not very lady-like."

I fought the urge to throw something at his pretty head, figuring there wasn't much point, what with him not being solid and all.

"Xander—" I warned.

"Alright, alright, I know your name is Katherine because it is written in very big letters on the tag of your bag. Simple."

"It's Kat actually." The urge to be argumentative was instant.

"Kat sounds like a pet. Katherine is much prettier."

I wondered if you could kill ghosts by smothering them with a wet towel.

"My friends call me Kat." Then I smirked back at him, "In that case, you can call me Katherine." *Ten points to me.* I mentally high-fived myself.

"Touché." He still seemed pleased with himself. "But that suits me fine."

"And the sitting? In the chair? You need to explain the sitting in the chair." I planted my hands on my hips awaiting a reasonable explanation, as if anything about this situation could be seen as remotely reasonable.

"I can't explain it fully to be honest. I think for some reason I can copy everyday actions like sitting or lying down. Maybe it's the same reason I seem to be standing on this floor instead of falling straight through it."

"Right." I said, fleetingly wishing he *would* fall through the floor.

"I seem to be able to choose the way I occupy a space," he shrugged slightly, "I know that's not a very interesting answer. Sorry."

"You sound like an expert on the whole being a ghost thing."

"I've had a long time to think about it. I'm not actually sitting in this chair. It only appears that way. I can't feel the chair."

"Can you feel anything?"

His eyes held an odd expression as they searched my face.

"Not the same way you can."

Lusty alarm bells clanged in my head again and I squirmed. Was he talking about the dream? I wrapped my arms around myself like a barrier. Ghosts couldn't flirt? Could they? Would they? Who did he think he was?

Xander's eyes narrowed.

"Are you okay?"

"Uh-huh. Fine. Why?"

"You seem uncomfortable all of a sudden. Was it something I said?"

"Nope. I'm good." *Resist Kat, resist.* "You were saying?"

A puzzled look flickered across his face.

"Uh—I was about to say I don't feel things the way I did when I was alive. The only thing I can feel when I touch things —you know, when my hand goes through them—is a tingling feeling like pins and needles. And heat. That's it."

"That's it?"

"Well, yes. What did you think I was going to say?"

I felt a bit silly and let my arms drop. Christ, was I so out of practice when it came to men that I assumed even a dead one was coming on to me?

"Nothing, I—you said something about me being able to feel and—er—" I trailed off awkwardly.

"You're lucky. I might have had a long time to think about it but you never get used to it. I miss being able to touch things, hold things, I even miss being cold believe it or not. And I miss hotdogs."

"You miss hotdogs?" I laughed and he nodded with a resigned, lopsided smile.

"What can I say, I loved hotdogs."

I tried to imagine what it would be like to not feel anything ever again, not the cool air on your skin or warm summer sun on your face. I imagined it would be like existing in a vacuum of nothingness. My smile faded as the full horror of it dawned on me.

"Now, can I ask you a question, Katherine?"

Uh-oh.

"Sure."

Xander stared straight at me.

"How did I die?"

I cringed inwardly. This was icky but I couldn't avoid it now. I crossed the room and sat in the armchair opposite him. He leaned back, shying away slightly.

"Is it that bad? Did I get hit by a train or something?"

"No, not a train."

"A bus?"

"No."

"Car?"

"Xander, please—" He shut up, shrinking with mounting apprehension. I bit my lip and steeled myself. "You were murdered."

Chapter Seven

I didn't elaborate. I simply waited for the awful words to sink in. The shock was clear on his face as he eased himself back in the chair. He let out a small whistle, eyes downcast and fixed.

"I wasn't expecting that."

"I'm sorry."

He lifted his eyes again, slowly.

"How? How did they—" he trailed off.

I told him the only facts I knew. That his car had been found on the side of a road at the edge of Runyon Canyon County Park. The window on the driver's side was down and his body was slumped sideways with a single bullet wound to the side of his head.

"Who did it? Who killed me?" His words were stilted.

"Nobody knows. There were rumours, but the police never charged anyone." I felt awful saying it, especially as his face crumpled with disbelief. "I'm really sorry.."

"Why? You didn't shoot me," he said bitterly, folding forward and covering his face with his hands. I didn't reply.

What could I possibly say anyway? He stayed silent. Minutes passed. I didn't know whether his mind was racing or whether he was in shock and I felt terrible but to be honest, I couldn't help noticing the clock was ticking closer to one o'clock. *Eeep.*

I shifted uncomfortably in the chair trying to think of a tactful way to say, '*So* sorry you were horribly murdered, but I really have to be going.' Before I had a chance to come up with a suitable exit strategy he slapped his thigh, a triumphant look on his face.

"That's it!"

"Huh? That's what?"

He leaned back again with a wide smile, spreading his arms expansively.

"That's why I'm still here after all this time. And more importantly, that's why you can see me when nobody else has been able to."

I had no idea what he was talking about but got the distinct feeling I was not going to be happy about whatever it was.

"Go on—" I said cautiously.

"You're a journalist, right?" he leaned eagerly towards me and I couldn't help shrinking back.

"How t—?"

He waved his hands dismissively.

"I overheard you talking on that little telephone. You're writing an article about me, aren't you?" His excitement was growing by the second, and so was the knot in my belly.

"Correct." I didn't like where this was going.

"Don't you get it?" He gesticulated at me again. "That's why I was drawn to you. It all fits. You're supposed to help me."

"Help you what?" *Please don't say it.*

"What do you think?" He was incredulous, as if he couldn't quite believe I could be so dumb. I wasn't, I had a horrible feeling I knew what he was getting at but I didn't want the words to be out there, where I was going to have to face them and try to find a way to say no.

"Katherine, you're supposed to find out who killed me so I can move on. Isn't that the way it works?" There. He said it. He'd obviously seen way too many movies. He might have been more attractive than Patrick Swayze, but I did not resemble Whoopi Goldberg in any size, shape or form and I didn't see a pottery wheel anywhere in my future. I didn't even like the Righteous Brothers.

I couldn't do it. Trying to solve a fifty-year-old murder case to save my career was one thing but helping a lost soul move on to the afterlife? That was way too much responsibility.

What if I failed? Most of the time I couldn't even manage to look out for myself, as the last couple of weeks had clearly demonstrated. What if I didn't find out anything new and he ended up stuck here, doomed to wander the mean streets of Los Angeles for all eternity? There was no way I was having that on my conscience. I didn't need it. I was carrying enough guilt already.

"No," I stood firm. "No, no, no, and a thousand more times no."

Xander was taken completely by surprise.

"What do you mean *no*?"

I stood and marched across the room to slip my shoes on, then grabbed my bag and turned towards him. I focused on his feet instead of his face.

"I mean, no. I'm sorry. I'm a journalist not a psychic. I'm writing an important story that could save my career and, seeing as you can't actually help me, I can't have you tagging along making things difficult so maybe you should go back to where you came from." Did I really say that? I sounded like such a bitch. Ugh, this was horrible.

"But you have to help me," he said, clearly desperate. "There's a reason you can see me, there has to be."

"I don't have to help, Xander," I was struggling to stand firm, mainly because he was really attractive when he was pleading. I needed to get away from him before I caved in to his sad expression and those puppy-dog eyes. "What I have to do is my job and that job is to write a magazine article. I'm sorry, but I'm late. I have to go."

"Go where?"

I opened the door, an unexpected lump sticking in my throat. I swallowed it down with difficulty as I stepped into the hallway and turned to face him.

"To see Quentin Millson."

He was in front of me in a millisecond.

"I'm coming with you."

"No, you're not." Before he could argue I shut the door in his face, finding myself standing suddenly alone in the quiet corridor. The wooden door shimmered for a second, like heat shifting in the air above a road on a hot day. Suddenly Xander materialised in front of me, his nose almost touching mine.

"Aaaahhh." Arms windmilling, I toppled backwards in fright and landed heavily on my bag, sending lipstick, pens and my cell phone sprawling onto the carpet. I seemed to be spending an inordinate amount of time on the floor. Xander stared down at me, arms folded. I gaped at him.

"You walked through that door." I was the queen of stating the obvious. I don't know why I was so surprised, I figured he could probably do it, but thinking it and seeing it in action were two very different things. Seeing it was frightening and quite disorientating actually.

"What did you think I was going to do? Stay in your room like a good boy?"

"That would be a start."

"You know, when I was alive women didn't go around telling their men what to do."

I laughed as I clambered up and started cramming my stuff back into my bag. "Firstly," I pointed out, "you're not my man. And, secondly, it's been a long time since you've been alive. Women have come to their senses since then."

"You can't stop me from coming with you to see Quentin."

I turned my back and started striding down the hallway.

"No, Xander—you're right. I can't stop you. It's a free country. Do what you want. If I say no, you'll probably pop yourself through the roof of my taxi anyway."

His long legs kept pace with me easily.

"I'll bet he knows something." His voice rang with certainty. "He always was a sneaky little creep. You'll see."

"I haven't changed my mind. This is not about you. This is about my article. I can't stop you coming with me, but I'm not asking him anything about your murder. Not yet anyway, he has his own story to tell."

"Are you serious? What kind of journalist are you if you're not going to ask the important questions?"

That was it. I'd had enough. I rounded on him furiously. "You want to know what kind of journalist I am? A bloody tired one. A jet-lagged one. And a very cranky one. I'm supposed to write a story about your sex life and Quentin's the only person around for me to talk to. So that's all I'm going to do today. Not that I have to explain myself, but if it's okay with you I'd like to gain his trust before I start asking him sticky questions about who might have shot you in the head. Alright?"

"My sex life?" Trust him to get stuck on that. "Why on earth would anyone be interested in my sex life?" He was seriously confused but I couldn't be bothered explaining the celebrity-hungry masses of the new millennium to him right that second.

"Grrrrr." I spun around and stomped around the corner, almost bumping into an elderly lady in a floaty purple caftan who had clearly heard me shouting because she flinched and shrank back against the wall. To be fair, to her I appeared to be yelling at myself like a lunatic. A nervous high-pitched laugh escaped from me, which didn't seem to reassure her much. I waved my notebook in the air madly.

"Just learning my lines." I moved past her and heard her mutter something at my back about 'too many drugs' but I kept walking.

"Quick thinking," Xander chuckled as he caught up.

"Shut up," I hissed, "don't talk to me. People will think I'm a crazy person."

"Don't worry about it," he said mildly as we made our way through the lobby. "There are plenty of *really* crazy people in LA, you'll fit right in."

I ignored him and faked a bright smile as I caught the eye of Marjorie, who was perched on one of the overstuffed Queen Anne chairs reading Shirley MacLaine's *Out on a Limb*. If only you knew lady, if only you knew. I whisked past her with a quick wave before she could stop me to chat.

"I haven't been in a taxi in a very long time," Xander sounded shaky all of a sudden, like a kid about to go on a scary theme park ride, "I don't like them, Katherine, they make me nervous."

I shot him an *are you kidding me* look, gritted my teeth and said nothing as I slid into a waiting cab, outside.

"You're ignoring me." He reluctantly climbed in beside me. I opened my notebook to check the address, deliberately not even glancing sideways at him. "That's very childish, you know." I continued to ignore him and leaned forward to speak to the driver.

"2231 Benedict Canyon Drive, Beverly Hills please." Settling back against the seat as we pulled away, I stared ahead, the model of obstinacy.

"I'm right about Quentin, you'll see," Xander muttered. I was determined not to answer him. This was not what I signed up for. What made it worse was the fact I was acutely aware of a mild heat radiating out towards me from Xander's—for want of a better word—body. And for some reason, the faint but delicious scent of warm bread and apples.

I cleared my throat and shuffled sideways, trying to distance myself without being too obvious. I could feel his eyes on me.

"Stop staring." I whispered out of the corner of my mouth. The taxi driver had a shiny bald head and a Tom Selleck moustache. He glanced back at me in the rear-view mirror.

"Did you say something, Ma'am?"

"Sorry," I leaned forward with a smile, "I was talking to myself."

The driver laughed and wiggled bushy eyebrows at me.

"That's the first sign of madness you know."

"Yes, so I've heard."

Sulking, I plopped back against the seat, with my arms crossed, to the sound of Xander chuckling beside me. It was overwhelmingly irritating.

"Oh, shut up," I muttered.

Chapter Eight

Quentin Millson's house on Benedict Canyon Drive was exactly as I imagined the man himself; overdone and full of its own self-importance, yet somewhat forgotten. We stood before the massive wrought iron gates, dwarfed by two enormous brick pillars topped with concrete cherubs. They perched like tiny, chubby sentries on either side of the broad driveway.

I peered through the heavy bars and down the tree-lined slope and made out the side of a large bougainvillea-draped residence. Sunset-hued bricks and Corinthian pillars peeped from beneath tangled flowering vines. The house couldn't have been more camp if it was dancing on a Mardi Gras float wearing a feather boa and leather chaps.

Despite its decadence, the property had a forlorn and tired air. It seemed to sag in its foundations like an aged drag queen at the end of a long night dancing in painful stilettos. Unimpressed by the shabby grandeur, Xander strode back and forth across the driveway.

"If anyone knows what happened to me, you can bet it's

Quentin. I think." He paused mid-stride. "Well, probably," He spoke rapidly, pushing a hand through his hair in agitation before pacing again. "He could never be trusted; I remember that much. The little worm knew everything about everyone, that's why he was so good at that gossip stuff."

"Will you stop marching around?" I studied the intercom instructions on one of the gate posts. The air-conditioning in the taxi had been on the fritz and the windows were stuck half open. I was overheated and windblown. "You're giving me whiplash."

"Sorry." Xander halted on the spot.

"If you insist on coming in with me, you have to promise not to talk. If Quentin thinks I'm acting weird, he'll stop the interview and kick me out. Okay?" I planted my hands on my hips and assumed my best school-teacher expression.

"But what if he's not telling you the truth? Can I tell you he's lying?"

"Xander. Please! You can't remember where you lived. What makes you think you'll remember whether he's telling the truth or not? This is not about you being—you know." I was still uncomfortable saying the M word to his face. "I told you; I'm only getting background stuff. Don't talk to me."

"Fine." He turned his back, thrusting his hands in his pockets and scuffing his feet on the road. "I do remember some things. I *could* help."

I rolled my eyes. It wasn't exactly leading-man behaviour. He was more like an aggravating kid brother.

I expected some kind of buzzing sound when I pressed the intercom but there was nothing, not even a beep. I pressed it again. Still nothing. Frustrated, I poked the small button several times in quick succession, hoping my persistence would be rewarded with a loud buzzzzzzzzz. Xander hovered over me.

"Bloody thing's broken." I sighed, exasperated.

"Great, you broke it."

"I did not break it. It didn't work in the first place."

"You broke it."

I was dangerously close to snapping.

"Xander—"

"Do you want me to try?" He stepped forward towards the intercom and without thinking I stepped back.

"Fine. Be my guest," I said, only to turn and see him grinning stupidly and waving his non-corporeal fingers at me yet again. He laughed.

"Kidding!"

Really?

"You do know you're being extremely unhelpful and immature," my voice was acidic, "not to mention annoying." A hurt expression shadowed his face.

"I'm trying to lighten the mood."

"Well, stop it! The mood's fine the way it is."

From behind me, a tinny voice weighed in to the conversation.

"Do you make a habit of talking to yourself in the middle of the street Ms. Alley?"

I froze and stared at Xander, eyes bugging and not wanting to turn around. He stifled laughter as he pointed at the intercom, unseen to anyone but me. Bastard.

A tiny TV screen had flickered into life and, for the first time, I noticed a square black camera box mounted—quite conspicuously actually—right underneath one of the fat cherubs. How did I miss that? Quentin Millson's equally fat face filled the little screen in grainy black and white. *Crap*. Way to come off like a complete whacko. I back-pedalled so hard I could hear a truck reversing in my head; *beeep beeep beeep.*

"Good afternoon, Mr. Millson, I'm Katherine Alley. Oh, of course you already said that, I mean *knew* that. I'm so sorry I'm late. LA traffic, I'm sure you know how it is. I was saying so a moment ago in fact, to my sister, on my hands-free." I waved my cell phone in the air, an electronic beacon of bullshit I was hoping he'd buy. There were several seconds of silence, no doubt while Quentin decided whether I was a lunatic or not.

"A word of advice, Msssz Alley," he drawled, distinctly unimpressed, "first impressions are everything in this business. You're lucky your reputation precedes you."

My what? My good reputation or my bad reputation? *Fuck*. Before I could question him, the screen faded to black and the massive gates groaned and swung inwards. They reminded me of a gaping mouth. I had a feeling I was about to be eaten for breakfast.

Suddenly nervous, I paused in the gateway. I shook both hands down by my side, rolling my shoulders back and tipping my head from side to side, stretching my neck like an athlete about to take a run up. While I took the time to prepare, Xander marched straight past me with long confident strides.

"What are you waiting for?" he called over his shoulder.

I was going to kill him.

For a second time.

By the time we navigated the meandering driveway and reached the front door, I was hot, sticky and not feeling at all like the well-groomed professional that had left the hotel a short time before.

I've always had a bone to pick with whoever first said, 'men sweat, women perspire and ladies glow'. I do not glow. I don't even perspire prettily. Unfortunately, thanks to my dad's genes, I am a full-blown sweat monkey. All I have to do is add a few extra degrees or the tiniest bit of exertion.

The wind-tunnel of a taxi ride and the long driveway trek

had caused my hair to arrange itself in stringy clumps on my clammy and still tender forehead. At least it covered the bruise I thought, huffing to myself as I touched it gingerly. Damp patches decorated the armpits of my suit jacket so it now resembled an overused dish cloth. Without checking, I knew I also had an unattractive perspiration moustache on my upper lip.

Xander however—due to his annoying non-corporealness—appeared cool and unaffected. I knew nobody could see him, but it still gave me the shits. Stupid movie stars. Even dead they managed to look better than everyone else. We faced the big double doors and I pressed the bell.

"Everything about this place is huge," I remarked under my breath as I gazed up at the multi-coloured lead lighting laid into each door. I smirked, "Do you think he's overcompensating for something?" Xander made a harrumphing sound then hunched his shoulders, sulking and chewing on his lip. "You truly don't like him, do you? What exactly did Quentin do to you again?" I couldn't help myself, "Oh that's right, you don't remember."

A deep furrow developed in Xander's forehead but before he could answer we heard the door's internal lock roll over with a clunk. I expected to be greeted by a maid or a butler or at least a half-naked Latino pool boy. The doors swung back and Quentin Millson himself was revealed, framed dramatically in the entranceway.

He couldn't have staged it any better and I stifled a smile. Short and rotund, with thinning but neatly-styled white hair, he was wearing heavy make-up and an incongruous dark purple Adidas tracksuit. He looked like an aged oompa-loompa who'd had a few too many nips and tucks. The enormous flower-filled vases crowding the hall behind him dwarfed him completely.

Quentin stood, poised as if for the paparazzi's benefit, and I briefly wondered if he was expecting me to curtsy. I glanced surreptitiously at Xander who was staring at him the same way you would a squashed frog.

"Mr. Millson, hello."

I stepped forward, thrusting out my hand. The heady scent of gardenias and a waft of liberal and effeminate cologne assailed my nostrils. Quentin regarded my hand coolly and had the audacity to wrinkle his nose in distaste before meeting my eager eyes with his little piggy ones.

"I'm sorry Ms. Alley—" His tone that implied he wasn't sorry at all. "—I don't like to touch ... people." He looked me up and down and I self-consciously smoothed the front of my smooshed suit and tucked my lank hair behind my ears. He fixed his gaze on my sweaty fingers. "You never know where their hands have been."

"Ugh!" Xander burst out, making me flinch, "He's more vile than I remember." I kept my smile firmly plastered on and made no sign of having heard. Thankfully, Quentin was completely oblivious. I dropped my extended hand hastily.

"Thank you so much for granting this interview, Mr. Millson. Very kind of you."

His nose was still twitching as he studied me. Maybe I had bad body odour after the hellishly hot taxi ride. There was no way he could smell me over the flowers and his own perfume but I clamped my arms to my sides regardless, imprisoning my armpits and any potential pong.

"Yes, well, as you can imagine I was *very* selective about who I wanted to share this information with." He waved a hand imperiously. "I was in negotiations with several other publications here in the States but in the end they didn't—" he paused and frowned, "—well, they weren't right, that's all. Anyway, your editor was smart enough to know when to jump on an exclusive story and she assures me that you are good. So, I suppose you'd better come in and—" he sighed dramatically and not altogether convincingly, "—get this over with." Before he'd finished the sentence he pirouetted, surprisingly nimble, and disappeared into the floral jungle, his words trailing behind him. We followed, ducking and diving around overblown blooms.

"See, I told you. Horrible," Xander muttered.

"Mmm-hmm." I whispered in agreement, pretending I was clearing my throat to cover the fact I was technically talking to thin air.

"Please, come in and sit down." Quentin waved me into a large, austere room. Entirely white and completely impersonal, it was at odds with the riot of flourishes that drowned what I had seen of the rest of the house. I obediently sat on one of the two modular couches, facing Quentin who was awkwardly arranging his body on the other.

He grunted under his breath as he clumsily tucked his legs up so he could recline to the side. Embarrassed for him, I averted my eyes. I was acutely aware of Xander, hovering behind me, glaring at the old man. Quentin lifted a pencilled eyebrow and glanced pointedly at my bag.

"Well, are you going to record this, Ms. Alley?" he said. "I have no doubt accuracy is of the utmost importance to a journalist of your calibre." I could have sworn I saw his lips twitch. Was he messing with me?

"Of course, Mr. Millson." I smiled in what I hoped was a winning fashion. "And please, call me Kat."

"I'd prefer not Ms. Alley, let's not get too familiar hmmm? Besides, Kat sounds like a pet not a person."

One. Two. Thre—

"Told you," Xander chimed, like juvenile clockwork. The strain of pretending he wasn't there was making me nervous.

"Ms. Alley it is then." My voice was a little too loud, too bright. "I'm sure you're extremely busy so we should get this over with, as you so eloquently put it." My laugh rang false as I fumbled in my bag for the palm-sized silver digital recorder I carried everywhere with me.

I leaned forward and placed it on the monstrous marble coffee table that crouched between the couches, pressing record. Metal clinked on marble and Quentin was bored already. Things were going swimmingly.

"So, Mr. Millson, going through my research I noticed that Xander Hill featured very heavily in many of your columns. Did you know him well? How did the two of you meet?"

"This'll be interesting," muttered Xander from behind me.

Quentin leaned back, focusing on a faraway point, his voice immediately suggestive of epic story-telling.

"Xander Hill was a very, very special friend, Ms. Alley. We became close not long after he moved here to Los Angeles, before he became successful. In fact, I was one of the first people to pick up on his talent.

"It sounds clichéd, I know, but we met at Schwab's Drug Store when he walked up, introduced himself and handed me a milkshake. Apparently, an actress friend had told him I was worth knowing." Quentin paused and patted his forehead with a white silk handkerchief.

"I didn't mind. He was very attractive, obviously, and remarkably funny and we quickly became friends. He would come to see me after auditions, upset over inevitable rejections of course. Unsure if he was ever going to make it. He was completely broke so I would often buy him dinner."

Xander's violent reactions made it hard to imagine the cosy scene and I expected to hear unequivocal denial expressed over my left shoulder. Instead, I saw Xander out of the corner of my eye, sidling around the couch, and keeping his distance and obviously perplexed. He skirted the entire room before coming to a stop behind Quentin. He didn't dispute a thing, but chewed his lip as he studied the top of Quentin's head, edgy.

"I already had some influence; nothing like my eventual success, that came later. After Xander was—" he paused, a grimace twisting his lips as he struggled with the words, "—after Xander was gone. But I was writing my regular column. I was respected, so I did him a favour. I liked him very much." He shrugged, his chin disappearing into fleshy shoulders. "I would drop his name in constantly, linked with various people. Some of it was true, some was not. The industry started taking notice. If a name is mentioned everywhere, eventually you start wondering, *who is this person*? It didn't take long before he was getting more auditions."

"So, it was thanks to you that Xander got his Hollywood break?" I asked. Xander's indignation flared and he glared at me over Quentin's head. I refused to meet his eyes.

"No." They spoke emphatically at the same time. Xander stopped short, mouth hanging open, surprised, as Quentin shook his head.

"Xander was exceptionally talented. He would have made it without my help, I have no doubt. He was incredibly driven. Very focused." He pursed his lips. "In fact, almost robotically so."

Xander paced back and forth behind the couch, distracting me. I leaned forward, trying to shift his movement out of my direct eye line.

"What do you mean?"

"Not making it was simply not an option, Ms. Alley. With most actors there's an element of needing to be adored, wanting the limelight. It's a distraction and was the downfall of a number of young performers I knew. Xander didn't have that. Not until later on. I think it went to his head eventually, but in the beginning he hated it. I would have to bribe him to go to parties, to be photographed. He didn't want to be famous, he wanted to be a successful actor. He was always focused on the next role, it had to be bigger, better. He wanted to be a leading man."

Xander snorted and my eyes flicked towards him involuntarily.

"He's talking like he was my best friend, like we spent time together," Xander growled. "Do you really think Quentin Millson is the kind of person I would have been friends with?"

Then it hit me. He didn't know whether it was true or not. Now my interest was well and truly piqued.

"Mr. Millson, why are we only hearing about your friendship with Xander now? In all my research, I came across only one early article you wrote about him, and he featured in your columns a lot, but nothing else—no photos together, no actual interviews—" I let the question hang. Quentin's right eye twitched as he regarded me judiciously, all the while twisting a bejeweled ring on one of his pudgy fingers.

"It wasn't common knowledge, Katherine." The use of my first name startled me. "But I promised Mitch I had a story to tell and I do. I've kept it to myself for this long out of respect for the dead, but I think it's time things were out in the open." He waved his hands with a small flourish, a sardonic half-smile on his face. "So, this is me, opening up." He finished with a high, false laugh.

"*Making* it up more likely." Xander stood directly behind Quentin's head, arms folded across his chest. "Think about it, Katherine, the man is a has-been. Whatever he's about to say, he's cashing in on my name. On my death. That's disgusting if you ask me."

I wished he would shut up but maybe he had a point. I wasn't sure how hard to push but Quentin *was* calling me Katherine. Maybe that meant we were friends now. I decided to risk a small fib. It wasn't like I could tell the actual truth. Xander's gut feeling about Quentin had to mean something, even if he didn't remember why.

"That's interesting, Mr. Millson. Only, I'm sure I read quite the opposite somewhere; that you didn't get on, that Xander wasn't exactly a fan of yours. I think it said, in fact, that he didn't like you at all."

I shrank back on the couch, waiting for an explosion. Quentin blinked rapidly and sucked a deep breath in through his narrow nose, lips pinched. He breathed out audibly. I prepared to reach for my bag, ready to leave in an instant if required.

"I think you have your facts wrong there, Ms. Alley." His voice was low and cold. First names were clearly back in their box. "I'm not sure what you think you've read, or where, but Xander and I were very close. We may not have seen each other much in the months before he was killed—" he scowled at the floor for a moment then glared back at me, all icy composure, "—for various reasons. But our bond was still intact, I assure you."

"He's lying!" Xander strode around the couch and stood beside me, staring Quentin down. His face was unrecognisable as he spat the words. Gone was the smooth matinee idol smile. In its place was an angry mask.

It wasn't a look I particularly liked. The ferocity of Xander's glare should have ignited Quentin's head into flames à la Nicholas Cage in *Ghostrider*. "I hated him, I can feel it. I don't remember why but I know how I feel about him."

Unfortunately, the intuition of a dead person, no matter how strong, didn't give me leverage. I could hardly say to Quentin 'a little dead birdy told me Xander hated your guts'. I had no idea why Quentin would make out they were close if they weren't? It didn't make any sense. I couldn't imagine him pretending to like someone if he didn't. The great Quentin Millson never held back. He had no qualms baring his sharp, white veneers to spray venom liberally at anyone deemed not worthy. I backtracked quickly.

"I apologise, Mr. Millson, I must have misread it. It was probably a silly piece of gossip. You and I both know better than anyone how out of hand the rumour mill can get sometimes."

"Yes," he hissed. Speaking of venom. "Well, if the Australian papers are anything to go by, I'd have thought you'd have learnt your lesson by now." *Ouch.* "A small tip, Ms. Alley —if you are going to trade in gossip, make sure it's true."

In that moment I wanted to tell him I'd learned my lesson and it was a mistake, honestly, and that I knew it was wrong and was sorry for everything that happened—but I had a feeling grovelling wouldn't endear me to him. So, I simply nodded like Luke Skywalker dutifully taking notes from an over-botoxed Obi Wan Kenobi.

After a lengthy pause, during which Quentin seemed more interested in his fingernails than whether I'd insulted him, I decided to give his story the benefit of the doubt and run with it.

"Mr. Millson, you said you didn't see each other much in the time before Xander was killed." He glanced up, nostrils flaring, one of his eyebrows arching in delicate enquiry.

"Mmm-hmm?" He inspected his impeccable cuticles again.

"Was there a reason for that?"

"Don't ask redundant questions, Ms, Alley," he snapped. "Of course there was a reason. There is a reason for everything. Another tip, dear—ask the question you really want to ask. Don't hedge."

I squirmed like a chastised five-year old. Half of me wanted to tell him to shove the redundant question up his arse and the other half knew I had to finish the interview if it killed me. There was a better chance of him eventually talking about Xander's death if I jumped through his hoops.

"*What* was the reason for not seeing Xander much before he died?"

"Much better." He sniffed as he straightened up an inch, touching his hand to the fine gold chain hanging around his chubby neck. He slid his thumb and forefinger back and forth along the tiny circular links.

Xander caught my peripheral vision. He'd moved across the room and was pacing again. I thought he'd be keen to fill in some memory gaps but maybe not. His obvious jitters told me he wished he was anywhere but here.

"To answer that question properly, Katherine, I need to tell you the whole story. So you can truly understand. I've never spoken about all of this before." Quentin sighed, "I know it's ironic, but I used to consider myself a very private man. Other people's lives fascinated me, but I couldn't bear the thought of the world knowing the ins-and-outs of mine. But I want to tell my story now, before it's too late. I want people to know."

Pretending to look across at the window, I chanced a quick glance at Xander. He was leaning back against the wall now, hands in pockets, one ankle crossed over the other. He was glaring blackly at Quentin again and hostility was coming off him in waves. It made my skin prickle.

"See, Katherine," he sneered. "I told you. He wants to cash in. He's nothing but a desperate old man."

I ignored him as Quentin continued somberly, "I tried to help Xander's career as much as I could. After a while, I didn't need to plant manufactured gossip about the starlets he was seen with. He managed to find them all by himself. It was easy, looking the way he did. I wrote about every one of them and leaked snippets of information about deals or meeting with

directors and casting agents. Nobody knew we were close, so it
appeared I was simply supporting a new talent. Which of
course I was," he added hurriedly. "Don't get me wrong,
Katherine, I helped Xander because I believed in him. His
talent was truly incandescent."

Xander was anything but incandescent; any blacker and
there would have been an eclipse. Quentin raved on, oblivious
and rich in praise. Smiling now, he told me about late night
dinners after filming as Xander's career shifted up a gear. He
spoke of the times Xander would spend the night, when they'd
had too much to drink and would wake dishevelled and hungover to share a cheap breakfast.

They would celebrate Xander's excitement at securing
small film roles and discuss how great he was going to be. They
would also argue over the string of starlets Xander continued to
traipse around Hollywood with; Quentin screaming he had
'too much talent for that' and Xander yelling that he 'needed to
do it for his career'.

It sounded more than a little *Brokeback Mountain* to be
honest. I'd heard of bromances, but this was pushing the limits.
Quentin hadn't come right out and said it, but suddenly everything clicked into place. I couldn't believe it hadn't already
occurred to me. The sexy secret. The whole reason for this
interview.

Xander Hill was gay.

Chapter Nine

What a scoop! Mitch was going to do backflips, although it wasn't exactly an earth-shattering discovery. Errol Flynn. Rock Hudson. Two of the sexiest leading men ever to grace celluloid and both of them had preferred pert-bottomed male stage hands over their glamorous female co-stars.

Despite the burgeoning sexual revolution in the late sixties and early seventies, in Hollywood it was still pretty standard to hide your sexual predilections, especially if you didn't fit the heterosexual norm. For a lead actor or actress, admitting you were gay was a career killer. And things had only marginally improved since then. Sure, there were several who had broken the mould but I knew for a fact there were plenty of others in the industry still too afraid to come out of the closet. It was the one thing I had never exposed against celebrities' wishes, despite having inside information. Chrissie would have terminated our friendship then and there if I had. Besides, I was absolutely an ally and I did have some moral boundaries. Not many, but some.

Now, I was no expert but I was pretty sure being gay wasn't something you'd be able to forget. Xander obviously didn't remember any of it. He clearly thought he was straight. After all, he had looked me up and down lasciviously with those gooey, sexy eyes.

"You and Xander were lovers!" I blurted at Quentin, excited. Xander, however, was less happy.

"Excuse me?" He stood bolt upright, bristling with testosterone. I stuck a finger in my right ear pretending to scratch it, blocking out Xander's indignant sputtering. Quentin smiled enigmatically for a few seconds then exhaled, all wistful drama.

"No, Ms. Alley. Xander and I were not *lovers*." A relieved *harumph* came from the other side of the room but Quentin wasn't finished. "We were more than that." He spoke with all the dramatic poise of a hammy soap actor, "We were partners. He was the love of my life."

That was it. Xander exploded from the other side of the room.

"What? LIAR! He's lying, Katherine." He charged towards the side of the couch, raging, stopping short, impotent and unable to do anything but tremble. His fists clenched as if he wanted to strangle the words from Quentin's throat. I ignored him.

"But why keep that a secret for all this time? And why the change of heart now?" Personally, I was enthralled.

Quentin shrugged.

"Like I said before, respect for the dead. Xander didn't want it known when he was alive. I suppose I didn't think I had the right to expose him once he was gone. I loved him." A disbelieving snort burst from Xander as he turned his back on Quentin in revulsion. "I'm sharing my story now, Katherine, because I'm getting old and there's no point in hiding it all anymore. To be honest, I think it's about time the world knew the truth about Xander. I've gone unacknowledged for too long."

"So, what happened?" I was warming to the story now. "Why did you stop seeing each other?"

"He scored his first lead role. Xander had just signed a three-picture deal with MGM when he came to me and said flat out that we couldn't see each other anymore."

"See," Xander spat from across the room, "I obviously came to my senses when I found out what a perverted cretin he was. Maybe he killed me for rejecting him." I was practised at ignoring him by now, so the comment barely registered.

"Did he give you a reason?"

"He said he'd been advised to distance himself by a director at the studio, someone who apparently knew about us and didn't think it was 'appropriate' for a popular and more specifically a straight actor to be spending the night regularly in the home of a *homosexual*."

"So that was it? He dumped you, just like that—without a thought?" Surreptitiously I shot a disapproving glare at Xander, who was still red-faced, fuming and now muttering *I was NOT a homosexual*, over and over.

"No, Katherine, he wasn't a bastard. He loved me and was upset, naturally. He said he understood it wasn't fair but that the studio was putting pressure on him. They did that back then—they still do." Quentin frowned. "It was important for his career, he couldn't risk everything for the sake of us and I understood that, I did. I didn't like it but that's the way things worked back then. If the studio told you to do something, you did it or you didn't work. Maybe you could argue if you were a big star, but Xander wasn't there yet."

"So, he just cut all contact?"

Quentin had started the interview in prima donna bitch mode but now he simply seemed tired, old and lonely. I found myself feeling sorry for him and I certainly couldn't picture him killing anyone.

"No, I saw him in secret, very late at night. He'd sneak over to my house or we'd meet somewhere, usually at a bar or a diner where nobody else in Hollywood would be caught dead. In the beginning I thought we could continue like that. Then he got involved with *her*." His lips pursed, pinching out the word as if it tasted horrid. A thrill coursed through me. I didn't even need to ask who 'her' was.

It was Xander who spoke first, in an urgent, hushed voice.

"Lola."

He was at my shoulder, leaning forward, a tight bundle of nerves. It was the first time he'd uttered her name. I repeated the name aloud for Quentin's benefit. Quentin nodded once, flaring his nostrils in distaste, his lips curled into the sneer he was famous for. The words came out slowly and emphatically.

"Yes, Lola. If it wasn't for that bitch—"

He didn't get to finish the sentence. Xander let out an almighty roar and launched himself across the room as if to tackle Quentin bodily from the couch. Of course—being non-corporeal—he dove straight through Quentin and the couch and the wall behind the couch, too.

It was too much for me to ignore this time and my reflexes reacted of their own accord. I screamed and grabbed at the couch either side of me, instantly regretting it and wishing I could reel the sound back into my mouth like you can do with the spool on a cassette when the tape has spilled out.

I needn't have worried. In the instant that I screamed, Quentin's face drained of colour and his hand was at his throat, eyes as wide as his facelift would allow, mouth hanging open.

"Quentin, are you alright?" I recovered and reached across the coffee table. My familiarity was unnoticed by him as he held his throat and stared at me. He expelled a short, sharp puff of breath and fanned his face, closing his eyes. Then he flushed, bright pink, the colour rushing back to his face as quickly as it had left.

My forehead creased. Had Quentin seen something? That would certainly complicate things. I was also more than a little concerned that Xander seemed to have completely disappeared into another part of the house. I expected him to come hurtling back through the wall at any second, on the attack.

"I'm fine, I'm fine," squeaked Quentin. "It was just a dizzy spell."

"You went so pale so quickly, you gave me such a fright." I hoped it explained away my reaction. I wasn't sure what I expected him to say next but I was hoping 'I'm feeling a little woozy because the ghost of my secret dead lover jumped through me' wouldn't figure into the conversation.

"Actually, I feel quite ill." His red-rimmed eyes watered and I noticed his hand shaking as he touched the handkerchief to his forehead. "Can we continue this another time? I'll let your editor know, we can reschedule. I still have so much to tell you, to show you, but I can't—" he trailed off as I reached for my bag and voice recorder.

"Yes, absolutely, of course." I was speaking way too fast and my heart was thumping in my chest. "Should I call someone for you?"

"No, it's fine, it's fine. I'll have Morag show you out. Wait here please."

Who the heck was Morag?

In the space of seconds, Quentin had hurried from the room and I was being ushered out of the house by Morag, who turned out to be a small angry-looking Scottish woman with tightly curled ginger hair and a lazy eye. She shut the door firmly behind me and I found myself outside the large double doors yet again, this time completely alone and harbouring a feeling not dissimilar to the one I used to feel after watching a *Melrose Place* cliff hanger.

As I called a cab and began the hike back up the long driveway, I also had absolutely no idea where Xander had disappeared to.

Bloody great!

A part from the sound of my hurried footsteps and matching breathing, the room back at *La Chateau* was disappointingly silent when I burst through the door. A million questions rattled in my head like lotto balls and I'd hoped to conveniently find Xander waiting for me. Not only was I poised and ready to rip into him about diving through Quentin (because clearly it was very rude) but, why did Quentin seem so convinced he was gay and secondly, did Xander remember Lola?

Quentin had simply said her name—okay, he'd also called her a bitch—but for Xander to react so violently, the memory of their relationship had to be fairly intact. If he didn't remember her, he wouldn't have cared, right? If Xander could answer the correct combination of questions, I'd be hitting the jackpot. Considering the luckiest I'd ever been was winning two dollars on an Instant Scratch-It, I didn't like my odds though.

"Hello? Xander. Are you here?"

My voice echoed in the emptiness. I'd honestly thought he'd return straight to the hotel. Where else could he have gone? Maybe he was mad I'd left him at the house? It's not like he'd needed a lift. What else was I supposed to do? He'd disappeared. For the second time that day. It had to be some kind of record, although what did I know? I was hardly an expert.

I waited, perched on the edge of the same chair he'd sat in earlier, one knee twitching up and down as I nibbled nervously on a fingernail. I half expected him to materialise in front of me, *whoosh*, and scare the hell out of me.

Twenty minutes ticked slowly past. Nothing. *Come on, Xander.* Where was he? Funny how a few hours ago I'd wanted him to go away. Eventually hunger pains and a vocal stomach drove me towards the door. I hadn't eaten since yesterday and, as I'd worn my coffee that morning, quite frankly I was starved and caffeine deprived. There was no point waiting around for him to reappear so I decided the best thing for me to do was engage in some overdue film research and grab a pizza.

I grabbed my purse and phone, thumbing the lumpy, ancient keypad to check for messages as I threw the door open and stepped blindly into the hall. Too late, I registered the vague outline of something big blocking my path before my vision swam, my arms and legs went all hot and fuzzy, and a blanket of nausea engulfed me. Off balance and disorientated I stopped dead, feet wide apart and arms splayed as I blinked rapidly and sucked back a mouthful of air. *What the—?*

"Are you okay?"

Xander's voice came from behind me but was compressed and distorted like he was underwater. I shook my head.

"Uurrghhh!" Did what I thought just happened actually just happen? I turned around, my vision clearing. Xander was standing between me and the doorway. "I walked through you, didn't I?" I managed to gurgle. My head was swimming and Xander peered anxiously at me.

"Yeah. Sorry about that."

"I feel sick."

"I think that's normal."

I'd recovered enough to shoot him a dirty look despite the fact I was relieved to see him.

"Do this often, do you? There is nothing remotely normal about the fact I walked through you, Xander. In fact, there's nothing normal about any of this. I mean, the popping in and out thing is doing my head in—you appear, you disappear, you appear and then you disappear again—and don't even get me started on that crap you pulled back at Quentin's house. That was unbelievably dumb, you know. You could have ruined everything. What were you thinking?" He shrugged and I planted my hands on my hips. "You don't know?" *Excellent.*

"He made me mad."

"Obviously."

"He said I was a homosexual."

"*Are* you a homosexual?"

"NO!"

"Are you sure?" I smirked and he glared at me. My hands shot up in surrender. "That's not what really made you mad though, was it?"

He scrunched his shoulders, clearly not ready to talk about it, so I sighed and tried an easier question. "Can you at least tell me what you were doing standing here outside the door? I've been worried."

"You have?" He glanced up again and grinned that grin— the lopsided one with the ridiculously cute dimples attached— and I consciously forced myself not to smile back. I glared instead and his face straightened. He cleared his throat. "I was trying to knock."

I stared at him, astonished.

"You were what?"

Slowly he repeated, "Trying to knock," and my eyes widened more.

"On the door?"

"Yes, on the door."

"But you're non-corporeal, Xander."

"I know that."

"How on earth can you knock on a door if you're non-corporeal, you idiot!" I was quickly discovering ghosts were able to do lots of alive-type things and the blush that furiously invaded Xander's cheeks was another one to add to the list.

"I'm not an idiot, thank you. I was thinking—since our visit to Quentin—I can obviously affect things in *some* way if I try hard enough. I made him ill. I just made you feel sick, didn't I? You can hear and see me. Something has changed. I thought I'd test it out, to see if I could touch something."

"How's that working out for you?" I arched an eyebrow. Xander shuffled his feet noncommittally. "No, I didn't think so." I inhaled ready to berate him again but stopped when I saw him peering at me sheepishly from underneath the fringe of floppy hair that hung over his eyes as he shoved his hands in his pockets again and kicked at the carpet with his toe.

A tiny smile flickered at the corners of my mouth before I could stop it, despite the fact I guessed it to be a well-practised look designed to get him out of all kinds of trouble. I wasn't letting him pull that one. I rolled my eyes in an exaggerated display to cover my amusement and quickly turned away, saying, "Forget it. We can talk about it later," as I stomped off down the hall. I stopped after a few paces when I realised he wasn't following, but didn't turn around. "Are you coming?" I feigned exasperation; glad he couldn't see my smirk.

"Where to?" His voice sounded small, like a little boy.

"How does dinner and a movie sound?"

Chapter Ten

An hour later Xander sat sulking in the armchair while I flopped on the floor munching happily on a slice of hot pizza, flicking through Netflix's movie catalogue on the in-house flat screen TV.

"This isn't exactly what I had in mind when you said dinner and a movie, you know."

"Sorry to disappoint you," I chuckled through a big mouthful. "But what did you think, that I was going to sit in a fancy restaurant with you like some loony loser, dining alone and talking to my imaginary friend?"

He wrinkled his nose disapprovingly at me.

"Didn't your parents teach you that it's bad manners to speak with your mouth full?"

I knew it was childish but I couldn't resist opening my mouth wide and sticking my tongue out. It was coated in mushed up dough and mozzarella cheese. Grinning at his disgusted face, I slowly and deliberately wiped my greasy fingers down the tracksuit pants I'd changed into, to add insult to injury. Xander shook his head as if I was a lost cause and kept talking.

"You could at least choose a movie I'd like to watch. Why would I want to watch my own movie, Katherine? I already know how it ends." He paused. "I think."

"This isn't a date," I said. "It's research. I still have a job to do remember. You're not giving me much to go on and I don't think watching *Jersey Girl* is going to help much either." I shook my head. "I can't believe that's your favourite movie. Seriously? Ben Affleck?" That man was haunting me.

I'd discovered while waiting for my pizza that one of the ways Xander passed the time over the last fifty years was sneaking unseen into cinemas. Not only was *Jersey Girl* Xander's favourite movie but he'd seen it six times. Here I was thinking it had gone straight to DVD.

"What? I happen to think Ben Affleck is a very talented actor. Extremely underrated."

"And very cute too, don't you think?" I said slyly.

"I AM NOT A HOMOSEXUAL, KATHERINE!"

"Okay, I'm kidding. Quentin must be making it all up."

"I have no idea why Quentin said those things. The man makes my skin crawl."

I stopped him.

"Xander, I know you're from a time when it wasn't really accepted. But things have changed. A lot. It's totally fine to be gay, or queer, or non-binary, gender-fluid, trans, or even completely asexual. Well, in most places anyway. Some places are still fairly horrible. Anyway, the point is, in civilised place, LGBTIQ+ people can even get married now. It's pretty great."

Xander stared at me.

"Now you're just trying to confuse me. Look, I have no idea what an LGBTIQ is or why we're talking about fluids," he shuddered involuntarily, "but if homosexuals want to be homosexuals, that's fine by me. I'm just saying I was most definitely not one. I can prove it." He gestured at me. "Take you for example. When I first saw you, I thought you were very attractive. If I was a homosexual I wouldn't have thought that, would I?"

My mind flashed back to my initial lusty thoughts about him and my cheeks burned. "Uh, I guess not," I stuttered. "Maybe you're bisexual. Hmm?"

"I am not. Of course, I've changed my mind about you now I know how bossy you are—"

"Very funny." Indignant, I threw a cushion at him and of course it sailed through him and bounced softly off the wall, coming to rest behind the couch. "I don't care, you're too young for me anyway."

"You're only a few years older than me."

"Younger is younger. I don't date younger men."

"Technically, I'm seventy-eight."

"Well, in that case, that's gross and a little too Anna Nicole Smith for me. No thanks. And what am I even talking about? You're not too young for me, Xander—you're too *dead* for me."

"That's not very nice. I was simply trying to make a point."

"Fine, whatever. It's great that you think I'm pretty," I flushed again and averted my eyes. "Just like it's nice that Ben Affleck floats your boat in whatever way you like but, if we can please get back to the topic at hand. I'm hoping watching your own movie might help jog your memory."

He frowned, dubious, and I clicked through to the landing page for *Chase the Wind*. I knew the film well, having seen it several times over the years. It was considered a cult classic, its popularity no doubt helped along by Xander's unfortunate demise and the love affair rumours surrounding the film. Nothing sells quite like a sex scandal.

The cover art was all glossy hair, shadows and tangled limbs, pretty raunchy even for the Seventies. Xander hunched into himself, uncomfortable as he stared at the TV.

"You mean jog my memories of Lola?" he asked and I nodded.

"What *do* you remember? It had better be something good for me to forgive you going all Patrick Swayze on Quentin." Xander's forehead wrinkled slightly and he shrugged, a blank look on his face. I found it unbelievably ironic that the one movie he hadn't seen was *Ghost*. I shook my head, smiling. "Never mind."

He surprised me then by sliding down out of the chair onto the rug where he arranged his lanky frame to sit facing me, cross-legged.

"Don't get too excited," he said. "I don't remember much. I mean I think there's far more I'm not remembering if that makes sense." My heart did a Flipper-worthy nose dive. I wasn't getting anywhere at this rate. I gritted my teeth and smiled encouragingly at Xander.

"I doesn't make that much sense, but I'm all ears regardless."

He leaned on his knees, inhaled and steepled his long fingers against his lips.

"I remember feelings mostly, lots of emotions, flashes of images, snatches of conversations out of context, the same as a lot of my other memories. My memories of her feel different though, like I know she's important somehow. I—I think I loved her."

"You *think* you loved her?" I was more than puzzled. "You mean you don't remember what your relationship was? You do know you were supposedly having a relationship with her at least?"

"No. I know we worked together. I remember running

scenes and filming but when I think of her, there's this over-whelming sense of attachment. I can only describe it as love."

"Everyone thought you were having an affair," I said bluntly.

"Is that what it is?" He seemed perplexed. "I don't know. That doesn't feel right somehow."

"What do you mean?"

Xander's eyes squeezed tightly shut, brows knitted as if trying to force the memory into its rightful place like a jigsaw puzzle piece from the wrong box.

"I'm not sure. I'm sorry. It's not only love I remember. There's so much sadness and anger—a lot of anger. But, I remember her kissing me once. Passionately. It must have been for a scene we were filming and it felt wrong—horrible." His mouth twisted and tugged down at one side, hands flat on the side of his face, fingers rubbing at his temples.

He looked up suddenly and his eyes were red, tears threatening to spill. "She's still alive, isn't she?" I nodded but didn't elaborate. "I've been to her home since I died. At least I think it's her home. It has to be. I find myself there sometimes, standing outside for hours—wanting to go in—knowing there's someone inside I want to see."

"But not knowing why?"

He shook his head. "I didn't even remember her name until today. Something Quentin said, it triggered some memories. Now I know it's her house. It has to be. I'm drawn there, but I can't go in."

"Why?"

"Something's blocking me, like an invisible wall." He shrugged then fell silent. I left him to his thoughts. It wasn't much to go on but at least it showed there was something between them. Although, if it was a love affair, it sounded like a pretty dysfunctional one.

"Xander, what about the bits of conversation you do remember? Even if they're out of context they might tell me something. What about the fight? You were seen fighting with her before you died. Did you know that?"

He nodded and his hands shook almost imperceptibly. When he did speak his voice was strained.

"I think I remember that. It was here, in this hotel?"

I tried not to hold my breath as he paused, wrestling with whatever memory was clawing its way out of his head.

"What was the fight about?"

"I don't know. All I remember is her crying and screaming at me to leave her alone, to stop harassing her."

"And you were angry—" I said quietly.

"Of course I was angry. You have no idea how it feels to be told by someone that they want nothing to do with you."

That's where you're wrong. I half-smiled, reflecting, but didn't speak. Xander needed me to listen. He was talking about anger but all I saw was hurt. For the first time I wished I could put my hand on his arm to comfort him. But what was the point if he couldn't feel it?

I'm so sorry." I felt completely ineffectual. He nodded, staring intently at the intricate pattern formed by the parquetry. We sat in silence as the minutes ticked by. Eventually Xander took a deep breath.

"There's something else I remember now." His head stayed bowed and he glanced up at me past lowered eyebrows. His eyes were flat and hard and the irises deeper, almost black. Unexpected prickles skittered up the back of my neck.

"Okay," I answered tentatively.

"There was money, a lot of money. She threw it at me." He scowled. "It was dark and I was standing outside in the rain. She was crying and she threw a wad of bills at me, saying she never wanted to lay eyes on me again.

"Why was she giving you money?" I frowned, puzzled.

"I honestly don't remember anything more than that, I'm sorry. I don't know what it was for. All I remember is being furious and feeling like I'd been kicked in the guts. Then she closed the door in my face. That's the very last thing I remember."

I was wide-eyed suddenly.

"You mean—?"

"Yes, Katherine. The last thing I remember before I died."

My pulse pummelled my skin as the tantalising thrill of his story sank in. I was ashamed to say I was having another one of those insensitive moments where excitement mingled with frustration and sympathy all at the same time. Nobody else knows this stuff. Nobody. My brain shifted into cheerleader mode, doing cartwheels and yelling triumphantly '*Gimme an S, gimme a C, gimme an O-O-P!*'

"So, she could have killed you," I blurted out. Lola was definitely a suspect in my books.

"No!"

"Why not?" I worried at the theory like a dog on a chew toy. "Come on Xander, you have to remember more than that. You're so close. Think." My voice raised half an octave and my hands took on a life of their own, flapping around. "She *might* have killed you. She was the last person to see you, and she obviously wasn't very happy with you." He flinched at that but I continued on oblivious, waving my hypotheses like pom poms.

"Was she paying you to go away? Or to shut you up about something? Was she your sugar-mummy and you needed money for new clothes? Ooh—maybe you had a drug problem." I was running out of ideas and the lack of forthcoming info was starting to infuriate me. The truth was dangling right in front of me, like a carrot, just out of reach and Xander was staring uselessly at the floor.

An irritated rush of air rumbled sonorously out of my throat. Xander lifted his head sharply from where it had been resting in his hands, clumps of hair sticking through clenched fingers.

"I don't remember! I'm sorry. I wish I could tell you more, I do."

I slumped back against the chair and sat silent for a few moments before finally sighing with resignation.

"It doesn't matter, Xander. If that's all you remember that's all you remember. It's more than I knew in the first place so at least we got somewhere."

"For the record, I don't think I had a drug problem," he said. "I don't even know what a sugar-mummy is so that's doubtful. I think it's much more likely she was simply paying me to go away. She was married and a big star. It didn't pay to have some young upstart hanging around causing trouble."

"I don't know Xander, I get the feeling it might have been more than that."

"Either way, I don't think she would have killed me. She probably didn't care enough to actually want me dead. She wanted me to go away, that's all."

"Okay, fair enough." There was a brief silence and I glanced away, at the image on the television screen. "Well, maybe we'll both have some answers soon."

"What do you mean?"

I'd completely forgotten Xander didn't know about Lola's moonlight cemetery visits. I pulled a figurative hamstring trying to remove my foot from my big mouth. I briefly considered sugar-coating it but, as my dad always said—direct is best. I squared my shoulders and met his gaze.

"Xander, there's every possibility I might see Lola sometime in the next few days."

"What?" The revelation didn't sit well. His eyes widened

and his nostrils flared. He sat to attention, his back poker straight.

"I'm waiting on a call to confirm it, but I'm pretty sure she's going to visit your grave. I'm going to try to speak to her."

He grimaced at the word *grave.*

"Why would she visit my grave, especially after all this time? She hated me."

It was my turn to shrug.

"Perhaps she feels bad. Come with me and you'll see her. Maybe you'll find out. Maybe we'll both find out."

He shook his head.

"I can't."

"Can't what? Come with me?"

"I can come with you but I don't think I can go into the cemetery."

"Oh," I frowned, "is it that weird energy blocking thing again?" Maybe it was an after-life rule—'must not go within fifty feet of own grave.' Xander shot me another one of those *are you really that stupid* looks, that I was beginning to know well.

"No. It makes me feel uncomfortable. How do you put it? It freaks me out. It's creepy. Why on earth would I want to go near where I'm buried?"

He shuddered and I started to laugh.

"Are you serious? You're a ghost and you're scared of the graveyard."

"I'm not scared. It's weird. That's my dead body you know."

I snorted. It was too hilarious for words.

"It's not funny," Xander pouted.

"I'm sorry Xander, but it is." I tried to compose myself and picked up the TV remote again. "How about you come with me when it's time and we'll see what happens, okay? I won't make you go in if you don't want to, but I think it's important that you come."

His eyes followed me apprehensively.

"And Lola will be there, in person?"

"I'm hoping so."

He paused before quietly agreeing, then he glanced at the remote poised in my hand.

"Katherine, I don't think I'm in the mood to watch a film now to be honest."

I turned away and pointed the remote at the TV, quickly hitting a few menus buttons and wiggling my eyebrows suggestively.

"Not even for Ben Affleck?" I'd figured I could get over my issue with Ben just this once. It was for a good cause after all.

Xander took in the title that flicked up on the screen and chuckled.

"*Jersey Girl*!"

"Yup... *Jersey Girl*." I winked at him, "It's either that or I educate you with *Ghost*." Xander surprised me by playfully poking his tongue out.

"I think one ghost in this room is more than enough to handle for the moment, don't you?" He grinned happily, a different person suddenly as he relaxed back against the chair.

This time I didn't hesitate. I grinned right back.

6 am. I was already awake, staring at the ceiling, tossing and turning, kicking the sheet around as though getting more comfortable would in any way stop my brain relentlessly ticking over. It was useless. There was nothing else to do but get up.

My lack of proper evidence surrounding Xander's murder had weighed heavily on me for days. It didn't help that my source list read like the cast of a Jerry Springer show —*sexy ghost, check; over-the-hill gay gossip columnist, check;* and hope-fully, *reclusive and apparently nutty movie star.* That list alone was unlikely to inspire confidence in the veracity of my story.

If I was going to somehow make this story work, I needed to get my facts straight about the entire investigation. I needed to know who all the suspects were, how the police ruled people out, what evidence they found. Exactly how advanced was forensics back then? I also wanted to know why Xander didn't appear to have a life before Hollywood.

I hadn't relied on my investigative skills or fact-checking ability since I started working for the magazine, to be honest. As a result, both were more than a little rusty. I wasn't going be able to fall back on the trusty old 'a source close to such and such', so I was going to have to put in the work. It had also been an age since I'd taken advantage of Freedom of Information laws for a story. I wasn't even sure whether they had the same thing in the States.

It all sounded like far too much effort and paperwork. There had to be a better way. In fact, I knew there was. I found myself perched on the edge of the bed, staring at the hotel tele-phone. I'd picked the handset up twice, only to replace it in the cradle almost instantly. This was not a phone call I wanted to make.

At least I didn't have a witness to my indecisiveness. Xander had disappeared the night before, right at the part in *Jersey Girl* where Ben Affleck was about to kiss Liv Tyler for the first time. He'd suddenly reappeared again for a few seconds before the end of the movie, standing right in front of the TV and making me drop my peanut M&Ms.

Then he'd done this weird dissolving slowly thing, staring me straight in the eyes with a resigned expression on his face, until he was completely gone. It left me feeling quite rattled. He hadn't come back yet and I was partly relieved. The thought of him sitting there all night watching me sleep was spooky.

Telling myself the end result would be worth the pain, I finally grabbed the phone and asked the concierge to put me through to Apartment Four before I could change my mind. I fought the urge to hang up as it rang and steeled myself as the person on the other end picked up with a bright '*Helloooo*?'

"Marjorie." I plastered a fake smile on my face, remembering a radio jock friend of mine telling me that you could *hear* a smile. "It's Katherine Alley."

The squeal on the other end of the line nearly perforated my ear drum and I yanked the receiver away from my ear.

"Oh my god, Katherine, how *are* you?" She immediately shifted into top gear. "Are you having a wonderful time? Have you interviewed anybody famous yet? How's your story coming along?" She paused, breathless from the barrage of questions and I laughed despite myself.

"If I answer those in order Marjorie—good, yes, yes and actually my story is the reason I'm calling. I think you might be able to help me out with something." This time I anticipated the squeal and held the phone away in time. I half expected the mirror in my room to crack and for dogs down the block to start howling.

"Oh my gosh, really?" She squeaked, so tightly wound I thought she might pop. "What on earth can I help with?"

I crossed my fingers.

"Marjorie, am I right in remembering your son works for the LAPD?

Chapter Eleven

The LAPD precinct in Downtown Hollywood buzzed with activity; harried officers yelling names, files passing from hand to hand. An eclectic panoply of faces lined the benches in the front lobby area, waiting to be seen. Despite the crowded space, the reception area was surprisingly chilly, especially after the heat of the street outside. The air-con must have been doing double duty. I shivered as I jostled my way to the desk, caught the eye of a dour blonde female officer and asked for Detective Brent.

It was clearly an imposition. She huffed then reluctantly showed me down a short corridor to an inner office, shooting me sideways glances as she walked. The wall panels were paper thin and shook as we passed them. We stopped outside a frosted glass door and I heard the tail end of Marjorie's unmistakable voice saying, 'Don't worry, son, I'm sure they don't think you're useless, it's probably because you're new,' and a deeper voice replying, 'Mum, I've been here five years.'

The blonde officer snapped her chewing gum and threw the door open without knocking. I was really hoping Marjorie's son would be a cross between Jimmy Smits and Christopher Meloni. Unfortunately, Detective Brent was unmistakably Marjorie's offspring, only taller and a little bit fatter, with a thicker moustache.

I caught Marjorie licking a palm and flattening her son's thinning hair as he clumsily attempted to wrangle his tie with fingers that were too big for the job. His white shirt strained at the buttons and damp patches circled his underarms. Two pink and plump faces swivelled my way, one decorated with a wide, excited grin and the other wearing the most unbecoming flush of purple embarrassment I think I'd ever witnessed.

"Katherine!" Marjorie shrieked, waddling towards me with arms out like a long-lost aunt. I succumbed to the squeeze. She was liberally doused in some kind of floral talcum powder and it puffed up my nose as I smiled self-consciously at Detective Brent over her ample shoulder.

"Mum, please!" He sighed heavily. "This is my place of work. Do you have to yell like a banshee?" Marjorie released me and rounded on him, hands on hips.

"Do you have to speak to your mother like that, Mr High-and-mighty-I-live-in-LA-now. Hmm? You're not so special I can't still give you a good clip round the ear you know." She punctuated her point by firmly folding her arms with a huff and turning back to me. "This," she jerked her lacquered bouffant sideways at him, "in case you haven't cottoned on, is my rude and ungrateful son."

Still an alarming shade of purple, he wiped his hand on his pants and shoved it at me. "Detective Brent, nice to meet you. Ms. Alley. Mum's told me all about you. You seem to have made quite an impression on her."

I shook his hot, clammy hand and started to mutter something self-deprecating but before I could utter a complete sentence, Marjorie blustered at him.

"Oh, la-di-da, what's with the formality, you big goose?"
She turned to me, lips pursed, head bobbling with disapproval.
"It's Barry. You can call him Barry. And Barry, this is Katherine
—you don't mind if he calls you Katherine, do you? There,
now we're all best friends." She smiled, glancing with expecta-
tion back and forth between the two of us. I laughed nervously
and Barry shuffled his feet. Several uncomfortable seconds
ticked past. Finally—

"So, Mum says you're hunting for information on an old
murder case. An actor I believe? Xander Hill? Never heard of
him myself, I'm not really interested in all that entertainment
rubbish. But, I managed to locate the case file in our archives."

"Yes, that's right." I was glad to be straight down to business. "Xander Hill. I'm writing a story on him. You know, fifty
years on, a bit of a retrospective, but I thought some background information on the case might be interesting." I crossed
my fingers behind my back against the tiny white lie. "Is that
possible?"

Barry motioned for us to sit as he strode purposefully
around the large wooden desk, sat down and opened a red
manila folder. His eyes flickered over the first page then he
leaned back in his swivel chair, clasping his hands behind his
head and blowing out a thin, whistling breath.

"I must tell you, this is a very old case, Katherine. A *very* old
case." He leaned forward, quickly tapping his sausagey fingers
rhythmically on the folder. "And, being as yet unsolved, I'm not
even entirely sure I can give you any of this information."

Great. Then he startled me by winking and slamming both
hands on the desktop with a loud belly laugh. "Nah, just
kidding, Katherine. Bloody hell, this case is colder than the
iceberg that took down the Titanic."

"Oh, Barry," Marjorie clucked in disapproval. Bewildered, I
frowned at him.

"So, can I see it or not?"

Barry's face straightened a touch.

"Technically, no. Not officially anyway. Not without going through a bunch of red tape." He lowered his voice to a theatrical whisper. "But, Mum said you just need basic information so, I won't tell if you won't." He stopped whispering and shrugged. "Not that there's much here to be honest." He tapped the folder again.

"What do you mean?" Confused by the rapid turns in the conversation, I was certain I'd misunderstood. "Is that it? How can you hold records for an entire murder case in one folder? That can't be right."

"Are you sure you've got the right folder, Barry?" Marjorie interjected. He threw her a look that clearly said *shut up Mum*.

"Sorry Katherine, this is it. Some transcripts and basic paperwork. Unless there's more stored in archives somewhere but if there is, it doesn't show up in computer records. All the old archived stuff is entered in and has a search code. I didn't find anything. I've been through this thoroughly and if you ask me, it was a bit of a half-arsed investigation."

"In what way?"

"Yes, get to the point Barry." Marjorie shifted from cheek to cheek in her chair, excited by the mounting drama. This time Barry ignored her, cleared his throat and passed me the documents.

"There were three initial suspects listed but the officers on the case didn't manage to locate a single witness to the actual crime, although that's not unusual. The only people interviewed were the suspects themselves and a couple of people who were witness to certain events that took place in the lead up to the crime. Even that information is fairly sparse. If I didn't know better, I'd say they simply couldn't be bothered."

"So, when you say events, Barry," I asked, trying to make

sense of the papers in front of me, "What kind of events do you mean?"

"Okay, well, look here." He turned the folder slightly and pointed to a passage of text. "There was an altercation with a Mrs Tennant at the Chateau Marmont." I nodded, indicating I knew all about that. "And there was some kind of stalker incident about a week before that, out at MGM Studios, involving a woman, a crazed fan, being thrown off the lot."

"A fan of Xander's you mean?"

"It seems so. The woman, a Mrs Temperance Martinez, got a bit too close and was causing some trouble. It turned ugly by all accounts so she was definitely a suspect."

"I've never heard about that."

"There's not much here. Apparently, she'd been following him around; too many bloody crazies in this town, I tell you. This one was under the delusion she was his wife." Barry chuckled, dismissing the information but I glanced up sharply.

"His wife? But Xander wasn't married."

Barry shook his head. "Hence the crazy. There are a lot of nutty people in LA, Katherine. You have no idea. Belie-eeve me. Nice fantasy though, I mean who wouldn't want to be married to a movie star."

I raised an eyebrow at him. Not me. And not to that one.

"So, why was she ruled out?"

"Says right there, she couldn't have done it because she was in the County Hospital psychiatric ward. Nervous breakdown."

"Oh, poor woman."

Barry shrugged as if it didn't matter, but the crazy stalker not-wife didn't sit well with me. Instinct told me not to dismiss her but it had been so long since I'd allowed myself to trust my instincts, I wasn't sure if I was seeing something that wasn't there simply because I wanted to. Either way, I moved reluctantly to the next page and another name I didn't recognise.

"Who's Jean Wittle?"

"Jean who?'

"Wittle."

I pass him several sheets of paper, held together loosely with a rusted paper clip. He shrugged and flipped through the pages.

"A secretary, it says here. She worked for a Zachariah Tennant." Realisation crossed his face. "Who, I'm presuming is the husband of the Mrs. Tennant that Mr. Hill had the afore-mentioned altercation with. Ah-ha!"

"Ah-ha what?"

"Well, there's obviously some kind of connection there."

I laughed.

"Finely tuned powers of deduction you have there, Barry." How on earth he got to be a detective was beyond me. I was about to give him the *"Hollywood Scandal for Dummies"* rundown when Marjorie saved me the trouble.

"Well, d'uh Barry. Where have you been all your life, under Ayers Rock? How are you supposed to help Katherine properly if you don't even know the story? Typical, just like your father, you don't know your bloody arse from your elbow." She rolled her eyes and took a big breath. "Okay, listen carefully. Xander Hill was supposed to be having a juicy affair with Lola Tennant, who was his co-star, even though she was much older than him, which is disgusting if you ask me. I don't like all this cougar business, never have, it's not natural. Are you following me?"

Barry's left eye twitched as she inhaled another big breath. "Anyway, they were seen having a huge fight at Chateau Marmont the night he was murdered. Some say she called off the affair but he wouldn't leave her alone, so she killed him to get rid of him. Others say her husband killed him in a jealous rage, which would be understandable of course, I mean I'd hope your Dad— god love him— in the same situation would have been so blinded with jealousy that he'd have done that for me."

"Off track, Mum," Barry tutted.

"Well, the police couldn't prove anything because of all the alibis and the like so nobody was ever charged. Nobody! And then the whole thing was dropped. Very strange if you ask me." Marjorie folded her arms at Barry. "See, I know the story."

I stifled a smirk as Barry went purple with indignation again.

"That's because you read those ridiculous gossip magazines, Mum."

"Ahem," Marjorie flicked her arched eyebrow in my direction and Barry flushed an even deeper shade of beetroot. I thought his head was going to pop.

"No offence, Katherine."

"None taken." I had to bite my lip to stop myself laughing.

"Well, then," Barry stammered as he searched the desk for a pen, avoiding my eyes. "I guess I'm up to speed now, aren't I? Thanks Mum. Okay, now where were we?" He shuffled the pages. "Oh, Jean Wittle, secretary to Mr. Tennant—"

"Yes, that's right," I glanced with amusement at Marjorie who'd already switched her attention to the handbag in her lap and was busy touching up her vivid orange lipstick.

"Right, Ms. Wittle observed a visit to Mr. Tennant's office by one Xander Hill. It resulted in—and I quote—*'lots of banging and yelling for around five minutes before an extremely agitated Mr Hill exited the office in a hurry'*. She states that she couldn't hear what the argument was about but that Mr. Tennant also left soon after, saying he wouldn't be back."

"Well, it doesn't take a genius to work out what they were arguing about." I frowned. "It must have been about Lola."

Barry rubbed at his chin, fleshy jowls shifting up and down like dough being rolled under the pressure of his fingers.

"Xander Hill seemed to have pissed a lot of people off if you ask me—pardon my French, Katherine," he said apologetically, more due to Marjorie's immediate clucking than my delicate sensibilities. I nodded absently, leafing through the remaining pages.

"That he did, Barry, that he did."

Marjorie chimed in, voicing the inconsistency that had nagged at me from day one.

"It's funny, I always got the impression Xander Hill was a nice boy. You know, a clean cut, good-looking, farm boy. That's how he came across. Polite—the kind of boy who'd be good to his mother, that kind of thing. He liked women clearly, but that doesn't make you a bad person does it? Anyway, he can't have been well-liked if this kind of thing was going on behind the scenes." She paused, shaking her head. "I suppose you can never believe all that celebrity hoo-ha. No offence Katherine, but famous people aren't always what they seem, are they?"

With that proclamation she reached into her bag again, pulled out her cell phone and started swiping frenetically, the intricacies of police work obviously not holding her interest enough to keep her from a game of *Fruit Ninja*.

I smiled. Wisdom popped up in the most unlikely places. It was true, I didn't know Xander at all, ironically even with access to the real thing. He was utterly inconsistent. Nothing made sense, least of all the contents of the red folder.

"So, let me get this straight," I turned my attention back to Barry, "the main suspects were Lola and Zach Tennant and the crazy stalker lady? The police interviewed all three of them, plus the secretary. That's it?"

"Looks like it."

"And they were all cleared, just like that?"

"Yes. Any evidence was circumstantial at best and they each had an alibi, although the Tennants' alibi was that they were with each other."

"Each other? That'd never be taken seriously, would it?"

I was rewarded with another shrug.

"They didn't question Quentin Millson at all?"

"Who?"

"The gossip columnist. Quentin Millson."

Barry scanned a couple of pages.

"No. Why would they have questioned him?"

I paused, not wanting to say too much, then fudged a little, saying vaguely, "Well, he knew stuff about everyone back then. He might have known something, heard something, maybe?"

Barry shot a withering look in my direction.

"The LAPD doesn't solve their cases with gossip, Katherine."

"You did say, in your opinion, it was a half-arsed investigation," I tossed back.

"I meant in terms of actual hard evidence." He spread out the remaining contents of the folder. "There's minimal evidence from the actual crime scene, there's paperwork here that hasn't even been completely filled out and even a new recruit could see the forensic report is incomplete."

"How does that happen? I thought you guys were supposed to write all kinds of reports and statements and stuff. Isn't there paperwork you need to fill out to say you've filled out paperwork? I don't understand how a murder investigation can have so much missing."

Barry shrugged again. He was going to get RSI of the shoulders if he didn't watch himself.

"Neither do I. It wouldn't happen now, but I have no idea how stringent paperwork procedures were fifty years ago. I'm not exactly an expert on 1970's police work. I'm seeing numerous blank spaces and the words 'insufficient evidence' repeated a lot."

"So, what *do* we have?" I huffed. "Anything?"

Barry ran his finger down the last page.

"No weapon located at the scene. No footprints either. Single set of tyre marks. It's noted that heavy rainfall seems to have washed the site clean; that's helpful. There's no written entry for whether gunshot residue was found on the victim's body, which is unusual, but traces were found on the interior of the vehicle. Not on the exterior however."

"So, what does that mean?"

"That means the shooter likely had his—or her—hand inside the open window when they fired the gun. Mr. Hill was shot at close range so it makes sense."

"Actually inside the car though? That's not close range, that's bordering on intimate. So why didn't they test the body for gunpowder?" I crinkled my nose at the word *body*. It felt weird to say, considering Xander was technically still around.

"Maybe the investigating officers thought it was redundant, considering they knew he'd been shot at close range. There would definitely have been traces on the body. Normally you'd still run the tests, look at the amount and pattern. That tells you more about what you're dealing with.

"I see what you mean about half-arsed. What else came up in forensics?"

"Nothing."

"Nothing? Aren't there heaps of forensic tests in a murder case? Or had they not been, I don't know, invented yet?"

"That's the strange thing. Los Angeles had the very first police crime lab in the United States; it was set up as far back as the 1920's. It's extremely odd that they didn't run all the tests under the sun in a case as high profile as this. Katherine, there wasn't even an autopsy ordered."

"I think the cause of death was pretty obvious, don't you?" I laughed.

"An autopsy doesn't only tell you the cause of death. Even back then, it would have ascertained the angle of the bullet entering the body, which tells you where the shooter was standing, even the height of the shooter. They could have found fibres or hairs on the body, possibly fluids." *Urgh, fluids.* I shuddered as Barry continued. "An autopsy tells the story of how a person died or in this case, was killed."

"What kind of police officer closes a murder case without gathering all the information?"

Barry mused for a few seconds. "I would say a police officer who had a reason for not wanting to solve the case."

I slapped my hand down on the table.

"Or a police officer who'd been coerced by someone to make the case go away?"

He smiled tersely, following my train of thought. "That's what I'm thinking."

My mind raced. Who would have had the influence and the money to bury a murder case? Quentin? Zach Tennant?

"Can we find out who was assigned to the case? Maybe speak to them?"

Barry tapped on the folder. "That's easy, their names are right here on the paperwork. Detectives Daniel Reisemann and Peter Croft. It's possible these officers aren't even still alive, Katherine. Remember, the case is fifty years old."

I waved my hand at him to backtrack. "Hang on. Daniel Reisemann? That name sounds familiar."

Barry frowned. "I can't see how you would know of him, he's a Los Angeles police officer, not even decorated." Then Marjorie piped up without taking her eyes off her game, showing she'd clearly been listening intently all along.

"There was an actor called Danny Reisemann back in the

mid-Seventies, I'm sure there was. Only made a few movies, bit parts mainly. Then again, I could be wrong."

I could kiss her and her encyclopaedic movie knowledge.

"Yes, I'm sure that's it. Could it be the same person?"

Barry made a *pffft* sound.

"I doubt it. Police detectives don't usually run off to become movie stars."

"Why not?" interjected Marjorie pointedly, "Ronald Reagan was an actor and he became President."

"That's not the same, Mum."

I leaned forward, excited. "Is there a way we can we check? Just in case."

Barry leaned back in his chair again and studied me. "Katherine, I'm getting the impression that what you're writing is more than a historical article. Is there something you're not telling me?"

Shit. I bit my lip. Marjorie lowered her phone and fixed Barry with a stern glare.

"Don't be silly Barry. It's not like Katherine is trying to solve the murder case, is it now?" She chuckled, shaking her head, and resumed her game. I met Barry's eyes and scrunched my nose.

"Well, actually—"

Marjorie gasped before Barry could say a word.

"Oh, my word! That's so terribly exciting—and so brave, Katherine. You'll be like that television show—*Castle*—with the writer and the police woman except clearly Barry isn't a woman. Maybe he can give you a badge. Barry? Can you give Katherine a badge?"

She clasped her hands, laughing, and I smiled but I was still looking at Barry. He was studying me intently and I braced myself to be kicked out or given some spiel about civilians having no business sticking their noses into police business. At the very least, I expected him to take back the red manila folder. I was tempted to make a grab for it and run, but didn't.

Barry didn't kick me out. He pressed his fingers together under his pudgy chin and narrowed his eyes. "I'll make you a deal," he said finally and I nodded, a little apprehensive. "I'll give you the information you need, if you let me know anything you find out. Keep me in the loop. I'm not convinced you're going to find what you need with so little to go on but, on the off-chance you do, I'd like to be able to take some of the credit."

I breathed a sigh of relief. "Of course, Barry. I can do that."

He joined his hands behind his head and smiled, wolfishly. "Okay. Then we'll see how useless the guys here at the precinct think I am." He winked and I smiled back with a hint of trepidation. What was I getting myself into? With that, Barry went all cowboy on me, swivelling dramatically towards his computer and drawling with a bad American accent. "Ah guess we'd bettah see if these gahs are still kickin'—"

I stifled a snort and held my breath as Barry typed, his pudgy fingers moving surprisingly quickly. "Sorry ladies," he suddenly banged the keyboard with his right hand for emphasis. "Detective Daniel Reisemann is not your movie guy, going by what's in the system. He was with the police force right up until he retired in 1984 and I'm sorry to say is now deceased. He died in 1991, aged 72. Heart attack."

There goes that lead. Surely it was too coincidental to not mean something, damn it. I wasn't giving up that easily.

"What about his partner, what was his name? Croft?"

"Let me see." More typing and clicking. "Peter Croft. Only retired from the force in 1995. He must have been a rookie on this case, like nineteen or twenty years old."

"So, he's still alive?"

"Looks like it."

"Well, he'd have to know something more about the case, wouldn't he? I have to talk to him."

"Alright. I'll see if I can get an address for you. I think this is about all we can do today. How about I copy this and meet you outside in a bit. Then I'll leave it with you."

I could barely contain my excitement. Finally, the possibility of something more concrete to go on. I headed for the door with Marjorie in tow as Barry went off in search of the photocopier. The air outside was hot and humid and the late afternoon sun washed across the cars that lined Wilcox Avenue. The heat of the pavement burned through the soles of my shoes and it took a few seconds for my eyes to adjust to the glare and for my skin to warm after the sub-zero temperature inside.

Marjorie chattered away beside me but I had trouble paying attention because of the questions racing around my brain. I made generic *mm-hhm* noises so she didn't think me rude but really, I was thinking about non-existent autopsies and stalkers and actor-detectives and gay actors who didn't think they were gay and how I needed to speak to Quentin again—soon.

"When do you think would be convenient, dear?" Marjorie stopped walking suddenly and looked up at me. I had no idea what she was talking about.

"Ummm—" Luckily my phone beeped loudly in my pocket, saving me from being caught out. "Sorry Marjorie," I shrugged apologetically, "hold that thought."

It was a text message from Leon. It simply read, *Tonight. 8 o'clock.*

Butterflies surged in my belly. This was getting real. A nervous thrill chased its way up my back but I couldn't help smiling as I flipped the phone shut. What on earth was I going to say to Lola? I scanned the other side of the street absently as I ran through possible scenarios, then fixed my eyes on a single figure standing motionless in between a blue sports car and a white pick-up truck, hands in pockets, staring intently at me.

Xander.

I smiled instinctively, and I lifted my hand to wave, but something in his face made me hesitate. His expression could only be described as malevolent. I don't think I'd understood the meaning of that word until now. Let me describe it. It's a mixture of anger and spite and hate and black roiling energy and at that moment it was coiled up inside Xander as he glared at me from across the street.

It startled me and my hand dropped. I froze and couldn't do anything but stare back at him, a gnawing confusion in my gut. All sound was sucked away as though I was caught in a vacuum filled with only the rushing thump of my heartbeat. We faced off in silence for three, four, five seconds and I couldn't help but be frightened. And then— before I could move or say anything—he shimmered and was gone.

It took me a moment to register that Marjorie was tapping me on the arm with an extremely worried look on her face. Barry was crowding in behind her, clearly concerned. The clamour of the street whooshed back and I gasped a big mouthful of air, my focus returning.

"Are you okay, Katherine? You've gone quite pale," Marjorie clutched my arm.

I nodded.

"You look like you've seen a ghost," added Barry, tentatively patting my other arm as he held out a thick yellow envelope with a sticky note attached.

I blinked at him.

"I'm fine." I took the envelope, my hand shaking. "Thank you for this. I'll call you if I find out anything or if I need anything else."

"No worries," he glanced anxiously at Marjorie who was

still fussing around me. "The address you need is on the post-it."

"Great." I turned to his mother. "Marjorie, I'm fine. I think I had a dizzy spell coming from the air-conditioning into the heat, that's all."

She folded her arms and eyed me suspiciously.

"Well, okay then—if you're sure. You can't blame me for mothering. It's what I do, right Barry?" I touched her pudgy arm in thanks and she smiled. "So, you'll think about that interview and get back to me?" she asked, the worry clearly over. It clicked. That's what she was talking about.

I tucked the big envelope into my bag, avoiding her eyes.

"Sure, Marjorie. Of course."

"Great." She beamed. "That's really great. I'm so pleased. In the meantime, do you have any other clues? Anyone else exciting to talk to?"

There was no way I was telling her about Lola or the cemetery. The mere idea of it would make her beehive explode. And knowing her, she'd want to come with me. The last thing I needed tonight was a side-kick tagging along. I didn't know when Xander was going to show up again. Or if he was going to show up at all. Or, considering what just happened, which one of his personalities I was going to get.

Chapter Twelve

Cemeteries are usually hushed and tranquil but, as the cab left me standing at the entrance to the Westwood Village Memorial Park in rapidly approaching twilight, the clatter and buzz that is Los Angeles enveloped me.

Granted, it was somewhat muted, as if the high-rises lining Wilshire Boulevard and overshadowing the park had lowered their voices, but it wasn't likely to be out of respect for the dead. It was more likely to be in quiet awe of the dead's collective star status.

It was ironic that the AVCO theatre complex on Wilshire was mere steps away. Throngs of movie-goers and tourists lined up day after day; fat mid-westerners with loud voices, gaggles of excited Japanese teenagers and other assorted travelling clichés, cameras in hand, all eager for a brush with fame.

Every one of them was completely unaware that, while they gazed up at the latest blockbuster on the screen, a who's-who of Hollywood royalty were taking the big dirt nap mere metres away. I glanced at the dimly lit cemetery map, posted inside the entrance, and then back at the dark green expanse of neatly clipped grass in front of me. It was dotted in a seemingly haphazard fashion with trees of varying sizes and shapes and a multitude of shining plaques.

A broad road circled the main lawn, lined with crypts and headstones. According to the map, Xander's grave was situated diagonally opposite, in the far corner. As I considered whether to follow the road left or right, apprehension slithered up my spine and coiled heavily around my shoulders. I shivered.

Normally cemeteries didn't bother me. Generally, I found them fascinating and peaceful, not even remotely scary. I even have a favourite back home in Sydney; Waverley Cemetery, found about half way along the meandering and picturesque coastal walk between Bondi and Coogee.

Since the late 1800's, it has perched on the edge of a wide, arcing bluff at the top end of Bronte, jutting out over an expanse of dark-blue sea with a massive drop off to the scruffy peaks of the Pacific Ocean and the jagged rocks below. It couldn't be more different to where I stood now. At Waverley, the banks of crowded gravestones, old and new, undulate up and over low rises, a riot of giant white crosses and angels and saints.

Dad used to take me there when I was younger. We'd roam the narrow crisscrossing paths, some paved and some worn by foot, and study the rows of headstones, mausoleums and marble slabs. Some were well kept; shiny, white and polished. Others were broken, overgrown and unloved, generations of family members and loved ones—who'd once left flowers and tended weeds— now gone, sleeping in their own graves.

Together we'd construct fanciful histories for the people buried there. We'd calculate how old they were; which loved ones were left behind; we'd discover tiny lives cut short and would speculate as to why, standing solemnly side by side and grieving for families we didn't even know. We'd trace the way whole clans had grown with each marriage and birth and then died off as branches of descendants in turn grew old.

It was never a game, never trivialised. It was my Dad's way of teaching me to pay attention to detail, to be creative enough to think outside the box, to imagine what might have been. But he always encouraged me to follow up with real research, so I would take my notes and sit for hours at the library, searching family records to see how close we were to the truth.

My versions were always a little off the mark. I had a tendency towards the romantic as a kid. My Dad was a little more prosaic. He'd say my natural curiosity and sharp mind would make for a perfect journalist but my imagination was bound to trip me up. Regardless, my memories of those moments with my Dad were nothing short of treasured.

At that moment, in the darkening LA cemetery, I didn't feel any of those things. Not curious, not imaginative and definitely not serene. I was shitting my pants. One pesky, amnesiac ghost shows up in my life, shattering all of my beliefs, and now cemeteries were ruined for me forever.

I felt certain someone dead was going to jump out at me. My nerves were frayed to the point of breaking. It could have been Xander or someone else—say Marilyn Monroe or Dean freaking Martin. I hoped desperately the fact I'd seen one ghost didn't mean they were all going to come out of the woodwork, thinking me some kind of mystical psychic conduit. Bugger that. What was I, Shirley MacLaine? The bloody Ghost Whisperer? Although, to be fair, if Marilyn showed up, I'd definitely have some JFK related questions for her—I mean, I'm not an idiot.

Regardless, as I'd told Xander in no uncertain terms, I didn't feel compelled to guide the deceased to the spirit realm. Unless of course they happened to be an extremely attractive but annoying movie star who wouldn't take no for an answer.

Any other ghosts would be told in no uncertain terms to find their own way to the light. I wasn't a metaphysical street directory.

Bolstered by equal measures of resolve and ghostbusting bravado, I set out to my left. I passed Eva Gabor on one side and Natalie Wood on the other, staying well away from the lawn. I didn't need the extra worry of ghostly hands bursting out of the ground to grab at my ankles. By the time I passed Marilyn unscathed, my nerves and breathing had settled somewhat, although I was still understandably jumpy.

I spotted Xander's grave from fifty metres away. Ten or so teenaged girls had set up camp and were sitting among piles of flowers and tributes. A veritable carpet of photos and trinkets spilled over from the four-by-eight-feet plot, swallowing up neighbouring graves.

I hid behind a nearby tree to watch undetected, until I decided whether to lay in wait for Lola to arrive or introduce myself to the gaggle of girls. I still had a retrospective to write for the magazine, whether I liked it or not. It would be sensible to chat to them.

If not for the cluster of miniature glass lanterns sitting atop it, each flickering with a tiny tongue of orange flame, I doubt I'd have picked out the headstone among the brightly-coloured clutter. Twin girls sat huddled together; the floral pattern of their near identical wrap dresses merging into a mess of silk petals as the fabric swirled on the grass. They were holding white candles and singing softly in unison, a melancholy song I couldn't quite make out.

I decided to wait, so I bent to put my bag on the ground at the foot of the tree, reaching inside for my notebook and digital recorder. When I straightened, *SWOOSH*, Xander had materialised right in front of me. He faced me in the semi-darkness, his voice shattering the quiet.

"This is creepy, Katherine and I'm not entirely happy about being here."

"JESUS CHRIST!" I instinctively grabbed for the narrow tree trunk and dropped both the recorder and book.

"Sorry, I didn't mean to startle you."

"Don't do that," I huffed back at him, my heart pounding. "You made me yell—really, *really* loud." I peeked around the tree to see several girls looking my way. "Great! See what you did, now they've noticed me."

Xander folded his arms and glanced in the direction of his grave, back at me and then back at the grave again.

"I said I'm sorry. Can we get this over with?"

I reached down to pick up my stuff, eyeing him warily. "So, which one are you? Good Xander or Dark Xander?"

"Huh?" The *Buffy* reference was clearly lost on him. He shifted his attention back to me. "What do you mean?"

"You're making me crazy, Xander. And you're starting to scare me. You appear, you disappear, you appear, you disappear. One minute you're all nice, then you go psycho on Quentin, then you're nice again and then *poof*, you're gone. And when you come back, you seem like you want to rip my throat out for running over your puppy or something. What the heck was your problem earlier?"

He stared at me, perplexed. "Earlier when? What are you talking about? I don't even have a puppy."

"I wasn't being literal about the puppy." I rolled my eyes. "About an hour and a half ago, I was at the police station trying to find out more about your case and when I came out you were across the street, giving me the evil eye. Did I do something wrong?"

I was suddenly aware I'd raised my voice again and turned to see one of the girls stepping away from the others, looking my way with a puzzled expression on her face. She was tall and blonde, with her hair in 1940's pin curls and a bright slash of red lipstick across her generous but downturned mouth. Of course, to her I must have appeared to be a crazy woman standing under a tree in a graveyard talking to myself. Or talking to the tree. I wasn't sure which was crazier and I shuffled my feet, feigning nonchalance.

Xander pursed his lips and shook his head.

"I haven't seen you since the hotel last night, watching the movie. I definitely wasn't at a police station today."

"Yes, you were." I hissed out of the side of my mouth.

"No, I wasn't."

I sighed theatrically. The blonde girl was still watching me so I pretended to scratch my nose to cover my moving lips.

"YES... you *were*."

"No, I wasn—" he stopped mid-sentence and frowned. "I don't remember being at a police station. Which one?"

I couldn't help a stab of irritation.

"Does it matter? The point is, you seemed pretty pissed off at me."

"Language, Katherine."

I stared frostily at him.

"Get fuc—" I started to say, before thinking better of it. I wasn't going to get anywhere swearing at him, even if the look on his face did give me a modicum of satisfaction.

"Did you find out anything useful?" He was still glancing uncomfortably back and forth between me and his grave site. I wagged my finger at him.

"Oh no, Mister. You're not glossing over it that easily. What I found out can wait. What I'm worried about is your Jekyll and Hyde act. You looked like you wanted to kill me today. It was scary."

"I'm sorry Katherine. I don't remember being there. I can't tell you where I was. But I certainly don't want to kill you."

"Fine, so if you don't remember being there you probably have no idea why you were so annoyed at me."

He shook his head again.

"Why am I not surprised?" I huffed, irritated. "See those girls over there? They're here to pay homage to you, the late, great Xander Hill. I'm sure if they knew what a pain in the arse you were—uh—*are*—were—oh, you know what I mean. If they knew you like I do, I'm sure they wouldn't bother."

Xander took a step back, a wounded expression on his face.

"You know Katherine, you can be so mean sometimes.

"Maybe I'm not a very nice person."

"I don't believe that."

I'm not sure why his words irked me but they did and I rounded on him, letting fly and not caring if the girls saw me.

"Xander, it doesn't matter what you believe because you don't know me. You know absolutely nothing about me, so you don't know what you're talking about. You know why? Because you're a ghost. That's it. Nothing but a ghost."

"Well, technically, yes."

"There's no technically about it. You *are* a ghost— completely and totally."

"I'm also a person."

I couldn't help it; the earlier scare, my frustration, and the sheer absurdity of the conversation I was having pushed me to my limit.

"No, you're not. You're not a person. You are person-shaped air with a bad attitude. Proper people are solid, Xander. You can't put your hand through a proper person, unless you happen to be Edward Scissorhands and are feeling murderous and—oh, look—" Without thinking I shoved my hands into his chest and waggled them around. His insides felt hot and weird, like electric pins and needles and I quickly yanked my hands

back out and waved them madly at him. "I don't see giant scis-
sors on these hands, do you?"

Xander hadn't moved but was staring at me, eyes wide with
horror.

"Are you crazy?"

"Probably, yes. And pretty murderous as it happens. And,
considering the last couple of days, are you surprised."

Xander recoiled visibly from my words. "I thought I could
tell what kind of person you were Katherine, but obviously I'm
wrong."

"That's rich coming from you. I don't know what kind of
person you are either, especially after today," I arched an
eyebrow at him. "Now, I'm going to talk to these girls until
Lola gets here. Are you coming?"

He stepped back, away from me.

"No."

I shrugged like I didn't care.

"Suit yourself."

And with that, I squared my shoulders and stepped out
from behind the tree into full view.

The blonde girl had stopped about twenty-five feet away,
most likely deterred by my crazy yelling and windmilling
arms. As I stepped into full view, she met my eyes and smiled,
friendly but hesitant.

Close up she had to be no more than seventeen; all clear
skin and white teeth with big blue eyes that were drowning
under lashings of mascara and liquid eye-liner. I expected her
name to be Britney, Tiffany or Amber but after asking whether
I was there to visit Xander, she introduced herself.

"I'm Poppy."

Close enough.

"I'm Kat. Hi there. " My accent piqued her interest as we drifted towards Xander's plot.

"You came here all the way here from Australia? For Xander?" She was wide eyed at the thought. "Wow, you must love him so much."

Before I could stop myself, I snorted, then covered quickly by feigning a cough.

"It's more of a professional interest."

"Actress?"

I shook my head.

"Journalist."

"Oh, you must be like, so smart. You're writing a story about Xander? Wow, that's like, so totally amazing." Was she for real? She sounded like she'd just walked off the set of *Clueless*. I decided my best course of action was to blend in.

"Totally." I smiled brightly back at her then gestured towards a square blue and red picnic rug and several bright cushions, nestled among the flowers and notes. "Are you guys like, moving in? When did you get here?" I fought the urge to roll my eyes. I sounded like an idiot but Poppy didn't seem to notice.

"A couple of days ago." She tossed her hair, all teen self-importance. "I come every year, but then I'm from here in LA. The other girls come from all over, out of state. This year's special, so everyone came. We had to get here early to get a good spot."

"A good spot for what?" I was worried. Were they expecting to see something? To conjure him up? Was there going to be a séance? By that time, a couple more girls had crept closer, listening in. Poppy's demeanour, and the fact they hung back from her, made it clear she was their leader. A pale, bird-like brunette, with cropped sticky-uppy hair and braces, stared at me like I was a total dummy.

"To be close to him of course." She plopped down next to the twins, who'd stopped singing and were staring up at me. The rug was strategically placed immediately in front of Xander's headstone. These freaky kids had staked their claim on prime graveyard real-estate; the piece of ground that put them within a few earthy inches of Xander's actual corpse. I was more than a little creeped out.

"Right. That's—uh—really special," I managed.

"Don't mind Wanda." Poppy rolled her eyes, "She can be a little obsessive."

I had to stop myself from pointing out that they were all camping out in a cemetery. I was pretty sure that qualified as obsessive. Nevertheless, the girls were eager to talk. They formed a straggly circle, cross-legged on the ground, leaving a space for me—all except Wanda who scowled at me from her post on the rug and refused to budge.

Feeling like an overgrown girl-scout, I squished myself into the circle as far away as possible from the patch of ground under which Xander's bones lay. Then I glanced over at the tree where I could still make Xander out, hunched and motionless but definitely looking our way. Shivering, I turned back to the excited girls and switched on my voice recorder.

"So, tell me girls, what was so great about Xander Hill?"

They clamoured over each other, voices shrill and excitable, hands clasped dramatically to their bosoms. '*Totally* gorgeous' seemed to be the most popular opinion, with 'sexy' and 'dreamy' running a close second and third. I didn't think the word 'dreamy' was part of modern teen-vernacular but its contributor, a pony-tailed redhead, was channelling Frenchy from *Grease* in a candy pink poodle skirt and tight black sweater, which explained it somewhat.

It would be sweet if it wasn't so deluded. Xander was attractive, but what if they knew that in reality, he was borderline schizophrenic. Then again, there's nothing like teenage infatuation to make a girl completely myopic. I myself was more than familiar with the affliction.

Flashback to 1999. Boyz-mania was sweeping the globe in the wake of worldwide hits, *When Will I Know* and *Take Me Over*. I was completely obsessed with super-blonde and androgynous lead singer Lars Ross and his twin brother, Marcus, the band's overly muscular drummer (I refuse to acknowledge the original third band member, Paul Tarrant, on the grounds that he was not very cute and had left the band by then anyway).

Like any boy-band fan worth her salt, I was convinced at the time that I would one day, inevitably, become Mrs Lars Ross, despite the fact I was fifteen with teenaged acne and a copycat crew-cut. I even camped outside their hotel when they toured, screaming hysterically and hurling myself at the window of their Toyota Tarago as they left (because God knows, that's the perfect way to a demi-god pop-star fall in love with you).

To this day, I harbour a secret fantasy that I will one day be called upon to interview Lars, upon his inevitable international come-back. As he sits opposite a much older, less pimply and clearly more desirable me, he will of course see instantly that I am his soul mate. We'll sell the photo rights to our wedding to OK Magazine and the rest will be celebrity connubial bliss.

While I identified somewhat with these girls; camping outside a swanky hotel was one thing, sleeping on a grave was entirely another. At least Lars was still breathing.

"Aren't girls your age supposed to be gushing over someone like Ryan Reynolds or Leonardo DiCaprio?" I asked.

"Ew, no!" Poppy wrinkled her pert Californian nose at me. "They're like, old. I mean, they are totally like, *forty*. That's practically dead."

"Sweetie, I hate to point out the obvious," I countered, "but Xander *is* dead."

She faltered.

"But that's different. Xander was just beginning. His star was rising, he had so much left to give and then—" her eyes welled with tears, threatening to turn her lashes and liner into wet, black goo, "—then he was gone. His star was snuffed out. Now he'll never be old. He's—he's—" she struggled for the right words, lip quivering dramatically as I stared at her, more than a little taken aback by the sudden flood of emotion.

"Forever young." It was Wanda, from behind me.

Wow. Poignant stuff. As if on cue, the twins start singing the Alphaville classic.

Forever young ... I want to be
Forever young.
Do you really want to live forever... forever... forever.
Forever young...

It was all I could do not to laugh. Don't get me wrong, I didn't doubt the depth of their adolescent emotions but it was all so dramatic. Maybe I was getting old and cynical. Hang on, I *was* old and cynical. I waited respectfully until the song and the sniffles died down.

"So, I'm presuming you're familiar with his movies?" Not that there was a huge back catalogue. Poppy's wrinkled forehead was the facial equivalent of the word *d'uh* so I tried a better question. "Do you have a favourite?"

Again with the clamouring, although this time they all seemed to agree on *Chase the Wind*.

"He should have won an Oscar, if you ask me. I'm sure he would have, if he hadn't been killed." This was from Miss Poodle Skirt.

From one of the twins—"He should have won posthumously, he was every bit as good as Heath Ledger in Batman, and *he* got one."

She was answered immediately with an indignant chorus of *he was way better than Heath Ledger ever was!* They all shrieked and glared at the poor kid like she'd committed a cardinal sin and she shrank, suitably chastened.

I decided to mention Lola, to see how much they knew. If they'd been coming here every year, they'd know if she'd visited. I leaned forward conspiratorially.

"Girls, can we get serious for a minute?" They quietened straight away, brandishing solemn nods. I paused for dramatic effect, quite relishing their rapt attentiveness. "What are your thoughts on who killed him?"

They all started to murmur and the thrill that raced around the little circle was palpable and delicious. Then Poppy straightened and stared me dead in the eye.

"Lola Tennant killed Xander Hill."

In unison, every head swivelled my way to gauge my reaction. I was surprised by her conviction. Since the police station I'd been trying to figure out who might have had the motive, money and power to kill the investigation. So far, Lola's husband was topping my list.

"Lola Tennant? Not her husband?"

All of them murmured in dissent and Poppy shook her head emphatically.

"No way," she said. "He had an alibi."

Puzzled, I narrowed my eyes at the small group of girls, all of whom were nodding vigorously. "But Lola had an alibi too," I argued. "The police cleared her. Her husband was a very powerful man in Hollywood at the time. You don't think he could have paid off the police?"

Poppy laughed derisively. "You watch too many crime movies, lady. That doesn't happen in real life."

I glowered at her. *Lady?* When I was seventeen, I wouldn't have dreamed of being such a smart-arse to someone clearly much older and wiser.

"Oh really? Okay, smarty pants. What makes you so sure it was Lola?"

Poppy chewed her lip and glanced around at the other girls all of whom instantly shrank back, a couple of them avoiding my eyes. Poppy moved to speak but Wanda burst out, "Don't, Poppy."

My eyes widened and I glanced back and forth between the two of them.

"Don't what?"

Poppy put both hands up in front of her as if to say to the others *it's alright* then took a big breath.

"We're sure Lola did it—because she said so."

Furious, Wanda jumped up from the blanket.

"Poppy, shut up! We're not supposed to tell anyone."

"It's okay," I interjected quickly, "I know she's alive. I know she visits." The two girls stopped dead in surprise.

"You do?" said Poppy. "How?"

I wasn't about to admit that the day before I'd thought she was dead. They didn't need to know this was a total fluke.

"I'm a journalist, remember? Of course, I know. Why do you think I'm here?"

"Well," Poppy pursed her lips, miffed, "I *thought* it was because you loved Xander and were writing a story on him."

"I am. This is all part of it don't you see." I tried to appease her. "It's romantic and tragic, all at the same time. A legendary Hollywood actress sneaking into a graveyard by moonlight to pay homage to her long-dead lover. I mean, *wow.*"

The girls all agreed. They were like a solemn circle of nodding dogs, the type you see on car dashboards, perpetually waggling their little heads.

"I guess," Poppy admitted grudgingly.

"So, can we get back to Lola confessing to murder? So, you've spoken to her—she actually said that?" I couldn't believe it was going to be this easy.

Poppy leaned in and beckoned me close. It was dark now and the meagre candlelight flickered, casting sinister shadows across her pretty face. The circle of girls tightened as she whispered theatrically.

"She comes late at night, always the night before his anniversary. She swore us to secrecy when we first started coming here a couple of years back and figured out who she was. That's the only time we've spoken to her. We try to respect her privacy."

"What did she say?" My hushed tones matched theirs. "I mean, what exactly did she tell you?" I couldn't help it, excitement coursed through me.

"She said she's visited here every year since Xander died," said Wanda.

I shrugged; I already knew that. "And?"

"And that she loved him, despite what he thought," added Poppy.

"And?" I was getting increasingly impatient. They all gazed at Poppy again, who paused for obvious dramatic effect. "What?" I demanded, looking from one girl to another. The back of my neck prickled. Poppy spoke slowly, rounding out her words for effect.

"She said that she was to blame. That his death was her fault."

There was a hush and I waited expectantly for more. Then, realising nothing was forthcoming, I sat upright. What a letdown.

"That's it? That's why you think Lola killed him?"

Poppy sniffed.

"Of course. She said it herself. Isn't it obvious?"

"No. I don't think so." I was disappointed with the anti-climax. "I'm sure she meant she was to blame for him being out there, in his car. He *was* found only a few streets from her house. Don't you think he might have gone to see her, after the fight at the hotel?" I was careful not to reveal too much private information but there was no harm in reminding them of the possibility. They pouted collectively, not happy with me trashing their pet theory. "Sorry, girls. I'm not convinced. That's why I need to speak to her myself."

The group let out a communal gasp and Poppy stared at me in horror.

"Speak to her? You can't do that. Nobody speaks to her. She asked to be left alone. If you speak to her, she won't come back."

I tried to sound sympathetic.

"I do understand that, but I'm a journalist. I've got to do my job."

"What, it's your job to intrude on people's lives?"

She folded her arms and glared at me. All traces of uncertain teenager had vanished.

"Of course not. Girls, this is not the same as paparazzi chasing after Princess Diana. I'm trying to figure out what happened and this was the only way I could get to see Lola."

I thought of Kelly Craig. Guilt flared in me and I was momentarily side-tracked by the ease with which I'd justified being here. I shrugged it off. This *was* different. I was writing a serious story so it was warranted. Wasn't it? Nobody could get hurt here. The girls drifted towards each other, crowding into a cohesive group, facing me, defensive and determined.

"Hang on a second." I leaned back. "How come you're so quick to defend her if you think she killed your beloved Xander? Hmm?"

Wanda stepped forward, scary in her intensity. "Because she's paying her penance. The guilt is what brings her here. She loved him, like we do. It was obviously a crime of passion."

I crossed my arms and raised my eyebrows at her.

"No, a crime of passion is committed in the heat of the moment. Like stabbing your husband with a carving knife over the roast pork because he criticises your gravy one too many times." They all stepped back, alarmed. "Don't worry, I'm not speaking from experience." I sighed. "Look, Xander was shot on the side of the road while he was sitting alone in his car. That's pre-meditated. Someone had to have followed him or known where he was going to be. So, either Lola killed him in cold blood or she didn't do it—simple as that."

I couldn't believe I was standing there arguing with a bunch of teenaged girls, but as I wracked my brain for something to say to get them on side, a ripple ran through the entire group. Some of them clutched hands as they murmured, staring at a spot way beyond me. They started backing away slowly and I fleetingly thought maybe Xander was behind me and for some inexplicable reason they could see him. But a quick check of the tree showed him still standing motionless underneath it.

I turned to find out what they'd seen. Not far away, only just visible in the darkness, was a small, white-haired figure moving inexorably towards us.

It had to be Lola.

Chapter Thirteen

S he was slight of build, almost swallowed by an enormous, moth-eaten fur coat. She walked with small, unhurried steps, seeming to glide across the grass like an apparition herself. Her shoulders were stooped, her back bowed by age. Her face showed no trace at all of her former beauty; mouth pinched, cheeks drawn, her pale skin as grey and translucent as vellum. Even in the flickering candle light, I could see the spidery blue veins crisscrossing her spindly hands and neck as she drew closer.

I wasn't sure what I'd been expecting of the former screen-goddess. Swept up in the mystery and tragic romance of it all, I'd forgotten how old she would be, but the sickly and unkempt figure before me was a shock. She drew closer, then stopped, touching a shaking hand to her lopsided and snarled chignon, a vivid blue silk flower fixed haphazardly to the side. The slash of scarlet lipstick on her mouth bled into the lines around it. There was a sadness about the little touches of vanity.

I took the girls' lead and moved further back. As we shifted,

Lola stepped forward to the foot of Xander's grave. She coughed, wet and phlegmatic, and huddled into her fur. Not once had she acknowledged the girls gathered there—or me— it's as if she didn't see us. Her eyes were set deep in folds of papery skin and directed at the ground. Poppy clutched my hand in the dark. I wasn't sure if it was to stop me stepping forward or a reaction to the sheer drama.

I could hear my heart's rhythmic thud in the hush that swallowed us. It was as though even the wind had ceased in order to still the rustle of the trees and the grass. Everyone was silent and respectful, heads down as Lola slowly lowered herself, stiff and awkward, to her knees.

I glanced over at the tree; towards Xander. He had moved much closer since I last checked but was still motionless, staring intently at the old woman, his expression unreadable. I imagined the reaction from the young girls if they knew their idol was standing right behind them. I squeezed Poppy's hand and leaned towards her with a theatrical whisper.

"What do we do now?"

She shouldered me away gently, glancing sideways at me with a scowl.

"We wait and let her pay her respects. Quietly."

My forehead crinkled upwards.

"For how long?"

This time Poppy glared forcefully at me.

"As long as she needs. Don't be rude. She usually takes a while and talks to him. Now shhhhh."

"Fine."

I moved to fold my arms then caught myself. Anyone would think I was the teenager, not her. I shoved my hands in my pockets instead and put my head down as if I was praying but, in reality, I was watching Lola from underneath my lashes and trying to come up with a way to introduce myself without scaring her off. Something told me blurting out '*Hi, I'm a journalist. Let's talk about Xander's murder*' was not the best way to go.

Her lips were moving rapidly. I could hear the faint murmur of her words, her voice husky and weak, but she was speaking too quickly for me to make out what she was saying. Oddly, it didn't sound like English and as she rocked back and forth slightly on her heels I saw she had a tangle of rosary beads twisted around her gnarled fingers. I wondered what she was praying for. Forgiveness?

Time ticked slowly past as we all stood in the dark and watched, the only light coming from the tiny flames on the headstone. They illuminated Lola's face with an eerie flickering glow. Her rapid speech slowed and eventually she became still and silent.

Then she reached deliberately into her coat and pulled out a small book, its cover tattered, the pages curled at the corners. She laid it deferentially among the other offerings and flowers. My eyes strained to see the title but the cover was too faded and torn. I watched her put trembling fingers to her lips and touch the ground. Nerves danced down my spine and then spun, tingling, into my lower belly as Lola struggled to her feet.

It was my chance, I had to move quickly. I stepped forward and instantly multiple hands grabbed at me as several of the girls hissed in protest.

"No! Don't."

Poppy was frantic. "Please!"

I shrugged them off and took another couple of steps. I moved into Lola's eye line so as not to startle her, but she didn't register my presence. Instead, she started to turn away.

"Mrs. Tennant?" My voice was oddly strangled. She kept moving, ignoring me completely, and I cleared my throat. "Mrs Tennant," I tried again, this time a little louder.

She didn't turn but her voice wavered out of the dark, thin and reedy.

"I'm sorry, I don't know that name. You're mistaken."

I could hear the girls behind me muttering to each other in outrage and I started to feel embarrassed as she shuffled away. I was intruding on an old woman's grief. What on earth was I doing? This was as bad as following Kelly Craig. I shrugged the feeling off, telling myself this was different, that I *needed* this story. I followed for a few steps and tried again; my voice more insistent.

"Lola!" This time she stopped and turned halfway towards me, gradually and deliberately, her gaze still fixed on the ground. "I know you're Lola Tennant." It tumbled out in a rush. My face was flushed, I could feel it, and I felt the sudden urge to apologise and back away, but it was too late. "I'm so sorry to intrude—" *Was I?* "—but I need to speak with you. It's important."

She raised her head finally and stared at me. Her eyes were a deep brown beneath the crêpey lids. "It's about Xander." I trailed off, redundantly. Of course, it was. A strange half-smile settled on Lola's face and she dropped her eyes again.

"I'm sorry, Xander's not here. He's gone."

Leon was right. She was crazy.

"Yes, I know that, but I—"

She interrupted as though I hadn't spoken.

"It was my fault you know. I left him alone. I shouldn't have left him alone." Her voice cracked. I had to know what she meant. I stepped closer.

"Mrs. Tennant, if we could talk elsewhere, talk properly, then perhaps you can explain it to me. Maybe I can help—"

"I'm so tired. I don't remember." She smiled faintly at me and began to turn away. Desperate now I reached out and touched her arm. She flinched and I retracted my hand.

"I'm sorry, Mrs. Tennant. I's just that I'm trying to find out—"

At that moment, Lola looked past me and took a sudden stumbling step back, her eyes unfocussed as if dizzy. Then they cleared, her face blanching.

"Are you alright?" I put out my hand again. "Mrs. Tennant —Lola?"

Wide-eyed and panicked, her eyes flittered to me then back to the space behind me. I heard some of the girls gasping— *What's wrong? What's wrong with her?*

Lola's mouth twisted and opened and shut as if she wanted to speak and her hand fluttered to her mouth. She squeezed her eyes shut and took another step backwards. When she opened them again, strangled sobbing sound broke from her.

"I'm sorry. I'm so sorry."

She wasn't talking to me. That much was clear. She turned and walked away surprisingly fast, clutching the fur coat around her and stumbling on the grass. The girls were in uproar, crowding in on me in righteous anger and indignation.

"What did you do? What did you say to her?" demanded Poppy.

I didn't respond. I was rooted to the spot, staring after Lola's rapidly diminishing figure. Damn it! I didn't need to turn around to understand what had gone wrong, I instinctively knew. I don't know how, but Lola had seen Xander. How was that possible?

When I did turn, Xander was standing right there, just as I expected. His fists were clenched, his face contorted. Tears stained his cheeks. His shoulders shuddered as he put his face in his hands.

I couldn't talk to him there. The girls were too incensed and focused on me. Some were crying, others like Poppy were glaring at me as if they were going to stone me to death. I'm

ashamed to say, I then made it all a hundred times worse. Before
I had a chance to consider how icky my actions were, I lunged
towards Xander's headstone, snatching up the raggedy book
Lola had laid there. I made a run for it, bolting with the phrase
'bottom-of-the-barrel' ringing loudly in my head.

I instructed my pesky new conscience to shut the hell up as
I raced towards the cemetery entrance. The girls howled furiously behind me, but none of them chased me. I was glad.
Their supple teenaged legs would have outrun me like a pack of
gazelle. Xander was waiting at the entrance when I reached it,
furious. He immediately berated me.

"You can't take things from people's graves, Katherine,
that's a terrible thing to do. What were you thinking?"

I stepped back, shocked. "You want to talk about the book?
Xander, Lola *saw* you. What happened back there?"

Confusion overwhelmed him. "I have no idea," he stammered, "I don't know how I even got that close. One minute I
was standing under the tree, the next minute she was right in
front of me. I felt so angry." He paused, "It felt like I was being
swallowed by it."

"You did a good job of scaring her off, that's all I can say." I
studied the book in my hands. Despite the worn and tattered
cover, I could read the title now. It was an old copy of *Peter
Pan*. Xander seemed so desolate and confused that I softened
the edge on my voice. "I still need to talk to her Xander, now
more than ever." I held up the book. "Does this mean anything
to you?"

He studied it without a hint of recognition. I tapped it
against my palm as I mulled things over. "I doubt she'll come
back to the cemetery again after this. I'll need to go to her
house."

Xander didn't answer. His eyes were fixed into the distance.
Vacant.

"Xander?"

He blinked, refocusing.

"What if she won't talk to you?"

"Well," I took a deep breath, "if she won't talk to me, I'll have to work with what I've got. I've got you—"

"Hmmph!" He grimaced.

"—I've got Quentin, and I found out some interesting information from the police today."

"Like what?" He eyed me, wary.

"I'm not entirely sure, I'm hoping to find out more tomorrow. We may well find out why your murder case was dropped so easily. One of the detectives on your case is still alive. He's retired but lives out in Pasadena. Your file has some big inconsistencies and I want to know why."

"Then I'm coming with you."

"Xander—" I was about to argue. The last thing I needed was to keep trying to act normal with a very vocal ghost interrupting every five seconds. I stopped myself. What was the point? He'd just turn up on his own. "Fine, but can we talk about it on the way home? I want to get out of here before those girls hunt me down and flay me alive for desecrating your grave."

"I told you it was a terrible thing to do, Katherine. Don't you have a conscience?"

It seemed I did. Or at least something vaguely conscience-shaped. It's not like I'd never had one. But I'd denied its existence for so long, it felt disconcerting now, like a shoe I really liked the look of and wanted to wear, except it didn't quite fit.

"Lola left the book for you, dummy. And you're standing right here, with me. Doesn't it make more sense that you actually get to have it, instead of it being left for your bones? Hmm?"

Xander shook his head and tossed me a disapproving look as he walked towards the street.

"However you want to justify it to yourself."

I gritted my teeth. *Grrrrrr.*

"I am not justifying."

"It'll come back to haunt you," he threw coolly over his shoulder.

I stopped, wishing I could give him a swift kick. "I would say it already has," I yelled after him. Xander turned and glared at me.

"Well, if that's how you feel, I'm not going to walk with you. I'll meet you back at the hotel." He paused before saying cryptically, "then again, maybe I won't." And, with that, he disappeared.

I poked my tongue out at thin air. "Oh, whatever." Then I stomped off in search of a cab.

Chapter Fourteen

Nearing my room, I yawned so hard I thought my face would split. The day had been so intense my adrenal gland was putting in for overtime. I couldn't wait to collapse face down into my pillow. As I stifled another yawn, I fumbled for my key.

An instant before it slid into the lock, Xander's head and shoulders burst through the door with a loud *Shhhhh*. Maybe it was the exhaustion, maybe it was the fact I was getting used to him popping out at me unexpectedly. Either way, he didn't startle me the way he usually did. Instead, I stood statue-like with my hand outstretched, simply staring at him quizzically as he protruded through the wood like the figurehead on a Spanish galleon.

"Yes?" I huffed. "Do you want something?"

"There's someone in your room."

"What do you mean there's someone in my room?" I took a hurried step back, alarmed. "How can there be someone in my room?" My voice escalated and he put a finger to his lips. I dropped to a whisper, hissing at him, "What kind of someone?"

"A woman. She's tall and scary-looking and she seems very interested in a red folder you left on the bed."

"Oh my god, that's the file I got from the police today." A horrible thought occurred to me. "Shit, this is like one of those mob movies where, as soon as someone gets close to uncovering something they shouldn't, they get taken out."

"Taken out where?"

"*Killed*, Xander – *killed*. What else is she doing?"

"Well, she's dancing, but there's no music—" he said with a creased brow, "—and she drank most of the tiny bottles in your little refrigerator."

Immediately I relaxed and chuckled at him.

"It's okay, Xander. I think I know who it is. You're right, she's pretty scary."

It could only be one person. Chrissie.

I'd met her on a press junket in London when I was twenty-two and pretty new to the game. We were sitting next to each other amongst twenty other journalists in a cramped, over-heated hotel room in Knightsbridge, waiting for our 10-minute turn with the talent.

The celebrity in question, Tate Martin, was the lead singer of hot new rock band *Red Rock;* a band still on the up-side of a meteoric rise. Shaggy haired and dirty-looking, he'd recently collaborated with another up-and-comer, Shanna Mortimer, and was rumoured to be sleeping with every female celebrity within a hundred miles who had a thing for bad-boys. He was also the proud owner of a raging coke problem and had kept us waiting for six hours.

When a platinum-blonde PR princess popped her shiny head through the door to sweetly inform us that Mr. Martin would be another hour and—even then—we might not get our ten minutes, Chrissie had immediately uncoiled her five-foot-ten, to-die-for body out of her chair with ophidian grace, and tossed her long blue-black bob over her vividly inked shoulder. She'd fixed the poor girl with a frigid glare, partly courtesy of her pale lilac contact-lenses

"You have got to be fucking kidding me," she'd thundered. The publicist had stared at Chrissie in shock. So had I and every other journalist in the room. We all knew her outburst had ruined any chance she had of getting an interview. It was common knowledge; you didn't mess with the PR bitch.

Before anyone could say a word, Chrissie had turned on her biker-boot-clad heel and thrown casually over her shoulder, "This is a load of bollocks. You can tell *Mr.* Martin; I'll make it up." She'd stopped and glared around the room at us all. "And if you mugs are going to sit and wait for him, you're more fucking stupid than he is. Now, if you'll excuse me, there's a tequila shot with my name on it waiting in the bar."

I'd loved her immediately and sheepishly grabbed my notebook and bag and crept passed the angry, stuttering publicist and the sweaty, whispering journalists. I'd joined Chrissie in the lift where she was in the middle of lighting up a cigarette. She'd winked at me and blown smoke from between lobster-red lips.

"Atta girl!" She'd thrown her arm casually over my shoulder. We'd been like Bonnie and Clyde, Laurel and Hardy, and Tom and Jerry—all rolled into one—ever since.

I opened the door without a sound and there she was. Eyes closed and airPods firmly in place, she gyrated wildly in the middle of the room, wearing a tangerine snakeskin miniskirt and holding a pocket-sized bottle of bourbon. The wooden heels of her blue cowboy boots clonked on the parquetry and the music was turned up so loud the driving beat—tinny and brittle—carried clear across the room. She was oblivious to my entrance.

My tongue curled around two fingers and I whistled. The piercing blast reverberated around the apartment, shattering her trance. She whirled around, beaming, and tapped sharply on her Apple watch. The music stopped.

"It's about fucking time."

I leapt at her, enveloping her in a full body hug. Xander was not so eager, circling us with feline wariness, all hackles and twitching tail.

"What the hell are you doing here, you mad thing?" I shrieked. "And come to think of it, how the hell did you get into my room?" I had a flash of déjà vu—La Chateau really needed to tighten up their security, although I'm not sure they could have kept either Xander *or* Chrissie out. Chrissie extricated herself from my arms and waved dismissively.

"I told them I was your secret lover, that I'd come to surprise you." She waggled her tongue lasciviously and I glanced sideways in time to see Xander's lip curl in distaste. "Nah, just kidding," she winked. "I spend half my life in LA, they know me here; I'm practically part of the furniture. I was worried about you, kiddo. Why else would I come?" She whirled around, putting on a posh accent. "The fahn-tahstic ah-mbience?"

Laughing, I turned to introduce her to Xander who was now leaning against the wall by the balcony doors, looking decidedly put out.

"Chrissie, this is—" I stopped dead, my arm frozen mid-gesture. *Crap.* Talk about auto-pilot. I was already so used to having him around I'd completely forgotten nobody else could see him. Chrissie stared at me expectantly and Xander folded his arms, smirking, as if to say *let's see how you get out of this one.* "— the incredible view from my balcony. Check it out."

Xander snorted and Chrissie shook her head and slapped the back of mine.

"Fuck the view. Flying visit, babe. *Fly-ing*. I have to be back on a plane in four hours. I'm not wasting time on scenery. Hurry up and get changed while I pee because, quite frankly my love, you look like dog's bollocks." She turned and headed for the bathroom.

"Where are we going?"

"Where do you think we're going, stupid?" she rolled her eyes and closed the door.

Of course.

"The bar?" I said it more for Xander's benefit than Chrissie's. So much for sleep.

"I don't like her." Xander shifted from foot to foot, his mouth drawn in a tight line. I gestured for him to turn his back while I changed.

"I don't care. She's my best friend. You don't have to like her."

"So, you're going to go out drinking?" Xander scowled at the wall. "When you have a crime to solve? Don't you have work to do—an article to write?"

"A few hours isn't going to make a difference, Xander. Besides, it's been a crazy day. I think I deserve a break. You don't have to come. In fact, I'd rather you didn't. Ignoring you is more difficult than you think. I get all discombobulated. You can turn around now, I'm dressed."

The dejected expression on his face when he turned to face me was so exaggerated, I had to stifle a laugh. I made a small *ta-dah* gesture, thinking the push up bra and sequinned mini-dress I'd poured myself into might elicit a positive response, but all I got was a melodramatic sigh as he stared at the floor.

"But, what if I get lonely here by myself? What if I remember something and I need to talk to you?" He lifted his chin and gazed dolefully at me.

"Oh no you don't. Those puppy dog eyes don't work on

me." I chuckled as I strapped on the pair of gorgeous but completely impractical sky-high heels Mitch had thoughtfully included in my surprise suitcase. He smiled then and fluttered his eyelashes at me. Hearing the toilet flush behind the closed bathroom door, I rolled my eyes and whispered, "Okay, you can come. But try not to be a nuisance."

Xander did this peculiar little jig, a huge grin on his face and I laughed out loud.

"What's so funny?' Chrissie emerged from the bathroom. "And, am I mistaken or were you talking to yourself out here?"

"Actually," I said, "this room is haunted. I was talking to the resident ghost." Chrissie didn't bat an eyelid so I carried on. "His name's Fred and he's going to come and have a drink with us, if that's okay with you."

"Fred?" Xander whispered, pulling a funny face as Chrissie cocked an eyebrow at me.

"You really have cracked, haven't you?" She shook her head at me. "Jesus, this is more dire than I thought. You need alcohol, STAT. Come on... Sky Bar, now. Can't have you wasting that dress. Crikey, Kat, are you trying to give me a heart attack? I can almost see what you had for breakfast. Hey, if you play your cards right—you, me, Fred. Let's get freaky." She cackled, gave my sequin-clad and barely-covered arse a resounding slap and grabbed her bag.

"Sorry, darl," I retorted as I trotted obediently out the door after her, "you're not my type."

Xander fell in beside me, shortening his strides to align with my teetering steps.

"So, what is your type?" He smirked and I coughed to cover my whispered reply.

"Alive."

He nodded slowly then ducked his head, speaking to his feet.

"You look beautiful by the way."

I glanced at him in surprise, which in turn caused me to stumble in my enormous shoes. Chrissie turned with lightning reflexes and grabbed my arm, holding me up.

"Clearly, you are out of practice my friend. That's supposed to happen at the end of the night, not the beginning." She linked her arm through mine and dragged me down the hallway leaving Xander—still smiling—trailing behind us.

C hrissie's friendship comes complete with an access-all-areas pass in every major city. Sydney, London, New York—the girl literally knows everyone. We strutted to the head of the queue outside Sky Bar, which didn't impress the fifty or so other people lined up in the slightest.

The colossal, bald bouncer was channelling Mike Tyson, lisping 'long time no see, baby' as we approached the door. The badge on his lapel said *Rolando* and he kissed Chrissie hello, holding her shoulders firmly and kissing both cheeks in turn. A gaggle of twenty-somethings in tight dresses screeched in ineffectual outrage. Rolando glared the indignant girls into silent obedience before waving us straight in.

I'll admit, being treated like royalty was a perk I'd always enjoyed back home. Shallow as it sounds; jumping queues, being seated at the best tables and plied with free drinks makes you feel somewhat special. Who wouldn't want that? But now, it was all too apparent how easily a person could get carried away, puffed full of self-importance. Now I felt guilty. I waved apologetically at the plebeian queue, mouthing *sorry, so sorry about that.*

Upstairs, the expansive deck overlooked a glittering expanse of LA lights. We ordered drinks and perched poolside on white-cushioned loungers surrounded by diaphanous drapes and pockets of lush green foliage. Hundreds of tiny candles reflected off the pool's glassy surface and the chatter around us blended seamlessly with the house music being spun by the DJ.

The crowd was eclectic and sexy; models, actors, musicians, business men. Wannabes abounded and the air reeked of desperation and Gucci perfume. They all had one thing in common; every person was on high alert, eyes constantly darting around so as not to miss anybody important. We didn't even register on their radars.

Chrissie downed her dirty martini in two swift gulps and signalled for another as I sipped mine and tried desperately to keep my eyes open. Xander sat stiffly on the end of my lounger, studiously ignoring Chrissie. What the heck was his problem?

"So, fill me in, babe." Chrissie waved her hand at me. "Are you really okay or do I need to feed you some Xanax?"

"I'm okay. It's helping to keep busy."

"And how's the whole Nancy Drew thing? Getting anywhere?"

I laughed.

"I haven't discovered any missing treasure or hidden passageways if that's what you're asking but, yes, I think I'm making headway. I can't believe what's fallen into my lap to be honest."

Chrissie's look said *go on*, as she guzzled her second martini. I told her about Lola and my visit to the cemetery, the half empty police file and filled her in on my interview with Quentin. When I got to the part about Quentin and Xander being lovers, she nearly spat her drink all over me.

"No!" Her eyes goggled in disbelief and I nodded.

"Yes."

"No!" Xander was righteously indignant once again.

"Yes," I repeated, without thinking. Chrissie blinked at me, perplexed.

"Why did you just say yes twice?"

I glared at Xander as if to say *thanks a bunch*. He glared back.

"I told you, I am not a homosexual, Katherine." He sniffed and stood up. "I'll leave that to your mannish friend here. I'm going for a walk." He stalked off in the direction of the bar and I narrowed my eyes and watched him go for a few seconds, wondering why he never disappeared when I wanted him to. Then I realised Chrissie was still waiting for an answer.

"Sorry, what?"

Chrissie leaned back and studied me, taking a long, deliberate mouthful of her drink. Finally, she pursed her lips and narrowed her eyes.

"You're acting extremely fucking weird, you know that? What gives?" She knows me too well so I tried to stay as close to the truth as possible without coming completely clean.

"I have a lot on my mind, Chrissie. This story is way more complicated than you can possibly imagine. Plus, jet lag, it makes everything else a hundred times worse."

She didn't buy it for a second.

"Mmm-hmm. Whatever you say."

"What?" I crossed my arms defensively across my boosted bosom.

"I've never seen you like this, Kat. You're all over the bloody place. If I didn't know better, I'd think you were on drugs or something."

I snorted.

"You'd know."

Now Chrissie folded her arms.

"Actually, I've been well-behaved recently. Been sticking to liquids. And we're talking about you, not me."

I took a long draught of my martini and grimaced at the saltiness before fishing out the briny olives one by one with my fingers and munching on them so I didn't have to talk. Eventually I ran out of olives as Chrissie signalled for a passing waiter-slash-Calvin Klein model to bring us yet another round.

"Is it any wonder I'm a bit wacko? Give me a break—my Dad died thinking I was a loser—" Chrissie opened her mouth to object immediately but I blazed on, "—so what do I do to honour his memory? Prove him right, that's what. My career is on life support with the plug about to be pulled, and here I am in exile— in bloody La La Land of all places—the pinnacle of normality, NOT—trying to figure out who killed some obscure actor fifty years ago, just so I can prove him wrong." I adopted my TV presenter voice. "Introducing the disaster that is my life."

The waiter sashayed up to our loungers with another tray of drinks, although the first had already gone to my head. I grabbed a martini and gulped at it, wiping my mouth indelicately with the back of my hand then slamming the glass down. The fragile stem snapped between my fingers with a chink. *Oops.*

"Whoa, slow down there, cowboy," Chrissie was vaguely alarmed as I reached out and picked up her drink. I waved her away and hiccupped.

"You're hardly the one to lecture me on alcohol consumption. Leave me alone. You're shupposed to be my friend."

"I *am* your friend, and I'm here for you, but that also means I get to tell you when to pull your head in. Your dad's gone, babe, you can't change what he thought. You can only change what you think of yourself."

I burped and lay back against the lounger. My shoes had begun to dig painfully into my toes so I kicked them off and tucked my legs underneath me, tugging self-consciously at the miniscule dress to ensure my bits were covered.

I vaguely remembered someone telling me once that you

can't see the stars at night in LA because of all the smog and the lights. I stared morosely up at the inky expanse of blank sky and wished I could drown in it.

"I feel like I'm stuck, Chrissie, in some kind of middle ground. What's the word?" I waved my hand. My vocabulary was drunk.

"Limbo?"

"That's it — limbo. I want this story; it could save me. But I feel guilty for pushing, for digging, and I don't know why. Everything was so much simpler when I didn't give a shit."

Chrissie scratched her head.

"I don't get it either, honey. This is hardly the same as before though. Quentin willingly gave you that information, Xander Hill is long-dead. I honestly can't see the harm."

At the mention of Xander, I surreptitiously glanced around and slugged more of Chrissie's martini. He was nowhere to be seen. "Yeah well, you should have been at the cemetery earlier," I continued. "I was awful. Lola Tennant's an old lady now and she's still grieving. I felt intrusive for the first time in my life. I really did."

"So, drop the story." Chrissie shrugged. "Stick to your original assignment. Problem solved." She stared pointedly at her near empty glass, still in my hand. I signalled the beleaguered waiter again. Maybe it would be more prudent to bring the bottles and shaker so we could help ourselves.

"I can't drop the story."

"Why not?"

"I can't, okay?" I wasn't about to explain that I was carrying the added responsibility of Xander's eternal soul. I couldn't drop the story. What would happen to him if I did?

"Right. If you're not going to tell me why, don't bitch and moan that it's too difficult. You can't have a foot in each camp, Kat. Either you're still a journalist or you're not."

I fiddled peevishly with the cushion ties on the lounger, blinking hard to re-focus my martini-squiffy eyes.

"Maybe I was never a journalish-t in the first place," I slurred. "I was more like a spy – a really shallow spy in nice shoes." With that, Chrissie put her fresh drink down, leaned across and slapped the side of my head. Hard. "Heeeey," I squawked.

"Enough with the self-pitying bullshit. Seriously. If you don't like the industry, why'd you get into it?

I glared at her in resentment, at least I think it was resentment; my eyes were goggling in their sockets and it was becoming harder and harder to concentrate.

"I happen to love this industry, thank you. You know how I feel about film and mus-shic and television and—everything— it's just—" I burped again and tasted olives and salt and sour stomach, "—well, it's not exactly earth-shatteringly important is it? We're not changing the world."

Chrissie groaned.

"Not this crap again. Come on, Kat, give it a rest. The world would be pretty fucking depressing if everyone only ever did serious, heavy stuff. Fun is important. What does that *Eat, Pray, Love* woman say? Bringing people joy and making them smile is equally as important a calling."

I rolled my eyes—or they might have rolled by themselves, I *was* a few martinis in.

"It's pop culture, not Jesus."

"Fine, then why didn't you follow your dad and do boring investigative stuff, if it's that much bloody better?"

I stared at her uncertainly. Why didn't I follow my dad?

"If you mus-ht know, I didn't think I was smart enough." *There*.

"Rubbish. You *know* you're smart. Otherwise, you wouldn't have gotten so bloody bored with all the blockheads you used to go out with." She snorted. "It used to drive me bonkers, listening to you try to dumb down your conversations. I never got it."

I wagged my finger at her again, all wannabe-Beyoncé attitude.

"Uh-uh. If I'm so sh-mart, why have I been so satish-fied with writing *fluffy rubbish?*"

"What," Chrissie bridled, "so entertainment reporting is for dummies? People who couldn't make it in *real* journalism. Is that what you're saying?"

I hiccupped and goggled at her a bit more.

"That's not what I said, but now that you mention it, it's not exactly rocket surgery." My metaphors were more mixed than my martini.

"I'll have you know, there are plenty of extremely intelligent people working as entertainment journalists." Her eyebrows shot up and her cheeks pulled inwards as if she was sucking half a lemon.

I knew she was referring to herself and I knew as her best friend I should have appeased her and told her how smart and fabulous I thought she was. But, unfortunately, at that exact moment I spotted Xander going off like a frog in a sock on the dance floor. His arms and legs flailed crazily in all directions, completely out of time to the music.

Then he started doing the robot.

I burst out laughing, spraying salty martini all over Chrissie. Of course, she thought I was doubled over with mirth at the mere idea that she might have had more intelligence than a goldfish and it clearly rankled. A lot.

"Well, fuck you and the horse you rode in on," she snapped. I tried to stop laughing but now Xander was doing the caterpillar across the floor. Clearly, along with *Jersey Girl,* he'd watched far too many 1980s music videos.

"Oh, come on, Chrissie, I'm not laughing at you. I didn't say you were dumb. You said it yourself; you get paid to drink with rock stars. Not to mention how many of them you end up in bed with." I snorted. "And their wives, for that matter. You don't exactly need a college degree to do that." Thinking back, my tact was clearly even more sloshed than my vocabulary.

Chrissie stared at me in silence for a few seconds before picking up her drink again, downing half of it in two impressive mouthfuls then placing the near empty martini glass gently back on the little round side table between us.

"Is that right?" she said finally in a quiet voice. "Funnily enough, I didn't fly half way across the world to be insulted because a mental cow—who's supposed to be my friend—can't get her shit together. It appears you're right, Kat. This industry *has* turned you into an arsehole." She stood up, reached into her purse, and dropped two fifties on the table. I regarded them with confused and unfocused eyes.

"But—where are you going?"

Chrissie leaned down and kissed me on the cheek.

"I've got a plane to catch—" she paused, "—and apparently some rock stars to fuck. Bye, Kat." With that, she stalked across the deck and down the stairs before I could say a word. Through my inebriated haze, I was still able to register two things. I should have eaten more that day and I had just been a total bitch to my best friend. *Good job.*

Muttering, *she was mean to me first,* I snatched up Chrissie's discarded glass so I had one in each hand and slumped against the cushions, both legs sticking out in front of me. My internal monologue grumbled drunkenly. She'd hit me on the head for god's sake. Honestly, who does that? Draining my drink, I then tipped Chrissie's upside down, slurping the last few dregs and letting the remaining olives tumble into my open mouth.

"I must say, you're the picture of elegance. You do know I can see straight up your dress?" Xander stood at my feet, a bemused look on his face, as I chewed.

"Pssssht!" I mumbled sloppily through bits of olive. "I've got more important things to worry about, Mister, than whether a stupid ghost can see my knickers." He took in the numerous empty drinks and his eyes widened. "Wasshamadda? Never seen a drunk lady before?" I waved the glasses I was still holding then clinked them together for emphasis. "Hmmm?"

"Where's your friend? I think she should take you home. You're drunk." He sat and eyed me warily as I finally surrendered the empty glasses, leaning over to place them gingerly on the table and nearly falling off the lounge.

"Gold star for Xander," I crowed as I regained my balance, "Yes, I am indeed as skunked as a drunk."

A small group of painfully-cool hipsters stood nearby, pointing at me and whispering, clearly under the impression I was talking to myself. I didn't care this time. I waved at them with a silly grin on my face then turned back to Xander. "Chrissie's gone." My smile faded and I let my hands flop in my lap. "I was nasty to her, so she left."

"Must be the day for it," Xander said, "You were mean to me earlier too, rememb—" he stopped when he saw the tears plopping silently off my chin and soaking into my dress. "Don't cry. It can't be that bad. Your friend seemed pretty tough, I'm sure she's okay."

I shook my head. "She's not as tough as she pretends to be. None of us are. You have to grow a thick skin in this business, otherwise you'd never cope." I laughed with no real humour, "You get abused by people a lot. But stuff still gets through, it still stings. I shouldn't have spoken to her like that."

"So, apologise," said Xander and I grimaced. The thought of doing more grovelling, thanks to doing or saying yet *another* stupid thing, made my head throb. Or maybe that was the martinis.

"I'll let her cool down first. I can't face her yelling at me again. Right now, I don't think she likes me very much. Great, there goes my last friend." I slid further down in the lounger, feeling sorry for myself. Xander stared off into the distance, thoughtfully chewing his lip.

"You know, everyone's an actor if you think about it," he said, almost to himself. "We only ever show other people what we want them to see and it's not always the whole truth is it?"

I sat up and squinted at him.

"Are you trying to tell me something?"

He turned to me with a little start, as if I'd interrupted some kind of important philosophical musings. He gave a tight laugh.

"No, Katherine, I'm not trying to tell you something. It was an observation is all."

"Oh." I flopped back down and he watched me for a few seconds before turning to face me.

"By the way—Chrissie's not your last friend." I widened my eyes at him and he smiled. "I'm your friend too."

The sentiment was so unexpected, and I was so drunk, that I immediately screwed my face up to stop more tears from erupting.

"Oh, Xander," I snuffled, "that's sweet of you." Overcome with affection, I leaned over to pat his non-corporeal knee and promptly toppled off the lounger, landing face down with a loud 'ooff' on the timber decking. At that embarrassing point, the duty manager—an officious blonde with enormous fake breasts, skin-tight white pants and a clipboard—came over and asked me not so politely to leave. Apparently, I was scaring the patrons who were actually *somebody*.

I muttered something about nobody being a nobody and

everybody being somebody even if they looked like a nobody and how the hell did she know I wasn't a somebody. Then, in case she decided to whack me with her clipboard, I gathered my purse and my shoes, gave her a sloppy salute and made for the stairs with Xander close behind me, his eyes bugging out of his head.

"Did you see the size of her breasts? How does she even stand up? The poor thing must get a really sore back."

For some reason this struck me as highly hilarious and, as we skedaddled out of the club like naughty children, I was practically hysterical; the alcohol, the exhaustion, the excitement, the argument—everything finally taking its toll. Rolando watched me stumble out through narrowed eyes, shrieking to myself like a nutcase, before making a note in his door book.

My first thought was that Chrissie's VIP status just got revoked and she was going to kill me. My second thought was a bit more visceral.

I was going to vomit. *Urgh.*

Chapter Fifteen

Barry's nondescript white station wagon was badly in need of a clean, a wheel alignment and one of those cardboard lemon deodoriser thingies that you hang from the rear-view mirror.

Ordinarily, a slightly malodorous car wouldn't bother me —in fact, I was the proud owner of one myself—but, post-martini-binge, I was feeling more than a bit average. I kept my breathing shallow so the smell of sweaty sneakers and old food wrappers couldn't invade my lungs and make me barf. Again.

Xander had disappeared the night before, not long after I'd staggered into the Chateau, carrying my shoes and with vomit between my toes. Nobody had batted an eyelid. I'm fairly certain they'd seen worse.

Every inch the gentleman, he'd stuck around long enough to make sure I got to my room. Futile really—not like he could have called for help if I'd fallen down dead-drunk in the lift— but sweet nonetheless. Then, lady-like as always, I'd passed out fully clothed on the couch with my dress around my waist.

I wasn't worried where he was, he'd undoubtedly reappear

at some point, but for the time being Barry and I were alone for
the thirty-minute drive to Pasadena.

"Sorry about the car, Katherine." Barry was sheepish,
leaning across and down towards my feet to grab a couple of
empty Pepsi cans, which he tossed in the back. "You did say you
didn't want to drive to Pasadena in the squad car."

"It's completely fine, Barry." I politely forced a nauseous
smile and twiddled the air-conditioner knob. Nothing
happened except a sickly rattle and a single puff of stale air. "I
would have felt a bit like a criminal, I think. Anyway, thanks for
picking me up and coming with me. You're an absolute
legend." I meant it wholeheartedly, but watched in amusement
as his neck and face flushed that familiar pinky-purple and a
self-conscious smile appeared.

He obviously didn't receive many compliments. I got the
distinct impression that despite his rank, he wasn't very highly
thought of at work. "I'm sure having a police officer of your
stature accompanying me will help me to get through Detective
Croft's front door." I didn't add that catching Ubers in the LA
traffic was melting my credit card, so the free ride was a definite
bonus.

"You can't call him Detective, Katherine." He frowned, his
blush fading. "He's retired. That means he's just a Mr."

"Oh. Sorry." I was taken aback by the unexpected nit-
picking.

"That's alright, you didn't know. I'm sure it won't matter
once we're there, but—"

"No, no," I interjected, uncomfortable now, "if that's the
rules, Barry, that's the rules."

Then he started to stammer. "I'm sure it's not important,
really."

"Oh, okay."

"Okay."

"If you say so."

"Right."

We fell silent. It was one of those awkward moments where nobody quite knows what to say next, so nobody says anything at all. After a few minutes, I snuck a surreptitious glance sideways at my uptight companion, studying him. Barry was clearly out of place here, projecting less the swagger of an LA cop and more the air of a nerdy accountant. Maybe that was why he didn't fit in. I didn't know much about Barry at all. As per usual, I had been so wrapped up in myself I hadn't bothered to ask him anything about himself.

"Barry?"

"Mmm-hmmm?"

"Can I ask you something?"

He swivelled his eyes towards me like they were on stalks, keeping his head facing straight, then fixed them back on the road ahead.

"I suppose so." He sounded wary.

"I'm curious, how did you end up here in LA?"

Barry became quite animated then. It was fate he reckoned. It had all started way back in World War II when his dad, an American GI, had swept his mum off her little Aussie feet with nylon stockings, cigarettes and fervent Yankee promises.

Between Mum and Dad, Barry had grown up on a diet of chilli-dogs, donuts and Hollywood private dicks. Humphrey Bogart inspired him to become a cop, but after ten years on the force in Sydney, arresting drunks and attending domestics, Barry was fatally disillusioned. He'd known even then where he was supposed to be. Where the excitement was. The City of Angels.

Trouble was, when he'd arrived after a long and drawn-out application process, he'd discovered it was all the same. He'd expected *LA Confidential*, what he got was street bums, junkies and the occasional celebrity stalker.

"This case I'm helping you with is the most exciting thing to happen since I got here," Barry admitted. He wasn't well liked, I was right. The LAPD was like a high-school clique—outsiders were treated with suspicion. Despite making Detective the year before, thanks to hard work and no social life, he still felt like the dorky new kid. "I'm certainly no Sam Spade." His face dropped.

"Clearly, they don't know a good cop when they see one. I certainly wouldn't have gotten this far without your help. You're pretty great in my books, Barry." I felt bad for him—and it was true—so I figured bolstering him up couldn't hurt. He flushed and adopted a gruff voice.

"We'll see, Katherine, we'll see." Then he clammed up completely and focused on the road. So much for bolstering his confidence. After a few minutes of uncomfortable silence, I realised our bonding moment was over. I'd embarrassed him way too much.

I slouched sideways, leaning my head against the car door and winding the window down so I could gulp in some more clean air. My mind drifted to Chrissie and our argument. *Ugh, what a mess.* I'd stared at my phone for ages that morning, willing my fingers to punch out her number, but in the end I didn't. I chickened out, but told myself it was simply because my migraine wouldn't have coped with her yelling *fuck off* at me. I sighed in self-pity, sank lower in my seat and glanced absently in the side mirror.

There was Xander, sitting in the back like he'd been there the whole time. He smiled broadly and wiggled his fingers in a secret little wave.

"Aaaah!" I jumped, my outburst startling the hell out of Barry.

"What? What is it?"

He glanced back and forth between me and the road, with comical alarm, his eyebrows sitting almost on top of his head. I thought quickly and scrunched one eye closed

"*Bee!* It was a bee. It flew in my eye."

Barry frowned and looked warily around the car, struggling to keep the car straight.

"Did it sting you? Is it gone?"

"No... and yes, I think so."

He turned his attention back to the road and I turned mine to Xander's reflection in the mirror. I shot him a one-eyed dirty look.

"What did I do?" He threw his hands up. I couldn't answer verbally, so I narrowed my eyes and impaled him with a telepathic *shut-up*. He simply grinned and gave me one of his infuriating winks. *Grrr.* I tried ignoring him by closing my eyes and feigning a nap, but Xander was clearly bored in confined spaces. Like a five-year-old. "Are we there yet?"

My eyes popped open. He couldn't be serious. "Are we there yet?" he repeated. I glared in the mirror with wide eyes that clearly said 'what are you playing at?' but a smile tugged at the corner of my mouth. He grinned and chanted a third time. "Are we there yet?"

I shook my head, a tiny little shake then clocked Barry looking at me funny so I pretended to bop to music, jerking my head in time and breaking into truly terrible beat-boxing sounds.

"It's a bit quiet. Feel like some music?"

Despite Barry's wide-eyes, I kept burring and popping. Xander, to my surprise and awe, took my cue and started rapping along with me. I have no idea how he knew the song, but he started improvising new words to De La Soul's *Ring Ring* in a way that was so macabre it was hilarious.

"Hey, it's my dead-day - sorry I scared you, boo – why dontchya leave your name six feet under – or I'll just walk through you."

What—a—lunatic.

The unexpected combination of Sixties movie star, questionable Nineties R&B, and *The Adams Family* humour sent me over the edge. I couldn't help it. I finally cracked and a small hiccupping giggle erupted from me like gas. I covered my mouth, trying to smother my mirth, but Barry was glancing sideways at me again. This time it was in fear, I'm sure. He must have thought I was nuts.

"Sorry." I attempted to straighten my face. "I was remembering something funny."

Xander found this excuse particularly comical and burst out laughing in the back seat, which immediately set me off again. I tried so hard to stop laughing that it came out like a strangled pig snort, which of course in turn made Xander hoot even more. This time there was no escaping it, I well and truly had the giggles, and Barry no doubt thought I had totally lost my mind.

"It must have been a very funny something." He gave a tight, worried smile before reaching forward and turning on the radio, clearly so he didn't have to converse anymore with the screeching mental person sitting next to him.

B y the time we reached *former*-Detective Croft's house, I'd managed to contain my hilarity. Barry still eyed me warily every few minutes in case I cracked up again, and I couldn't blame him for being skittish. I clambered out of the car to find Xander already standing impatiently by the little front porch. He hummed *Ring Ring* under his breath.

I bit my lip to stop myself giggling and gazed across the

lawn at the pretty Californian bungalow. It had high white-washed gables and pale green weathered paint. The wide sash windows were thrown open, and dated but snowy-white lace curtains drifted out into the breeze. The lawn was neatly clipped and velvety camellias bloomed in the curved flowerbeds, heavily laden with scent. It was a lived-in home, worn and past its prime, but pleasant and welcoming nonetheless.

We reached the porch and I could hear the faint chatter of a television set and the chink of cutlery on china, through the screen door. The inside was light and airy and I could see long fingers of warm sunshine reaching into the front hallway from open windows in the other rooms.

A man's voice called out, repeating the score of whatever game was being televised, then the sound was abruptly muted. I almost loathed knocking, not wanting to disrupt the normalcy inside. Barry saved me the trouble, rapping sharply on the screen then puffing his chest out and glancing sideways at me.

"Maybe you should let me start the ball rolling, okay?" He rocked back and forth on his heels, sliding both his hands into his hip pockets.

I shrugged. It was fine with me. A rangy silhouette filled the screen door.

"Can I help you?"

Barry put on his best officious voice.

"Afternoon, Sir. Are you, or did you used to be, Detective Peter Croft?"

I rolled my eyes as the silhouette chuckled.

"Well, I'm still Peter Croft." He had a relaxed drawl, his voice deep and smooth. "Who are you?"

"I'm Officer Brent from the LAPD and this is Katherine Alley, she's—um—she's with me. We'd like to talk to you about a case you worked on a very long time ago. A murder. One that happened fifty years ago, to be exact."

I shuffled my feet anxiously thinking, 'please don't close the door, please don't close the door'. At the same time, I could hear Xander muttering behind me, *'come on... come on.'* I felt disingenuous letting Barry make out I was with the police, but was certain that—if we mentioned the word *journalist*—the door would slam in our faces. I didn't want to chance it.

The screen door clicked after a lengthy pause and swung slowly outwards. Peter Croft stood solidly in the doorway, every inch the retired police officer. His seventy-odd years had been more than kind; a weather-beaten face, scruffy white stubble stark against dark, coppery skin. He reminded me pleasantly of an elderly Denzel Washington. We all peered up at him as he directed an impenetrable gaze first at Barry then at me, then again at Barry. His shoulders rose as he inhaled slowly and drew a tight line with his mouth.

"I knew someone would come one of these days." He exhaled sharply. "To be honest I thought it'd be sooner. You'd best come in."

I exchanged pensive glances with Xander as we traipsed into the house. Peter busied his wife with refreshments and we all sat perched on the edges of sturdy, economical couches, tense with anticipation until cool drinks arrived on a wicker tray, icy and fragrant. His wife, a buxom woman with her greying afro cropped close and a gentle face, quickly made herself scarce.

Pictures in mismatched frames lined the walls and huddled in clusters on well-polished side tables - a wedding photo in black and white, faded baby pictures, children at varying ages; laughing on birthdays, solemn in graduation caps. A pair of photos hung side by side across the room, both unmistakably Peter Croft in full police dress but taken at opposite ends of his life. One showed a young man, face bright and full of optimism and eagerness. In the other his jacket was heavy with medals and coloured ribbons, the lines on his face showing the burden of the years.

Small talk was made briefly; we asked about his family and answered questions in return about the traffic on the drive over, passing comment on the terrible state of roads in LA. I complimented the décor then pointed at the uniformed photographs on the opposite wall.

"You were a policeman for a very long time, Mr Croft. And decorated too, I see."

He gazed at me for a long time.

"Yes indeed, young lady. I was." Then he smiled. "I think it's what they call a distinguished career." He fell silent and bowed his head, elbows on his knees and hands clasped, forehead resting on his knuckles. The silence stretched uneasily until Barry broke it by clearing his throat.

"Mr Croft—"

"Peter, please."

"—uh, Peter. We've got some questions about the Xander Hill murder case—1973—I'm sure you recall it. We've been doing some research for uh... for a police study, and we found some inconsistencies. There were some problems with the case that lead us to believe it wasn't ultimately conducted as it should have been."

He trailed off uncertainly and glanced at me as the room settled into silence again. When Peter finally looked up, his brow was deeply furrowed.

"That case has been like a weight around my neck for fifty years." His voice was heavy with regret. "I never should have let it happen. Danny said it would be fine and I was new to the bureau—young, stupid. Easily swayed, I guess. Things were tougher back then for a black officer. But it wasn't fine. Not fine at all."

"Peter, the procedure for—" Barry started. I lifted my hand

to stop him, motioning for him to take notes instead. He flipped open a small black notebook. I spoke gently to Peter, taking a less officious tack.

"Mr Croft—Peter—it seemed to me that there was a lot of information missing from the case file; things that weren't done. Like an autopsy, for instance. I mean, that seems a pretty important thing to miss." I took a stab in the dark. "Would I be right in thinking somebody wanted the case to go away?"

Peter nodded.

"Who was it?" I held my breath.

"It was Zach Tennant."

I wasn't surprised but Xander jumped up from the couch and paced the room, furious.

"Bastard! So, *he* killed me... and he got away with it."

I ignored him with difficulty, paraphrasing him instead.

"So, are you saying, Peter, that Zach Tennant killed Xander Hill and paid off the police?"

"No, no." Peter put his hand up. "Tennant didn't kill him. It's much more complex than that."

Xander stopped pacing and stared at the man, as puzzled as I felt. Barry scratched his head, perplexed.

"I'm sorry, I'm confused." I leaned forward. "If Tennant didn't kill him, why did he want the case to go away?"

"He wanted it over, wanted to protect his wife. Looking back, he clearly thought she'd done it—that she'd killed Hill—but he gave her an alibi anyway. He claimed she was at home with him the whole time. We had nothing else to go on, we investigated every possible angle, whether she'd hired someone to do it, that kind of thing. We came up with nothing. It all dragged on and on with no more leads and the papers, well, the papers were hounding them relentlessly, you know how they are." Barry shot me a look and I felt my cheeks flush. "Eventually, Tennant came to see Danny at the precinct."

"Danny? He was your partner?"

"Sure was."

The hairs on the back of my arms tingled with nervous static.

"So, what happened? What did he want?" I prodded him, although I was way ahead, already piecing it together in my head. I should've known to trust my instincts by now.

"Danny had an agenda the whole time, from the very beginning of the investigation, that's why he didn't order an autopsy. Autopsy results would have been too hard to make disappear. I questioned him but he told me it was a waste of time; it was obvious what the cause of death was. He told me to smarten up, that things were different in the Detective Bureau. Our time was premium and we shouldn't waste it on what was evident." Peter paused and shook his head, lost in unpleasant memories. "He was a bully—and, unfortunately, I believed him."

Barry interjected, pen at the ready.

"So, Zach Tennant paid you both off. How much? What was it worth?"

"There was no money. It was never about that," said Peter. I leaned over to touch Barry's hand.

"Don't you get it?" I said to him urgently, saving Peter from further explanation, "Danny made a deal. He didn't want money, he wanted fame."

"What?" Barry clearly had no recollection of the conversation with his mother the day before.

"Detective Daniel Reisemann." I waved my hands at him, then repeated, "DANNY Reisemann—the actor your Mum mentioned. Remember?"

"Bullshit." Barry's blatant disbelief was borderline comical.

"It's true." Peter shrugged.

"I told you." I smirked with satisfaction.

Xander had faced the window through the entire conversation but now he turned and laughed bitterly.

"The things people do for fame, huh?" He stopped short, clearly remembering something, but when I raised a quizzical eyebrow at him, he turned away.

"Well, there you go." Barry slapped his knee in amazement. "Police officers *do* become movie stars. I'll be buggered. But two things I don't get—what did you get out of it and why do records say Reisemann was with the force right up until he retired?"

Peter let out a short mirthless laugh.

"Me? I got nothing, Officer Brent. I wouldn't go as far as to say movie *star* either. Danny was envious of the way people lived in this town, all the movie people. He knew all the dirty little secrets, said none of them deserved what they had, said it was easy money. He closed the case on the condition Tennant gave him parts in all his movies, that he'd make him famous. He quit the force a few weeks after he closed the case and was going to pay me for keeping quiet, when he got rich. Problem is, it never happened."

I was puzzled.

"Why not?"

Peter laughed again, this time warmly.

"Because Danny was a terrible actor. He made five movies with Tennant over three years, all pretty small parts but he couldn't complain. Tennant was holding up his side of the bargain. Then Tennant died. All the stress finally got to him, I guess. His wife had pretty much gone into hiding, so he'd lost his biggest star. His films had been consistently losing money. He dropped dead of a heart attack on set. Nobody else would hire Danny because he was so bad and he didn't even have good looks to rely on. Eventually he came crawling back to the force, got reinstated and never talked about it again."

"And you never said anything either." I let out a low whistle.

Peter shook his head, suddenly seeming so much older than before.

"I convinced myself I hadn't done anything wrong. I hadn't taken any money; all I'd done was stop investigating. I tried to make amends by working overtime on other cases, refusing to let them drop. I worked hard, you can see from those photos, I became a decorated officer. But even that stuck in my throat, I felt like a fraud. You know, in the back of my mind there was always that thought, that I could have solved it if I'd kept trying. If I hadn't been so weak."

He sighed, rubbing at his face. "After Danny retired, then passed away, I thought about talking. It had weighed on me for so long. But then I thought maybe there was no point dragging up the past after so many years. What purpose would it serve apart from hurting my family? The closing of the case seemed legitimate. Everyone involved was long gone. Nobody else remembered. It was only my own guilt eating away at me so I decided in the end to continue letting sleeping dogs lie, so to speak."

He trailed off and fell silent once again, lost in thought. I didn't know what to say, or even whether to say anything at all. I couldn't assuage fifty-year-old guilt with platitudes and I certainly couldn't tell him Xander had been stuck ever since, most likely as a result of his silence. And was there any point in revealing that his main suspect still lived, hidden away in the Hollywood Hills. I didn't think so. To my surprise, even Xander was quiet. I expected him to rant about the injustice but he faced the wall, his expression hidden from view, hands shaking slightly. Fuming, I was sure.

"Sir, I need to come clean with you about something," I said tentatively, realising that if I was to use any of this at all I had to be honest with Peter. He smiled at me, obviously tired but his eyes still crinkling.

"Sir? Whew, it must be big. Well, it seems like the day for it. Go ahead girly."

"I'm not actually with the LAPD I'm afraid. I'm a journalist. I—" I faltered. "—I didn't feel right not saying."

Peter didn't bat an eyelid, only smiled again.

"I figured as much. You're far too smart and pretty to be a cop." He surprised me with a wink.

"Can I take that to mean you're okay with me using this information for my article?" I was still hesitant.

He put his hands on his knees and pushed himself up to standing.

"Lady, I'm old and I'm tired of carrying this around with me. I'll repeat whatever you need—to whomever I need to—come what may."

I stood as well, not daring to believe how well this had gone.
"Are you sure?"

"You have my word."

I shook his hand as Barry too climbed to his feet.

"Actually, Mr Croft," he was suddenly all officious again. "Let's not jump the gun, eh? I reckon that'll depend on whether we uncover any new information that could lead to reopening the case, don't you?"

"What do you mean?" I interrupted, puzzled.

"I'm saying, Katherine," Barry cleared his throat, "unless we solve the case and are required to make all this known, there's probably no point turning someone's life upside down after all these years. Wouldn't you agree? I'd say talking to us has eased the burden somewhat already." He nodded knowingly at the older detective, who gave a tiny nod of his head in return. Knowing the permanent pole up Barry's backside, I'd expected it would be strictly by the book from here on in. I was surprised to say the least. He wasn't completely uptight after all.

And he was right. If I didn't find out anything new about Xander's murder, I was simply going to write a story about secret gay love, despite Xander's continued denials. In that case, was the fact it had been buried relevant? Did printing it warrant the turmoil it would bring to former-Detective Croft and his family? If I was honest, no.

I felt like patting myself on the head. The only other time in my life I'd been happy to sit on scandalous information was when I'd been trading it for something more salacious. Clearly, I was growing as a person. Besides, if I did happen to stumble on the killer and reopen the case, it was reassuring to know Croft was prepared to talk. It was win-win as far as I was concerned and I didn't even have to feel dirty.

"There's one last thing I need to know, Peter," I hedged. His eyes crinkled again as he spoke.

"You want to know who I think did it?"

I nodded, my stomach swirling. Peter's expression turned serious as he scratched at the silvery stubble on the side of his face. "There is not a shred of doubt in my mind, to this day—" he paused "—that Lola Tennant killed him. Now, if you don't mind, I think my lunch is calling." He gestured towards the hallway, every bit the gentleman. Barry and I turned to go, murmuring assent and our thanks.

"We'll get this all straightened out, I assure you." Barry shot Peter a quick salute and I shook my head, my eyes rolling before I could stop them. Peter caught me and his lips twitched. He was back to looking like Denzel and he patted my arm gently before turning to Barry.

"No doubt you will." He shook Barry's hand firmly as they reached the front door. I glanced back at the window to assess Xander's reaction, but he was gone. My stomach sank. I had no idea when he'd disappeared but I imagined his head was reeling. How hard it must have been, listening to your own murder dismissed so easily, as though it didn't matter. We climbed back into the car and Barry turned to me.

"So, what do you think?"

I mused for a couple of seconds.

"We still have no real proof as to who killed Xander, but we're closer, that's for sure." I shrugged. "Peter was pretty certain Lola did it, and Zach Tennant was so convinced his wife committed murder that he bribed the police. Nobody does that without good reason."

"Okay, so what now?"

"Now? Now I go to see that wife."

Chapter Sixteen

Considering Hollywood's often sordid history, it wasn't surprising to find a bus tour dedicated to death and scandal, kind of like a *Movie Star Homes Tour* for the morbid and deeply disturbed. I managed to book myself on the next one heading out that afternoon. I figured it was the easiest way for me to not only check out where Xander died but also to get within walking distance of Lola's house.

Waiting for the little bus to depart from the tour depot on Sunset, I worried about Xander. He'd appeared and disappeared a number of times since heading back from Pasadena that morning; twice in the car and once back at the hotel. He only appeared for a few minutes and each time I might as well have not been there.

He'd been troubled and angry, staring into the distance or at the floor. At the hotel, he seemed to be talking to himself, except I couldn't hear him. It was as if someone had pressed his mute button. Then he'd flickered like a faulty television set and disappeared again.

He was clearly getting worse. I chewed my finger nails,

anxious. It was happening more often and for longer and I had absolutely no idea what it meant. I was hardly a ghost expert. I considered asking the tour guide if John Edwards' house was on the itinerary but thought better of it, due to the fact he looked a lot like Lurch from *The Addams Family* and was creeping me out. I made a mental note to ask the concierge about local new-age shops when I got back. There had to be books on this stuff, right?

The window seat beside me on the bus sat empty when we pulled away from the curb, which was lucky because a few minutes into the tour a peculiar warm sensation radiated against my side. The heat increased rapidly until it was border-line unbearable. I was about to yell to the driver that I was certain the bus's fuel tank was about to go kaboom, when I heard Xander's faint voice as if coming from a radio that'd been turned down low. His figure took shape beside me, his voice getting stronger, until the heat suddenly dissipated and he was sitting there, solid as you like, half way through a sentence.

"—no idea why you would behave like this."

I stared at him, confused—and glad I took the aisle seat so I looked like I was simply gazing out of the window. The other passengers were either chatting among themselves or listening intently to Lurch, who was running through his spiel on the tinny PA. I felt sure I could speak to Xander relatively unnoticed.

"Pardon me?" I whispered.

"So now you're talking to me?"

"What on earth are you going on about?"

He folded his arms and narrowed his eyes.

"I've been trying to talk to you since we left the hotel but you've been ignoring me. I don't know what I've done, but it's pretty rude, Katherine."

"Wait a minute. You just got here."

Xander stopped short, uncertain.

"No, I've been with you since the hotel, we walked all the way here. You mean you haven't been able to hear me this whole time?"

"Or see you. Xander, you've been disappearing and reappearing so much today you're making me dizzy."

"I have?"

"You don't remember?"

He shook his head in confusion.

"The last thing I remember before we left the hotel is being in Pasadena, at the old detective's house."

I frowned again. Something was way off.

"Is there something you're not telling me?" I had a sudden thought. "You remembered something important when we were there, didn't you? You've been weird ever since."

He looked away and I thought he was about to open up, but when he turned back his eyes were flat.

"There's nothing. I didn't remember anything new." He stared at his fingers, knotted in his lap. I didn't believe him but what could I do? I couldn't force it out of him.

"Fine, whatever. I think something's happening to you though. It can't be right, all this disappearing, memory lapses, the weird personality shifts."

He was unresponsive and surly, so I sat back against the seat, studiously ignoring him. Two could play at this game. I had no idea how, but I was going to figure it out, with or without Xander's input. Eventually he lifted his head and glanced out of the window as if only just realising we were moving.

"Where are we going now and why are we on a bus?"

I hesitated and chewed my lip.

"Uh—"

"You don't need to sugar coat it, Katherine; I can take it. Tell me."

"Well—" Fine, if he wanted it straight up, I'd give it to him, "—this is what's known as the *Dark Side Tour*. I'm on my way to speak to the woman who might have murdered you and I thought it would be fun to stop past where you were shot on the way. As well as taking a quick peek at where lots of other famous people either died or did very bad things. Cool? Cool."

He stared at me for a second, dumbstruck, then wrinkled his nose in distaste.

"There is something seriously wrong with you."

I smiled broadly and shrugged.

"You asked."

"Why on earth are we going to where I died?"

"In case it triggers something in your memory, dummy. Maybe there are some left-over energy vibrations there or something. I don't know how it works. Don't argue, I'm willing to try anything at this point."

Xander wasn't convinced—or happy—but I didn't care. Caught up yapping to him, I'd missed the *Viper Room,* where River Phoenix had overdosed and shattered my teenaged heart into a million pieces; I'd also missed the spot on Sunset where Hugh Grant was busted with Divine Brown, although I wasn't as bothered about that. There was still plenty to see however, on what turned out to be a three-hour tour, with Xander's murder site the very last stop.

Fascinated, I pressed my nose to glass as the bus wound its morbid way past the house in Beverly Hills where Sharon Tate was murdered by the Mansons, and the toilet block where George Michael was arrested. OJ and Marilyn Monroe's houses in Brentwood were next, then Michael Jackson's in Bel Air. We whizzed past countless other grisly and sordid settings, before heading towards our final destination.

. . .

There was nothing to mark the scene of Xander's death. It was basically just a patch of gravel, the road on one side and grass and dry scrubby trees leading into the county park on the other. I never would have found it on my own.

When everyone piled off the bus with their cameras, I distanced myself from the group, pretending to examine spots on the ground like someone from CSI. As soon as Lurch turned the other way, I ducked into the dense scrub and crossed my fingers against a head count when the rest of the noisy group re-boarded the bus.

I was in luck. Once the bus had pulled away and was completely out of sight, I emerged from the bushes, picking bits of dried leaf out of my hair. Xander stood motionless by the side of the road with his eyes closed. I cleared my throat.

"Uh—what are you doing?"

He didn't move.

"Trying to sense something. Shhh."

I stood in silence for a few minutes, waiting and taking note of the fact there were no houses on this particular stretch of road. Patience was not my strong point.

"Are you feeling anything?" I prodded.

Xander opened one eye and peered at me for a few seconds before scrunching his nose. "Not even a tingle. Sorry. I don't even feel mad. Nothing."

"Well, that was a wasted trip." I sighed. Xander, however, was oddly cheery.

"Not at all! I got to see where Harry Houdini died. He was standing in the driveway as we went past. He waved at me."

"Really?" My eyes widened.

"No, I'm kidding."

"Xander!"

"What? You've got to admit, that was funny. You should have seen your face. I'm funny—right?"

"XANDER!" I glared at him. "We've got more important things to worry about than whether or not you're bloody funny. I'm trying to find out who killed you; this is serious."

I tutted and took out my map, turning it round and around to get my bearings. Lola still lived in the same house, the one she'd shared with her husband. It sat on Palo Vista Drive, which ran directly off Mulholland about a mile up the road.

"Sorry," Xander was contrite. "I kid around when I'm nervous. I know I'm not being much help."

"It's okay, don't worry about it." I tucked the map into my pocket and started walking. Xander jogged a couple of steps until he caught up and I smiled grudgingly at him. "I suppose it was a bit funny."

"Only a *bit*?" He grinned.

"Alright, you win. It was hilarious." I laid it on thick. "I am utterly blown away by your comedic timing and sparkling wit."

"Okay, now you're mocking me."

"No, no. I mean it. You should definitely be a comedian—" *pause for effect* "—Not!"

It went completely over his head. "Not what?"

"It's called sarcasm," I chuckled. "It's a 'not' joke."

"If it's not a joke then what is it?" He stopped walking and actually scratched his head, puzzled.

"I didn't mean it's not a joke. It's a joke, it's—" I stopped, floundering for an explanation that made some kind of sense. "What you do is you say the opposite of what you really think and then say 'not' after it to show you actually meant the reverse." Explained that way it sounded stupid.

"I don't get it." Xander's brow wrinkled. "Why wouldn't you say what you meant in the first place?"

"Because it's supposed to be funny. You try one."

"So, if I said 'I'm not very attractive, not'—would that be right?"

I mentally juggled his sentence.

"Technically I suppose so, because clearly you are extremely attractive. So, by saying 'I'm not very'—wait a second, you're trying to get me to tell you how attractive you are, aren't you?" I snorted as he waggled his eyebrows at me. "Nice try, Mister. Regardless of whether you are *butt-ugly* or not, you had your timing all wrong. You have to pause before you say 'not' and then say it all dramatic, like this – '*Not!*' See?"

"I still don't get it."

"Sweet baby Jesus!"

"What's a baby cheese?"

"Huh?"

"You said 'sweet baby cheeses'. Is that like a tiny cheese?"

I resisted the urge to facepalm myself.

"Are you serious?"

"No. I'm kidding," he deadpanned. "Was it funny?"

I laughed, unable to hold it in any longer.

"Shut up, Xander," I grinned as I began to march up the hill again.

"No, seriously, was it funny?"

"You're an idiot."

"Yes, but am I a *funny* idiot?"

And that's the way it went—on and on, all the way to the top of the hill. Luckily Xander fell into subdued silence about fifty metres before we reached Lola's house—and about thirty seconds before I was about to lobotomise myself with a spoon rather than listen to any more of his lame jokes.

. . .

The heavy iron gates marking the entrance to Lola's property were in stark contrast to those at Quentin's home. Rusted and tangled with wisteria, they sagged from cracked and dishevelled brick pillars and didn't quite meet in the middle

Snarled vines crisscrossed between the gates, negating the need for a lock. Beyond them lay wild, unkempt gardens, broken paving and a surprisingly small Mediterranean-style villa, rendered in faded and peeling blue stucco. Like dogs and their owners, houses in Hollywood clearly grew to resemble their occupants.

Xander walked up to the gates and stood, staring silently at the dilapidated house. I hovered beside him, following his eyes.

"Is this the house you remember—that you've been to before?"

He nodded, focusing intently on one of the low windows. It was mildewed and cracked in one corner, the curtains behind it drawn and hanging unevenly as if multiple hooks were missing.

Movement caught my eye and my nerves jittered but it was only a fat tortoiseshell cat, twitching its ears and sunning itself on the broad window sill behind the glass. I moved my hand back and forth in front of Xander's face, scared he was going to flip out on me—or turn evil. "Are you okay?" I whispered, not wanting to startle him. He didn't answer me, but his expression was relatively calm so I relaxed—for now.

I pulled at the vines covering the brick pillars, searching for an intercom of some kind. There was none. I was fairly sure they had them in the sixties and seventies. As a very well-known celebrity, why would she not have one installed? Seemed strange. Regardless, at least it meant she couldn't be forewarned and lock me out. I inspected the impenetrable knot of vines across the gate. How the heck was I going to get through them?

"There must be a side entrance, Katherine." Xander spoke quietly, as if reading my mind and without taking his eyes off the house. "Nobody's gotten through those gates in years by the looks of them. You said your friend's brother makes deliveries here. Then there must be another way in."

If Xander had been corporeal, I would have kissed him.

"Maybe it's down the side of the house," I tried to peer through gaps further down the wall. "Are you coming?"

"No, I told you, I can't go in. I've never been able to."

I glanced quizzically back at him.

"But she's seen you now. Maybe it'll be different."

Xander shook his head sadly.

"It's not. I don't even need to try. I know. This place is filled with her energy. I can feel it already, guilt—and sadness. She's protecting herself. I'm telling you, there's no way I'm getting through those gates."

"What do you mean protecting herself? From what?"

When he turned to me, his mouth was hard.

"From me."

"Why would she—?" Xander shot me a glare that said 'she had damn good reason' and I backed up a few steps in uncertainty. *Okay then*. It was like playing split-personality roulette and right now I didn't feel like waiting around for the nasty ball to drop. "So, you'll wait here?" I waited a split second for a response, but he'd already shifted his attention back to the side of the house. I shivered involuntarily and turned swiftly to go, searching for a break in the wall or another gate.

"Katherine—"

I stopped short of breaking into a jog and whirled around.

"What?"

"Katheri—Kat—before you go in. I need to tell you something."

The uncharacteristic use of my nickname unnerved me. I took a few tentative steps towards him.

"You never call me Kat. What is it? Is it bad?"

"I don't think you're going to like it."

Foreboding slithered around my feet and I felt the fluttery beginnings of panic in my gut. His tense expression made me more than a little uneasy.

"Spit it out, Xander."

He hesitated, staring at me. "I wasn't entirely truthful with you on the bus."

"About what?"

"I did remember something, back at the detective's house. Something important." *I knew it.* "I didn't want to believe it of myself, that's why I didn't say anything. I thought I might have been imagining things—twisting events in my mind, confused. But I'm not."

"Twisting what? Is it about Lola?"

"No, it's not about Lola." His continued hesitancy pulled my nerves taut to the point of snapping.

"Then what? What are you talking about Xander?" I snapped, exasperated. Finally, his lips curled in disgust and he rubbed his hand hard across his eyes before pushing the words out through gritted teeth.

"Don't make me say it—I have to show you." Before I could say anything, he stepped quickly towards me and placed his hand in the middle of my chest. It passed straight through me and I gasped as I felt a jolt of electricity. My head pounded for a second, then a wash of images filled my head.

Tangled limbs and bed sheets. A man's laughter. Hands entwined. Naked skin and sweat. Xander's eyes. And a much younger, but unmistakeable face. It was Quentin Millson. I felt heat and longing and then something else. Something dark and cold and hateful.

Frightened, I jerked backwards and Xander withdrew his hand. I felt dizzy and sick and I glared at Xander confused and angry at the violation.

"What the hell was that?" I demanded.

"It's what I remembered."

"Quentin?"

"He was telling the truth, Katherine."

"Huh?"

"I was his lover."

He spat the word 'lover' as if it were venom and pressed the back of his hand to his mouth.

"Excuse me?" My voice rose an octave, "Are you saying, after all your furious denial, that you're gay after all?" I shook my head, still trying to shake off the sick feeling. I'd thought it was going to be something terrible. "Xander, there's nothing wrong with—"

Xander rounded violently on me, his eyes dark and his mouth still twisted with distaste. "I am not—I *was* not—a homosexual."

"Wait, you just showed me—"

Xander closed his eyes, drawing in a deep shuddering breath.

"I said I was his lover, Katherine, but I was not *gay*."

I was so confused. Was he saying he was the victim of some kind of casting couch coercion? I knew how rife that had once been, even recently, until the Weinstein scandal had brought it all down like a house of cards. So many young actors and actresses caught up in it. I moved towards Xander, sympathetic. It wasn't his fault.

"Okay, so you were pressured into having sex with him but—"

"No," he cut me dead. "Don't you get it? It was so much more than that. I used him, Katherine. For nearly two years, I slept with him in secret. I made him fall in love with me, made him believe I loved him, to get what I wanted. The lengths I went to—" he paused, clenching his fists and screwing up his face. "I lied to him and I was disgusted with myself the whole time. What kind of person does that?"

Now I got it—and the awful darkness I'd felt. And he was right, it immediately changed the way I saw him. I was so dismayed, all I could do was stare at him, speechless. My hands balled at my sides, nails digging into my palms. Then I found my voice. And it was strident.

"You think being with Quentin was disgusting? Xander, if that's the truth, you're the one who was disgusting. What you did was blatantly manipulative. You deceived someone who cared about you. You did things that were completely against your own moral judgement, whether that judgement in itself was right or wrong, purely for your own selfish gain, to help your career. How could you?"

To be honest, up until then I'd still been sitting on the fence regarding Quentin's big reveal. Teasing Xander had been amusing but I'd actually suspected Quentin was exaggerating somewhat. Judgmentally, I'd thought him a lonely, attention seeking old has-been, trading on what was more likely to have been a fling, if anything.

Having sex with someone to advance your career, even blurring the lines of sexuality, was nothing new. It had always happened. But making someone fall in love with you, faking a whole relationship—for years—that was different, at least in my eyes. That took commitment and I'm not talking the matrimonial kind. *I'll take sociopath for a hundred, Alex.*

Suddenly, it occurred to me that if this was the truth, Quentin had motive enough to have killed Xander. The bastard abandoned him—for a woman no less. Now, *that* was the definition of a crime of passion. I was back where I started, with no real clue about who might have done it. I couldn't look at him. I shook my head and started backing away.

"Kat—"

I stopped him.

"Don't call me Kat. Not now."

"Katherine, listen to me. I have to tell you everything."

I reeled. There was more?

"Go on, what else?"

"I didn't just use Quentin for my career. It was more than that." He paused. "I used him to get to Lola."

"Lola? I'm not sure I understand. Why? How?"

"I don't remember." Xander shrugged and averted his eyes. "All I know is, it wasn't good."

"You lied to me."

"I wasn't lying, Katherine." His tone was desperate, "I had no memory of it. Not until now."

I put my hand up. "Just stop." I didn't want to know any more. Not yet. So, I turned and I walked away.

Chapter Seventeen

I blindly followed the perimeter wall, stalking around the corner of the property. I was desperate to get away from Xander, so I could think. Overgrown crabgrass tugged at my ankles and I stumbled, grazing my palm on the cracked and broken surface of the wall. Once out of sight, I pressed my back up against the cool bricks and slid to a crouch, gasping, my head reeling.

Shit. Was Xander the villain in this story after all? I was starting to panic. I took a long, slow breath. *Calm down, Kat, you're being over-dramatic.* This was not an episode of *Charmed* and I did not need to vanquish Xander. He wasn't evil, he simply wasn't a very nice person. Clearly. Maybe that's why he was stuck; Heaven had a policy on refusing entry to arseholes.

Xander was definitely not turning out to be the person I thought he was. Then again, all I'd had to go on were old magazine articles, PR spiel and Hollywood hearsay. Of all people, I should have known that someone's public face was nothing but a cleverly constructed mask, one that made them seem special. Their true face hid underneath, hoping desperately not to be found out by people like me. Most famous people lived in fear that their ordinariness could be revealed to the masses at any second; that they'd be outed as simply human —damaged and broken and weird. No different to everyone else.

The Xander I'd expected was a reflection of his shiny, plastic image; a black and white photograph with a showgirl and a cocky smile. The black moods, the sudden displays of violent temper and the menacing countenance, the arguments recounted in the case file; clearly that was the real Xander Hill. Or was it?

Hadn't I seen another, more unexpected side too, full of humour and silliness? He'd been polite and sweet on occasion, tender even. I'd seen fear and frustration and regret—and I'd seen sadness. Was he faking all of that too? He was an actor after all.

The lies and half-truths swarmed in my head like angry bees. How was I supposed to know? I couldn't process it all right then so I stood up—still confused and furious—and followed the wall again. Finally, I came to a narrow gate. No intercom here either but this gate was locked with a heavy brass padlock. I knew I was in the right place; the grass in front of the gate was patchy and worn with traces of thick tyre marks. Unlike me, Luis must have had a key.

I didn't hesitate. I grabbed the bars and hoisted myself up, swinging my body awkwardly over the top and hoping Lola wasn't the owner of some kind of vicious dog. The metal bruised my hip bones and as I dropped to the ground on the other side, my left hand slipped and my right arm was nearly yanked out of its socket.

I swore under my breath and rolled my shoulder a few times, reminded that it was exactly this complete lack of coordination that led my junior gymnastics coach to suggest to my mother that I try out for chess club instead.

I skirted the house with trepidation. It would have once been beautiful, I'm sure. Now, after years of neglect, it was nothing but a cracked and peeling shell. The front entrance was set into a wide, tiled alcove that was heavily littered with dead leaves. They skittered, dry and brittle, in the breeze and I kicked them aside and took a deep breath before rapping sharply on the faded wooden door.

Minutes passed before I heard the sound of movement behind the door. I was about to knock again when a thin voice called through the wood, clear and lucid and with surprising gumption.

"Whoever you are, you're trespassing. Get off my property before I call the police."

"Mrs Tennant? Lola? It's Katherine Alley, I spoke to you at the cemetery last night." A long pause. When Lola spoke again her voice shook.

"Go away. I think I made it very clear last night I didn't want to speak with you. Get off my property and leave me alone."

"I know you saw Xander last night." I cocked my ear at the door as I paused but there was complete silence. "Lola. I know you saw him. I know other things as well." Desperate, the words tumbled out of me. "I know about the money and I know your husband made a deal to make the case go away. Please, you have to talk to me. It's important. For Xander's sake."

Okay, so it wasn't exactly *for Xander's sake,* but if it got her to open the door I was at peace with the tiny white lie. I held my breath again and waited. Another minute passed—nothing. I was about to give up when the clunking of locks stopped me. The door inched slowly open, the wood sticking in the frame.

It creaked, heavy on its hinges. Lola pressed a troubled face to the gap, her eyes searching my face.

"I thought I was seeing things," she whispered fearfully, "that I'd finally gone mad. He was really there?"

I nodded. "He was there."

Lola moved away from the door, still guarded but tugging it further open to let me in. I stepped over the threshold and waited while she fumbled at each lock with trembling, arthritic hands, painstakingly securing the door behind us. The first thing I noticed about the house was the unmistakable and acrid smell of numerous cats.

She turned and shuffled down a dim hallway, beckoning for me to follow, her hunched and bony shoulders protruding from a ragged black house dress. Her hair hung loose. Patches of pink scalp showed through but it still trailed down the middle of her back, thin and ashen and matted in places. Sickly coughs rattled her tiny frame and she stopped occasionally, steadying herself on the wall before continuing down the corridor.

She ushered me into a large but stuffy central room. Once it would have been opulent and beautifully furnished but now there were old books and yellowing newspapers, their pages curling, heaped on sagging sofas and strewn haphazardly across the ornate but filthy coffee table. Bare walls surrounded me, yet stacks of framed black and white photographs sat on the stained carpet, propped up against mildewed skirting boards.

Four unkempt cats; two tabby, one grey and fluffy and another one white with a painful-looking scab on its nose, immediately wound around our legs, mewing plaintively. I spotted three more, two curled in sleep on the faded velvet sofa and the fat cat I'd seen from outside, still sprawled in the window.

Overflowing litter trays squatted in one corner, pungent

and offensive in the airless room. Lola fussed around several bowls caked with tinned cat food and saucers of souring milk, before turning her attention back to me. I gazed around at the sorry state of the house, saddened.

She perched tensely on the arm of one sofa and motioned for me to sit opposite. She didn't offer me a drink, hospitality either forgotten or not warranted. Her arms wrapped tightly around her frail body and her eyes darted around the room before fixing suddenly on me.

"Is he here?"

"He's outside," I said. "He can't come in." Her brow creased. "He's not sure why, but he can't come through the gates. He thinks your energy is blocking him somehow."

"This can't be real." Lola touched a shaking hand to her temple. "Why has he come back? Why now?"

"He hasn't come back. He never went away."

"What do you mean?"

"Apparently, his spirit—or whatever you want to call it— has been stuck here since he died."

Both hands flew to cover her mouth.

"Oh my god. No."

As her face crumpled, her eyes slipped out of focus. She rocked back and forth, her mind battling with unseen demons, lips moving rapidly without sound. Minutes slipped passed as I watched, uncomfortable but not daring to intrude. She'd forgotten I was there, lost in private pain or mental fog. Finally, she looked up at me, eyes clear.

"So, Ms. Alley. Katherine—" her voice was husky and broken with age and pain "—what exactly is it you want to know and why? What has this all got to do with you?"

As soon as I uttered the word 'journalist' she flinched, her mouth tightening. I explained that Xander had come to me, that I was trying to help him find out what happened that night. When I said that, she eyed me curiously.

"You mean he doesn't remember?"

I shook my head.

"Xander doesn't remember much at all. Fragments, bits and pieces of memories, but no, not who killed him. I was hoping maybe you would be able to shed some light on it. I know the police cleared you, but I also know about the deal your husband made with Danny Reisemann."

Relief seemed to settle over Lola's face. Then her lips pressed tightly shut and she hugged her ribs, shaking her head.

"No, I don't know who killed him. I'm sorry, I wish I did. It certainly wasn't me." A bitter smile curled her lips. "My husband never believed that, though. Right up until the day he died, he always thought I'd organised Xander's murder, that I was actually capable of that. When Zach made that deal, he thought he was protecting me."

"Could your husband have killed him?"

"No. He was here—with me—that entire night. Our alibi wasn't a lie. Although, if there was one person with a good reason to want Xander dead, it was Zach. Like everyone else, my husband believed I was involved with Xander romantically. An affair would have affected my career and—in turn—his films and his reputation. He couldn't have that."

She laughed, but it was without humour. "You see, he loved me obsessively but there was no passion, no real love. I was a belonging. I made him money. Bribing the police wasn't about protecting me, he was protecting an asset. It gave him something to hold over me so I'd never leave. It didn't matter that I didn't do it. He thought I did and so did everybody else, so he took care of business."

I leaned forward, wanting to backtrack slightly.

"So, are you saying you weren't involved with Xander?"

She looked at me sharply.

"No. I wasn't. But it was easier to let Zach believe I was."

"I don't understand. Easier than what?"

"The truth."

The fragments Xander had been able to recall tumbled around in my mind, attempting to arrange themselves into some kind of order. Trying to make sense of them was like trying to knit with wet spaghetti.

"Is this something to do with the money you gave Xander?" I asked after a short pause. She snorted and immediately broke out in racking coughs.

"*Paid* Xander you mean?" she managed to splutter before pausing for breath and fixing me with a calculating stare. "What did Xander tell you?"

I attempted to explain with what little detail I had.

"Only that you threw money at him the night he died. That you said he wasn't getting any more. He thinks you might have been paying him to go away, to leave you alone."

"Xander was blackmailing me, Katherine. He knew something about—" she paused, "—my past. Something that could have destroyed my career, my life. He was relentless."

"Can you tell me what it was?"

A derisive laugh broke hoarsely forth from her.

"Don't you think if I was prepared to talk about it, I'd have refused to give Xander the money? I would have let him talk."

"That was fifty years ago. He's dead. No offence, but everyone also thinks you're dead." She flinched at that. "How can it possibly matter now? I apologise for being so blunt, but I get the feeling we're running out of time."

"Running out of time how?" Lola's face paled and she moved from her position perched on the arm of the sofa and sat among the faded cushions.

"Something is happening to him. He keeps disappearing,

again and again; for longer periods each time. His memory is patchy at best, and his personality, well it's different sometimes."

At that she laughed again, still with no real humour. It was a hollow, empty sound.

"That sounds perfectly like Xander. He was never what he appeared to be."

"Lola, this isn't about whether or not he had some kind of bloody personality disorder. I think he's fading away."

"I don't know what you think I can do about that." Her chin jutted, stubbornly and I exhaled sharply out of sheer frustration.

"You can tell me the truth, tell me what you know. It makes no difference to you now, surely."

She fixed me with a cold glare.

"Does it occur to you that I might be quite happy to stay 'dead'. I certainly don't need to be back in the press. What is the point of stirring it all up now? How does that help anybody? How does that stop whatever is happening to him? You asked what the money was for and I've told you, Xander was blackmailing me. That's enough." She closed her eyes for a few seconds and rubbed at her temples with shaking hands.

There was one thing I didn't quite get.

"Why *do* people think you're dead?"

She sighed.

"Isn't it obvious? I wanted to make sure people left me alone, forever. I'd been quite content to live my life quietly, out of sight. But I was nearly out of money. Everything Zach left me was gone, eaten away over the years. So, I came out of hiding I suppose you'd say, to make that god awful show."

"Orion Point?"

Yes. Aside from the money, it was a mistake. I couldn't cope with the pressure and I resigned. But it had all started up again, the rumours, the hearsay. Two nervous breakdowns later, I'd had enough. I posted my own obituary, in the Los Angeles Times. Nobody checked, nobody came knocking. I got away with it. Terribly sad, don't you think?"

I studied her face. It was blank. Resigned. As if she was talking about somebody else. The words 'I got away with it' echoed uneasily in my ears.

"Can I ask you another question?" She pinched her mouth and raised an eyebrow as if to say *do I have a choice?* "If Xander was blackmailing you—if you were so angry about it—why do you still visit his grave? The girls at the cemetery told me you go every year. They told me you said you loved him. How is that? I'm sorry but none of this makes any sense."

Lola started to cough again, spittle hitting her lips and the back of her hand as she held it to her mouth. Struggling to her feet, she moved to the window as the coughs subsided. She pulled the corner of the curtain aside.

"Why can't I see him now?"

"I don't know, but he's there," I shrugged. When she turned, her eyes were red.

"I did love him, Katherine. Before he turned on me, we were quite close. We'd been working together on a film and he seemed to be a lovely young man. I cared about him very much. He had no real friends here in Hollywood, no family." Her eyes darkened for a second and she paused. "I took him under my wing, so to speak. But then it became much more than that."

"In what way?"

"I began to suspect he was in love with me. I'm ashamed to say I didn't discourage him. I was flattered. I convinced myself I was starting to have feelings for him. He was young and beautiful and would gaze at me with such adoration. You have to understand, Ms. Alley, my marriage was not perfect. I had success, I had money, I had everything except love."

"It was at a dinner, at another director's house, that I tried to kiss him. Zach had been particularly uninterested in me that evening and I cornered Xander in the kitchen. I assumed, of course, that he'd respond in kind. I had thoughts of a passionate affair. But he reacted badly, he was horrified. He backed away from me with such a strange expression."

"That's when he told me—" she stopped, her frail voice trembling. Hunching over, her eyes darted as she assembled her thoughts. Then she abruptly straightened, avoiding my eyes. "—he told me I'd misread his feelings. That he adored me, yes, but we were friends, nothing more."

She was lying. I wished I hadn't told her about Xander's amnesia. Addled as her mind might occasionally be, I could tell she was deliberately curating her story, rearranging events.

"And that's when he turned on you?"

Lola's face reddened. I could see the cogs in her mind turning, as she threaded her story together. She was the consummate actress. I had no way to tell what was fabricated and what wasn't.

"Not exactly. After that, I refused to see him. I was mortified as you can imagine. Humiliated. But he seemed intent on proving to me that we were friends. He became obsessive; would call at odd hours wanting to talk, visit our house uninvited. He was at every social event we went to. It bothered Zach, understandably. It wasn't normal."

"So, what did you do?"

"I asked him to stop. I told him it wasn't appropriate, that he had to leave me alone. It was then that he threatened me, said he didn't want to hurt me but I was giving him no choice. He told me what he knew—what I'd done—and said he'd go to the papers unless I spent time with him, that he knew people. But if I let him be my friend, he'd keep quiet."

"That's all he wanted, not money?" I was more than a little

confused. "He was blackmailing you to spend time with you? That's a bit creepy." Creepy and not making any sense at all.

She sighed deeply, her breath rattling.

"He was lonely. He said he had nobody else. I agreed, for a while. Everyone thought we were involved, of course. But Xander scared me. He was so intense, and he'd broken my trust. I didn't *want* to see him anymore. I still cared for him but I didn't want him to be a part of my life, it was too—complex. The press got wind of our relationship and eventually Zach confronted me; he said I needed to choose between my career and Xander before it ruined me. So, I told Xander I couldn't see him at all. I told him I didn't care about him. I offered him money instead—to keep him quiet—and he took it, but it wasn't enough. He still wouldn't go away."

"I told Zach that Xander was obsessed and wouldn't leave me alone. I even lied and told him Xander had demanded I give him money or he'd go to the press and tell them everything about our 'affair'. It was lies on top of lies and all it did was make things worse. So, in answer to your original question, Katherine, I go to visit him every year because I feel guilty."

"What is there to feel guilty about?" I frowned. "You say you didn't kill him and he was the one blackmailing you. I don't get it." Lola moved the curtain aside again and pressed her hand flat to the dirty glass, peering out through the filth.

"If it wasn't for me, Xander would never have been out on that road. He was here that night—we argued. Whether I pulled the trigger or not, it's my fault. He died thinking I didn't care about him, which was a lie. If I hadn't been so worried about my career—" she trailed off, her voice thickening with tears. "I never got over it you know. It ruined everything anyway. The papers were so brutal." She laughed bitterly. "I suppose he had friends in the press after all. I became fearful of leaving the house. I couldn't work until years later and even then; it was a struggle. Zach's work suffered too and he died a few years later, still believing I'd had an affair. I never forgave myself for all of it."

I couldn't get past the phrase, 'friends in the press'.

"Lola, what do you know about Quentin?"

Her brow knitted and she blinked at me.

"Quentin Millson?" She recoiled as I nodded. "He was the worst of them all. After Xander died, he printed the most horrible things about me. He was convinced I was a murderess. He belittled my work, attacked my husband. This whole town hung on his every word, beastly man."

"I can tell you why. I found out something nobody else knows." I trod carefully. "He wasn't just Xander's friend. They were involved, for a long time, before he even met you."

"What?" She gasped, her face a mask of shocked disbelief. "What do mean involved?"

As I recounted both Quentin's story and what Xander had told me outside, her forehead creased and her mouth opened and shut wordlessly before setting into a thin line.

"More lies. No, I wasn't aware. But I'm not surprised." She closed her eyes and—when she reopened them—they were hard and flat. "Don't you see, it had to have been Quentin. He must have done it. He killed him. If he thought Xander had left him and—well, seeing him with me. It's obvious, isn't it?" Her hands fluttered to her throat. "My god, I had no idea. I don't think the police even questioned him. Why would they? All this time, we didn't know."

"Nobody knew," I said. "It's not that clear cut though I'm afraid. Yes, Quentin would've had motive. Nobody would ever have connected him to Xander like that. But nobody knew about your big secret either. I guess that gave you motive, too."

Suddenly she spun to face me, grabbing the curtain with one hand to steady herself, terrified eyes wide.

"Does he know I'm alive? Quentin. Does he know?"

I stood and moved quickly to the window. I touched her arm tentatively and she flinched, like she had at the cemetery.

"He doesn't know." I had no idea what she thought he could do to her now but I soothed her anyway. She took a full breath and turned back to the window, shaking.

This was getting me nowhere. I was going around in muddled circles. Between Quentin's story, Xander's lies and revelations and now Lola, I was choked with contradictions. I needed the whole truth, not the fiction gumbo with a little fact on the side I'd been served so far. But I'll admit, now it wasn't just about finding Xander's killer. Now I had to know what her secret was. What had she done that was so terrible? I guess old habits died hard.

"I hate to say this—" I couched it in a soft tone. "But have you thought maybe he was murdered because of something to do with your secret? Maybe somebody else knew. Help me figure it out, give me something more to go on. If Quentin was involved, I might then have a way to get to him." It was worth a try but she was vehement.

"It had nothing to do with it. If Quentin knew anything he would have printed it years ago. Trust me, nobody else knew." She was beyond frustrating and involuntarily anger crept into my voice.

"So, despite admitting that your secret led 'inadvertent-ly'—" I made sarcastic quote marks with my fingers, "—to Xander's death, you're still not going to tell me. Even if it could help him?"

She snapped, surprising me with her aggression.

"Don't you dare tell me this is all for Xander," she hissed. "You're a journalist and you've got a story to write. That's what this is about." I stepped back, shocked into silence as she spat at me, pointing with a gnarled hand, her shoulders shaking.

"Xander already knows my secret. If he doesn't remember it, I'm glad. He's better off not remembering. Believe me, it would only bring him pain. Maybe it's best that he disappears. At least then it will be over, he'll finally be at peace."

"But you don't know that—" I interrupted, but she ploughed on, talking straight over the top of me, her tiny voice ferocious.

"You're all the same. What gives journalists the right to decide what people should know about someone's private life? If it wasn't for people like you, I wouldn't have had to be worried in the first place."

How could I defend myself against that? She was right. I'd made it clear to Xander that helping him was not my priority, that my story was the most important thing. Yet, here I was trying to convince Lola that what I cared about was helping Xander. What rubbish. Maybe I hadn't learnt a thing.

"I think you should leave now." Lola crossed her arms tightly across her chest. "I'm not saying another word."

"But—"

"I'm sorry. No."

She escorted me back to the door and I stood feeling frustrated and—to be honest—disgusted with myself. I stared at her as she went through the process of unlocking the door. I hoped she'd change her mind at the last second. I was so close. Would it make a difference to Xander? I didn't know, but what if it did? What if it changed everything?

She wouldn't look at me and, despite feeling conflicted, I couldn't believe that fifty years on she still wouldn't be honest about whatever it was Xander had over her. Surely it didn't matter anymore. But if it didn't matter, why was I so desperate to know? As I stepped outside the door, she put a restraining hand out.

"Can you tell him something for me?" Tears threatened to

spill as her hand gripped my wrist, bony fingers digging into me. I nodded and put my hand over hers. Her voice dropped to a whisper. "Can you tell him I never meant to hurt him?"

"I'll tell him." What else could I say? As I stepped outside, she let go of me and moved to close the door. She stopped suddenly, once again pressing her face to the thin gap.

"And tell him that I forgive him."

"But—" I was confused, "—how can you forgive someone who ruined your life?"

"Because, I ruined his first."

What did she mean by that? She stared at me sadly as the gap closed and the heavy door thudded into place. I expected to hear the clunking of locks rolling over, one after another. All I heard was the unmistakeable sound of sobbing through the wood. Tears sprang to my eyes unbidden and I scrubbed them away, sniffing. What on earth was I going to do now?

Chapter Eighteen

After an awkward taxi ride, where the driver kept attempting cheery small talk only to be met with my morose, preoccupied stare, I sat in the lobby of The Chateau for an hour all on my own, slumped on one of the stripy chaise longues, watching the evening parade traipse by. Star-spotting didn't particularly interest me, I simply wasn't ready to face Xander yet. What would I say to him?

I wasn't entirely sure how angry you can be at someone who has no memory of being an arsehole, and who feels bad about it once they've remembered. Did I even have a right to be angry? He'd done nothing to me. Yet I still felt betrayed. Maybe he deserved to be murdered.

As soon as the thought crossed my mind, I regretted it. Nobody deserves to be murdered. Agitated, I leaned on my elbow and chewed my nails, nibbling them painfully right down to the quick. I couldn't have been further from figuring out who killed him. All I'd uncovered was a liar and a con man.

I was a complete hypocrite of course. How dare I be angry at Xander? I was only in LA because I'd nearly ruined Kelly

Craig's life. Up until a few weeks before, I would have sold my own Grandmother for a good headline, whether it hurt somebody or not. If I wasn't careful, my high horse was going to trample me to death.

Right then an enormous bottom, tightly wrapped in paisley denim of all things, flumped onto the end of my chaise and nearly squashed my feet.

"Katherine!" It was Marjorie. "Aren't you all relaxed! It's about time you took some time out, the way you've been rushing around. Barry filled me in on all the excitement this morning. I must say, he thinks you're a little strange. I told him all creative types are like that. Isn't that right?" She was so exuberant she actually grabbed my feet with both hands and wiggled them. Then, seeing my face, she stopped and patted me gently. "Oh, honey-bun, you must be exhausted."

She appeared to be waiting for me to say something. A bright smile decorated her face, her cheeks puffed out like she was storing nuts for the winter. I was so emotionally wrung out; all I could do was stare at her and nod. Instead of taking it as her cue to leave, Marjorie pounced. "I know what. While I've got you here—all comfortable—maybe it's the perfect time for our little chat. What do you say?"

I couldn't bear it. I couldn't even fake politeness. I heard a loud groan and, as I slapped a hand to my forehead, I realised it was coming from me. It wasn't intentional and I instantly wished for a rewind button. Marjorie wasn't so terrible, she just had bad timing. Insulted, she stiffened and clasped her hands in front of her. "My apologies, Katherine. I didn't mean to be a bother. Maybe another time, then?"

"Sorry, Marjorie," I backtracked, "Uh—maybe. I have so much to get on with. This story takes precedence over everything else. It's import—"

"It's fine, really." She stood abruptly with a terse smile.

"Good luck with everything." With that she turned and flounced away in a puff of lavender scented talcum powder, leaving me feeling awful. Unable to stall any longer, I unfolded my legs from the chaise and dragged myself upstairs.

Xander sat motionless in one of the armchairs in the main room—hands in his lap, staring at the wall. He didn't look deep in thought, simply blank.

"Hi." I stopped in the doorway, hesitant. He didn't answer me. I took a few steps towards him. "Xander?" Without turning his head, he spoke so quietly I almost couldn't hear him.

"When you go to heaven, and you're at the pearly gates with St. Peter—you know, the guy who weighs your soul and decides whether you get in or not— if you can't remember being a terrible person, do you think he would give you the benefit of the doubt and let you in anyway?"

I smiled despite myself and moved towards the coffee table, sitting down on the edge facing him, elbows on my knees.

"Somehow I don't think it works that way."

"Then I'm going straight to hell."

"Don't you think if you were going to go to hell, you'd already be there?"

"Maybe I am. Maybe that's what this is. Hell, limbo, whatever. I remember enough now to know that I was not a good person, Katherine. I did bad things to people. Maybe I deserved to die."

I turned my head away, guilty that I'd thought the very same thing literally moments before. After a moment or so I met his eyes again.

"Xander, the way you treated people—Quentin, even Lola —the things you did, yes, they were bad. But they didn't give someone the right to shoot you in cold blood. Nobody deserves to die that way," I attempted to jog him out of his funk, "Well, except for axe murderers, child molesters and maybe the guy that wrote the Hamster Dance song."

It worked. I was rewarded with a lopsided smile. We sat in companionable silence for a while until finally he spoke again.

"What did she tell you?"

I sighed.

"She told me you knew something bad about her past and you were blackmailing her with it."

He nodded slowly.

"I thought as much, I knew it was something awful. Why else would she be giving me money? What was it? I don't remember."

"That's the thing, she wouldn't tell me. Once I told her your memory was a bit wonky, she clammed up, said you were better off not remembering."

"Oh," his voice was despondent, "I was hoping you'd be able to tell me. I thought maybe it would help bring some memories back."

"I'm sorry, she flat out refused. To be honest, I don't know which parts of what she told me were true and which weren't." I grumbled with frustration. "But she did say it wasn't about the money. Apparently, it was—"

"About her," he interrupted, "I wanted to be *with* her."

"That's right," I nodded, "You do know that's a little bit stalker-ish."

"I wish I could explain it. I remember the money making me incredibly angry. It didn't have to be like that, I didn't want the money. All she needed to give me was time. I didn't have anybody else. But she wouldn't."

"Why would you feel you needed to blackmail someone into spending time with you? How is that even a real friendship? Lola told me she was very fond of you, even loved you. But then you got obsessive and wouldn't leave her alone, so she had to cut you off. And for the record," I couldn't let it slide, "how can you say you had nobody else? You had Quentin, remember?"

Xander whitewashed my point completely, focusing only on what Lola had said.

"Really? She said she loved me?"

"Yes."

"I don't believe that. She couldn't have or she wouldn't have abandoned me."

"Like you abandoned Quentin?"

He growled and punched a fist into his open palm.

"Yes, Katherine—I get it. The same way I abandoned Quentin. I suppose it was karma, isn't that what you're saying? God, I wish I remembered more." He fell silent for a few seconds, staring at the floor, then he jerked his head up sharply. "You shouldn't help me anymore, I'm a bad person. I don't deserve your help. I need to leave you alone."

I sighed. "You're not the only one who's been a bad person Xander, believe me."

He looked at me, puzzled, so I filled him in on the last few months. I told him about Kelly and how my first instinct when I heard she'd attempted suicide was that it was an even better headline than the first. I admitted that the second the thought ran through my head, I knew something was seriously wrong. I'd become somebody I barely recognised and I'd crumpled like a two-tonne wrecking ball had ploughed through me.

"My dad was right. I'm a terrible journalist and a terrible person."

Xander was still frowning.

"I didn't know you were that kind of writer. Is that the

kind of work you like? Revealing people's secrets whether they want you to or not? So, you're like Quentin?"

I scrunched my face, suddenly embarrassed.

"When you put it that way it sounds awful. I mean, I also —" I paused "—no, you're right. It is awful. Do I like it?" I took a sharp breath in. "I mean, I used to. I liked the challenge of finding out things other people didn't know, or want you to know. I liked the perks. After a while, I even enjoyed the notoriety."

"What do you mean?"

"Celebrities and their publicists hate me as much as they need me, Xander. One day they'll be on the phone trying to sell me a story, the next they'll be begging me not to run something. I get abused as much as I get praised."

"Doesn't that upset you?"

"It stopped bothering me after a while. It meant I was good at my job. You know, when I was in London once—this is going back a few years—Elton John invited me to one of his lavish parties. I was thrilled. It was completely unexpected, especially because I'd published a particularly scathing story criticising his latest hair piece. Once I got there, I was summoned—like an audience with the Queen. In front of everyone, Elton told me I was a vile human being and he poured an entire bottle of Cristal over my head."

Xander's eyebrows shot up,

"That sounds humiliating."

I laughed.

"It was, but I wore it like a badge of honour." The disappointed expression on Xander's face saddened me. "Ah, my dad used to look at me like that." Hot, unexpected tears pricked my eyelids.

"At least you still have the chance to make things better. I can't do anything about the things I did. It's too late for me.

"No, Xander. It's too late for me as well." My throat unexpectedly tightened. "Dad died a few months ago."

His eyes widened. "Kat, I'm sorry. I didn't know."

"What makes it worse," I continued, "is that we argued right before he died. My dad was a journalist too, an exceptionally good one. A—" the word stuck in my throat, "—*proper* journalist. The last conversation I had with him, he told me he was embarrassed by what I was doing and that if I didn't smarten up, he wanted nothing to do with me. I didn't listen. I told him to go to hell." Tears spilled down my cheeks and I wiped them roughly away. "That was the sum of my relationship with my dad in the end."

Xander was gazing at me sympathetically.

"I can imagine that would be terribly hard. I'm sure it was all said in the heat of the moment, but not being able to apologise, well—" He trailed off and I nodded. "At least you remember your parents though. I don't even know whether I got to say goodbye, I don't remember them at all. When I try to think of my family, all I find is a big black nothing in my head. It's blank."

I sniffed.

"Trust me, right now I wish I could wipe the memory of that conversation from my head."

"But, think about it. You're still here. You're still alive, in the world. You can still change. Aren't I proof that your father is no doubt up there somewhere, watching you? He'll see it, I promise."

I shook my head.

"But I'm still doing the same thing. Remember me saying I wasn't interested in helping you, that all I cared about was my story? You should have seen me go after Lola, trying to get her to tell me everything. I was like a bull terrier. Do you think I've changed at all?"

Xander leaned forward and stared directly in my eyes. "Yes, I do. I know this story is important to you, but can you honestly tell me you don't care at all about me—about how learning the truth might affect me?"

I gazed back at him, my heart pounding against my ribs. He was right. I did care. Very much. I didn't want him to disappear.

"No, I can't tell you that."

He smiled. "Kat, you haven't written the story yet, so how have you hurt anybody?"

"I haven't."

"See? Maybe in the process of helping me, it helps you."

I thought for a second, scratching my head uncertainly. "Xander? What if it's not too late?"

"Too late for what?"

"For you to make amends - to make things better."

"I'm dead. I think that qualifies as too late."

"But what if that's why you're still here, why I can see you, why all this is happening?"

He laughed doubtfully but I could tell I'd caught his interest. "I think you've seen too many ghost movies. I'm not sure that's realistic."

"What exactly about any of this is realistic?" I snorted at him.

"Good point." He smiled. "But don't you think I'd need to at least know what I'm making amends for? I still don't know *why* I behaved that way. How can I make it better if I don't know the truth?"

"I don't know either. It was just a thought." I shrugged.

Xander stood and assumed his usual hands-in-pockets pose.

"Don't worry about it, Kat. Focus on what you need to do. I've bothered you enough."

"Where are you going?" I stared at him, alarmed

"Don't panic, I'll be back. I need to think. I need to remember. I'm so close, I can feel it." He gestured at the clock. "I'm going to leave you to sleep."

I stood too, as if I was going to block his way to the door.

"But, where will you go?"

"I'm a ghost, aren't I? I can go anywhere I want."

He winked at me, turned around and walked straight through the wall, leaving me chuckling. Xander was right, sleep sounded good.

Exhausted, both mentally and physically, I clambered into bed. My mind churned relentlessly, but eventually I drifted into a restless sleep, troubled with mixed up images of Xander calling out to me, *You left me. How could you leave me?*

At 2am I woke with a start. This middle of the night crap was beginning to be a habit. My throat and head were heavy and thick, like I'd been crying in my sleep. I rubbed at my face and sat up, instantly wide awake.

"Xander?" I called out into the main room but there was no response. I swung my legs out of bed and padded into the living room. Empty, just as I thought it would be. I stood redundantly in the centre of the room. Stupid insomnia. The TV remote caught my eye and I was instantly torn between in-house movies and the red folder on the desk. Weighing up the importance of solving Xander's murder against watching *Titanic* for the hundredth time, I grabbed the folder and plopped down cross-legged on the rug.

What was I missing? The files made even less sense when I was sleep-deprived. There had to be something I wasn't seeing. I studied the papers one by one, and then in different orders, trying to find a connection. But there was nothing.

Frustrated, I kicked the folder away with my bare foot and flopped back onto the rug, throwing my arms above my head and staring up at the maze-like pattern embossed on the ceiling.

How had Dad done it? How had he managed to find the right threads to pull a story together so it held? All I seemed to be able to manage was tangling them up in knots. I'd never felt quite as lost and alone as I did right then. So, I did the only thing that made any kind of sense. I checked the time and I called Mum.

It was dinner time in Sydney and I tried to picture her sitting alone at a table that once accommodated a whole family, Dad at its head. More than likely she'd avoided the dining room and was sitting with her plate on her lap, in front of the television with Magda—her scruffy little Scottie dog—stretched across her slippered feet.

"Sweetheart, what on earth are you doing calling from the other side of the world? This will cost you a fortune, you silly girl." Apart from a slight delay, she sounded as though she was in the next room. It was such a Mum thing to say and I immediately started to snuffle uncontrollably. "What's wrong? Has something happened? Has that scrawny editor of yours been awful to you again?" she demanded, my tears instantly triggering her maternal alarm.

"It's okay, Mum. I'm fine. Nothing's wrong." I wiped my face with my sleeve, glad she couldn't see me.

"Rubbish." She was strident. "You don't ring your mother in the middle of the night—yes, I know what time it is there—when nothing's wrong." She softened her tone. "Come on now. Talk to me, darling."

"I needed to hear your voice, Mum. That's all." It was true. Comfort enveloped me like a warm cardigan and I curled on my side on the rug, my knees tucked up and the phone pressed into my ear. She murmured softly, a homely, soothing sound.

"Well, that's lovely, Katherine." She never called me Kat. "It's wonderful to hear your voice, too. I've been thinking of you every day, wondering how you're getting on. It must be a blessing to be away from everything."

I admitted it was but that I was still struggling, that the remorse I felt had changed everything. I wasn't sure I could do my job anymore, at least not the way I used to and maybe that was a good thing but I didn't know how else to be. I told her how confused I felt and that I wanted to do things right this time but this story had become so complex, so huge, that I felt quite simply overwhelmed

"I can't make sense of it all, Mum. I have all this information but none of it fits. I don't know where to start to be honest. I don't know if I'm cut out for this kind of stuff. Maybe Dad was right, all I'm good for is covering movie premieres and best-dressed lists."

She tutted.

"Your Dad never said that to you and you know it."

"He may as well have."

"Katherine, stop it. Your Dad was hard on you because he could see where you were headed. He knew you could do better. That's all. He loved you very much."

"I know, I know," I mumbled through more tears. I heard my Mum take a long breath in on the other end of the line. She exhaled slowly and audibly. I snuffled some more, miserable but aware enough to know I wasn't the only one missing him. It was a long moment before she spoke again.

"Do you know what your Dad used to do when a story was troubling him?"

"Dad had trouble with stories?" I snorted, finding it hard to imagine.

"Of course, he did. Quite often in fact. He'd stay up all night sometimes, wracking his brains, poring over documents, tearing out what little hair he had left." She laughed. I hadn't heard that sound for months and it made me smile.

"That sounds familiar," I sighed, 'except the hair part, I still have hair, clearly."

"When he was stuck, he used to write everything down in a letter."

"To who?"

"To anyone, I don't think it mattered to who. To me, to you, to someone involved in the story, to the Pope for all I knew. The point is, he wrote down all of his questions, the things he was stuck on—and he asked for assistance figuring it all out. He used to say getting it out of his head helped."

"And then what? What did he do with the letter?" I wasn't sure I understood.

"He slept on it. Literally. He'd put it under his pillow and sleep on it and, more often than not, he'd wake up in the morning with some clarity." She paused. "Darling, why don't you try writing a letter? To your Dad."

I rolled on to my back and stared at the ceiling again, silent. It couldn't hurt. If nothing else it would give me something to do while I couldn't sleep. Dad's theory made sense, I had to get this stuff out of my head or I was going to go mad.

"That sounds good, Mum. I'll try it."

We chatted a bit more and I asked how she was managing. She told me her friends had made her take a cooking class with them and she hadn't poisoned anyone yet. She cried a little and brushed it off then put Magda on the phone. The little dog snuffled and licked the receiver and whined at the sound of my voice and I said '*go get her, go get her*' and laughed at the sounds of her racing around the living room on stumpy legs, barking her silly head off.

Mum insisted on getting off the phone, saying I'd regret my bill when it came in, despite me explaining it was a company phone. She made me promise to take care, not to talk to strangers (too late) and to make sure I tried the letter thing because it always worked for Dad.

So, I did. I wrote him a letter. It went on for page after page after page. My hand kept cramping and I'm certain I rambled, but I started from the beginning, because what better place to start. I told him absolutely everything, even about Kelly—how ashamed I was and that he was right, it was a shitty job and I could do better. I wanted to do better, but I was scared I wasn't good enough. That I'd never been able to get that long-ago overheard conversation out of my mind.

Then I wrote about my story. I outlined the facts, even copied lines from the case. And I told him that nothing made sense; the blackmail, the lies, the sex, the missing information, the dead ends. I wrote it all down, every detail. I wrote that I wanted to get to the bottom of it, but I didn't want to hurt anyone. Not again. But I was confused—in the end, wouldn't it be justified if it helped solve a crime?

I also wrote about Xander. I said Xander was not who I thought, that everything pointed to him being less Jekyll and more Hyde. But I added that I hoped I was wrong, that I'd seen something more between the shadows. I expressed my worry that he was running out of time, disappearing. Should I even care? I wondered if Dad could tell me where Xander would go —or if he would cease to exist. Become nothing.

I asked him, 'surely there must be a reason for all of this?' For being sent to LA in the first place, being able to see Xander. For finding Lola, even meeting Marjorie and in turn, Barry. It was all too neat, too convenient to be a coincidence. There had to be a purpose, a grand plan of some sort.

I laughed as I wrote that bit and I knew Dad would too, wherever he was. Was that really me, the sceptical Katherine Alley, spruiking a higher purpose? I finished my letter by saying *why not?* If believing meant there was a chance Dad could hear me, I was a convert, well and truly. Because I missed him desperately and wished he could know how sorry I was. For everything.

By that time my pages were soggy with tears. I signed off, 'your loving daughter, Katie', found an envelope in the complimentary *Chateau Marmont* writing set on the desk and sealed it all up. I tucked it under my pillow, thinking *come on, Dad, work your magic.* He was right, my head already felt lighter. With that I snuggled down, took a big contented breath and fell into a deep, dreamless, and altogether lovely sleep.

I slept solidly until ten a.m. and, when I woke, brain magic happened. My Dad was a genius! I scrambled out of bed and sprawled on the rug, riffling through the discarded folder from the night before until I found what I needed; the stalker who was thrown off the studio lot the week before Xander died —the woman claiming to be his wife.

The statement listed her as Temperance Martinez, twenty-four, last known residence—Clark County. There was no record of how long she was in the psychiatric ward. Nothing was followed up. Once she was deemed crazy and no longer under suspicion, the police must have simply crossed her off their list.

Nobody knew anything about Xander's life before he came to LA. It was a great big blank. He could have been married. He lied about so much—whether he remembers it now or not— there was every chance this poor woman was telling the truth. I punched Barry's number into my phone. He answered quickly, heard my voice and instantly became flustered.

"Katherine, how are you? Good to hear from you, good to hear from you. What can I do for you?"

"Barry, I need you to try and find some old records for me. Can you access old marriage records, things like that?"

"Yes, that's easy. They're public records. You can access them yourself if you know where to search, you don't need the police to—" he changed tack quickly, "—although, you know I'm more than happy to help of course. It's probably much, much quicker if I search for you, knowing the system and all that."

"Thanks, Barry." I smiled to myself. "That would be great. I've got something else I need to do today so it'll save me some time. I need you to look for marriage records for a Temperance Martinez, I'm not sure if that's her maiden name or her married name, I'd say sometime between 1955 and 1965. Her address at the time of her committal was in Clark County, that's in Wisconsin, right? So, try there first then widen the search if you have to."

"Wisconsin's a bloody big state, Katherine," he puffed his breath a little.

"I know, Barry, but I don't have much more to go on that that. Can you do it? It could be important."

"It's the woman from the case file, yes, the crazy fake-wife?"

"That's the one. I thought it might be worth checking her out. You never know. There's something about her that I can't let go of. I need to trust my instinct on this one."

"Okay, you're the boss. I'll see what I can find—if I can find anything at all—and I'll call you later."

I thanked him and rang off, still wrapped in thought. If this woman was his wife, it meant he'd abandoned her when he came to LA. Of course, Xander was from Iowa not Wisconsin, but weren't they neighbouring states? And how easy is it to lie about where you're from? It wouldn't be the smallest lie he'd told.

She could have come to find him and he'd denied knowing

her. Meaning it was his fault she ended up committed to a mental hospital. Could she have had a father or a brother who wanted revenge? It was another theory—another straw to grasp at. But right now, I needed all the straws I could get.

With that out of the way, I put in a quick call to the concierge and made a vague excuse about needing a psychic and quick. He didn't miss a beat, immediately pointing me in the direction of Spellbinders Bookstore, a metaphysical shop on Melrose. It was quite well-known apparently, with Shirley MacLaine becoming a regular customer after The Bodhi Tree closed down. With a testimonial like that, it was exactly what I needed. I hoped to God—if he existed—they had a resident ghost expert.

Chapter Nineteen

Dreadlocks have always grossed me out. I find myself imagining all sorts of little crawly creatures that could live undisturbed in the matted hairy tentacles. As I browsed the wooden shelves of Spellbinders Bookstore, the impressive set on the tall black man standing next to me made me want to itch my head like crazy.

According to the concierge, the store had been a fixture on Melrose since the nineties, but didn't become really popular until after the demise of its main competition, the famous Bodhi Tree. Now it was Mecca for those eclectic LA spirits fascinated by mysticism and all things spiritual and otherwise otherworldly. I was a little out of my depth, being a recent convert and all. Regardless, the meditative tinkle of strung chimes, the faint smell of incense, and the sound of soft but earnest conversations soothed me. Simple as it sounds, it felt nice.

The assistants at the counter were busy, but I didn't mind browsing. I'd always been so blinkered to this world that the breadth of book titles amazed me. The tiered shelving was all

solid wood and gave off an organic vibe, if there was such a
thing. I trailed my fingers across the myriad of printed spines
seeing everything from yoga to angels to astral projection
written there. I saw titles on totems and trances and crystals,
but nothing about ghosts.

"You seem to be searching."

It was the dreadlocked man. He had a gentle, leathery face
and his deep voice sounded like a hum. I wasn't sure if he was
being literal about the searching or implying that I sought my
life path so I just blinked at him.

"Huh?"

"You seem as though you're looking for something in
particular. Can I help you find something?" As he spoke, his
eyes focused above me as if he was examining tiny flies dancing
around my head. It was a touch unsettling.

"Oh, right. Um—do you work here?"

"No. But I'm here a lot. I know where everything is." He
smiled and dipped his head slightly. I glanced over at the
counter. The assistants were still busy, but they looked my way
and smiled encouragingly.

"Okaaay." I was reluctant "Do they have any books on
ghosts?"

"Ghosts or hauntings?"

"Aren't they the same thing?"

"No, no, no. A ghost is a manifest sentient spirit, a
haunting is simply a residual energy imprint—very different
things."

Riiiight.

"Uh—then I mean ghosts."

"Ghosts? Hmmm." He closed his eyes and steepled his
fingers in front of him, inhaled deeply then exhaled with
another loud 'Hmmmmmmmm.'

I leaned away from him, pulling my chin back on my neck

like a startled tortoise. I was about to make an excuse to leave when his eyes popped open and he broke into a wide, benign smile.

"Over here."

He proceeded to show me books on clairvoyance, books on séances, books about famous ghosts. Nothing was even remotely what I needed. I cracked my neck to the side, irritated.

"Do they have anything on what happens to ghosts if they, you know, hang around for too long? That's what I want. Specifically."

A strange expression crossed his face and he gazed intently at me.

"You're troubled."

"What?"

"You feel great pain and guilt."

"Pardon me?"

"I can see it in your aura." His eyes flittered above my head. "You are trying to assuage your guilt by helping another."

He was freaking me out, partly because he was so obviously right, but how the hell did he know that? I glanced around quickly and lowered my voice.

"Listen, Mister. I don't know what you think you can see buzzing around up there, but whatever it is, stop it. I'm sure it's incredibly rude to analyse someone's aura thingy without asking first. I just need a little bit of help with a ghost. Okay?" The man smiled at me again, his bushy eyebrows dancing.

"Of course, follow me." He turned and strode towards the back of the shop without turning around to see if I was behind him. I was a little thrown, but I trotted obediently along, ignoring the curious glances of the other shoppers. He ducked his head through a narrow wooden door and I followed, suddenly finding myself in the open leafy garden behind the building. He spread his arms expansively, welcoming me into the lush, peaceful space.

Two simple white chairs sat underneath the biggest tree I had ever seen. It towered almost three stories high and its dark green, heart-shaped leaves draped low and thick. I stared up at it in wonder.

"Man—now that is a tree."

"It is the Karma Tree and it holds all the knowledge in the world. The Karma Tree welcomes you."

Something about the space made me feel I could say anything, so I smiled and peered up into its branches.

"Thank you, tree. It's nice to be here." Was I actually talking to a tree?

He gestured to the two chairs and we sat facing each other, this strange man and me. He stared and smiled, smiled and stared, until I began to feel vaguely uncomfortable. He was waiting for me to start talking—after all, I was the one with the questions. Finally, I cleared my throat and began. "Okay, so I have this *friend* who seems to have come into contact with a ghost. I mean, a real bona fide, honest to goodness ghost." I waited for him to pooh-pooh me or laugh, but he only nodded. "Right. So, this ghost," I continued awkwardly, "has been hanging around earthbound for a very long time."

"How long exactly?"

"Like, fifty years long."

More nodding.

"Mmm-hmm. Go on."

"For a while now he's been disappearing on and off and he doesn't know where he goes. And it seems to be getting worse."

"Anything else?"

I hesitated.

"Yes. This person—this ghost—he was murdered."

The strange man's eyes widened and he pursed his lips,

inhaling sharply and then making a clucking sound with his teeth and tongue.

"Murdered? And let me guess, he doesn't remember anything about it?"

"That's right. He remembers very little from when he was alive actually. How did you know?"

"It's pretty standard ghost ideology. When a person dies as the result of a traumatic event, they generally block out all memory of it."

"That makes sense. People do that when they're alive, too."

"Exactly."

"But why would he have forgotten everything else as well? This ghost has even forgotten his own personality."

The strange man frowned.

"What do you mean?"

"Well, when I—I mean when my *friend*—first encountered him, he was very pleasant. Friendly, even funny. But he's since found out that when he was alive, he wasn't a very nice person at all. In fact, he did some quite horrible things."

"I see."

"But he's also had episodes where he's appeared to my *friend*, in quite a menacing manner, but then has no recollection of that either. It's very confusing."

"Can I ask how exactly he was murdered?"

"He was shot." I wrinkled my nose at him. "In the head."

"Aaaaah. That could explain many things."

"Like?"

The strange man pressed his fingertips together and narrowed his eyes.

"There is a part of the brain called the hippocampus—"

"The hippo-what-nus?"

"—campus. It's responsible for processing long term memory as well as being linked to emotional memories and responses. If this ghost was shot in the head and the hippocampus was damaged, it's not a wonder his memories are fragmented."

"So, what do you think?"

"I think it's fascinating."

"No, I mean, what do you think is happening?" I made an exasperated squeak. "I'm worried about him."

"Your *friend* or the ghost."

I narrowed my eyes.

"The ghost. I honestly think there's something wrong with him. He might disappear completely and I don't know how to help him. I never believed in ghosts before; I don't know what I'm supposed to do."

"You mean your *friend* doesn't know what to do?"

He smiled beatifically at me and bowed his head.

"I think we both know what I meant." I laughed then, giving up the pretence. He looked up with the odd smile still on his face and shrugged softly, his hands out, palms upturned.

"I don't think there's anything for you to do. It's not your path to fix this. It is a very troubled spirit."

"To coin a phrase—*well d'uh*." I felt a little like I was talking to Yoda.

"Tell me," continued the man. "What did he do in life, this spirit?"

"He was an actor."

"Ahhh. And so it becomes clearer—or less clear depending on how you look at it. An actor naturally has many faces, you see. If he doesn't remember his death, his behaviour, or who he really was, it's possible he is blocking out the persona that caused him the most pain. What you see most of is the face that gave him pleasure, the most peace. Possibly that would have been his public face—his image."

"So why do you think he has such strong feelings about

people, without knowing why? And why do I keep getting glimpses of—let's call it his *bad face*? He's really scary when he's like that."

"When you have no memories, you have no choice but to run off gut feelings. They are not linked to memory, they are purely instinctual. Perhaps the reactions you see are based on the way these people made him feel on a cellular level. As for his *bad face*—there could be a number of reasons."

"For example?"

"What you are seeing could be anger echoes, a violent echo of a memory or feeling he's been suppressing. You see it because in the end he can't deny the truth behind what happened to him or what he himself did. He needs to acknowledge it so he can make amends, if possible, and move on."

I knew it. It wasn't too late, Xander was supposed to make things right. But how the hell was he going to do that? How do you make up for blackmailing someone fifty years ago and ruining their life?

"The disappearing is worrying," the man continued. "Can you tell me more about that? Is there anything else happening?"

"A lot actually. Sometimes he appears, but I can't hear him, or I can hear him, but can't see him. Other times he says he's been talking to me for a while, but I don't even know he's there. He's aware of being there though. Oh, and sometimes he flickers."

"He flickers?"

"Yes, like a broken TV set. On, off, on off."

"And this is happening more often?"

"I've only known him for a few days, not quite a week, but it's increased in that time. He says it's happened before, but not this often."

I sounded like a patient describing everyday symptoms to a doctor, but there was nothing everyday about what was happening to Xander. According to the strange man, it was as I thought—he was about to disappear for good.

"It would be my opinion," the man sighed heavily, "that something pivotal is occurring which means he's running out of time. The universe gives us limited time to work through certain karmic issues."

"What happens if he runs out of time?"

"I would think he will simply fade away."

"Fade away? Where to?"

"To nothing."

The thought horrified me.

"Could it be linked at all to finding out who killed him? You know, avenging his murder?"

"Is that what you're trying to do?"

"Yes."

He mused for a moment, looking up into the depths of the mighty tree.

"No. I don't think that matters in this case. Dead is dead. Of course, there are certain situations where how someone died does matter, after their death. But it doesn't sound like this is one of them. If this spirit did terrible things during his life, making up for them is much more important—karmically speaking. Whoever killed him has their own karmic path. That's not your, or his, concern. What about the person he wronged? Is this person still with us?"

"Yes, she is."

"You know her?"

"Well, sort of. I've spoken to her."

"Why has he not made amends with her before now?"

"Uh—because he's dead." *D'uh.*

"I meant in a spiritual sense, of course." He chuckled, rather annoyingly if I'm honest.

"I told you; he didn't remember anything. It's hard to make

amends when you don't know you did something wrong. Right?" I was confusing myself.

The man dipped his head again.

"True. Is there anything you can see—any reason at all— that your spirit friend might not get the chance to make amends with this woman now if he wanted to?"

I thought for a second.

"Mmmm. No. Apart from the fact she doesn't want to talk to—" I stopped, remembering Lola's frailty and the sickly coughs that wracked her body the day prior. Why hadn't I seen it before? "Wait." My heart was suddenly in my throat. "I think she might be dying."

The strange dreadlocked man nodded sagely.

"Then your ghostly friend had better hurry."

I was ushered back into the shop, the man gliding calmly behind me. I had no idea who the swami-like guy was—he could have been a complete fruit loop for all I knew—but it didn't matter. He was a life saver—or should that be afterlife saver?

I thanked him profusely then ducked around shelves and display tables, making a beeline for the exit. Despite the urge, I didn't run, not wanting anyone to think I was a shoplifter bolting from the store with a bunch of pilfered crystals and incense in my purse. When I reached the door, I turned to wave one last time. But the man was gone, nowhere to be seen. I peered around the high shelves. I could see all the way to the back, but he had definitely disappeared.

"Can I help you, honey?" The query came from a stoned-looking woman in canary yellow harem pants. They had bells on the bottom and they jingled as she shifted from foot to foot in front of me, a human tambourine.

"No—I mean yes—that man, the one with the dreadlocks. Did you see where he went?"

Her face lit up and she turned, looking around the shop and grinning widely.

"You saw Marcus? You're lucky, not many people see him these days."

"Sorry?"

"Marcus. He's our resident ghost." She placed a hand gently on my arm. "He only appears to people when he has something important to share. Did he help you?"

It was another one? Oh, great. Clearly, I really was turning into *The Ghost Whisperer*.

"Yes, he helped me." I sighed. At least I knew he was speaking from experience. I glanced around one last time and smiled, sending out a telepathic 'thank you'.

Once on the street I tried frantically to wave down a cab, with no luck. I grabbed my phone out to order an Uber instead, only to find the nearest driver at least twenty minutes away. I couldn't wait—not now. I broke into a run. I was puffing within two blocks, a stitch tearing savagely at my side, but I kept running. I needed to get back to the hotel as quickly as I could.

I was so ill-equipped for cardiovascular activity that I overheated quickly. My skin was literally humming. After about a minute I realised the continuous humming was not my exercise-retarded body but my cell phone buzzing in my back pocket. What an idiot. I slowed to a walk as I reached for it. It must have been buzzing on my butt for ages because it had registered three missed calls from Barry. I caught it before it went to voicemail a fourth time.

"He—llo?" I panted into the phone.

"Hello, this is Officer Barry Brent of the LA Police Department." His tone was officious on the other end. "Could I please speak to Katherine Alley?"

"It's me, Barry. You rang my cell. Who else is going to answer it?"

"Oh, Katherine. Hello. Of course, I was just wanting to make sure, you know. You never know who you could be revealing important information to. Are you okay? You sound like you're under some kind of stress."

"I've been running—and I'm really not used to running. Something important has come up, I'm on my way back to the hotel. Have you got something for me?" My nerves were jangling. How the hell did detectives do this all the time?

"You'd better sit down, I found out something very interesting."

I walked faster, I didn't have time to sit down.

"I'm sitting down," I lied, "spit it out. What did you find?"

"I searched for that marriage record you wanted; for Temperance Martinez? It took me quite a number of enquiries, but I finally found it registered in Jackson County, also in Wisconsin. There was some confusion because it wasn't her only marriage. The records I found indicate that after she was released from the psychiatric hospital here, she settled back in Wisconsin and eventually married again."

"Okay, but I don't care about that one. Tell me about the first one."

"Of course. Martinez was indeed her first married name. And her first husband's name was Alexander, Katherine. Alexander Martinez. I don't think there's any doubt that's—"

"Xander."

I wasn't sure whether it was from running or hearing it confirmed but bile rose suddenly in my throat. *He was married —and he left her so he could come here to be an actor and do all those awful things.*

Nausea hit and I doubled over in the street, trying to breathe.

"Are you sure?" I had to ask. "How can you be sure it's him?"

"Yes, I'm sure. I did a bit of detective work myself. I cross referenced the name Alexander Martinez with other records in that county and elsewhere in the state. It took a few hours, but it paid off."

I crouched to the pavement and leaned against a shop front, horribly dizzy.

"What did you find?"

"I found a record that matched from 1943 and—"

I interrupted him, confused.

"1943, but I don't see wh—"

"It was an adoption record, Katherine. Alexander Martinez was given up for adoption when he was six years old. The mother's name on the adoption record was Maria Lolita Martinez."

I went completely cold, my hands shaking violently. Barry continued on blithely, "Martinez was the maiden name of—"

"I know who it is, Barry. Thank you."

I hung up the phone.

Chapter Twenty

I burst through the door of my hotel room, hoping he'd be
there—hoping against hope that he wasn't still off somewhere thinking.

"Xander!" I yelled into the stillness. "Xander, are you here?
Please tell me you're here." Shock and confusion engulfed me.
One minute I'd been set to race back here and tell him he had to
make amends and *fast*. The next I was trying to process both
the fact he was married and that I'd discovered Lola's big secret.
Xander clearly wasn't the only one needing to make amends.
How was I going to break it all to him? What an incredible
mess. Desperately, I yelled one more time, standing in the
middle of the empty room, fists clenched.

"XANDER!"

"What?"

I whirled around. He was sitting in the armchair, casual—
as though he'd been there all along. But he hadn't.

"Xander, my god." My words tumbled over themselves. "I
don't know where to start." I stopped short, registering the
thunderous look on his face. "What's wrong?"

He glowered at me.

"What do you think, *Kat*?" He said my name hard and loaded with sarcasm. "I remembered. Almost everything."

His face frightened me. Why was he so angry at me? I stepped back.

"*Almost* everything?"

"I remembered enough."

"Xander—"

"Let me guess, Katherine," he spat as he stood up, "you were going to tell me some hippy at the spiritual store said I need to make amends for the bad things I did? That it's the only way I'm going to be able to move on—*find the light*?"

Despite my fear, I couldn't help but throw a little sarcasm back.

"Actually, it's the only way you're going to be able to stop yourself disappearing into nothingness, but same-same, I guess."

He laughed bitterly and turned his back.

"Maybe I don't want to make amends. Maybe I want to disappear into nothingness. Besides, I'm not the only one who needs to make amends. If at all."

"That's what I'm trying to say, if you'll let me talk. I *know*. I know everything. I didn't just go to Spellbinders, I also had Barry track down some old records for me. I had a hunch. I know you were married and that you left your wife to come here, to LA. And I also know the reason why."

When he turned, his face was awash with anguish and rage. He was struggling to hold it together. "I know Lola is your mother," I finished, stepping towards him. The change in his expression ripped at my heart.

"*Was*." His fists balled by his side and his nostrils flared as he battled to find words through gritted teeth. "I was six years old, Katherine. Six years old. I wasn't a baby, who wouldn't remember. I loved my mother—I needed my mother." His voice cracked. "She abandoned me. She left her only child so she could come to Hollywood—to be a goddamned actress."

"Xander—" I was appalled but he raised a hand to silence me.

"Let me tell you what I remember."

"Okay." I nodded and sat down.

"We'd lived in Watertown since I was born. I don't remember anything before that. We'd walk past the orphanage on State Street often, although I didn't understand what it was at the time. All I saw were lots of other kids there—like a big picnic was going on every day.

"She used to say how sad it was that none of the children had parents and would squeeze my hand tight. I asked if I could play with them each time we walked past, but we were always in a rush. I was never allowed.

"Then one day she took me there in a taxi. I remember being so excited because I'd never been in a taxi before and I was going to get to play with all those kids. That's all you care about when you're six. She let another woman lead me into the yard and went inside for a short time. When she came back out, she climbed quickly back into the taxi. I thought maybe she'd forgotten her bag. And then when it pulled away, I thought maybe she was going to visit a friend and would be back to get me that afternoon. But she never came back, Katherine. She just left me there."

I struggled to hold onto tears and my throat ached. Unbidden, an echo runs through my head—*the things some people will do for fame.* Indeed.

"I'm so sorry, Xander. Really."

He kept talking, oblivious to my words, his brow furrowed as he dug deep for the memories. "It was years before I saw her again. I was nearly twenty-six. Even then it was only in a film.

I'd had to leave the orphanage when I turned eighteen and I ended up in Black River Falls, up in Jackson. I needed work and a sawmill there was hiring. I worked there for a few years— keeping to myself—before I met Temperance." His voice cracked. "She was a waitress, a sweet girl, blonde and pretty. I fell in love with her, which was a miracle in itself, I never thought I'd ever trust another woman.

"I was such a roughneck. I don't know what she saw in me. But she married me anyway. When I asked her how I could make her happy, she laughed and said I already did. All she ever asked was that I took her to the movies every week. I had no interest in the cinema, but she loved it. It was a small thing. How was I to know it'd change everything?"

"When I saw my mother up on the screen, it was a shock. I knew it was her, she was unmistakable. Temperance said I went white. I told her I was feeling ill—how could I tell her the truth? But I asked Temperance about the woman on the screen —Lola, as she was calling herself then. Temperance told me she was a real big star."

"I couldn't believe I hadn't seen her before that but—like I said—I had no interest in movies. I worked in a sawmill for pity's sake. Temperance didn't suspect anything. She'd show me pictures in magazines; I think she was happy to have a sudden common interest. Apparently, my mother had only recently been discovered, but was hugely successful already. How had it taken her so long to make it? I didn't understand it. Or why she hadn't come back."

"From then on, she was all I thought about. I'd sit in the movie theatre, showing after showing, over and over, the same films. Temperance got bored and stopped coming with me. Eventually, she found my fixation strange. In the end, I wouldn't even go home to Temperance, I couldn't even touch her anymore."

"It wasn't long before she got tired of having no husband. I came home one night to find her with another man, in our bed. I didn't even care. I felt nothing. I packed a bag and left for Los Angeles. I knew I had to find Lola; she was my mother." He turned to me. "I thought, surely she'd be glad to see me?"

I met his eyes for a second and then looked away, at the floor. I couldn't answer him. He shook his head and continued, walking back and forth across the room.

"When I got to L.A. I figured out pretty quickly I wasn't getting anywhere near her. I was smart enough to know that if I approached her directly, I'd scare her off. I could be arrested. I did see her a few times in those first weeks though, at fancy restaurants, stepping out of cars outside nightclubs, dressed to the nines."

"In the meantime, the women here liked me. I never had a shortage of beds. They were all wannabe actresses and models. They'd all tell me I should act, that I was easily attractive enough. That's when I knew what I had to do—to get close to her." He paused. "For her to love me again."

"Is that when you met Quentin?" I spoke carefully, not wanting to push too hard.

"Yes." He scowled. "I'd been to a few auditions, but things weren't happening quickly enough for me. I'd been offered some bit parts, but nothing substantial. An actress I'd been sleeping with on and off had told me who Quentin was; that if you wanted to be seen, have the people who mattered take notice of you—you made sure you got into his column."

"Why didn't you simply become his friend?"

"It wouldn't have been enough, Katherine. I needed to know he would do anything for me. I needed to build a solid career quickly if I was going to be able to get to know my mother again. So, I seduced him. It was easy. He was an insecure and scared little man, that's why he hid behind his column."

"So you played on that insecurity." I shook my head at him, disappointed. Xander rounded on me.

"I made him feel good about himself. I didn't treat him badly; I wasn't awful to him. I pretended I—" he struggled to get the words out, "—I pretended I loved him. Considering I'd never acted before, I was exceptionally good at it. Yes, I used him. But he never, ever knew that, even after I ended it."

"Don't try to make out that what you did was okay, Xander. You should be ashamed."

He stepped towards me.

"I am ashamed, believe me. I already told you; I was disgusted with myself the whole time. The things I did—"

"I'm not talking about having sex with a man, Xander. Christ! I'm saying you should be ashamed of using somebody like that, being so manipulative. Quentin didn't deserve that."

Xander was quiet, his head down. "I know."

I sat back, confused.

"Wait, you said you hated him. You were adamant that you always hated his guts. At the house—what you showed me—"

When he lifted his head, his eyes were filled with anguish.

"You don't understand. The problem was that I hated myself."

Boom! Spellbinder Tree Man—Marcus—was right. Xander was reacting to instinct, not memory. The hatred he remembered must have been the way he'd felt about himself when he was with Quentin. Xander exhaled heavily before continuing. "I was so relieved when I didn't have to do it anymore. When I'd finally made it. It took almost two years—far longer than I'd planned—but finally I landed a big part opposite her. It was all I wanted. I didn't need Quentin anymore, so I lied to him. I told him the studio had advised me to cut ties."

"Quentin told me that, remember?" I was terse. "What I don't get is why you continued to go to such lengths, sneaking around to see him. Why didn't you break it off completely?"

"I didn't want to put him offside. I was enjoying my success; I liked the attention it gave me. People were being good to me, praising me. I'd never had that in my life." He grimaced. "They weren't big on praise at the orphanage. Quentin could have destroyed that in an instant if he'd wanted to. I couldn't risk it, so I let him think I still loved him—that my hand was being forced. I saw him in secret—regularly enough to keep up the pretence—but once I started spending time with Lola, it got messy."

"How?"

"Quentin was jealous. He thought I was spending too much time with her off set. When the rumours of an affair started, he got angry. It was so difficult to appease him, especially towards the end. I took to avoiding him, which made him worse. He thought she was stealing me away. That I was obsessed with her."

"You kinda were," I pointed out cautiously.

"She was my mother. Didn't I have the right to want to be near her? I'd missed out on so many years with her—" he trailed off, his voice strangled.

"Xander, she didn't even know you were her son. The time you were spending with her was an illusion."

"Don't you think I knew that?"

"So why didn't you tell her who you were straight away?"

He didn't answer me at first, still pacing back and forth, agitated. But suddenly he turned and sat in the other armchair, finally meeting my eyes.

"I was afraid." His expression was frank. "I was afraid that, if I told her who I was before she had a chance to get to know me, she would reject me. I thought if I could get her to like me

—to care about me—when I did tell her who I was, it would all be okay. She hadn't recognised me at all when we first met. Why would she? I'd told everyone I was from Iowa, that I'd grown up on a farm. Part of me had fantasised that she'd know me immediately, that I would be unmistakable, a mother's instinct. But how could she have, I was more than twenty years older—a man, not the little boy she'd left."

"So, what happened?" I was still tentative, not wanting to upset him.

"We got to know each other well. What do you say these days? We *clicked*. But then she began to have feelings for me." His face twisted in a rictus of discomfort. "Romantic feelings. I didn't even see it until she tried to kiss me. It wasn't for a film, I remember now. It was at a party and she told me she was in love with me. She threw herself at me."

"Lola mentioned that when I talked to her," I interrupted. "I have a feeling the version she told me was somewhat different though."

"I don't doubt it. I panicked. It was too bizarre a situation —my own mother, in love with me. Wanting to *make* love to me. I had no choice but to tell her who I was. I thought if she cared about me the way she said, it would be all right. I believed that once she knew I was her son, it would fix everything, that she would be pleased I was there."

"But she wasn't, was she?"

He shook his head and again, I desperately wanted to touch his hand, to comfort him. I cursed the fact I couldn't. Instead, I softly touched the arm of the chair he sat in.

"No." His face twisted into the same mask I'd seen before— sadness, anger, hate, all mixed together. "She panicked, too. She backed away, staring at me like I was about to attack her. I remember trying to take her hands, saying, 'It's me. Mom, it's me.' But she wouldn't let me touch her. All she could say was 'don't call me that', over and over."

"I was devastated. I couldn't understand why she wasn't happy. She told me nobody knew about me, not even her husband, and that she couldn't risk anyone finding out. It would destroy her. Nobody would understand a woman who abandoned her own child to be an actress. I got that, because I know I didn't."

"So, you blackmailed her."

"I never meant to; it wasn't my original intention. I just wanted to know my mother, to be part of her life. I started visiting her at home, I made sure I got invited to the same parties, the same premieres. Her husband didn't like me—it was clear—and he made her tell me to back off. So, she did. She made it very clear I wasn't wanted. She gave me no choice, Katherine."

"I understand that's how you felt, but you can't—"

He laughed without mirth, harsh and full of resentment, interrupting me.

"The blackmail didn't work anyway. It changed everything. She kept seeing me, I mean she had to. But I knew she didn't want to be there. She wouldn't answer any of my questions about why she left, why she didn't take me with her. I would shout at her to talk to me, to explain. I wanted to understand, but she gave me nothing."

"The whole of Hollywood was buzzing, we were always together, people assumed we were involved. The press hounded us relentlessly. Printed all kinds of things. Even the idea of it made me feel sick. I hated it, but she insisted on making no comment at all. To deny it meant explaining the truth, and she wouldn't do that. Yet again, her career was more important than me—her son."

"Xander, I know how hard it must have been, but why

didn't you leave her alone? It must have hurt terribly—I can't imagine how much—but why blackmail her? Knowing she didn't want a relationship with you, why didn't you just leave?"

He stared at me in disbelief.

"Why should I have? She abandoned me." He stood, his fingers clenching and unclenching. "SHE *ABANDONED* ME, KATHERINE! I grew up in a children's home because of her. Do you have any idea what that was like? Why should she have been allowed to go on living her fancy life, as if I didn't exist? I wasn't going to let her get away with it. Whether she liked it or not she was going to acknowledge me, even if it was only between us. She owed me that much."

"But in the end, Zach got in the way didn't he."

Xander's lip curled instantly in distaste.

"Her husband believed we were having an affair, like everyone else. She refused to tell him the truth. He told her to choose and she did—she chose him. She chose her career."

"I'm so sorry."

Xander rubbed a hand across his eyes and sniffed dismissively.

"She offered me money—lots of it—to keep quiet, to go away. And I took it at first. But then it made me furious, that she thought money would make up for it all. As if that would make it better. If she thought I was going to go away that easily she was mistaken."

My heart was hammering painfully in my chest, but I wasn't sure if it was echoing Xander's heartbreak or from the mounting sense that the unfolding drama was leading to something big. Like, *murder* big.

"So, you kept pursuing her? That's why you fought that night; here at the hotel?"

He nodded and when he looked at me his eyes were rimmed with red.

"That's why we fought and that's why I followed her home. I wanted more, Katherine. I wasn't giving up. All I wanted was my mother's love, didn't she understand that. I didn't want her money."

"But that's the last time you saw her. That's when she told you she never wanted to see you again. And that's the night you were killed."

"Yes." The word came out as a hoarse whisper. "I was so angry when I left. I screamed at her through the closed door that I was going to the papers—that I was going to tell them everything."

"Xander, that gives Lola motive. Don't you see? Don't you understand what you're saying? If she thought you were going to go to the press, she could have followed you that night. There's no way she would have wanted that to come out."

He stared at me; brow heavy as the thought weighed down on him.

"I'm not sure, Katherine. I remember it was raining hard, it was difficult to see. I was so furious my hands were shaking. I must have pulled my car over to wait out the rain." He growled in frustration as he dug for memories that were long buried. "I —I don't know."

I took a deep breath then exhaled slowly. My heart ached for the little boy who longed for his mother, but what it made him do as a man was difficult to reconcile. Was it possible Lola killed him? It seemed too big a coincidence that an hour after Xander threatened her, he ended up dead streets away from her home. Or, was it Quentin? Hell hath no fury like a lover scorned. Watching Xander's anguish, it was clear finding his killer was not his priority.

"Xander, you know what you need to do, don't you?"

"I need to make amends for what I did." He closed his eyes and, when he opened them, he blinked rapidly as if processing it all before looking at me. "What about my mother, Katherine? Doesn't she have to make amends too?"

"Maybe you both need to, I don't know." I quoted the strange man from Spellbinders. "But Lola has her own path to tread, and you can't control that. For you to be able to move on, I think you need to let go of your anger."

"How exactly do I do that?"

"Forgiveness is a start—" I shrugged "—and maybe letting Lola know you feel remorse."

He nodded reluctantly. "Do you think she'll see you again, Katherine? What if I still can't get inside?"

"I don't know, I guess we'll find out. But to be honest, I don't think Lola is the only person you wronged. Whether Quentin knows you lied to him or not, he was hurt by all of this too. The most important relationship in his life was a lie. He needs to know the whole truth too. All of it."

"No, he doesn't." Xander was adamant. "It wouldn't do anything except hurt him more. You were right, he doesn't deserve that. Quentin is the one person in all of this who did absolutely nothing wrong. I took advantage of him. Maybe I can make up for that now."

"What if he's the one who killed you, for leaving him?" I suggested, cocking one eyebrow at him. Xander laughed softly. He didn't take me seriously at all, but I hadn't ruled it out myself.

"I really don't think that's likely. Quentin was petrified of guns, trust me. Let him believe I loved him, what harm could it possibly do me now? But tell him the truth about Lola, then maybe he'll understand everything. It might bring him some closure."

"Are you sure?"

"I'm sure."

"See, you can't be all bad, Xander." I smiled. "You're making amends already."

He didn't smile back.

"Don't be nice to me Katherine. I don't deserve it. I need to accept that my mother didn't want me. She didn't love me. I should have accepted that a long time ago. And why would she? I was an awful person. Maybe I should be happy to fade away into nothing."

He seemed so sad that I reached out without thinking to touch his hand. The air crackled slightly—like a tiny electric shock—as my hand passed through his, but I didn't flinch. I held my hand there. It was the closest I would ever get to touching him.

"I don't believe that. She told me she cared about you. That she forgives you. You have to believe me."

He shook his head and moved his hand away. A chill wrapped around my hand where his was a moment before and I curled my fingers into my palm.

"What if I can't forgive her? Accepting it is one thing, but I don't know if I can forgive her."

"You've got nothing else to lose, Xander. But we have to hurry."

"Why?"

"That's what I've been trying to tell you. I'm fairly certain you keep disappearing because you're running out of time." I paused and took a breath, unsure how direct to be. "I think your mother's dying."

Chapter Twenty-One

Lola's front door stayed firmly shut this time. I knocked and knocked with not even the faintest response. The place was eerily quiet in the late afternoon light. I'd left Xander at the gate again and for some reason I had butterflies going in alone.

"Lola!" I pressed my face up against the heavy door, "Lola, it's me Katherine. Please open the door." Silence. I tried again, banging so hard on the door that I skinned my knuckles. "Lola! I need to talk to you. Please." All I heard was the faint sound of a cat meowing plaintively from behind the door.

I picked my way around the house—through weed infested gardens—to one of the windows. A dull yellow light shone behind the closed curtains and I could make out the edge of the room through a crack. There was no sign of movement when I rapped on the glass.

"Lola." Nothing.

"She's in there. I can feel her." I heard Xander's voice behind me and whirled around, startled. He stood nearby, staring at the window with his hands by his side.

"How did you get in here?"

"I just can today." He shrugged. "Whatever was blocking me before is weaker. But this is as far as I can get."

"That can't be good." I glanced back at the window. "I'm worried." I knocked on the window again. "Lola, I know you're there. Please, let me in."

"I don't think she's going to let you in this time."

"Why not?"

"She's scared. I can sense it. Everything feels different this time, the energy around the house, it's coming from fear. It's strange, I can feel it pulsing. It's weak, but then it rallies and gets stronger, like a heartbeat."

Xander followed me back to the front door. I reached into my bag and grabbed my notebook. Scribbling '*I know everything*' along with my phone number, I tore out the page and folded it in half. He frowned at me as I slid the folded note underneath the door.

"So, what now? We wait?"

"What else can we do? I'm hoping once she sees my note, she'll call. She has to, right?"

Xander stared at the house.

"I'm not so sure."

To be honest, as we headed back toward the gate, neither was I.

W aiting sucked. By nature, I'm not a patient person. Since getting back from Lola's, my pacing had practically worn a track in the oriental rug in my room.

I'd managed to reach Quentin again and he'd agreed to see me the next day but until then I was at a loose end, waiting and praying for Lola to call. After being subjected to game after game of eye spy and watching me munch my way through the entire mini-bar, even Xander got sick of me and disappeared.

And so it was that I found myself alone, at 11pm, contemplating the adult movie channel and musing on the fact porn stars seem far more fastidious with their waxing regime than my own haphazard efforts at intimate grooming.

I could have worked on my article but it seemed pointless to spend time on a retrospective when it had become so much more and I wasn't ready to start committing everything to paper until I'd worked it all out. I'd been studiously ignoring the latest spate of check-in voice mails and text messages that had arrived from Mitch so that I didn't have to fib about how close I was to filing it.

I knew I'd been staring at the adult movie channel for too long when I recognised one of the girls by name and thought, 'ooh, I like her, she's the one with the—'. Anyway, the phone finally rang and I dived for it. Just in case it was Mitch, I feigned a massive yawn and a sleepy voice thinking, if I pretended she'd woken me up, she'd go away and call back later.

"*Mmmm-nnn-hello?*" But it wasn't Mitch. It was Leon. "Hey! You're calling late. What's wrong, did you miss me?"

"Chica, I can't talk." His usually soft voice was all urgency. "But I have a message for you. My brother called—that lady he works for, the actress you've been talking to— she's in the hospital."

I sat bolt upright. "What? When?"

"A few hours ago. He found her in the house and called the ambulance. Chica, she's asking for you."

I scribbled down the name of the hospital and rang off quickly.

"Xander!!" I shouted into thin air. I had no idea if he could hear me but it worked last time. "Xander! I mean it. I need you.

NOW!" I spun around in the room to see if he'd appeared. "Come on, come on. XANDER!"

Nothing. *Great!*

Exasperated, I grabbed my bag and bolted out the door. As I raced down the corridor, Xander materialised right beside me, keeping pace and scaring the absolute crap out of me as usual. I stopped dead and yelled at him.

"Bloody hell, Xander, you're going to give me a heart attack one of these days if you keep appearing like that. Jesus! You should feel my pulse."

Xander folded his arms with a sly smile, "I would imagine your racing pulse has far more to do with what you were watching, young lady." He pressed his lips together pointedly, "Hmmm?"

"Were you spying on me?" I blushed, embarrassed. "I thought you were gone. I—I wasn't. I was—"

Xander chuckled heartily and I narrowed my eyes and growled.

"You drive me bonkers, do you know that?"

"Indeed I do." He straightened with mock pride, then his smile faded. "I'm teasing, trying to lighten the mood again. You know—considering."

"Oh." I sobered instantly. "Then you already know where we're going?"

Xander nodded, sadly.

"It's time."

Chapter Twenty-Two

Admissions at Cedars-Sinai was chaos when we arrived. It took the Duty Nurse a while to notice I was at the counter. Eventually, she told me the room number and we practically ran down the sterile corridor.

Surrounded by machines and tubes and wires, Lola was tinier than before, nestled like a sickly baby bird in the centre of the wide hospital bed. Her eyes were closed. Scraps of caked make-up clung tenaciously to her lips and lashes but her skin was a deathly grey. A drip fed into her alarmingly thin right arm, and tubes wound up both nostrils. I couldn't tell if she was breathing or not. Only the beep of the heart monitor was assurance she was alive.

Xander stood at the foot of the bed, staring at her. I was too frightened to touch her, not even sure she'd wake, but she'd asked for me so I tried.

"Lola," I murmured, laying my hand lightly on her arm. No response. I pressed my fingers against her skin, more firmly this time. "Lola?"

Still nothing. I shook my head at Xander.

"Let me try," he said.

"But she might not be able to see you, or even hear you."

He moved to the other side of the bed, still staring down at her.

"She will." He leaned forward, his eyes roaming her face, then reached out, laying the flat of his hand on her cheek. I drew a breath and held it. "Lola?" He spoke her name first—hushed and hesitant—before taking a long, trembling breath. "Mom?"

I'll admit, I expected the tender familial word to bring her immediately out of unconsciousness in order to gaze lovingly at Xander with maternal recognition. I'd clearly watched too much daytime television. It didn't happen. He tried again and again, each time a little louder—but there was nothing to show she could hear him at all. The heart monitor maintained its slow, monotonous blip until eventually Xander gave up. His lips pressed together in a bitter line.

"See, Katherine, even now, when it's almost too late, she doesn't want to speak to me."

"She's unconscious. What do you expect?"

He slumped against the wall and railed sarcasm at me with a wave of his hand.

"A motherly hug? A cookie? Rays of heavenly light and forgiveness? I don't know, a god-damned explanation?" He took a deep, calming breath, exhaled and sat up. "What do we do now?"

I offered a wan smile and shrugged.

"I guess we wait."

And so we waited and watched, like sentinels, on either side of the bed. I'm not sure whether we were waiting for her to stir or waiting for her to die. Xander was motionless, staring fixedly at Lola as I in turn watched him.

An hour passed in complete silence, apart from the hiss and

sigh of the ventilator and the rhythmic pulse of Lola's heart monitor. Her chest rose and fell almost imperceptibly and several times the machine registered a slowing of her heart beat. Each time it did, Xander shifted into transparency before flickering and returning to normal when her heart beat rallied. He was lost in thought and, if he felt himself fading, he didn't show it.

I must have dozed off because his voice—strident in the quiet room—made me jump.

"She looks different, you know. Smaller. She used to be so vibrant and strong. So beautiful. I loved her very much, Kat. I can't understand why she didn't love me back—why she *couldn't* love me back. A mother is supposed to love her child, isn't she?"

Of course, a mother was supposed to love her child. I didn't understand it either. I was lucky enough to grow up with two parents who loved and encouraged me. I couldn't imagine either of them being willing to abandon me as a child, no matter what the reason. How did you rationalise that kind of selfishness?

I knew my father was embarrassed by me. That he'd wanted nothing to do with me because of my actions—my behaviour. He'd had a reason. I couldn't blame him, yet it had still caused me such distress, even as an adult. It gave me some small understanding of Xander's pain but I didn't know how to answer him. As I tried in vain to formulate a response, a hoarse whisper from the hospital bed shook us both.

"Alexander?

Expecting him to be beside Lola in a second, I was surprised to see him press back against the wall, wide-eyed and fearful. Watery eyes flickered behind her half-opened lids and her hand searched the bed beside her, weak fingers reaching for him.

"Are you here?" Her voice wavered, reedy in the quiet

room. Then, a barely audible whisper. "I need to hear your voice."

Xander didn't move or speak. For some reason, he simply stared at her in abject horror. I leaned forward and touched the back of her hand.

"Lola, it's me. Katherine."

Her deep sigh rattled with disappointment.

"I thought I heard him. I thought he was here. I hoped —" she faltered. "It's too late, isn't it?" She turned her head and gazed at me, eyes red-rimmed and heavy. "It's much too late."

I glanced at Xander. He was hunched slightly, head down, hands clenched at his sides. "He's here Lola," I said gently. "He's standing beside you."

She moved her head from side to side, her gaze darting around the room, passing over him. "I can't see him. Why can't I see him?" Her voice was weak and hands fluttered at her sides as the heart monitor sped up. "Alexander?"

Xander stared sullenly at the floor. I reassured Lola again that he was there, that he could hear her, even if she couldn't see him. I wasn't sure she believed me.

"I need to tell him I—" A sob broke forth from her and the heart monitor beeped sharply in alarmingly quick succession.

"Xander!" I hissed, "For god's sake."

"Tell her I want to know why she left me."

He didn't look up, directing his words to the ground.

"Ask her yourself. Isn't that why you came—so you can talk to her?"

He shook his head.

"I can't."

I turned back to the bed. Lola was watching me with a pained expression, mascara tears streaking her face like ink spilt on dry parchment.

"He doesn't want to speak to me. And, who could blame him?" She attempted a thin smile.

"He wants me to ask you something."

"He wants to know why?" She sighed. "Which 'why' does he want to know? Why I left him? Why I didn't come back? Why I turned him away when he came to me?" She turned her face away and closed her eyes, taking a belaboured breath. "So much to say, but—" She stopped.

"—but still it continues," Xander muttered, glaring at her.

"Please Lola," I said, "he needs to know."

She opened her rheumy eyes and stared at the ceiling. A deep exhale rattled in her throat. "I—" she coughed and gestured weakly to the tubes that fed into her nose, "—I want to, but I don't think I—"

Her eyes started to close and I turned to Xander, desperate.

"Do the thing."

"What?" he looked up at me sharply.

"The thing! Like when you showed me what you remembered." I flapped my hands at him. "You know—you said you sometimes absorbed people's feelings when you felt lost or lonely. Maybe if you get close enough—if you touch her—you'll be able to see it all, what she wants to tell you."

I could tell from his face the idea terrified him.

"I don't think I can."

"Xander, this might be your last chance. To get the answers you need."

He stared at me for a long second, then pushed himself away from the wall and approached her bedside. Hesitating momentarily, he leaned down and rested his hand lightly on her forehead. An almost imperceptible glow radiated around the edges of his palm and, as it did, Lola's lips parted. She sighed a breath of relief. At the same moment, Xander's eyes closed and he took a sharp breath in.

He began to speak. I knew immediately it wasn't his words he was sharing.

"I was sixteen when I fell pregnant with Alexander. My parents had moved to America from Agua Caliente—in El Salvador—a few years before that. They settled in Racine, in Wisconsin, of all places. We weren't your typical South American immigrants; my father was qualified as a doctor. He had a good job, we had a nice house. I went to a good school. But still we were judged, because of where we were from. Because we weren't white."

"Both my father and mother were killed in an automobile accident not long after I turned fifteen. It changed everything. I had no other family, nowhere to go. I couldn't go back to El Salvador on my own. One of my father's colleagues, Dr. Anthony Tyrell, took me in, to live with his family."

"Things were fine for a while, as fine as they could be. I missed my parents, but I was cared for, and at least my education continued. It meant I had some chance of looking after myself once I graduated. I could make a good life."

"I knew Dr. Tyrell's wife, Joanna, didn't like me. She made that very clear whenever we were alone. I was an embarrassment. Dr Tyrell was more than kind to me though, and so was the rest of the family—especially their eldest son. His name was Alexander, too. He was blonde and athletic and he made me laugh. He brought me sunshine again."

"I'm sure it's obvious where this is going. Alex and I fell in love. Or at least what we thought was love. We were children, what did we know of love? When I found out I was pregnant, he said of course he would marry me. He said we would have our baby and everything would be okay."

"It wasn't. The Tyrells were a respectable family. There was no way Joanna was going to let her seventeen-year-old son marry some little South American slut. He was destined for Harvard. Dr. Tyrell wasn't going to kick me out onto the street though. He was a good man."

"I was allowed to stay. But Joanna had conditions. Alex was sent away—kicking and screaming—to a school in up-state New York. He swore he'd come back to me, but I'd learned by that point not to rely on anybody else's promises."

"I became the maid. I was taken out of school so nobody would see my growing belly, and I was put to work until I was too heavily pregnant to mop floors or make beds. When it came almost time for Alexander to be born, they tried to persuade me to give my baby up. They told me it would be the best thing for everyone—that I could go back to school. My child would have a chance at a better life and no-one would have to be shamed. Everybody could move on."

"I refused. It was my baby, my only family, and I wasn't ashamed. Joanna refused to keep me in the house any longer and made Dr Tyrell choose; his family or me."

"He drove me across two county lines. I gave birth to my son in a women's shelter in Watertown, Jefferson. My suitcase contained clothes, a handful of photos, and my mother's jewellery. The envelope Dr Tyrell handed me before he drove away held five hundred dollars. He said it was the only way he had to say sorry."

"Alexander was the most beautiful baby I had ever seen. I know a mother is biased, but he was. Everybody who saw him said so. He was so full of charm, and hardly ever cried. He was so placid. It made it easy for me to work. I took him with me everywhere, wrapped tightly against my body while I took every job I could find."

"I stayed at the shelter and washed dishes, took jobs sewing, cleaned people's houses. I made sure to feed myself well so that

I could feed him, while I saved every dollar. By the time Alexander turned one, I was able to afford a tiny room in a boarding house in town."

"It was tough when he was small. An unmarried mother was scandalous. I would sometimes get turned away from work when they realised, I had a child but no husband. There were always the men who wanted to take advantage, who would make promises to look after Alexander and me—simply to get into my bed."

"I didn't need anybody except my little boy. He gave me the comfort and love I needed. He gave me the determination I needed to survive—the determination to make sure he had a good life. It was my one and only goal. It was the only thing I cared about."

"So, I worked and I worked and I worked. But I never seemed able to do more than make ends meet. We survived, yes, but that's all. I wanted better. I wanted more for my son."

"Alexander was five years old and already in school when a man by the name of Herb Freeman came to stay at the boarding house. He was from California, he smoked fat, pungent cigars and said he was in the movie business. He oozed charisma and told me how beautiful I was. I hadn't been with a man in years and, although I knew he was married, I took him to my bed."

"The affair lasted several weeks, the amount of time he was staying in town for location research. Herb told me again and again that I should be in films, not scrubbing floors. He said he could get me started, that I didn't even need to know how to act—my looks would get me by."

"Herb said he would set me up in an apartment in Hollywood, that he would help me. He was infatuated and he dazzled me with stories of parties and film stars. In the end, the only thing that caught my imagination was the money he said I could make."

"When I said yes, I would go—that I would pack up Alexander and follow him back to Los Angeles, he said no. He and Alexander liked each other, boyish gifts had been bought, handshakes and hugs had been traded. But, no. He said Alexander would be a hindrance to me. Nobody would hire an unmarried actress with a child. Where would he go while I was working? It wouldn't work."

"I refused. I said there was no way I would leave my son and that Herb could leave. He shook his head at my stupidity and did just that."

"But the seed had been planted. After that, no job seemed big enough. No matter how hard I worked, the money wasn't enough. All I could see were the holes in Alexander's shoes, the darned patches on his pants, our meagre meals and his hungry little face when he asked for seconds and I had to say there were none to be had."

"For months afterwards, I would take out my purse and run my fingers over the silver lettering on Herb's business card, wondering if it could work, wondering how long it would take me. Wondering if I could do it. Then I would feel my son's chubby hand in mine or hear him laugh, or feel his breath on my cheek as he slept and I would resolve—*No. I won't leave him.*"

"Of course, you know that I did. I told myself it was temporary. That as soon as I had made enough money and a name for myself, I would come back for him. I told myself he would be safe, that it would be worth it. I told myself I was doing it for him and I packed his belongings into a taxi and took him to the children's home. I left him there, playing with some children in the yard. I didn't even tell him I was leaving. I was such a coward. I couldn't face lying to him if he asked whether I'd be gone long. I simply signed the papers and left without saying goodbye, trying desperately to ignore the pain in my heart."

Xander's voice trailed off, his eyes still closed, brow furrowed, the channelled memories clearly painful. Suddenly Lola coughed violently again, her frail body convulsing. My tears flowed freely as the heart monitor beeped rapidly and I thought *No, not now—not yet.*

I was about to call for a nurse when Xander's eyes opened. His face was tear-stained and sorrowful, but I saw no trace of anger as he lifted his hand from her forehead. He sat in the chair by the bed and reached down to take Lola's hand. His fingers closed around hers—solid flesh on solid flesh, and her body arched upward with a sharp inhale.

My eyes widened—what was happening? How was it possible? Xander squeezed her hand.

"It's okay, Mom. I'm still here."

Her fingers gripped his tightly, then her face relaxed as she sank back into the bed, breathing heavily. Her eyes stayed closed, as if feeling him was enough. The monitor slowed, regaining its rhythmic blip as her breath settled. I stared, gobsmacked, at Xander's hand. He followed my gaze, flashed a brief, sad smile at me then returned his attention to Lola.

When she opened her eyes, it was with the knowledge that the ghost of her dead son was really there, holding her hand. But knowing doesn't necessarily prepare a person for reality. Her shock was manifest, her other hand flew to her mouth as she uttered a tiny frightened sound from between quivering lips. Xander said nothing and she squeezed her eyes shut again, pressing her mouth tight, restraining a strangled cry.

Just as I had at the cemetery, I felt like an intruder, as though I was witnessing something I shouldn't. I pressed myself back against the chair, willing myself invisible but not wanting to miss the exchange. The difference between this and the many other private moments I'd muscled in on over the years, was that I knew Xander wanted me there.

When Lola's eyes opened again, they were clear and focused. A quiet strength settled over her that wasn't there before, as though she was drawing it from him. Mother and son gazed at one another in silence as minutes ticked past, each studying the lines of the other's face. Her fingers tightened on his.

"I was dreaming—that we were talking." Even her voice was stronger.

"It wasn't a dream."

"You saw it. You saw it all?"

Xander nodded and she took a deep, relieved breath.

"I wanted to come back, I swear to you," she said, her eyes searching his.

Xander shook his head in disbelief.

"But you didn't. Why?"

"Because it took too long. To make it, to get where I wanted to be. I couldn't come back with nothing, without having done what I set out to do. It would have made leaving you pointless. I couldn't do that. Every time I thought I couldn't bear it, that I should come back to you, something told me I was so close, that if I waited a little longer. I had to keep trying so that I could justify it all.

"But it took so many years before things started to happen for me. America had entered the war by then of course and I had no idea it would affect the film industry so much. There was no work. Herb, the man who said he would help me, ended up running a munitions factory so I worked there in between auditions. I scraped through. Nothing changed until I met Zachary and he began to write roles specifically for me. So many times, I wanted to give up and come back. I missed you so desperately—"

"Don't you think I missed you?" Xander interrupted. "I

had no idea why you left. I was a little kid. I thought you didn't want me—that you didn't love me."

"Of course, I loved you."

"Then how could you abandon me? Do you have any idea what my life was like?" Xander pulled his fingers from her grip and backed away from the bed. She reached out to him with a sob.

"I'm so sorry."

"You're sorry? You could have come back for me at any time. You chose not to."

"Please, you have to understand. The more time passed, the harder it got. Zach built my career, I owed him so much, I couldn't walk out on him."

"But you could walk out on me?"

"Alexander, I thought you would have been adopted, that a good family would have taken you in. You were such a lovely boy, I felt sure that would happen. I thought if I came back and took you away from that, it would be worse— "

Lola trailed off and Xander glowered at her.

"That's a lie. How can you lie like that? Why didn't you check? I was in that orphanage until I turned eighteen and they practically threw me out. I wasn't their responsibility anymore. I was nobody's. I was alone."

"I didn't know."

"You didn't care."

Lola sighed deeply. It was the sound of complete resignation.

"I cared very much. I thought about you every single day. But, by the time I made it, by the time I had the money and was successful enough to come back—I'd left it too late. You were an adult by then. I thought if I came back then, you would hate me—that you wouldn't be able to forgive me for leaving, and who could have blamed you. I couldn't forgive myself. So, I convinced myself you had found a family—that you were loved and safe, that you didn't need me."

"You were wrong."

"I made a mistake. I know that now—and I've carried that guilt with me all these years, believe me."

"I can't. I'm sorry." Xander shoved his hands in his pockets and stalked away from the bed before turning suddenly. "If you felt that guilty, why did you turn me away when I finally found you? Explain that."

Lola's face, ashen until now, flushed and her lips quivered.

"I have no explanation, other than I was scared."

"Scared of what?" Xander asked, incredulous. "Of me?"

"In a way, yes. I was scared of losing everything. More than I'd already lost. I'm sorry, I know it mustn't make sense. It's not an excuse and I know it doesn't make anything better, but I'm trying to explain. It had taken me years to get to where I was when you found me. I was a different person. This place, this industry, it changes you. You of all people should know that. I'd done things, behaved in ways I wasn't proud of, for what? For fame? For money? At such a cost. I'd already convinced myself I'd lost you forever. All I could think was, if I lost everything else, it would all be for nothing. I knew if people found out the truth it would be the end of me—the money, the recognition, the houses, my husband. It would all be gone."

"But you would have had me."

It amazed me how a statement so simple could be so loaded, but there it was.

"Yes," she murmured. "I would have. I made the wrong choice. A terribly wrong choice. And then, when you were—" her voice cracked, the word *killed* like a stone in her mouth, "—when you died, it was too late. I thought I would go mad with grief and guilt. I have never forgiven myself—never wished for anything more than to be able to go back." Again, she reached a feeble hand out toward him. "I'm sorry, Alexander. So, so sorry."

I expected Xander to rebuke the simple apology a second time. After all, how could the word *sorry* make up for a childhood ruined, a life twisted by loss? But, to my surprise, he took his seat by the bed and entwined his fingers with hers once again. He sat quietly, eyes downcast. Lola closed her eyes, inhaled deeply and then breathed out, her frail body sinking visibly into the be—a palpable expression of relief. When she spoke again, she was barely audible as she struggled once more for both breath and words.

"I don't expect you to forgive me. I don't have the right. But I needed to tell you the truth—that it was all for you. That I never forgot about you, not for a single second of any day. Even though I wasn't with you, I read to you every night, just like I did when you were small—hoping that somehow you would know. I carried your favourite book with me all these years."

Xander lifted his head and exchanged a look of under-standing with me, his eyes red-rimmed.

"*Peter Pan,*" he whispered.

I nodded and reached into my bag, taking out the small, tattered book. I held it out to him, but he was reluctant to let go of Lola's hand. Her breathing was laboured again and—although her eyes were closed—they moved under the lids as if darting to catch memories.

"Can you read it, Kat?" asked Xander. "I don't think it matters which part."

I tried to swallow; my mouth suddenly dry with nerves. Me, read it? Now? The most important book of his childhood, reading it aloud as he shared what could be his mother's last moments—and it didn't matter which part? Was he serious? Of course, it mattered.

As I turned the curled and yellowed pages, Xander laid his forehead on Lola's hand, held tenderly in his. I chose a random page and started to read to them. As I told the tale of magic and fairies and pirates and crocodiles, I was reminded of my father reading to me as a child. I remembered talk of tooth fairies and Easter bunnies and my eyes blurred with tears, but I kept reading out loud, about lost boys and absent mothers and never quite growing up. Xander was right, it didn't matter which part I read.

"*Never say goodbye,*" I recited quietly, the words catching in my throat despite myself, "*because goodbye means going away and going away means forgetting.*" I stopped, unable to continue, but they didn't seem to notice. Lola lay still—very still—and Xander's head remained bowed. I gently closed the book.

Sitting in silence, I marvelled that they were able to connect like this. Not only after so many years apart but considering one of them was actually dead. I'm no ghost expert but I'd hazard a guess that Xander was only able to touch Lola's hand because she was so close to death herself.

Her pulse ebbed and flowed and I watched as Xander's physical presence echoed it the same as before. Each time he faded in and out and in again, I wanted to reach out and touch him myself—like I had wanted to so many times over the past week. To see if—just maybe—he was solid. But I refused to intrude this time.

After a while Xander stirred, lifting his head from her hands.

"I forgive her, you know," he said, and I smiled in answer. He rubbed at his face and gazed down at Lola. "Do you think she forgives me?"

"I'm the wrong person to ask, Xander. Although I'm not sure there's anything for her to forgive. Not really."

"What do you mean, of course there is. You said it before, I need to make amends."

"Maybe I was wrong. I didn't know everything when I said that." I attempted to articulate my thoughts in a way that made sense. "Yes, you wronged people and you lied—a lot—and maybe you need to make amends for those things. But the situation with your mother was not your doing. She abandoned you, whatever her reasons."

"All you wanted was to find her and be close to her. She could have made it all better once she knew who you were, but she didn't. She made the wrong choice and you paid for it. Xander, you reacted out of hurt, not malice. Did you handle things very well? Probably not, but the blackmail and the arguments were not things you set out to do when you came to find her, were they?"

"No. They weren't."

"I think she needed your forgiveness more than you need hers." He seemed doubtful so I tried lightening things up a little. "Hey, at least we can be pretty sure she didn't kill you."

His smile was wry.

"True. Although, I'm beginning to think finding out who killed me doesn't matter."

"Speak for yourself," I straightened up and shot him a look that said *are you kidding me?* "I haven't given up on wrapping this little mystery up just yet, buddy."

Xander laughed.

"Can't let it go, huh?"

"Nope, I'm too curious for my own good,"

"You know what they say about curiosity, don't you?"

"I guess you'd better save me a spot up there then, hadn't you," I chuckled and pointed upward. "I might be joining you real soon."

Xander stared at me with a funny smile and I stared back.

We fell into an uncertain silence until eventually, Xander broke my gaze and stared back down at Lola.

"I can feel her slipping away." He glanced back at me. "Do you think this is it? What happens now?"

He was asking me? My belly suddenly felt like it was full of bats. Not butterflies, but whopping great big, flappy bats.

"I don't know. I guess—uh—if you see a light, go toward it?" I offered, lamely.

"I'm scared," he said, and I felt terrible for not having a better answer. Terrible for wishing he'd disappear only days before. Terrible all around, in fact. I didn't want him to go.

"I know." The lump in my throat was like a giant boulder, squashing my words, "But I'm here, okay?" He nodded and held tight to Lola's hand.

"Can you read to me, Kat? Please?"

I opened the book again and started reading, not even sure of the words I was saying, blinded by tears. I read and I read and I read, acutely aware of the slowing beep of the machine.

When it happened, I was still unprepared. I don't think you can ever be prepared for the moment somebody dies, even when you know it's coming. The continuous unbroken tone that rings out for a stopped heart is like a punch to the gut. I dropped the open book in my lap with a start.

Xander gripped Lola's hand tightly, gazing at her lifeless face. He was perfectly still, frozen in that moment. And—as I watched—he slowly faded away. It's what I expected but still, a sob wrenched forth from me as he disappeared completely. He was gone. Something broke open in me and I let myself cry unchecked. Not only for him. I cried for my Dad too, for Lola. I cried for Kelly Craig. And I cried for myself.

Two nurses bustled in, answering the alarm call as I stared at the vacant chair. They busied themselves with the checks and formalities that come with death. They were wholly unaware that not one but two people had moved on to the after-life.

One of them, a brackish black woman in her forties with tightly scraped hair and a Southern accent, asked me if I was family and I said *technically, no*. She said *either you're family or you ain't*. I told her I wasn't but that Lola didn't have any family and had asked for me—to which she pursed her lips, made an *mm-hmm* sound and handed me a form to fill in.

"Sorry for your loss." She sounded anything but sorry. She turned on a squeaky rubber-soled heel and marched out of the room. I shook my head at the lack of compassion in some people and immediately flashed back to my own reaction upon hearing about Kelly's suicide attempt. Was that really me? I flushed, my cheeks hot with shame at the memory as I pulled the pen from the clipboard and started to write.

"Well, wasn't she a ray of sunshine——*NOT!*" Xander's voice rang out, strident, from across the room, scaring the bejesus out of me and causing my pen to jerk across the page in an inky scrawl.

"Aaaahhhhhh!" I shrieked. Xander sat there, in the chair by the bed, as if nothing had happened. "Xander! What the hell— why are—but—" I was totally flummoxed but so inordinately happy to see him that I launched myself across the space separating us to grab him in a hug. Too late, I realised my error and that horrible, hot fuzz feeling assailed my senses as I tumbled headlong over the chair and landed in an emotional heap in the corner.

I clambered to my feet, rubbing my head as Xander looked on, amused as always by my uncanny ability to fall on the floor for no real reason. Nurse Cranky-Pants stood in the doorway glaring at me, not quite so entertained. By way of explanation, I clutched at my chest and sniffed dramatically. "I'm sorry, Sister, this is such a difficult time. I'm beside myself." I eyed her hopefully as she clucked her tongue at me then left the room.

"Very good," said Xander, "You could be an actor, you know."

"Not bloody likely," I countered. "Actors are a pain in the arse." I smiled, questioning. "So—you're still here."

He smiled back.

"I'm still here."

"Do you have any idea why?"

A shrug.

"I guess I have unfinished business."

Chapter Twenty-Three

The version of Quentin that answered the door was a far cry from the one who'd greeted me on my first visit. The make-up and the garish tracksuit were gone, and the diva attitude seemed to have been shelved along with them.

Quentin seemed smaller, shrunken somehow and his face was drawn. He smiled when he saw me though. It was a tight, tentative smile and his eyes were wary.

"Katherine, my dear, thank you so much for coming back. I'm terribly sorry about my behaviour the other day. Incredibly unprofessional of me." He ushered me through the massive doors once again and Xander trotted obediently behind me, his attitude also completely changed.

"Perfectly understandable, Mr. Millson, I—"

"Quentin, please." He interrupted me quickly and I smiled back at him.

"Quentin, it's fine. You had a bit of a turn, that's all. It was no problem to reschedule the rest of our interview. I'm glad you were happy to talk to me again."

"I don't quite know what came over me, Katherine. It was

most strange. It was almost as if—" he paused "—no, it doesn't matter. This is always a very difficult time of year for me, you understand."

I threw a disapproving glance Xander's way and he had the decency to look abashed. Quentin led us past the white room and opened a door into another, more surprising room. It was as if a cluttered suburban lounge room had been picked up and plonked, *Wizard of Oz* style, into the middle of the palatial home. Numerous mismatched photo frames crowded the side-table tops and a massive television set dominated the room, hooked up to both a DVD player and oddly, an Xbox 360.

"This is the nicest room in the house, I think," Quentin sat, squashing himself between the homey and worn cushions that filled one of the sofas and gestured for me to sit also.

"It's definitely cosier than the other room," I agreed. He called for the angry-looking Morag to arrange some refreshments and, while we waited, he attempted cheery small talk.

"So, Katherine, how are you enjoying Los Angeles?"

"It's great, thank you. I've been here quite a bit before actually. It's one of my favourite places."

"Ah—" He nodded then fell silent again. *Awkward*. He was saved from making further idle chit chat by the arrival of tea and biscuits. But once Morag left the room, he didn't waste any time. He'd clearly summoned me back for a reason. "Your article? Going well I presume?"

I decided to ease him in slowly, risking a quick, surreptitious glance at Xander before I spoke.

"Actually, Quentin, it's going beyond well. I've managed to do a lot of background research and—thanks to you—I have plenty of new information of course. That's going to be sensational. I spent some time at the cemetery where Xander is buried, talking to some of the fans there. They gave me some lovely comments."

"Those girls are there year after year." He chuckled with clear affection. "Quite lovely that they think so much of him, considering they're so young. It shows that a talent like Xander's transcends time, don't you think?"

Xander smiled, enjoying the kudos, and I had to work hard not to roll my eyes. I murmured half-hearted agreement instead as Quentin went on. "I'm so glad I've been able to help you understand what Xander was truly like, Katherine. People will be suitably shocked, of course, but I cannot emphasise enough how important I think it is for the truth to finally be told. It's important for today's LGBTIQ youth to know this kind of history, I firmly believe that. I know your editor will be very pleased with the exclusive. And of course, I understand it means I'll have to kiss my quiet life goodbye for a while." He fluttered a hand round. "But I'm prepared to make that sacrifice, you know, in the name of authenticity, my dear."

This time I couldn't resist a wicked little dig.

"I'm sure being back in the public eye will be quite a difficult adjustment," I said, "especially after enjoying relative anonymity for a while now."

"I wouldn't quite say anonymity, Katherine," Quentin sniffed at me and I smothered an amused smile.

"Anyway," I continued, "I'm sure you'll manage just fine and I'm glad you feel that way about the truth. You see, I've been able to uncover some other very interesting information that I'm not sure even you know."

Quentin's shoulders tensed and he leaned back with a nervous twitch of his eyebrows. "Really? Do go on."

I didn't want to hit him straight between the eyes with the full story, it could have sent him into shock and he'd only just recovered from the other day.

"Well," I began, "I wanted to get some background information on the murder case in addition to the more—how can I put it—personal stuff. I have a friend in the L.A. Police Department and he was able to let me see Xander's case file."

Quentin's face froze in a tight smile.

"I wouldn't imagine there would be much of interest in it, Katherine. It's not as if the police managed to find the killer. Even though it was completely obvious to everyone else."

"You mean, you think Lola killed Xander?" I leaned forward.

"Of course she did it. Who else? It's common knowledge they were involved and they were seen fighting in public, right before he was killed." His face coloured rapidly. "The fact the police did not arrest her—" he trailed off, frustrated.

"You hated her, didn't you." It was a statement more than a question. Quentin stared at me; his mouth was tight. It seemed as though he wasn't going to answer. Then he growled unexpectedly.

"It was her fault I lost him."

I frowned, unsure where to go next, how to tackle things.

"Are you really certain they were romantically involved?" I said eventually and he pulled a face.

"Don't be so naive. Why else would Xander have left me, so easily? He was obsessed with her and she—well, she was married. Why would she have spent so much time with him and risked the scandal if there wasn't something between them?"

"What if it was something else?"

"Like what?" His eyes narrowed.

I glanced at Xander who stood by the door, poised and annoyingly serene. On the other hand, I was surprisingly nervous. I plunged on regardless.

"Quentin, there were a number of things in Xander's case file that didn't fit. There were things missing that should have been there and other information that seemed to lead nowhere.

I started piecing things together myself. I had a hunch." Quentin was eyeing me warily but he said nothing. "I'm not sure if you're aware, but there was a woman initially under suspicion, a woman who claimed she was Xander's wife."

"The woman who was stalking him?" Quentin laughed and waved his hand at me dismissively. "She was crazy."

"No," I said. "Actually, she wasn't."

He stopped laughing abruptly.

"Excuse me?"

"I found their marriage record. She was telling the truth. She was Xander's wife. Or, I should say, the wife of Alexander Martinez. That was Xander's real name."

"No. It's got to be a mistake. I'm sorry, I can't believe that. Even if this were true, why wasn't it discovered at the time?"

"One of the police officers on the case made it all go away. It was never investigated properly. That's why they were never able to pin the murder on anyone." Quentin stared at me. "It's true, Quentin. I'm sorry. Xander left his wife to come out here to L.A." I hesitated. "I can prove it."

"How?"

"I found other records—all linked."

Quentin was thoroughly confused by now. His hands shook and he'd pulled his handkerchief out to wipe at his forehead. He pursed his lips.

"What other records?" he said curtly.

Xander was pacing now. I felt terrible dropping such a bombshell, but Xander was right—Quentin still thought he'd been abandoned in favour of Lola. He was consumed by hurt, even now. At least this way he could understand why it happened. He could be left believing Xander really cared for him.

"Quentin, I'm sorry to say this so bluntly —and I'm sure this is going to come as a shock to you—but, the other record I found is an adoption record from 1943. Xander was given up for adoption when he was five—by a woman named Maria Lolita Martinez."

Quentin stared at me in bewilderment, his eyes searching mine for a few seconds until realisation dawned. His face blanched.

"You're telling me Lola Tennant was his *mother*?" He fell back against the back of the sofa, aghast. "I—oh, dear god." He put his hands to his face then dropped them to his lap and looked up. His eyes met mine, but his mind was enmeshed in long ago memories.

I waited as he struggled to process the information, his eyes darting unfocused around the room. He pulled himself together and his eyes refocused on me, his face wet with tears.

"How can you be certain it's them? The names are different. I mean, this is all speculation." He wasn't going to like what was coming next. I took a deep breath before continuing.

"I'm certain because—up until yesterday—Lola Tennant was still alive. She confirmed all this herself."

"No." He shook his head, pooh-poohing me. "That just proves this is all nonsense. I know for a fact Lola Tennant died —a long time ago."

"I'm afraid she didn't," I assured him. "She wanted people to think so. She even faked her own obituary. She died yesterday afternoon, at Cedars-Sinai. You can call them and check. I was there when it happened. I saw her, spoke to her."

Quentin's face gradually morphed from a mask of disbelief to an expression of deep distaste.

"She's definitely dead now, though?" he asked and I nodded, a shiver running down my spine at the chill in his voice. "Good. What did the old bitch have to say for herself?"

I explained everything to Quentin—except for the true motive behind Xander's affection for him. I told him all Xander wanted was to know his mother but that Lola rejected him again and again. When I told him about the strange form of blackmail an odd expression crossed his face.

"That's why they were always together? That's why they were fighting?" Sudden comprehension marked his voice.

"Exactly," I answered. "It didn't matter to her in the end what he threatened. She didn't want anything to do with him. She was too scared of what she could lose if people found out."

"I always thought—" Quentin's throat choked as he spoke "—I thought he didn't love me anymore, that she'd stolen him away, seduced him. Why didn't he tell me? I felt so betrayed." He became distraught, a sudden sob breaking forth. "That's why I—that night, when he went to her house—oh, what have I done?"

What?

I sat up straight. Out of the corner of my eye, I saw Xander react at the same instant. "Quentin—" I urged "—what are you saying?" It took a minute for him to compose himself. Xander stood beside me now, tense.

"What does he mean?"

I made a tiny shrugging motion and we waited for Quentin to speak again. He sucked in a shaky breath.

"I followed Xander that night. I was dining at the Chateau and I hadn't seen Xander for several weeks. But there he was, at the hotel with *her*. I saw them argue and leave separately. I wanted to speak to him. But I soon realised he wasn't going home. He was driving to her house."

A sick feeling sat heavily in my stomach. Beside me, Xander's tension was palpable as Quentin dabbed his handkerchief to his face. "I heard Lola screaming at him from where I stopped my car, just a few houses up. I could hear how upset Xander was, but couldn't make out what they were saying."

His voice rang with bitterness as he added, "I thought it was a lover's tiff and it crushed me."

"It was raining, but I could tell Xander was crying when he got back in his car. I called out to him, but he couldn't hear me over the downpour. I followed him again. I was hurt and so very angry. I figured I'd confront him once he got to wherever he was going. He parked his car a few streets away, on the side of the road." Quentin's voice quavered, his throat tightening. "He was still visibly upset; his window was open and he didn't seem to care that the rain was pouring into the car."

My whole body shook from the adrenalin that coursed through me. I knew where this was going, or at least I thought I did. It couldn't be anything else. Quentin got up from the sofa and walked slowly over to a set of drawers. Among the photos was a small, ornate silver box and Quentin opened it, taking out a tiny key. He unlocked the top drawer, took out another box— this one wooden—and returned to the sofa.

Eyes wide, Xander backed away from the couch as Quentin opened the box. His hands trembled violently. Quentin's voice was thick and hoarse as he reached into the box and took out a small, black pistol.

"I wanted her to be blamed. After all, it was all her fault."

"What did you do?" I stared at him in dismay. "It was you? You killed him?"

"No!" Quentin's head jerked up. "No, you misunderstand me. I didn't shoot Xander."

"What? But you have the gun—"

"Katherine, Xander killed *himself*."

My head snapped around. Xander had backed up against the wall, his eyes fixed on Quentin in horror, mouth gaping.

"No! God, no—" His arms wrapped around his shoulders as if he was trying to retreat into himself before he stared wildly up at the ceiling, then at me, in complete confusion. Then realisation hit. His lost memories rushed over him, crushing him like an avalanche. He threw his head back and roared in anguish.

My mind was a riot. I was vaguely aware of Quentin's almost hysterical muttering about *seeing the gun* and *not being able to get to the car in time to stop it,* but all I could focus on was Xander, who had crumpled to his knees, moaning. I badly needed to comfort him, but Quentin was staring at me, confused and waiting for me to say something. He was completely oblivious to Xander's presence, while I was watching him fall apart.

"Quentin," I managed to stammer, "you're saying Xander shot himself and you took the gun? Why on earth would you do that?"

"I told you. I wanted Lola to be blamed." His voice rose as he stared at the gun. "I panicked—I'd watched the man I loved kill himself over her. I didn't want people thinking badly of Xander. I hated her so much. I wanted her to pay. I had no idea she was his mother. That makes it so much worse —the pain he must have been in." He dropped the gun on the floor with a clatter and covered his face, crying unchecked.

I was at a loss. I leaned on my knees, trying to compose myself, a part of me simply glad the gun hadn't been loaded. The last thing we needed right then was a bullet ricocheting off the wall and hitting one of us. Imagine the headline.

Xander was slumped against the wall, eyes closed and finally quiet, his head in his hands. I couldn't imagine what he was feeling. I slowed my breath while I tried to figure out what to do next. Quentin saved me the trouble. He was surprisingly calm when he spoke.

"Katherine, I understand you can't keep this information to yourself. I don't expect you'll exclude this from your arti-

cle. I imagine you'll also need to inform your police officer
friend. I want you to know I'm prepared for the
consequences."

"You want people to know the truth?" My eyes widened.
"Everything?"

"It's not about what people need to know. I imagine all
Xander wanted was to be acknowledged. If you print the entire
story, then he gets that."

"You really loved him, didn't you?" I studied him carefully.
"For you to go through all of this, you must have really loved
him."

"He was the love of my life," said Quentin simply. "I wish
he hadn't felt he had to lie to me the entire time." He smiled,
wistful. "It makes me wonder whether he ever did really
love me."

Xander was staring at Quentin, the man he purported to
hate only a few days before. The man he used for his own
twisted gains. He nodded gently then, and I knew he was giving
me permission.

"I know for a fact that Xander did love you, very much."

"That's a lovely sentiment Katherine, but you can't
possibly know such a thing."

"Quentin, do you believe there is something after this?" I
asked, gesturing around the room.

"What are you trying to tell me?" Quentin snorted. "That
you're in contact with Xander's spirit?"

"Actually—" I hesitated, feeling like an idiot "—yes."

"Thank you for trying to make an old man feel better," he
said with a mirthless chuckle. "But that's going a little far,
Katherine. Even for me." He wasn't going to be easily
convinced, so I shrugged at Xander as if to say *what now*?

Xander spoke softly without taking his eyes off Quentin.

"Tell him to read my letters again."

I frowned at him. *What letters?* But Xander just gestured for me to go on so I did, despite my confusion.

"Quentin, what if I said to you that Xander wants you to read his letters again?"

Quentin narrowed his eyes. "How on earth do you know about them? They're private. Nobody knows about our letters. Who told you?"

"I told you. Xander." I shrugged. "I know it's hard to believe, but Xander is here with us—in this room—right now."

Quentin jerked as though I'd slapped him.

"He's here?" His head whipped back and forth, frantically peering around the room. "This can't be real." Tears filled his eyes again and his chin quivered.

"It's been hard for me to understand too, trust me. But I promise, I'm not trying to fool you or scare you." I reached out to touch his hand. "You should know that I think you've helped him a lot," I continued gently. "Xander had no memory of how he died. Maybe now he can move on."

"This is a bit much to take in." Quentin was obviously shaken.

"I understand, but this isn't a joke, I wouldn't do that. Xander really is here."

"Tell him I said thank you," Xander murmured.

"He said to say thank you," I repeated for Quentin's benefit.

Quentin gazed around the room again, then nodded sadly.

"Anything; I would have done anything." Suddenly, he wrapped his arms around himself, got up and said to me almost brusquely, "I think you should go now, Katherine. I promise I'll be in touch, I meant what I said about this information, but I need some time alone right now."

"I understand," I stood too. "Of course."

We were ushered out quickly and the last thing I saw was

Quentin's crumpled face, tears streaming, as he closed the door. Xander stood beside me in silence, his hands as usual in his pockets, head bowed.

"You never told me about the letters," I said.

"I might have been a liar, Katherine, but I was a good actor and I was nothing if not thorough. The letters made me more convincing."

My brow furrowed.

"But were you never worried someone would get hold of them, that you'd be found out?"

"No, never," he answered. "I knew without a doubt how much Quentin cared for me. He would have protected me with his life."

"I'm not sure that's something to be proud of, Xander."

"Believe me, I'm not proud of it. But the letters served a purpose. Even now they serve a purpose. They helped you convince Quentin that I'm really here and now he no longer thinks I betrayed him. He can read those letters and go on believing I felt that way. With what he did for me, not only when I was alive but after—" he paused, struggling, "—after what I did to myself, I owe him that much."

I was silent as we made our way up Quentin's driveway toward the road. Xander was uncharacteristically quiet too. Eventually I had to ask.

"About that—"

"About what?"

"What you did. Are you alright?"

"No. I'm not." A deep exhale. "I remember it all now."

"Are you ready to talk about it?" There was a long pause but he didn't reply. "We have to talk about it Xander. You're still here, despite everything. We have to figure out what you need to do to move on."

"I know, but not now. Can we just not talk now?"

"Xander, I don't know what else you're supposed to do. What if you're stuck? I—"

"Katherine, stop!" He halted in the middle of the driveway. "I mean it, I'm not talking about it. You've got everything you need now, haven't you? Every dirty little secret. Isn't that what you wanted? Don't pretend this is about me. I keep forgetting, you're a journalist. Do what you want with the information, I'm sure you will anyway, but for now just leave me alone."

I backed up at his stinging remarks, my arms instinctively crossed across my body.

"That's not fair. You know I—"

"I said, leave me the hell alone!"

"But—"

"No."

And with that, he disappeared.

I burst into tears. I was too upset to be angry, but all the same I thought to myself—

God, I hate it when he does that.

Chapter Twenty-Four

Suicide had always been something beyond my comprehension. Before then, I'd struggled to imagine ever being so sad, or overwhelmed or that desperate that I'd consider ending my own life. But Xander had, and so had Kelly Craig and unfortunately so many others. Xander, because of how Lola made him feel. Kelly, because of the way I made her feel. The parallel sickened me. I understood now why my dad was ashamed of what I was doing with my life. I was ashamed of myself.

I guess I was one of the lucky ones. I'd never sunk to such dark emotional depths that being dead—ceasing to exist— was better than being in the world. But, I could see how easily it could have been me, with a few different twists and turns in my life—with different choices. I certainly understood fear and insecurity, and feeling terrible about myself. But mostly I'd cocooned myself in a cushy, unchallenging life, so that I'd never had to face the really bad stuff.

I had turned myself into an unfeeling, superficial arsehole to avoid risking failure or pain. Maybe that's why some artists were lost to the darkness, because they opened themselves up emotionally—they took risks, whatever the cost—that's what it meant to really be alive... and it took them over the brink.

Two days had passed and Xander still hadn't reappeared. My hotel room was horribly quiet and empty. I shouted his name into the silence at intervals, hoping he'd hear me. All I got in return was a flat echo from the bathroom tiles as my redundant voice filled the space.

I had no choice but to sit and write. I finally returned Mitch's calls and assured her that no, I hadn't been kidnapped by some weird new-age cult. I was in fact working and the article was—yes—going to be mind-blowing and more importantly on her desk very soon.

In between typing and pacing, I ventured out occasionally for food or coffee, at first expecting Xander to materialise beside me in the elevator or on the street. As the second day drew to a close, I expected it less and less. I had no clue whether he was staying away on purpose, had moved on to the great beyond or had simply faded away into nothing. I knew he had no reason to stay anymore, the mystery was solved. But I wanted him to come back—if not for himself, for me.

I reminded myself that—regardless of whether I saw him again—I was flying back to Australia two days' later. It was over. Xander was right, I got everything I needed. What else was there to do?

Despite everything, I put off calling Barry to fill him in because I knew once I did there'd be no going back. If the LAPD reopened the case—although technically it wasn't a murder case anymore—it would all come out, whether I liked it or not.

I'd written two articles. I wasn't one-hundred-percent sure which one I'd give to Mitch. Both were explosive, although times had changed. As far as readers were. Concerned, the more gratuitous the story, the better. A retrospective revealing a Hollywood star's hidden homosexual relationship would pale in comparison to an exposé headline that screamed, '*HOLLY-WOOD STAR WHO BLEW HIS BRAINS OUT WAS SECRETLY GAY, SECRETLY MARRIED AND SECRETLY IN LOVE WITH HIS MOTHER!*' I knew Mitch would want the Jerry Springer-esque version to run, but I figured what her circulation figures didn't know wouldn't hurt her.

I seemed to have developed a fully-grown conscience. Not just a few guilty twinges—a *bona fide conscience*. I figured I always had one, it had just been napping, Sleeping Beauty-like, and had needed a kick up the arse to wake it up. Either way, it was fully conscious now and dancing the fandango. As a result, stripping someone else's life bare without their permission didn't sit well with me anymore. It was one thing to want answers, to solve a mystery— entirely another to shout what you find to the entire world. If I ran this without consent, all it showed was that I hadn't learned a damn thing.

Something Lola had said to me weighed heavily. '*What gives journalists the right to decide what the public needs to know about my private life?*' It was a fair call. What gave me the right? I could justify it all I wanted, say it didn't matter because she and Xander were dead and it couldn't hurt them, but I couldn't lie to myself. It didn't make a difference that they were both dead. I did not have the right to tell their story.

Quentin was a little harder to convince. He wasn't happy at the thought of protecting Lola, but was relieved at the thought of keeping the gun hidden in that little wooden box—at least for a while. I had no doubt he'd be satisfied as long as he still got to tell multitudes of journalists and television chat show hosts about the passion that ran deep between he and Xander.

"I'm impressed, Katherine," he lisped down the phone line to me. "Gossiping is easy, anyone can gossip. Discretion is so much harder and much more valuable, trust me. If you decide not to run the full story that's your choice. I'll go with whatever you decide. But you do know, the truth has a funny way of wanting to be told." Mystified, I asked him what he meant. "Life doesn't like loose ends, Katherine my dear," he said. "It likes to make everything right in the end, to balance things karmically. When that happens, you'll know. And I'll be here, waiting."

He sounded like he'd been talking to my friend at Spell-binders. I rang off and stared at my phone. Then I dialled Chrissie's number.

"Don't hang up," I rattled off as soon as she answered. Chrissie's usual feline greeting was replaced with a sleepy and crotchety response.

"Christ, Kat. Do you know what fucking time it is?"

"Uh, no." I cringed. "What time is it there?"

"Not a fucking clue. But I was asleep." Chrissie yawned expansively.

"Oh. Whoops." I tried to sound suitably apologetic.

"Yeah, well, at least I'm not drunk, right?"

Urgh.

"I am so sorry I said that." The pause on the other end was so lengthy I assumed the phone had cut out. I was about to hang up and redial when I heard her dramatic sigh crackle down the line.

"I've been called worse than a drunken slut before, darl," she said. "And hey, I might be sober, but I can't tell you whose bed I'm in. Where the hell am I?" She covered the phone, but I heard her stage whisper, "*Who the fuck are you?*" before coming back on the line. "Nope, no idea."

I started to laugh.

"Am I forgiven then?"

"I suppose so. We're even anyway. I did call you a mental bitch."

"Yes, but there's so much truth in that statement."

"Fair call," she sniffed. "Now, what's up, chicken little? And make it fast. I have no idea who this slice of delicious next to me is, but I might make the most of being awake and take a bite."

Not keen on listening to the muffled advances taking place on the end of the line, I got straight to the point.

"You know that giant black book of yours?" I likened it to a Yellow Pages, only the hefty tome was filled with the phone numbers of every rock star, actor, writer, director, reality TV personality and celebrity in the entire universe.

"Nnmph-hhmm, yup." Her answer sounded suspiciously like it was coming from under the covers.

"Oh, for god's sake, Chrissie, can you get off whoever that is for one second? This is important."

"Okay, yes," she huffed more clearly. "What do you want my book for? Whose number do you need?"

"Kelly Craig."

Chapter Twenty-Five

Asking for forgiveness is not easy, especially when it's for something exceptionally awful. The next morning, Kelly Craig's agent intercepted my call with a curt, 'Kelly has nothing to say to you,' but I persisted, calling back several times and managing to get across the fact I was calling to apologise.

Kelly herself didn't say much. She wouldn't have got a word in edgeways, even if she wanted to. I filled the air with a lengthy apology. It sounded far too feeble and meaningless so I ended up pouring my heart out to the poor girl. I talked about my dad and my own fear, and the importance of a working moral compass. I talked about the fake plasticity that's part and parcel of the entertainment industry and admitted to her that I was caught up in it all—in the shine and sparkle and manic ego stroking.

I told her the industry is like a great big turd rolled in glitter and—if you examine it too closely or you poke it too hard—well, you can imagine what you get... covered in shit. So, nobody looks too hard or pokes it, they just blindly go along with the fake glitter. When I started waxing lyrical about karma, she started clearing her throat uncomfortably and I realised I'd held her hostage on the phone for almost twenty minutes, talking at her about poo and glitter and the universe. I really was mental.

In the end, I echoed Lola's words—that I didn't expect her to forgive me, but I wanted her to know how truly sorry I was. She said, 'Okay,' and disconnected the call. That was it. It took a while for my hands to stop shaking after I hung up the phone.

"That was brave of you."

I almost didn't want to turn around in case I was imagining his voice. I squeezed my eyes shut on the tears that suddenly threatened and spun slowly in the chair. I opened my eyes. Xander was standing in the bathroom doorway, the same spot he was in when I'd first laid eyes on him.

He appeared different somehow. Neater. Sharper. He was wearing a suit instead of jeans and that crumpled old checked shirt but that's not what had changed. I studied his face, trying to put my finger on it, but fell short of figuring it out. We stared at each other in silence for a minute, until I couldn't stand it any longer.

"Hi." It seemed the thing to say and he smiled a strange, serene smile.

"Hi," he replied.

"You're here."

"It would appear that way."

"Where have you been?"

"Around."

"Around? Is that code for 'I have no idea, I was floating around in nothingness?' Or were you avoiding me?"

"Neither." Still with the spooky smile.

Right.

"Okay, see I was happy to see you a second ago, Xander. But now you're irritating me, as usual. Are you going to tell me where you've been or not? And what's with the suit and the creepy serial killer smile? Hmm?"

I folded my arms and glared at him expectantly, only half joking. He laughed. It was deeper and more resonant than usual and I stared at him curiously but—in that instant—he seemed more like himself again. Not completely, but enough that I relaxed.

"Okay, okay. I was up there." He pointed at the ceiling.

"Huh? Up where?" Before you point it out, I really was that slow on the uptake. He wiggled his eyebrows to indicate about as high up as you can go.

"Up *there.*"

"Up *there,* there?" I goggled at him. "You mean, like, *Heaven,* up there?"

"Yes, Kat. Like *Heaven* up there. Where do you think I'm pointing to? The roof?"

"There's no need for sarcasm," I huffed. "How was I supposed to know you went to Heaven?" Then the full weight of what he was saying flooded my little atheist brain like a religious tsunami. "Oh, my god! XANDER! Crap, can I even say God now? Christ—"

I fumbled my words again, trying to remember which words are supposed to be blasphemous from my minimal Sunday school lessons. I flashed back to one of the scary nuns spouting '*thou shalt not take the lord's name in vain*', and then I gave up, threw my hands in the air and said, "Holy shit! You were in *HEAVEN*?"

"Well, technically the place *before* Heaven. It's kind of a sorting place. They don't actually call it Heaven up there, by the way."

I excitedly moved to stand, but he motioned for me to stay put, instead crossing the room and sitting on the couch across from me.

"But I don't understand," I practically shouted at him. "If you managed to move on, you know, to Heaven or whatever it's called, then—hang on, what *is* it called?"

Xander laughed at me.

"It doesn't matter what it's called, Kat."

"Fine, don't tell me. I don't understand what you are doing here if you finally got unstuck. You got to *go towards the light!* What happened?"

"I can't tell you too much, I'm afraid."

"Is your memory going all kaplooey again?"

"My memory is fine, thanks." He pulled a face. "I'm just not allowed."

"Are you kidding me? That sucks."

"I can tell you I'm going to be fine, but things are a bit more complex for me than most people."

"Why?" I asked.

"Because I took my own life."

"Oh. Right."

There was a small awkward silence until Xander finally cleared his throat.

"It goes against the natural order of things, apparently. I have a lot of working out to do up there. In any case, I wasn't even going to be allowed to do that until you did your part. So here I am."

"Me? What do you mean?"

Xander smiled at my confusion.

"Come on Kat, you had to know all this wasn't only about me."

I stared at him blankly and he sighed melodramatically.

"Do I need to spell it out for you?"

"Uh, yeah," I nodded. "I think you do."

"Okay, remember when we first met, I was adamant the reason you could see me was so you could help me find out what happened—help me move on? I'm not the only one who needed help, you did too. You can't tell me you haven't figured that out."

I felt a bit like I was playing out the denouement of an episode of quasi-evangelical family drama, *7th Heaven,* but it actually did make sense.

"Sure, but I still don't get what 'my part' is."

"You just did it." Xander smiled beatifically as if talking to an idiot child.

"You mean apologising to Kelly?" My brow furrowed.

"Why do you think I'm here? They're letting me say goodbye."

Then it clicked. Of course. "That's it? That's all I had to do?"

"Yup," Xander nodded. "Don't underestimate how important that was. To you and to her. We're all connected, Kat. Making amends, it's all checks and balances." There was that idea again.

"It wasn't brave, you know," I said.

"Yes, it was," he answered. "Admitting you're wrong is hard, trust me, I know."

"I had to do it. It was—"

Xander cut in, speaking the words at the same time.

"The right thing to do."

I smiled at him through tears I had no hope of stopping this time. Without thinking, I leaned across to put my hand on his. I touched warm skin.

I TOUCHED WARM SKIN!

My fingers zinged with energy and heat but it was unmistakably solid skin and flesh. I gaped at Xander, who was mirroring my shocked expression.

"What the fuck?" I had no other words and, for once, Xander didn't scold my language because I'm certain he was thinking the very same thing. We scrambled to our feet and he started laughing, grabbing at my hands and squishing them, feeling my fingers and my palms and my wrists.

He was solid. I could actually touch him.

I succumbed briefly to the exploration, staring at him before placing my own hands on his chest. I ran my fingers over him, feeling his arms, strong under his jacket and shirt, squeezing his shoulders. I reached around and threaded my fingers into the hair at the nape of his neck.

It wasn't erotic, it was simply the physical expression of the pent-up need to comfort each other we'd both felt for days. I'd wanted to touch his hand and hold him so many times in the past week and been unable to. To touch each other now was a blessing.

As Xander placed his hands tenderly on either side of my face, I wrapped my arms around his waist and pressed my palms into his back. I tilted my chin to look up at him, my eyes meeting his. Slowly he dipped his head as he gazed at me and pressed his lips, gently but firmly, against mine for just a moment. A long, spine-tingling moment. Then—

"Thank you, Katherine," he murmured, his lips still so close to mine I could feel the warmth of his breath. "For everything."

I scrunched my eyes closed, still reeling from the tenderness of the kiss, and gulped a deep breath. "Uh-oh," I managed to say. "This is the goodbye speech, isn't it?"

"Almost," he rested his lips against my forehead, "but not quite." He closed his arms around me and I pressed my cheek into his chest. We stood there like that for a while. I fancied I could hear his heart beating, but I knew that was impossible. If it had been there, it would have been strong and solid and reassuring. I also couldn't help thinking fleetingly, *Mum would die if she could see this.* Most of all, I felt calm and serene and for the first time in a long time, really, *really* okay.

"I don't think I'm going to publish it, you know," I said finally, my words muffled through a mouthful of jacket. He kissed the top of my head.

"None of it?"

"Only Quentin's side of the story." I tipped my head back to look up at him. "That is, if you're still okay with that."

"I'm more than okay with it. His story is true, whether my feelings were real or not. There's a time for truth and there's a time for doing the right thing. They aren't always the same thing."

"I'm learning that."

Xander stepped back and took my hands.

"I know you are. Do me a favour though, don't delete the other story will you—the full story?"

"Why?" I shot him a funny look. "Do you know something I don't?"

He shrugged one of those infuriating shrugs, dropped my hands and backed away further into the bathroom doorway. Suddenly it came to me—what was different. He had a shadow for the first time. Its lanky shape stretched up the wall and I half expected it to take on a life of its own and dart across the room, with Xander giving chase. His voice yanked me out of my Disney daydream.

"It's time for me to go."

"I don't want you to." I wanted to stamp my foot at the injustice of it all and Xander pulled a face, reproachful.

"Don't be silly, Kat. You know I have to."

"But what am I going to do without you? Who am I going to boss around?"

"I'm sure you'll find someone."

"Who am I going to pass my lame jokes on to?"

"I think we both know your lame jokes are best not passed on to anybody."

"But—"

"Kat."

"What?" I was sulking now.

"I have a message for you," he said.

I was instantly wary and my eyes widened at a terrible thought.

"Am I in trouble? From God?"

This time Xander's laugh was rich and sonorous as he bent almost double, his eyes crinkling with mirth. My serious face made him laugh even harder.

"You're so funny." He straightened, wiping his eyes. "No, you're not in trouble from God. It's a little closer to home than that." I backed up a step, hardly daring to breathe. Xander's smile softened reassuringly and he nodded. "Your father asked me to tell you that you're better than you think you are," he said. "And, that you should have stuck around for the end of that damned conversation you overheard. He *always* thought you were smart enough to do whatever you put your mind to."

I stared at him, mute and fighting back tears. There was a lump in my throat the size of an apple as he continued. "But it should never have been about him. *You* have to believe in your ability. Because if you do, it'll keep you on the right track. He said to remember how you were as a kid."

Xander had become a watery blur in front of me as tears rolled down my face unchecked. "He also wants you to know that despite what he thought of the work you were doing, he never stopped being proud of his daughter—his Katie."

I couldn't hold it back any longer. I howled out loud, covering my face with my hands, crying into them with sloppy sobs. Xander waited patiently as I cried and then gradually pulled myself together, taking jerky little gasps of air and wiping my running nose on my arm like a five-year-old. I'm definitely the ugly-crying type and as soon as I cry, my eyes distend like marshmallows. I blinked puffily at Xander as I drew in a shuddering breath and exhaled, calming myself.

"Did he say anything else?" My voice was shaking.

"He also said to tell you the Tooth Fairy is definitely real, but you were right—the Easter Bunny, not so much."

"What?" I stifled a hiccupy giggle.

"And," Xander continued, "he warned me you might not believe me. He said, 'my Katie might ask for proof that it's really me'."

"And?" I stared at him.

"So—" the corner of Xander's mouth twitched "—he said for me to remind you of the time when you were a toddler, when he found you running around dragging your Noddy toy behind you, and the bell had come off his little hat, yet—"

My eyes widened in horror. No, he couldn't have told him *that* story.

"Xander—I believe you. I believe you! You can stop now."

Xander continued on blithely, clearly relishing the moment.

"—yet, somehow, as you ran along on your chubby little baby legs, that bell was still jingling. How long exactly were your parents at the hospital, getting that little bell removed from your—"

"Nose! Getting it removed from my nose." I was laughing but on the verge of complete mortification. Xander clearly found it hilarious.

"Right. Your *nose*. What did he call you again? *Tinkerbell*?"

I burst into embarrassed giggles and laughingly sent a threat toward the ceiling.

"I am going to bloody-well kill you, Dad."

As our laughter subsided and my cheeks faded from scarlet

to not-quite-so-scarlet, Xander and I found ourselves facing each other in companionable silence. I was trying not to think too hard on the whole after-life thing. It was way too much for my brain right now. I was also trying not to think about the fact, the first real connection I'd felt in years was with a seventy-year-old dead guy. Even I knew that spoke volumes about my emotional state. I had to sort my shit out.

Instead, I told myself I'd simply helped a friend who was in trouble and now that *friend* was able to move away somewhere nice. Like, really nice. That was enough for me. There would be plenty of time for theosophical chat (and therapy) when I got home, over a bottle or three of vodka with Chrissie, who would probably argue that God is a woman because who else would create Ryan Gosling, right?

Xander was smiling at me but a single tear tracked down his left cheek. The sight of a man in tears was a particular Achilles heel. I welled up again immediately.

"Please don't." My voice was thick as my throat tightened. I tried to think of something else to say, anything to drag things out. "So, I was thinking. If I ever interview Ben Affleck again, I'll make sure to say hello for you. Okay?"

"Don't be silly." Xander chuckled and wiped his face roughly. "I wouldn't want to put you through that kind of trauma." I laughed too, or at least I tried to through my snuffles. "Bye, Kat."

"Bye," I whispered.

"Be good."

"Never." I smiled a watery smile.

I expected it to be a serene goodbye, with him calmly fading away into transparency the way he had before, but instead he started to glow. It was almost imperceptible at first. His skin became iridescent and his hair seemed to move and lift as if coming to life. Gradually, he was bathed in shimmering sunlight, despite the curtains being closed.

Then he got brighter. And brighter. And even brighter. I blinked a few times against the light, my hand shielding my face involuntarily. He was glowing almost white hot now. Even his eyes were glowing. It was totally freaky.

"Uh, Xander—"

The exact moment I thought—*oh my god, he's going to explode*—there was a flash of intense light and heat, a big whoosh—then he was gone. Completely gone.

I stared at the vacant bathroom doorway with a deep sigh. Then I checked my eyebrows hadn't been singed off and said to the empty room—

"Well. That was different."

Epilogue

I gazed around my room at the Chateau Marmont one last time, immeasurably sad to see no physical evidence that Xander Hill was ever there. It was all filed away in my memory; those chocolate fondue eyes, his laugh, the lanky way he walked, always leading with the hips, his patent disapproval every time I said the word *fuck*.

The handful of photos Mitch had given me before I left were sticking out of the top of my handbag. On top of them was the one I'd printed out—the behind-the-scenes still from *Chase the Wind*. The brooding two-dimensional image didn't do him justice at all.

Nobody would ever believe me. Not that it mattered and not that I planned on telling anyone. Quentin was the only other person in this with me. He'd been sending me stuff to support my story; copies of the letters and the small collection of photographs he'd had hidden away for years.

In the process, we'd struck up quite the friendship. It was a little one-sided, mainly consisting of Quentin peppering me with questions about my time with Xander and whether or not he'd talked about him much—but I didn't mind. Behind the camp and bitchy façade, he was simply a lonely old man who'd never recovered from having his heart broken.

I'd filed my story by email that morning. Mitch was beside herself with glee, of course. It was exactly what she'd asked for and more. Sex, gossip, name-dropping and a scoop that would blow all of the other magazines—with their tired old James Dean stories—out of the water.

"And this, Kat, is why I didn't fire you," she'd drawled down the phone only an hour earlier. "You are too, *too* good. We'll have *Pop Vulture* back up online before you know it darling, and who needs Channel Five—we'll start talks with the 1 Live Network, get you another TV spot."

I told her that actually I was thinking of taking some time off to reassess things. That maybe celebrity gossip wasn't my calling after all. To which she started having a conniption and said, "What on earth are you talking about, you were made for this. Don't do this to me, Kat. Is it money? It's the money, isn't it? Honey, let's talk turkey when you get back."

It wasn't the money. It was me. I didn't know if I could do it anymore. I briefly considered the option of launching a brand-new career in political correspondence, except I already knew that the Parliamentary structure confused the hell out of me. Even *Question Time* on the TV bored me to tears. I'd be asleep in minutes, drooling on myself. That would never work.

Maybe I could move to the country and get a staff reporter post at a regional paper, like the *Border Mail* or the *Echuca Gazette* and write articles about sheep and school fetes and jam making. You know, get back to my roots, write about what's real. No, that was not likely either.

The problem was, I still loved entertainment. I loved film and television, I loved the arts and music and theatre and— believe it or not—there were a lot of artists out there I admired greatly; they weren't all total wankers. It was the inevitable bull-shit that came along with it all that I couldn't cope with any longer. But, I still wanted to write. Time out would do me good while I figured it out, whether Mitch liked it or not.

I grabbed my bag and room key and headed for the elevator down to the lobby. The bell boy would go up and get the rest of my stuff while I checked out. I leaned against the elevator wall, running through final checks in my head. Plane ticket, check. Passport, check. All of my loose ends were tied firmly in a knot as far as I could tell. I'd sent a thank you note down to Con-X to Leon, tied to an alien bobble-head, saying *I owe you, big time.* And, I'd put in a quick call to Barry a short while before.

I'd thanked him profusely for all his help and filled him in on Quentin and Xander's love affair, to which he'd said '*well, bugger me*' about five times before realising his pun and saying, '*sorry, Katherine, poor choice of words*'.

I'd told him that— even though we didn't end up solving the crime—I couldn't have written my story without him. At least the second half of that sentence was true. Barry had spluttered and coughed, but I could practically hear him puffing with pride before he got all serious and said, '*it was a noble attempt at sleuthing, Katherine, but detective work is actually much harder than people think it is, you know*'. He said he'd been happy to help, before adding cheerfully that his Mum would be pleased it all worked out well for me too, and had I managed to call her back yet about that little interview?

Oh dear. Marjorie. Eek.

The elevator opened on the ever-swanky lobby. It was busy as usual and I gazed around as I waited my turn at the desk. If only these walls could talk, I mused. And the couches and the beds. Oh, my lord—if only the beds could talk! Wait, there were some things nobody needed to know. I did wonder though what other scandals and secrets still lay undiscovered, protected by the sacred mantle of the Chateau Marmont.

Tom Cruise's double was manning the check-in/out desk again and dripping politeness and efficiency, clearly remembering my grumpiness on arrival. I attempted amends by grinning cheerfully and answering all of his questions in as chirpy a manner as I could muster. Yes, my stay was fantastic. Yes, I loved L.A., but no, I didn't get to see Universal Studios unfortunately. My bad.

I handed my key back to him and he took it gingerly, clearly frightened by my bipolar impression of The Joker. As I turned away from the desk to wait for my bags, he stopped me.

"Oh, Ms. Alley. Ma'am—" he said. "I almost forgot. A package arrived for you this morning."

It was a large brown envelope, stuffed to the hilt. I imagined it was from Quentin, although he'd said everything had been emailed through. Puzzled, I turned it over. The label on the back had *Baden, Baden & Corfield, Attorneys at Law* printed on it, with a Beverly Hills address. Was Kelly Craig suing me after all? Maybe I made it worse with my rambling attempt at an apology. Why would she hire a lawyer here in L.A. though?

I ripped open the end of the envelope and a stack of black and white photos fell out and scattered on the floor. I dropped to my knees to retrieve them and gasped audibly when I realised what they were.

"Is everything okay, Ms.Alley," Tom-clone said, stepping around the desk to assist me.

"Everything's fine," I assured him, quickly gathering up the photos before he could see them. I carried them over to one of the lobby's plush sofas and sat down, hardly able to believe what I was looking at.

The woman in the photos was unmistakably Lola Tennant,

although she was far younger than in her films. It was the little boy on her lap and in her arms, that held my attention.

Xander's five-year-old smile was even more charming than the one I knew. His dimples threatened to swallow his cheeks and his eyes flashed with childhood cheekiness. In one picture his face was puffed out with breath, aimed at a row of candles on a cake. Lola gazed at him with what can only be described as complete adoration. It was a perfect mother and son moment. Seeing it, the tragedy of all that time lost was even more acute.

I reached into the envelope and extracted a wad of papers. The official letterhead informed me that Baden, Baden & Corfield acted on behalf of Lola's estate and that she'd asked for all of the enclosed documentation to be forwarded to me upon her death.

Stunned, I stood there holding not only copies of her birth and death certificates but also Xander's birth certificate and adoption papers. They were held together with a large paper clip. In front of them all was a folded piece of creamy note paper with my name on it in a spidery scrawl. I opened it. All it said was this.

Dear Katherine
Make sure you tell it all and tell it right.
I owe my son that much.
L.T.

I stared at the note and the pile of photos beside me on the sofa, incredulous. She had given me permission. Well, bugger me, as Barry would say. I stuffed everything back into the envelope and sat there, clutching it to myself, not quite sure how to react.

Part of me wanted to jump up and down and scream and race for a phone to call Mitch and yell, 'Stop the presses!' But I didn't. I sat there, holding the package, until my suitcase arrived from upstairs. I thanked the porter and got up, in a bit of a daze quite frankly, and made my way towards the hotel exit.

I had absolutely no idea what I was going to do. Maybe the whole thing didn't need to come out. Then I remembered Quentin's little gem—'*the truth has a funny way of wanting to be told*'. Maybe it does.

Devil-Chrissie appeared in a puff of red glitter on my right shoulder and whispered, '*Maybe you should write a book.*' I rolled my eyes and flicked her away like bothersome sparkly dandruff. She reappeared, in angel-white, on my left shoulder and said, '*seriously, babe—you should totally write a fucking book,*' and I thought to myself, actually that's not such a bad idea.

Maybe I didn't need to decide just yet. Maybe I could sit on it for a while. I had a moment of déjà vu. Xander Hill had been dead for fifty years—it wasn't like he was going anywhere. I smiled to myself. Not anymore, anyway.

In the meantime, I had to admit there was something I still felt terrible about. I was reminded of it as soon as I stepped outside. Marjorie was standing in the driveway, in a too-snug bright orange pantsuit, waiting for a taxi. It was time to do the decent thing.

I offered a bright hello and she responded with a tight little smile and a nod. I couldn't blame her, I'd been pretty rude. I tried again.

"Marjorie, I'm so sorry I haven't managed to get back to you this week." I may as well have been prostrate on the ground, I was creeping that hard. "But, I have to thank you for getting Barry to help me. I was just saying to him on the phone this morning that I wouldn't have been able to write my story at all without your help."

The little fib made her smile a bit wider, but she still wasn't won over. "I was thinking—" I pulled out all the stops "—

maybe we can share a cab to the airport and have lunch when we get there. We can do that interview if you like. You know, ask me all those questions you've wanted to ask. Anything at all —I'm all yours. It'll be fun."

It worked. Her smile lit up the hotel forecourt and she grabbed me in one of her talcum powder hugs before I could avoid it.

"Oh, Katherine, that would be wonderful. Of course, don't apologise for being busy," she pooh-poohed. "You've had so much on your plate. I completely understand. I am so excited! There's so much I want to know, your life must be so glamorous—and it's going to help my reporting skills so much, you know. I mean I'm just learning, but—"

My left eye twitched. What had I gotten myself into? I sucked it up and smiled as she kept talking and our suitcases were loaded into the taxi. She bundled into the back seat and I climbed in beside her, thinking at least I had some time before we got to the airport to gather my strength for the onslaught.

No such luck. Marjorie had already whipped out her notebook and a pen, press conference-style. After instructing the driver to head for LAX, she turned to face me.

"So, Katherine," she said excitedly. "I've been dying to ask you—"

"Yes?" I mustered as much enthusiasm as I could.

She took a deep, preparatory breath, pen poised at the ready.

"Do you know Ben Affleck?"

Oh. My. God.

Acknowledgments

I started writing *Dead Famous* because one of the best jobs I've ever had was writing celebrity news for a gossip magazine, and everybody says—write what you know. My obsession with Hollywood goes back to the early 80s, to Sunday afternoons with my Nan, watching old movies on TV. I spent years dreaming about being a movie star, a pop star, a literary star, any kind of star really. Well... almost any kind. Whether it's film and television, music, or writing—the world of artists makes sense to me. So that's where a lot of my stories live.

This book is one step on a long and circuitous writing and publishing journey and, as such, there are numerous people to thank from different phases of the often-torturous trek.

Seeing this book realised has been a long time coming, and there are people who were in my life for the laying of its foundations, and the building of it, hour by hour at the laptop, who are no longer part of my circle. Because that's what life does—people come and go, for whatever reasons, and you give and take from each other what you each need. That becomes part of your story.

So, thank you to:

Those lost partners and friends who were there through the early writing of this book—you know who you are. Your support, your belief, even your disbelief (I do love to prove people wrong)—it all gave me what I needed to finish these pages and to hang on to loving them for long enough to finally get here.

My family—my sisters, Kylie and Clare, and my Mum—who are all voracious readers and have devoured everything I've written since primary school. To my Dad, who is not a voracious reader but who passed on his wannabe rock star vibes to me, and that's gotta be worth something.

Team Ninja—the incredibly talented Emma Grey, Nina D. Campbell, and Anjanette Fennell (my fabulous agent). Between us—the unwavering support through incredible ups and downs, the thousands of pages read, the endless cheerleading—has been a life-raft in the sea of uncertainty that is trying to make it as a writer. I am so blessed to call you my friends and to be riding the rollercoaster of inspiration, passion, inevitable disappointments, and equally as inevitable successes with the three of you.

Divorce Crew—my ride or dies. Sommer Tothill and Matthew Lowe. Thanks for the mems, the memes, the laughs, the tears, the gossip, the wine, the dirty talk—and most of all the friendship. To say I might not have made it without you is a gross understatement. Except you're not gross. You're hot AF. Just saying. D.C. Forever.

Random, but important—author, Nick Earls, for reading very early chapters of *Dead Famous* years ago and telling me to keep going. I kept going. Screenwriter and showrunner, Vicki Madden, whose brilliant take on character changed everything for me (and for everyone I talk to about character).

My beautiful, smart and funny daughter, Nikita, whose love for books and stories—even the trashy ones (actually mostly the trashy ones)—fills me with motherly pride. And I don't generally do motherly anything. Thank you for being willing to read all the things that come out of your mother's brain—you know, the dirty things you don't want to think about your mother thinking about. Hope I haven't scarred you. I'm sure you'll be fine.

Finally—thank you to Kat Alley. Who is fictional but not fictional. Me but not me. Who is simply the funniest and the loveliest imaginary friend. Alley Kat, Alley Kat... babe, I can't wait to discover what's next with you.

About the Author

Ruby Fox is an award-winning Australian fiction writer, screenwriter, and storyteller, who also still dreams of being a rock star —but, let's face it, that ship has probably sailed.

Ruby writes all the things but has a particular penchant for tricky tales, comedy that stabs you in the feels, rom-coms, stuff that is high-camp and scary as f*ck, and LGBTIQ stories. If there's magic, pop stars, or vampires in the mix, all the better.

She likes hot yoga, tattoos, and cheese but not in that order. Mostly the cheese comes first. Her dog, Lola, is the love of her life and—by the time you read this—she could be living literally anywhere in the world. She hasn't made up her mind yet.

Find and follow her on Instagram and TikTok
@therealzerofox and on Facebook @realzerofox

Want a sneak peek at *Dead Perfect* - Book 2 in the Kat Alley Series? Receive an exclusive excerpt and keep in the loop with news by subscribing at www.therealzerofox.com

Ruby would love you to leave an honest review of *Dead Famous*, wherever you get the books you love.

f facebook.com/realzerofox

⊙ instagram.com/therealzerofox

♪ tiktok.com/@therealzerofox

Ingram Content Group UK Ltd.
Milton Keynes UK
UKHW012102050723
424591UK00001B/8

9 780645 564860